A FASCINATING NOVEL DRAWN
FROM THE LIVING FABRIC
OF HISTORY

"Absorbing . . . Costain's skill at giving intimate insights into a great historical character has never been better shown. Betsy . . . should certainly take her place as one of literature's charming feminine characters, if not a newly revealed flower of history . . ."

Christian Science Monitor

"Costain paints a tremendous canvas filled with warm color and life . . . As those know who have read his many vigorous re-creations of the past, Costain has a magnificent talent for breathing life into history . . ."

Chicago Sunday Tribune

THOMAS B. COSTAIN

THE LAST LOVE

AVON
PUBLISHERS OF BARD, CAMELOT, DISCUS, EQUINOX AND FLARE BOOKS

With the exception of actual historic personages, the characters are entirely the product of the author's imagination and have no relation to any person in real life.

AVON BOOKS
A division of
The Hearst Corporation
959 Eighth Avenue
New York, New York 10019

Copyright © 1963 by Thomas B. Costain.
Published by arrangement with Doubleday and Company, Inc.
Library of Congress Catalog Card Number: 63-15486.

ISBN: 0-380-00215-9

First Avon Printing, January, 1975.

AVON TRADEMARK REG. U.S. PAT. OFF. AND
FOREIGN COUNTRIES, REGISTERED TRADEMARK—
MARCA REGISTRADA, HECHO EN CHICAGO, U.S.A.

Printed in the U.S.A.

Contents

THE
LAST LOVE

BOOK ONE
A Guest in the House

Chapter One

1

The Marquis de Las Cases, who professed a leaning to letters, hunched his thick shoulders over the rail and stared at the rocky islet. "Have we been crossing the Styx all these months?" he asked his companions. "Surely this is hell which now faces us!" He grinned with appreciation of his own wit and said to his son Emmanuel, who stood as always behind him; "Make a note of that, my boy. I think it's quite good."

The Bertrands, the Montholons and the mercurial Gourgaud were as much appalled as he was by the prospect but his remark was allowed to drop without comment. None of them liked Las Cases and wondered why the emperor had included him in his party. Madame Bertrand whispered to her husband, "Conceited little man!" Gourgaud rubbed his chin with nervous fingers and indulged in speculations as to the slim possibility of escaping from this volcanic prison house.

Madame Montholon was the only one who heard the light footfall on the deck behind them and turned to see the emperor approaching. She indulged in a fleeting but intimate smile over her plump shoulder. This was a habit which annoyed Napoleon very much, because of the implications which might be drawn from it. There had been too much sly whispering about them on the long voyage.

Curiosity had finally taken the upper hand. He could wait no longer to see this obscure island about which they had speculated so much. His valet Marchand had seen to it that he wore nothing but white, except, of course, for the low shoes of black leather. The southeast trades, which bombarded the island, ruffled his no longer abundant stock of hair. He took a few steps only toward the rail, his eyes fixed on James Roads with a rigid intentness.

The roadstead was filled with ships. There were the frigates which had accompanied the *Northumberland*, all flying the

3

flag of the Royal Navy, their masts bare, their decks filled with busy figures in white. There were in addition a few deep-sea trading vessels and quite a large number of fishing craft. The Man of Destiny's eyes smoldered as he took in this display of sea strength. If it had not been for the British Navy he might have accomplished all his objectives many years before. Had he been able to protect his armies in crossing the Channel, he would have sent them over from Boulogne without any hesitation, knowing how weak the land defenses of the obdurate island had been at the time. Why had it been impossible to find better commanders than the incompetent and overly cautious French admirals? Jeanne d'Arc was born to save France in the Hundred Years' War. Why could not another Madame de Clisson have been sent to inspire his sailors to fight as well as his soldiers fought on land?

Back of the hulls and masts of the shipping loomed up the mountainous line of St. Helena. An appalling sight! No gentle, warm Elba this; where, had he controlled his ambition, he could have spent the rest of his life in ease and with a certain degree of dignity. The gamble of the Hundred Days had been a costly one!

A furious anger boiled up inside him. He, emperor of a victorious France, the master of Europe, who had moreover placed himself voluntarily in British hands, was he to be treated as a prisoner of war? How could he have anticipated they would display their perfidy so glaringly?

How could civilized people exist on this volcanic islet? There was something mysterious, something fearsome and blood-chilling about the high-piled and tortured rocks which jutted up straight from the sea.

"France! Fickle France!" he said to himself. "How long will you allow this to go on? I found your throne vacant and still filled with the stench of the stupid Bourbons and the filthy wigs they wore! I raised it to a glory such as the world had never seen. France, France, let the world know that Napoleon is your true head! Demand his release!"

The members of his party waited for him to speak. He seemed calm enough on the surface. Finally he raised the telescope which hung around his shoulders on a twisted cord of white velvet. With uncertain fingers he adjusted the sights to the harbor of Jamestown pressed in between two towering walls of black rock.

After several moments of observation, he lowered the glass.

"There's a quay behind that iron arch," he said in a low tone. "It is filled with people. They are waiting for a sight of the man who might have been their master. I suspect they think I'll be taken ashore in chains." He dropped the glass. "I shall refuse to go until nightfall. They are not going to exhibit me like a trained bear!" He stepped back a pace. "Bertrand, tell that admiral fellow what I've decided. We'll go ashore by the light of the moon."

Gourgaud, who always found it hard to curb his feelings, took it on himself to make a comment. "Does the moon ever deign to shine on this ghostly pile of slag from the furnaces of Satan?"

2

The Balcombe family had assembled about the table for the evening meal. Because of the importance of the day and the excitement which had gripped the whole island, the two boys had been allowed to stay up; William, who was eight, and little Alex, who was four. They sat on each side of their mother and, being very well brought up, had little to say. Already, in fact, the eyes of little Alex were beginning to show the first signs of uncontrollable sleepiness.

The head of the house, looking about him with an affectionate glance was filled suddenly with a sense of his blessings and forgot the main topic of the moment. He had already explained that the ex-emperor of the French would not come ashore until after sundown and that he intended to ride back to Jamestown to watch. Now his thoughts had taken a different turn. "I suppose they still say at Carlton House that I married beneath me," he mused silently. "Ha, those red-nosed wine swillers, I wish they were here! Has any man a prettier or more affectionate wife? Where are there children to equal these of mine?" He smiled to himself as he raised his second glass of port and admired its deep coloring. It might have been said that he had a Georgian face, jaw more conspicuous than the brow, the eyes very much alive, the hair a mass of dark close curls. His white stock was immaculate but his coat and his braided weskit had a suggestion of age about them.

The second daughter was not much interested in her food. She fidgeted about until her father, who understood the signs, realized she had something on her mind. Finally she spoke up.

"Papa!"

"Yes."

"Papa, I think I'll go with you."

Before the head of the house could declare himself, Mrs. Balcombe took the matter in hand. "You are *not* going with him, Betsy. It's entirely out of the question. You will have to go to bed at your usual time."

Betsy frowned as though she did not understand the reason for such finality in the maternal dictum. "But, Mamma—"

"No 'buts,' young lady," said Mrs. Balcombe. "You're going to bed as usual and there's no use saying anything more."

"But, Mama, I have something—something *very* important I want to say about it."

William Balcombe smiled up the length of the table at his wife. "I think, my dear, we should hear this very important communication."

"Well," said Betsy, seizing the opportunity instantly, "when I grow up—when I'm married and have children of my own—they'll know I was here when Napoleon Bonaparte came. Aren't they going to ask me questions and questions and questions? They'll want to know—oh, *everything!* What am I going to say to them? *That I was sent to bed early?*"

"You may be worried about what you'll say," declared her mother, who was now smiling broadly. "But I'm not. You'll think of things to say, dear child. You always do."

"Betsy," said Mr. Balcombe, in his quiet-spoken way. "I'd like to take you, child, but I'm sure no women will be there. It may be a noisy crowd. Might even develop into a bit of a riot, you know. It wouldn't be safe for you. I'm sure your mother doesn't want to go. Nor Jane."

Jane, who was two years older than Betsy, faced her across the table. It was clear that she was not so much interested in the matter as the rest of them. Her mind, apparently, was on other things at the moment. In the past year she had been growing into a young lady, graduating from the wearing of pantalettes and becoming deeply concerned with such major concerns as parties and dresses and beaux. She was slender and had a brunette prettiness; and was in every way a sweet and pleasant young lady.

Betsy was quite different. In her fourteenth year she already showed the beginnings of an exquisite beauty. With this rare heritage, however, she was still a tomboy and much more concerned about her pony and the sports in which she indulged with her friends than with bothersome considerations of dress and appearance. Her hair was a mass of close fair curls but it never occurred to her that it demanded any further attention after the combing she gave it on rising. It must be acknowledged that Betsy was untidy, a burden which her usually gentle mother found hard to bear. Her eyes, quite large in a heart-shaped face, were a bright and vibrant blue; but as one result of an active summer her cheeks were tanned brown and there was a small cluster of freckles on her nose.

Sarah Timms, the colored servant who looked after the two sisters and helped with the serving of the meals, came in to distribute plates for the dish of stewed veal already on the table. She was a comfortable figure in a loose dress of broad colors and with a purple cloth wrapped around her head. She loved purple and would not wear anything else. She had warm and loving eyes.

"Miss Betsy," she said, "yu mammy right. Dis Bom'part, he terr'ble man. He get at yu an' tear out yu heart. An' eat it!"

"I did not ask for your opinion, Sarah," said Mrs. Balcombe. She was an indulgent mistress, but, after all, there were limits which had to be enforced.

"No'm, mistuss. My 'pinions nevah ast. But allus give."

"Yes, they're always *give*, Sarah Timms." Mrs. Balcombe sighed. "I really believe I've heard you express your views on every subject under the sun."

The ample and tenderhearted Sarah's concern at the moment was all for her charge. Betsy had fallen into the kind of despair that the very young can engender over small matters. "You goan eat veal, chile?" she asked.

"No," answered Betsy. "You know I don't like stewed veal. It's stringy and it has no taste."

Her father regarded her sternly. "Now, young lady, you know how hard it is to keep fresh meat on an island like this. We're lucky to have veal. I don't know what we're coming to. The number of vessels stopping here seems to shrink all the time. Perhaps we'll do better with this distinguished visitor in our midst. You'd better powder into that veal like a good girl."

"Perhaps Mamma will let me have an egg instead."

"No eggs!" decided Sarah. "We's gonna be sho't on eggs. Dis Bom'part he eats on'y chickem and soon all chickem on island be gone. Den where eggs cum fum?"

William Balcombe expected to assume the responsibility for the supplies needed in the Napoleonic household. His eyes began to twinkle.

"I must say that's a slant that never occurred to me. Perhaps I better look into it." He poured himself another glass of wine. "Sarah, are you really afraid of this man?"

"Cose I'se 'fraid. Dis night I'se goin' do like eve'yone in Jamestom. I'se goin' to bed and covah mah haid in blankit. He ain' goin' git at me!"

Mantee Timms, Sarah's husband, who was a general handyman about the place, came in with more dishes. He was not of much use and had careless habits with his shirts, which always seemed to be out. His hand trembled as he placed the dishes in the center of the table.

"Tee!" said Mr. Balcombe, sharply. "You been at the brandy again?"

"Huh, suh?" Mantee always needed to have a question repeated at least once in order to get a full grasp of the meaning.

"You heard me, Tee; have you been at the brandy?"

"No, suh, mas'r. No brandy. No, suh. None tall."

"Then why does your hand shake? Is it because you're afraid of this man Bonaparte too?"

Mantee was so eager to grasp at any excuse that he did not need to have this suggestion repeated. "Das it, suh. Yas, suh, das it. I'se 'fraid o' dis Bonumpart."

"Then you have no wish to go into town tonight to see him?"

"No, suh!"

Sarah had moved around the table to stand behind Betsy. "I's knew yu not eat veal, chile. I make johnnycake. Yu want now?"

"Yes, Sarah, please. But I must have sirup with it."

"Dey's sirup foh yu, chile."

"For me too, I hope," said the head of the house. "I like sirup."

"On'y nuff foh one, Mist' Ballum."

Mrs. Balcombe had made a discovery. "Betsy!" she said, sharply. "You've got that dog beside you. How many times must I say he's not to be brought to the table?"

Betsy's voice took on a pleading note, as she laid a protecting hand on the head of the small pug dog she had smuggled in beside her. "Please, Mamma. You know Snooky hasn't grown as fast as the others. They pick on the poor little fellow and don't let him go near the plates. He'd starve to death if I didn't look after him."

"But not at the table, Betsy Balcombe! Have you given him anything off your plate?"

Jane knew that her younger sister had broken this rule by giving her pet some surreptitious bites of the unwanted veal, so she came to her aid by asking their mother a question. "Did I tell you I was in Teach's shop yesterday, Mamma?"

The well-meant red herring served its purpose. Mrs. Balcombe turned at once to the older daughter. "I didn't know you were going into town, Jane. Why didn't you tell me?"

"Well, Mamma, I just wanted to have a quiet look around all by myself. I'm getting *so* tired of white. I've worn nothing else for five or six years and I *do* want my new dress to be something different."

The mother of the family became so completely engrossed in the point raised by Jane that she turned sideways in her chair and indulged in a slight frown. Betsy took advantage of this by carrying the dog to the side door and putting him out on the porch with a friendly pat. "Don't you worry, Snooky," she whispered. "I'll see you get plenty to eat tonight."

"Jane," declared Mrs. Balcombe, "I'm not sure anything will suit you as well as white. You look so girlish and pretty in it."

"That's just it, Mamma! I don't want to look girlish any longer. I saw"—with a sudden enthusiasm—"a really lovely India muslin. It's the new dusky shade, you know. They call it *graine de réséda*. I just love it."

Mrs. Balcombe gave some thought to the problem. "I'll go in and look at it, Jane. But, mind, I'm not promising."

The head of the house rose to his feet, reluctantly pushing the port bottle to one side. "Time to start for town, if you'll excuse me, my dear," he said. "I know a man's opinion is of no value but it seems to me this muslin would suit Jane very well. She's growing up, you know. Tee, bring Conquistador around. I'll ride him in tonight." His voice rose to a shout of

9

exasperation. "Your shirt's out at the back again! If you aren't more careful, I'll send you to the stables for good!"

He passed Betsy at the door and paused to drop a hand lightly on her head. "Sorry I can't take you."

3

The next morning Betsy was the first one up as usual. It was a very few minutes after six and not a sound was heard from the kitchens, and in the stables only the clucking of chickens and the lowing of cattle. By half-past six she was bathed and dressed and her hair had been brushed into a pleasant enough order. She hurried out into the sunshine, carrying a bonnet in her hand.

The dogs heard her at once. They swarmed out from their sleeping quarters under the porch and began to dash along madly at her heels, barking furiously. The hutch in the stable door was open but it was several moments before the almost benign face of William Pitt was framed in it.

He gave her a low bow. " 'Mawnin', Mees Bess," he said.

Before proceeding further it will be necessary to cast back for a quick survey of the domestic household. There were half a dozen servants in all and technically they were slaves, although they enjoyed much freedom of action and habit. Sarah and Mantee had been left on the island by a slaver captain because of illnesses both had developed on the voyage from Africa, and William Balcombe had bought them at a nominal figure. After they had been with the family for a few years, Sarah had raised the point that they should have a surname to demonstrate further the solidity of their marriage, and Mantee, with complete indifference, had agreed. Sarah had often heard nostalgic references at table to the beautiful home the Balcombes had once enjoyed on the Thames and she selected the name of that river as suitable for herself and the phlegmatic Tee. Gradually the name was corrupted to Timms, which suited her just as well.

The stable man had been close to death when he was put ashore from a slaver. He was an extremely tall man, perhaps as much as six feet eight, and William Balcombe was interested in him despite his deplorable condition. "There is a race of very tall Negroes somewhere in the central part of

10

Africa," he said. "From the Mountains of the Moon, I think. I'm sure this poor fellow comes from there. We should take him in." The purchase was made for a pound and the tall captive recovered with surprising speed. From the very first he had a manner about him. He carried his small head on his long arched neck as though it were birth and merit which elevated him so much above other men, and not a matter of bones. "I think he must have been a chief or at least a medicine man," commented his owner. They gave him the name of Caesar, and then fell into the habit of calling him Caesaraugustus.

He was assigned to the care of the horses and he seemed to be very happy in the stable and in the company of his four-footed charges. But one day Betsy, who often acted as a go-between, came to her parents with a request from him.

"Caesaraugustus thinks he should have a surname too. Like Sarah and Mantee."

"What name does the old chieftain want?" asked her father.

"One day he heard you talking to the curate and he made out enough of what you were saying to know it was about a very great man."

"Which curate?"

"The Rev. Godefroi Eustace Stodgkin."

"Oh, *that* one." Mr. Balcombe had small liking for the opinionated Mr. Stodgkin. "Who were we talking about?"

"William Pitt. Caesaraugustus says he was head man in *his* country just as Mr. Pitt was head man in England. He seems to think he's entitled to the name."

"Why, that uppish old rascal!" William could not refrain from smiling, however. He pondered the point for several moments. "I don't suppose the Great Commoner, if he were alive, would have any objections to this use of his name. He might even be pleased." He nodded to Betsy. "Well, William Pitt it is. I'll be glad to have a shorter name."

"Not shorter, Papa. We are not to call him William. It must always be William Pitt. He makes quite a point of that."

It was clear that William Pitt did not approve of dogs. He scowled at the noisy pups and shooed them away from the entrance into the stables with a hint of impatience. Betsy was disturbed by his appearance. His eyes were heavy and his feet seemed to drag.

"Are you ill, William Pitt?" she asked.

The tall slave nodded his head slowly. "Not well, Mees Bess. Not sleep."

She turned her attention to the dogs. "Now see here. You can't come in, any of you. You'll waken the whole household. Down, down! Yes, Snooky, I mean you too. Play with your brothers for a change and don't be such a mope." She turned back to the stable man. "Is my old Tom in a good humor this morning?"

"Ole Tom eat slow. If ole Tom eat slow, ole Tom in bad 'ummer."

The pony was not quite finished with his morning ration of hay and did not deign to look up when Betsy reached his stall. He even struck the boards behind him with one hoof, as though to say; "Have a care. I am in no mood for being petted or any such nonsense."

In the meantime the family of dogs had found another way of getting in. They came scrambling around her, fighting and yelping madly to let their mistress see how smart they were. The pony's whole face wrinkled with disapproval. "Is it right," he seemed to ask, "for a gentleman to be interrupted at his meal by a pack of silly dogs?"

"My fine Thomas Didymus," said the girl, insisting on running a hand over his long nose, "you are not to be so cross. When I get up this early so you can have your morning exercise, you should be grateful to me and not surly. If you belonged to some people I could mention, you would soon find out how well off you are here. Isn't that so, William Pitt?"

"Thas so, Mees Bess," answered the tall native. He peered over the side of the stall. "You eat hay fast, you Tom." Then he addressed the girl. "Does I lam 'im fum behin' or does I coax him wi' ca'att?"

"Please, William Pitt, don't hit poor Tom. Offer him a carrot."

Tom lost all interest in his hay when he saw William Pitt appear in front of his stall with a carrot in his hand. He nickered with delight and came out as soon as the bars were lowered. He gobbled the carrot and he even made no protest when the towering native saddled him.

The ride which followed was a particularly pleasant one. The pony found it to his liking to stretch his legs and went up over the hilly trails at a brisk pace. When they returned half an hour later, he put on a whirlwind finish down the slope to the stable door, where William Pitt waited with a bucket of water.

"Betsy, Betsy, Betsy!" cried Mrs. Balcombe, appearing on the side porch of the house. "How many times must I warn you not to ride so fast? Some day you'll be thrown and they'll carry you in with every bone in your body broken."

"Oh, pshaw, Mamma," called the girl, in her gayest mood. "I won't get thrown. I'm a pretty good rider, you know. Besides, I'm in *such* a hurry."

She did not mention her reason for hurry. Without further explanation of any kind, she took the path which skirted the other side of the house, and the next glimpse her mother had of her she was walking briskly down the steep road to the main drive. She had seen a spot of color at the gates which resembled the red coat of a soldier.

She was whistling exuberantly as she went down to investigate, reaching all the high notes with a sure sweetness. Betsy had a low-pitched voice and thus did not sing so well as Jane, who was a soprano of limited range. But her whistling was much commented on by the islanders, being such an unusual accomplishment in a girl.

It turned out that she had been right. The wearer of the scarlet tunic was standing outside the gate, his rifle slung over his shoulder. He was gazing up the road with the immobility of a British soldier on sentry duty.

Betsy said to herself, "I *knew* this was going to be an important day."

The Briars, a mile and a half up the road from Jamestown, was one of the prides of the island. The property of William Balcombe was like a strip of old England, scooped up from somewhere in Kent or Sussex, carried over thousands of miles of water by magic carpets or some such means, and then dropped into a narrow niche between the bare, black, forbidding rocks of St. Helena. Everywhere else the prospect was bleak and chilling and the soil was as unyielding as a steel buckler. But at the Briars it was always green. The land ran back to what would have been a grim background of volcanic rock except for a waterfall which came down the cliffside and was generally blown into foam before it reached the ground.

Although this quiet home, where an English merchant lived with his family, had an avenue of banyan trees and the orchard produced oranges, lemons, pomegranates, and mangoes, there was a preponderance of the shrubs and flowers and

13

fruits of England, roses and hollyhocks and geranium, even some of the trees so familiar at home, willow, oak, and many varieties of fruit. The grass lacked the spongy quality of the native matgrass, it was healthy and very green and as Anglo-Saxon as white cliffs and cool rains.

The house was of frame construction and in height two stories only, with a covered porch extended across the full front. It was wide enough to hint at comfort and spaciousness within, but the number of rooms could not have exceeded eight or ten. Behind it were stables and domestic outhouses. At first glance, however, one did not see the main house. The eye traveled inevitably to a wooden pavilion standing at one side and on higher ground. This was approached through terraced gardens which gave an impression of lavishness and a well-screened privacy. At some points of view only the peaked roof was visible. This had been used by the Balcombes as a guest house and many notables had stopped there while waiting over for ships, even the now illustrious Duke of Wellington.

It did not take Betsy long to reach the stone pillars which carried the single word BRIARS. She peered out through the severe pattern of the wrought-iron gates, finding her view completely blocked by the soldier's stiff red back.

"Good morning," said Betsy. "What are you doing here?"

The sentry was taken by surprise. He turned his head and studied her through the metal bars.

"On sentry duty, miss." He ran a forefinger under his tight collar. "Road's being guarded for miles. I'll be here most of the day."

Betsy jumped to a conclusion. "Then *he* is going to pass. The emperor."

"Gen'ral Bonaparte, miss."

"Oh, dear, yes. I forgot. It's an order, isn't it? Could I be sent to jail for calling him that?"

"I won't be reporting you, miss."

"Do you mind stepping a little to one side? I'm coming out. No order against that, is there?"

The sentry grinned. "Not as I knows of."

She stepped through and let the gate swing to behind her. For a moment she studied the tall and motionless figure in its uncomfortable and uncompromising red cloth.

"I'm going to stay here and see him pass."

"Well, I suppose it's awright. But sort of make yourself

14

scarce when you see Johnny Craps coming—ex*cuse me, miss*. I mean the gen'ral."

Betsy was beginning to feel thoroughly at home with this new acquaintance. She asked, "What's your name, please?"

"Private Knock, miss."

"Knock? Isn't that a rather odd name?"

"Never heard anyun else as had it, miss. Don't ast me how we got it. I don't know. My father didn't know. *His* father didn't know. We just had it give us. Some of these noddies I'm sojering with laugh at me. And these fussocks of officers grin when they gives me orders. Gal-go-raily, I'd like to bash in a head or two! Some day I may up and do it."

After a moment the soldier stared down at her over the barrel of his gun. "What's *your* name, miss? If ye don't mind telling me, that is."

"Not at all, Private Knock. My name is Lucia Elizabeth Balcombe. But I'm always called Betsy."

Betsy seated herself on a mound of grass at the side of the road and proceeded to ask him all the questions which came into her mind, which were many. The sentry, watching her out of the corner of an eye, answered her as best he could. Sometimes she was puzzled by what he told her, chiefly because his vocabulary was strangely different from anything she had ever encountered. "What do you mean by that?" she would have to ask, or she would say, "You do use the oddest words, Private Knock."

She had picked some ripe plums the day before, tearing a rent in her skirt in the course of climbing the tree, and she now found they were still in her pocket. She tossed them up to him and he crunched them gratefully in his strong teeth.

"Coo!" he said. "They're banging good. I never got much in the way of fruit in Lunnon. 'Cept as I was able to steal some off the barrows."

What interested Betsy most was that he had seen the emperor the night before at rather close range. She questioned him eagerly about his impressions.

"Yus, he passed as close as ten feet. Never looked at anyun. I got the idea he'd have been pleased to order us strung up, all in rows. Ev'y mothers' son of us. If you get a look at him now, miss, you'll see what I mean."

"Oh, I'm going to stay and see him, you may be sure."

He indulged in a grin. "You know your mind, I can see. You know, miss, I've been looking for'ard to when they'll transfer us some're out of this banging heat. But there's one thing I'd like to stay long enough to see. I'd like to see you when you grows up into a young leddy, Miss Betsy."

At this point the sentry came abruptly to attention. He clicked his gun into proper position on his shoulder and stared straight ahead of him.

"Here they come," he whispered. "Get back ahind that pillar so they won't see you talking to me. 'Gainst orders. Keep your eyes wide open, Miss Betsy. There he is, Gen'ral Bonaparte, old Johnny Craps hisself!"

And so Betsy Balcombe saw Napoleon Bonaparte for the first time, by peering cautiously from behind the stone gatepost. He did not see her. His gaze seemed to be fixed with a surprising intentness on the Balcombe domain.

She watched him until the mounted party with him passed out of sight on the road which led up to Longwood.

"I'm not afraid of him," was the thought which took possession of her mind. "He has a strange look, but very sad."

4

Betsy interrupted the breakfast that her parents were enjoying together by bursting in with her news.

"I've seen him!" she declared.

William Balcombe looked up from the kedgeree he was eating; a common dish in St. Helena because of the abundance of fish. Although there was no bacon, no sausage, no kidneys on the table—in fact, none of the classic dishes of a fine English breakfast—Sarah Timms had a special gift for the first meal of the day. There was a loaf of bread right out of the oven and smoking hot, an array of small containers with the most delectable of jams and jellies, and a pot of coffee filling the room with the most agreeable of odors. The dining room was on the east side and so had the benefit of the early sun. It was warm and bright and cheerful.

"Do you mean Napoleon?" asked the head of the house.

"Yes, Papa. He was riding up the shore road and I was behind the gates. So I saw him as plain as plain."

Although none of the other children had yet come down, Betsy seated herself in her usual chair. She reached for the bread. Holding up the piece she had secured, she emitted a cry of triumph. "The crusty end! I've haven't had it for—oh,

16

for weeks and weeks. One of those greedy little brothers of mine always gets it."

"The little fellows like the crusty ends," said Mrs. Balcombe.

"And so do I. And so does Jane. And you. And Papa." Betsy let the subject drop and proceeded to eat the bread with relish.

"Now tell us your impression of Napoleon," said her father.

"He looked—well, like a schoolteacher. You know, kind of stern and very sure of himself. And not willing to have any back talk at all. But I liked him."

"Then you'll be able to calm the fears of poor Sarah and the rest of the servants. They sometimes seem inclined to listen to you. They won't listen to me, although I got much the same impression as you did. Of course, I didn't get a close view of him."

Betsy began to draw on the information she had received from the sentry. "You weren't as lucky as Private Knock. He saw the emperor very close."

William Balcombe, having finished his kedgeree, frowned at this. "And who is Private Knock?"

"Oh, I haven't told you about him, have I? I saw him as soon as I went out this morning. He was on sentry go at our gates. So I went down to find why he was there and we had a long talk."

"Indeed. Don't you know, child, that young ladies should not have long talks with private soldiers? Or talks of any kind!"

"Oh, Papa, he was just filled with interesting things to tell me. You see, he was born in London and he joined a group who called themselves the Kincher Coes. They were a pretty bad lot, I'm afraid."

"Kincher Coes," said her father in a reflective tone. "That would be a corruption of the old cant term, I suppose. Some time ago—oh, several centuries—the crooks of England used to call their girls kinchin morts and their boys kinchin coes. So this interesting sentry had been a kinchin coe!"

"Oh, yes," said Betsy eagerly. "And they got into trouble. I think it may have been stealing fruit from barrows or the quarts of milk left on area steps. The bobbies were after them—"

"Bobbies?" said Mrs. Balcombe, who was beginning to show symptoms of shock.

"The police, my dear, the police," said her husband. "It's largely a London term but surely you've heard the word used."

"Well, anyway," went on Betsy, "Private Knock thought he had better get himself out of trouble, so he took the shilling."

"That means he enlisted," explained Mr. Balcombe for his wife's enlightenment. "And so, Betsy, this private soldier had a close look at Napoleon. How did that come about?"

"He was on sentry duty. On the steps of the cackle-tub—" Betsy stopped abruptly, wearing an expression of dismay. "Oh, please, Mamma, I didn't mean to say that."

"And what," in the sternest of terms, "is a cackle-tub?"

Betsy knew from the ominous expression on her mother's face that she was in serious trouble. She hesitated. "It's a name they have for—well, for a church."

"Betsy Balcombe! That is blasphemy! How *could* you say such a thing? How can you expect to go to heaven if you utter such terrible words? Tonight you must say your prayers twice and you must beg the Lord to forgive you. I hope He will."

"Come, come, my dear," commented the head of the house. "I think Betsy is very much at fault. She should never use such words. But"—he could not keep himself from smiling—"there's a lot of cackling goes on in churches when a committee of women get together. Not to mention what we suffer from church choirs."

Mrs. Balcombe's pretty face was flushed with indignation. "Mr. Balcombe, must it always be this way? Must you feel called upon to stand up for the child, no matter what she says or does?"

Noticing that his plate was empty, she rose and carried it to the sideboard for a second helping. Ordinarily she always felt a sense of satisfaction in using this particular piece of furniture. It was of the period of James I and quite authentically ugly in a heavy oakish way, being as stoutly built as the legs of a cavalryman. All of her best furniture had been broken in the passage out from England with this one exception. She cherished it beyond its just deserts but she had no

18

room in her mind for anything approaching satisfaction at the moment.

Returning to the table, she placed the replenished plate in front of her husband. "I expect you to agree, Mr. Balcombe, that Betsy must go to her room at once. And stay there until I say she can come down."

The girl's face was a picture of dismay. "But, Mamma! please let me tell you first what I was going to say. I noticed something when the emperor—I mean General Bonaparte— passing. It was *very* strange."

Mrs. Balcombe hesitated. "Well—if it's something we ought to know."

"He acted in a funny way. I couldn't see much more than his head because of the dip in the road but, as soon as he caught sight of our place, he became—very watchful. I think he must have turned in his saddle as he rode by, because there was his face for the whole distance staring up here. Now why was he so interested?"

"Perhaps," said William Balcombe, helping himself to marmalade, "he heard that the Duke of Wellington occupied the pavilion once."

The girl shook her head emphatically. "No, Papa, it was more than that. He was studying the place. Just as though it was a battlefield."

"Still he may have heard about the duke," said Mrs. Balcombe. "Everyone talked about the way he enjoyed himself here. He was such a kind man. I'll never forget what fine eyes he had."

"Most observing eyes, my dear," declared her husband. "He most certainly observed you. It's no wonder his men always call him the Beau. They say right now that Napoleon's old flame Grassini—the great Italian singer, you know—is in Paris and that our duke—"

"That will do, Mr. Balcombe," interrupted his wife. "There are things that even our Betsy should not hear."

Betsy, strangely enough, had not been paying close attention to what her parents were saying. She was busily pursuing her own thoughts.

"You know, Mamma and Papa," she said, "something occurred to me when I saw him riding by. I thought how odd it would be if he wanted to stay here too." She indulged in a throaty laugh which could not be described as a giggle, although it belonged somewhere in that classification. "Just think! Napoleon sleeping in the same room as the Duke of Wellington! Wouldn't that be funny?"

"Yes; that would be most peculiar," declared her father, thrusting back his chair and getting to his feet. "Well, I must hie me down to the marts of trade. The offices of Balcombe, Fowler and Chase do not begin to clatter noisily until I arrive." He kissed his wife and then leaned over to give Betsy an affectionate hug. "I'm sure if Napoleon does come here, he'll admire you, my dear, quite as much as the Iron Duke did. I bid you *adieu*, my fair ladies."

He was scarcely out of the room when sedate footsteps on the stairs announced the approach of the older daughter of the house. Jane was a picture of neatness. Her hair was combed back perfectly, her dress was so starched that it rustled loudly.

"You are early, my dear," said her mother, as Jane took her place at the table.

Jane looked at the remains of the loaf. "But not early enough, it seems. Who got the end?"

"I did," answered Betsy. "And *my*, how I enjoyed it!"

"There was a lot of talk going on down here. What was it all about?"

Betsy answered eagerly. "I saw Napoleon this morning."

Jane did not seem too much interested. "Oh! Where?"

"Down on the road to Longwood."

"Isn't it funny he should be up so early?"

"I read somewhere that he won his battles that way."

Jane's interest in the topic was exhausted. "Mamma, could we go into town today? I want you to see that material before it's all sold."

"Well, dear, perhaps I can spare the time. And, Betsy, I'll suspend your punishment and let you go too. *If* we go."

"Thanks, Mamma. But, really, I think I ought to stay here. Just in case something happens."

A sound of irate barking from all the pups in concert took Betsy to the side porch. They heard her voice raised in expostulation and Mrs. Balcombe went out to investigate. The girl lost interest at once in the canine controversy and turned in a suddenly grave mood to face her mother.

"Mamma, it's a good thing you have Jane, isn't it? She's so sweet and just the kind of daughter you like to have."

Mrs. Balcombe regarded her with an equally sudden gravity. "Betsy, dear child, you don't think that I—that I have a preference for Jane?"

"I wouldn't blame you, Mamma. I must seem like a great nuisance at times."

Her mother leaned down and put an arm around her, hugging her with a sudden emotional tightness. "Betsy! Betsy! It's not true, little girl. I love you as much as I do Jane, even if I am sharp with you sometimes."

"Well, I seem to do so much thinking about things and I always feel I should tell you about it. For instance, Mamma, surely the time has come when we, Jane and I, ought to be told about Papa and his family."

A slight note of sharpness resumed possession of Mrs. Balcombe's tongue. "Now, Betsy, you know we're not supposed to talk about that. Your father doesn't want it."

"But we don't even know if it's true what people say."

"How do you know what people say?"

"Why, don't you suppose they ask us questions? I guess they're afraid to say anything to you or Papa, so they come to us, to Jane and me. All the women you know come to us. They speak in low whispers. They want to know if it's true that Papa—"

"Please! Please! Let's not talk about it. Your father prefers not to have it discussed. I don't know why. But he does."

"Mamma, there's nothing to be ashamed of. He ought to be proud. When we were at school last year in England, all the girls used to talk about us, Jane and me. They seemed to think we were—well, like princesses in disguise."

"What do you and Jane say when these women ask you questions?"

"We say we don't know. That's all we can say, isn't it? But *you* must know, Mamma. Surely you must."

"Please, Betsy. Your father has asked me not to talk. Not with anyone. Perhaps when you get a little older he may think differently about it. But I'm not sure. Something happened that I don't know about. I think it left a mark on him."

"I wouldn't have brought it up except I got to thinking. If

21

Napoleon did want to come here, we could meet him on equal grounds, couldn't we?"

"You do have a way all your own of looking at things," said Mrs. Balcombe, with a rather strained smile. "Now be a good girl. Run along and find something useful to do."

Chapter Two

1

At five o'clock that afternoon the sun had lost so much of its triumphant height in the sky that it looked to be nearing the point when it would suddenly drop behind the jagged edge of the western hills. The air had become cool. The trade wind from the east was stirring the leaves in the overhanging trees and even causing the branches to twist and toss and to fill the air with the half rustle, half song which the natives sometimes called the "sonther." Mrs. Balcombe, seated at a table containing the remains of a substantial tea, was glad she had her cashmere shawl over her shoulders. It was a beautiful thing of many colors. All her husband had told her about it was that "it had come on a deal." It was doubtful if even Napoleon's first wife, the slightly tragic Josephine, or his second mate, the daughter of the illustrious house of Hapsburg, had possessed its peer.

She sat between her husband and the Rev. Godefroi Eustace Stodgkin, who had dropped in for tea and a parochial talk. William Balcombe had groaned when he arrived home from town and found this guest ensconced at the round deal table under a clump of sheltering trees. He had no liking for the new curate.

The visitor was tall and bony, with a prominent Adam's apple and such a degree of shortsightedness that his eyeglasses were as thick as the pebbles which boys skim on water. Also he was a bachelor. He had remarked once that he was waiting for the Balcombe sisters to grow up and would then decide which one he would marry. When this reached Betsy's ears she had said to herself. "I don't know how Jane feels. *But it won't be me!*"

As usual the visitor had been doing all the talking and what he had to say seemed to begin invariably with some such phrase as, "I am against it!" "I cannot accept such reasoning," "I refuse to believe," or "Never, never!"

Mrs. Balcombe's mind was not on his discourse and she was the first to see that a party of horsemen had come to a stop on the shore road below their entrance.

"They're turning in," she said, in an anxious tone. "If you will excuse me, Mr. Stodgkin, I will run and see if anything needs to be done." She rose from her chair, spilling a ball of wool out of her knitting bag.

"Who are turning in?" asked the shortsighted clergyman.

"I think it is Napoleon Bonaparte and his escort," replied Mr. Balcombe. He had indulged in a bath since his return from town, keeping the curate waiting while he did so, and was now wearing a fresh suit of clothes and a new cravat. He felt ready for any emergency.

The jaw of the young clergyman shot out at a belligerent angle. "I do not condone war," he declared. "I have nothing but contempt for great military leaders. I shall refuse to make the acquaintance of General Bonaparte. If you don't mind, Mr. Balcombe, I shall leave by the side road and pay a call on that woman over there. I can't be polite enough to name her by name because I don't know what her name is. I can only follow the lead of others and speak of her as the Veiled Lady." He paused and then added in a decided tone, "I am going to be very firm with her!"

Mr. Balcombe sighed audibly. It was becoming difficult to be polite to this man of unqualified prejudices. He glanced briefly to the south where a rise in the rocky structure of the island, somewhat similar to that which made the Briars so pleasant, allowed the smallest glimpse of a gable window in a cluster of trees. He was in the habit of glancing at it frequently because he shared the interest of all island inhabitants in the mysterious lady who lived there, and who was never seen even at the small gable window.

"You are going to be firm with her, did you say?" he asked. "What has the poor woman been doing?"

The new curate untangled his sharp knees and got to his feet. "Mr. Balcombe," he said, sniffling from the head cold which never seemed to desert him, "I do not condone such unusual happenings as the arrival of a woman in a veil who proceeds to rent—through a lawyer, mind you, who never sees behind the veil and who refuses to state her name—a house on this island."

"The lawyer in question," interjected William Balcombe, "gave a favorable report on her in all other respects. He said she spoke in a cultured voice. He knows her name but is under instructions not to divulge it. The bank did not need to question her when she called there. Advices had already reached them from England which satisfied them about her. In a financial sense at least. It is no secret that she receives remittances quarterly."

"Such considerations do not weigh with me," declared the curate. "She refuses to see me—"

"She refuses to see anyone, Mr. Stodgkin."

"But"—emphatically—"I represent the church. She *must* see me. Do you realize that she has never once set foot in the church? Why? It—it is intolerable not to know, so we can be of aid and comfort to her. That, Mr. Balcombe, is our duty."

"She never sees anyone but also she is never seen. It's clear she has good reasons for wanting to be left alone."

"I have called three times. Each time that maidservant, who does not speak English with any degree of intelligibility, has said no to me. That is why I say the time has come for the utmost firmness on my part."

"Don't be too hard on her," urged Mr. Balcombe. "I'm sure she's an unfortunate who has had a tragedy in her life."

"I do not condone—" began the curate again, but before he could define what exactly it was he had set his mind against, he saw that the mounted party was already halfway up the drive and that a man in a distinctive three-cornered hat rode in the front. He hurried away by a side path.

At the same moment a figure in brown and yellow emerged through the trees and came to the table in a breathless state.

"You see, Papa, I *was* right," said Betsy. "I knew he intended to come in on his way back. Papa, was that the Rev. Something Something Stodgkin I saw skittering around behind the house? What a trial he must have been to you!"

"I don't mind telling you, Betsy, that I am beginning to find him intolerable."

The girl bent over and picked up the ball of wool. "I wish Mother would be more careful with her knitting. Now I'll have to follow this all the way through the house until I catch up with her. And I'm in such a hurry!"

"Why, my dear, are you in such a hurry? It won't be

necessary for you to put in an appearance."

Betsy smiled confidently. "You think not, Papa? Let me point out that you had a French nurse for me for quite a few years and that I learned to speak pretty good French. Do any of the rest of you speak it at all? I'm sure I'll be needed to act as interpreter. And I think I should look my best."

The two sisters shared a bedroom, a pleasant corner of the house with two windows and a southeastern exposure. When Betsy burst in to change her dress, Jane was standing before a long mirror on one wall; a rather cheap one which had been acquired to take the place of the valuable Georgian gesso glass which had been broken into a hundred pieces on the ship. The afternoon in town had been fruitful. She had a length of the dusky muslin draped over her shoulders and was studying the effect.

"Jane," said Betsy, wriggling out of her dress and letting it fall on the floor. "Are you ready for company? *Great* company?"

"I think so," said the older sister calmly.

Betsy had run to a tall walnut chest-on-chest (which had been very much damaged also) and was rummaging furiously for what she would need. She had stepped out of her pantalettes, revealing the fact that they were a mere sham, covering her only from knee to ankle, and her first care was to select a fresh pair. It is always premature to speak of the figure of a girl of fourteen, as so many things can happen in the process of further growth. But the trimness of Betsy Balcombe cannot be passed over without notice. Her legs were slender and they were softly and beautifully feminine. They had, in fact, none of the awkward chubbiness of that age.

When sufficiently clothed to risk showing herself at a window, she went to the front of the room and looked down at what was going on below.

"Jane!" she said in a muted tone. "Come and look. Here he is, outside our house. Napoleon Bonaparte. He's riding a beautiful black, and *my* how dignified he looks. Admiral Cockburn is on foot beside him and all the others are walking too—dukes and princes and generals, I suppose. Jane, this is what old Tuddelbury back at school used to speak of as an *historic moment!*"

Jane, looking over her shoulder, seemed dismayed. "Oh,

oh!" she whispered. "Will we be expected to go down? Betsy, I'm afraid! Aren't you?"

"No. I don't think there's anything to be afraid of."

"But will we have to curtsy to him? Will it be necessary to go right down on one knee?"

Betsy was not at all concerned. "I don't know, I'm sure."

Sarah Timms came into the room in a flouncing haste. "Bose you wanted. Down'stahs," she announced. "Miss Jane I see's you ready. Miss Betsy, I mus' look you ovah." She patted and pulled at Betsy's dress and then, taking a comb, worked carefully over her abundant blond locks. "Theah!" she said, finally. "Now I'se satumfied. But Miss Betsy, doan you go talking lot down theah."

"Sarah, do you know what an interpreter is?" asked the younger daughter.

"No'm. I doan know 'bout terpriters."

The girl began to laugh. "Well, Sarah, that's what I'm going to be downstairs. That means I'll do *most* of the talking."

2

Admiral Cockburn had effected some manner of introductions with his smattering of French. Everyone was standing in a rather strained group, with Napoleon in the center. Having dismounted, he had lost much of the imposing dignity he had enjoyed while in the saddle. The assorted counts, barons, and military officers, who made up his party, were watching Mr. and Mrs. Balcombe in a cool appraisal.

"The daughters of the house, General Bonaparte," said the admiral, when the two girls paused in the doorway. "Miss Jane Balcombe. And Miss Elizabeth Balcombe."

Both girls curtsied with stiff uncertainty. The Comte de Bertrand, on Napoleon's right, leaned closer to whisper in his ear. "The younger one speaks French, sire. The older one—ah, sire, is she not charming?"

Napoleon's eyes swept over Jane and came to Betsy. There they stopped. He leaned a little forward in the absorption with which he studied her. Then he leaned back and whispered in Bertrand's ear.

"*Ma foi*, Marshal," he said. "Are you becoming blind? The older one is pretty, yes, but look at the other one. *La petite*."

"Miss Elizabeth Balcombe," said the admiral, "will act as interpreter for us. Will you—ah, take charge, Miss Betsy?"

Much of the assurance which the girl had felt on descending the stairs had deserted her. There was an anxious flush on her cheeks. "I am willing to try, my lord," she said, "but my French is quite limited, I'm afraid."

Napoleon understood something of what was being said. He smiled at the fourteen-year-old girl. "You must let me judge, Mam'selle Betsee," he said. "You are not afraid of me?"

"No, Your Highness. At least, I don't think I am."

"Where did you learn to speak French?"

"I had a nurse from Brittany when I was a small girl. I spoke nothing but French with her for several years."

"I am sure you found it a great pleasure to learn something of our very graceful tongue."

Betsy was recovering enough of her usual composure to give him an honest answer. "I liked it when I had my old nurse, Your Highness. But later, at school, well—"

"Yes, how did you like it at school?"

"We had French teachers there, Your Highness. And they made the language seem—well, kind of excitable."

The stern expression on the face of the Man of Destiny seemed to become somewhat more pronounced. He frowned at her. And then, abruptly, he began to laugh. "Ah, my child. You have spirit. You say what you think. That is good. I like to see it. I have done it all my life, mam'selle. See, we must make a bargain between us. We will always say to one another what we think. It will be an understanding, a game perhaps. And now," he turned to the situation confronting him, "will you tell your parents, mam'selle, that I have a request to make? It will take a long time to finish the additions and repairs to this dreadful place, this Longwood. It will be a matter of weeks. Perhaps even of months." He gave his shoulders an impatient shrug. "What am I to do? I cannot spend another night at that impossible inn."

Admiral Cockburn had been following the conversation with some difficulty. "I regret, General Bonaparte," he said, "that you found it so hot and uncomfortable."

"That was not all. The food! *Ma foi*, it is hard to believe that even English cooks could produce such abominable messes." He turned back to Betsy. "And so, mam'selle, I must make this request of your parents. Could it be arranged for me to stay here until this—this dreadful place in the hills has been made fit for human habitation? I would be quite content with the summerhouse I see up there. It looks cool and inviting."

Betsy conveyed the suggestion to her parents. They spoke together briefly in low tones. Then Mr. Balcombe nodded his head.

"Tell General Bonaparte we will be glad to give him possession of the pavilion. For as long as he needs."

A gratified look took possession of Napoleon's face when the girl translated this for him. He nodded his head several times. "M'sieur and Madame are most kind," he said. "Please tell them, *ma petite*, how grateful I am. And please make it clear that I will strive to render my stay as little difficult for them as possible. My servants will see to my needs and will, of course, prepare my meals."

"When does he want to come?" asked Mrs. Balcombe.

Betsy conveyed this question to him and Napoleon cried out emphatically. "Now! At once! Ah, that dreadful room! That stifling heat! I hope never to set foot there again!"

After another consultation with her parents, Betsy reported; "Papa says you are to consider this your home at once. They will consider it an honor if you will be their guest at dinner tonight."

"I shall be happy to dine with them," answered the ex-emperor. "How can I repay them for such kindness?"

"It will be a family dinner, Your Highness. My sister and I will be of the company. But not our brothers. They are having their supper inside now."

"How many brothers have you, mam'selle?"

"Two. One eight. And one four."

"Four!" Napoleon's manner suddenly became grave. "Then he is the age of my little son, the King of Rome. I think it will be a pleasure for me to see this small brother." He appeared lost in thought for several moments and then he shrugged his shoulders and spoke to Bertrand. "Will you see to things at once? Have my camp cot brought up without fail. I think, if our very nice little interpreter will accompany us to the pavilion, we can decide at once what other things will be necessary."

Betsy led the way through the grounds and up to the relatively high position where the pavilion stood. Napoleon paused in the shade of a grape arbor which covered the entrance to the thickly planted gardens beyond.

"How peaceful it is," he said, with a sigh. "And so very cool. Do you have this breeze all the time?"

"Always, Your Highness. The trade winds seem to blow straight across our property. In winter we would like them to stop because it is cold and raw then. But they never do."

"Perhaps I could stand here and raise up my arms to the skies like Joshua and command them to stop." There was a smile on Napoleon's face which suggested he half believed what he was saying. His eyes became attracted to the waterfall in the background. "How extraordinary! Doesn't the water ever reach the ground?"

"I don't think so, Your Highness. We are very proud of it. My papa says there is nothing quite like it anywhere. Even at Carlton House."

Napoleon leaned over and gave her ear a light pinch. "How lucky for me, *ma petite*, that you had a French nurse."

There were chairs in the garden. Napoleon seated himself in one and motioned Betsy to take another. "Make what arrangements you think necessary," he said to Bertrand. "And now, mam'selle, we shall have a talk."

"If it please Your Highness, may I ask a question?"

"Of course."

"What should I call you? It has been announced that it's to be General Bonaparte but that—that doesn't sound right."

The ex-emperor turned in his chair to look at her more closely. It was a frail piece of furniture and squeaked alarmingly.

"And why, *ma petite*, does it not seem right to you?"

"You were emperor and should always be called that. I can't address you in any other way without feeling you will be offended."

"And you don't want to offend me?"

"Oh, no, Your Highness."

Napoleon had often asserted that with him the human passions never mounted higher than his throat. But at this point in the conversation he made it clear that such was not the case. The skin of his face, generally so white and cool, suddenly showed a flush of anger and this spread rapidly to the fine marblelike expanse of his brow.

He got to his feet and began to pace up and down. His arms were not locked behind his back as was invariably the

30

case when he fell into deep mental concentration. Instead they swung back and forth without keeping in accord with the rhythm of his steps. It was clear that his emotions had been deeply stirred.

"There is no General Bonaparte!" So ran his thoughts. "He ceased to exist when I left Egypt. His place was taken by the First Consul and then by the Emperor. If he existed today, it would be as a shadow, as a spirit, wafted along those hot roads to the Pyramids. Or perhaps on that ship which took me back to France. General Bonaparte has been obliterated by the achievements of the First Consul and the glory of the Emperor.

"But these English, these cold, carping storekeepers and bankers and builders of ships! They know the most cunning ways of offending me. They say they never acknowledged me as Emperor and that I shall always be General Bonaparte to them! They are determined to keep alive the picture of that scrawny, starving young officer who came up out of the revolutionary maelstrom! This I most solemnly swear: I shall never acknowledge the name. I shall refuse to answer when so dressed. I shall return unopened any notes or letters delivered in that name. They may be from these petty officials or they may be from the Emperor of Austria or the King of England. It will be all the same to me. Never, never will they be opened! Even if it means they will put me in close confinement or even in a solitary cell. General Bonaparte has ceased to exist!"

Then he noticed that Betsy had risen and was standing undecided beside her chair, holding her bonnet against her skirt. She looked very much upset.

Napoleon's mood changed. "She thinks she has said something to annoy me," he thought. "On the contrary, this child has been the only one with the decency to see it is all wrong. And she has had the courage to tell me so."

He returned and dropped into his chair so abruptly and heavily that the creaking of the wood became positively alarming.

"You say you don't want to offend me."

"Yes, Your Highness."

"I am happy you feel that way. It has been customary to address me as sire."

Betsy was silent for a moment. Then her lips parted in an involuntary smile. "S-i-r-e?" she asked. When he nodded, she

31

paused again. She seemed afraid to speak. "But—but, Your Highness, are you sure there isn't a mistake? In English we have a much different use for that word."

"Indeed? What may it be?"

"With us it means—the father of a horse."

Napoleon was annoyed. He looked at her severely, suspecting she was making a joke at his expense. Then he managed a smile, a rather bleak one. "This is my fault," he said. "I told you to speak frankly. But, ah, what an abominable language! I shall have to train you to a proper appreciation of French."

"I am afraid," said Betsy, "that I am a failure as an interpreter."

"No, no! not at all. I think you a great success. But I am afraid you will have to learn to accept my rudeness and not feel hurt. Rudeness is necessary in a ruler. Even—an ex-ruler."

Some minutes later Mrs. Balcombe, standing at the outside door of the kitchen, motioned to her husband to join her there.

"Listen," she said.

A sound of voices reached them from the direction of the pavilion garden. Mr. Balcombe listened for a few moments and then shook his head. "It's the general talking to Betsy. But I can't tell what they're saying."

"Of course you can't. But they have been jabbering away like this for half an hour. Sometimes they actually seem to be quarreling. Then they begin to laugh instead." She gave her head a shake. "That Betsy! We certainly have an odd child."

"There are a lot of words which could be applied to our younger daughter. But I don't think 'odd' is one of them, my dear."

3

The Comte de Bertrand had left, accompanied by all the members of Napoleon's train. They were to return as soon as possible with the supplies needed to make him comfortable in the somewhat primitive pavilion. Napoleon seemed to have dismissed the matter from his mind. He lay back in his chair and continued to talk with Betsy.

"I don't want you to get into trouble, *ma petite*, over what

32

you call me. Suppose we leave it this way: you will say 'sire' when no one is within hearing who might object. At other times it will be wise for you to address me in accordance with their orders."

"Yes, sire."

The conversation went on from one thing to another. They discussed the burning of Moscow, and, as it happened, the girl had read enough on that subject to ask intelligent questions. There was considerable talk about the members of the Bonaparte family and the parts they had played. It was Betsy who introduced the most controversial of subjects by asking what he could have done instead of surrendering himself into the hands of the English. Despite the fact that his audience was made up solely of a fourteen-year-old girl, Napoleon went into this problem with the utmost seriousness.

"I could have gone on fighting," he said, "but I sensed that the French people were war-weary and I doubted if their resolution would have sufficed to win me a stalemate with the allied armies. And—yes, I must say it. I was weary myself. I knew it would have been necessary to shoot a good many of the French leaders to keep the assembly under my thumb. Could I have succeeded in this sufficiently to keep the struggle going for the balance of the year? Frankly, I had doubts.

"If I had fought on, they might have been willing to compromise for the sake of peace. I might have been allowed to resume the throne. They might even have allowed me to have my son back." He remained silent for several moments and then sighed deeply. "I would have been satisfied with that. I had seen enough of fighting. But I realized how heavy the odds were against me."

Betsy was listening with intense interest. Living so far away from the scene of the European struggle, the people of St. Helena depended on what they could get in the way of reading matter. When a ship from England put in at the island, there was always a scramble to get letters, to claim the months'-old newspapers, the pamphlets and books. The girl had devoured all that came into the Balcombe household, all judged proper for her eyes. Her mother made it a rule to read everything first, and Betsy had been fully conscious that Mrs. Balcombe was a severe censor. Even at that, however, certain names had strayed into the restricted area of her reading—Marie Walewska, La Bellilote, Grassini, Mademoiselle George of the Paris theater. She had, also, gained a surprisingly clear understanding of the state problems and of the campaigns.

"But why didn't you get on a ship for America, sire?" she asked him.

"I made a great blunder in not doing that," he conceded. "I could have lived there in great comfort as my brother Joseph will certainly do. Gradually a great many Bonapartists would drift across the Atlantic to join us. We would have lived on our memories. It would have become like the Elysian Fields. Do you understand, my child, what I mean by that?"

"No, sire," answered Betsy.

"The Elysian Fields are a stretch of high land in Parnassus to which warriors are translated without dying. They live there forever in great honor."

Betsy frowned slightly as she thought this over. "Would there be anything for you to do on these plains but—well, to sit around and talk?" she asked, finally.

"I'm afraid not. You have put your finger on the weak point, my child. Could men of action be content for long to do nothing but talk about the past?" There was a protracted pause. "I am not sure the Americans would have had much sympathy for us. They are people of action in their own way. For a time perhaps we would be lionized, but after that there would be a long period of silence and neglect while we—we rusted away. Still," he continued, "I was guilty of a bad error of judgment in throwing myself on the mercy of the English. They have none, these hard, selfish people!"

Finally they came back to Betsy herself. All through the conversation he had been watching her, and now he said abruptly: "You are too pretty to be English. The women of England are fitted for nothing better than to become the wives of shopkeepers."

Betsy could not let this pass. "No, no, no, sire!" she exclaimed. "That isn't fair. Nearly all my friends at school were pretty. And they were bright and nice."

Napoleon gave a scornful gesture. "Pouf!" he said. "I've known many English women and they've all been the same. Always dull and with faces like pastry just out of the oven."

Betsy had discovered that the tie on one of her pantalettes had become loose. She bent over to tighten it. Napoleon watched her with an amused smile.

"You are the one exception, Mam'selle Betsee. But there's a fault I must point out in you. You should not wear those absurd things."

"I hate them!" cried Betsy, straightening up. "But we have to wear them until we are fifteen, at least. It's such a silly fashion!"

"How much longer must you be a slave to it?"

"Another year. Unless I can talk Mamma into letting me discard them sooner. I'm afraid that's not likely. Mamma is a believer in rules."

"French girls no longer wear them," asserted Napoleon. "They went out with the Bourbon kings. Together with many things equally wrong and foolish."

"I didn't know that." Betsy seemed rather puzzled. "But I think French women were foolish to give them up. They have thick ankles and should be glad to hide them."

"French women are beautiful!" declared the Man of Destiny, frowning imperiously. "They are clever. They are fascinating. And they do *not* have thick ankles. A girl like you should not criticize them. *Ma foi,* how many have you known?"

"Quite a few, sire."

"And did any of them have thick ankles?"

"Yes, sire. All of them did."

He leaned forward to rest his arms on his knees and for several moments regarded her with an air of serious study. He was thinking: "What an extraordinary little creature. Most girls of her age would say nothing but 'yes' or 'no' and look frightened and stupid. But here she is, talking to me with more frankness than any of the members of my train."

Betsy was beginning to look disturbed. "I am sorry, sire, that I seem bold to you."

"I am not charging you with boldness. I am charging you with intelligence. And with courage." The pallid cheeks of the captive lighted up completely at this point. "Now that we are so deep into the subject, I will make a confession. You are partly right. Many French women are heavy. Let me tell you the full truth about feminine beauty. You don't find it in England. No, no, never in England! Rarely do you find it in France or Germany; although my second wife was fresh and pretty. No, it is necessary to go to Italy. Ah, how lovely they are, the women of Italy. I mean when they are young. You know, Mam'selle Betsee, I am not French by birth. The people of Corsica are Italian. My sister Pauline, who is the most beautiful woman in the world, is the perfect Italian type. She is a sensible woman, that one. She devotes herself to her looks and doesn't bother her head about politics."

He paused and then began to laugh. "So, French women have thick ankles! You really do say what's in your mind. And here am I, after knowing countless fascinating French women, agreeing with you. I see we are really going to live up to that agreement we made."

4

After dinner the men moved out to the front porch to take advantage of the evening breeze. The port was placed on a table there, convenient for use. Admiral Cockburn joined his host in obeisance to the rich and heady wine but Napoleon sniffed at it scornfully.

"Is it true, my lord admiral," he asked, "that Englishmen sometimes drink as many as five bottles of this at dinner?"

The admiral picked his way carefully through the much obstructed roadway of his knowledge of French. "There are five-bottle men, General Bonaparte. But they are—er, exceptional. You must understand, I don't mean to speak of them as admirable. Few men ever aspire to such a high—er, rating. Three-bottle men are more general. Even two-bottle."

Napoleon, bowing and rising to his feet, said to himself: "I should have waited a few years more. Surely a few only were needed for all Englishmen to drink themselves into the grave." He announced aloud his intention of taking a brief stroll in the gardens before going to bed. Captain Poppleton, a young officer of the 53rd Regiment, whose duty it was to keep the Captive always in sight, materialized instantly from his station in the gardens. He began to follow at a discreet distance.

Mrs. Balcombe had not accompanied the men to the porch and so Admiral Cockburn faced his host alone. He glanced across the table, noting the broad lines of Balcombe's somewhat florid face. "There could be truth in the story they tell about him," he thought. "Certainly there's a Hanoverian hint in the cut of his jib. Which one of them could have been his father? Old King George himself?"

After a rather long stretch of silence while he turned this

over in his mind, and Balcombe continued to sip his wine in full enjoyment, the admiral brought his attention back to the problem which faced him. "I'll be glad, Balcombe," he said, "when I'm relieved of this duty. It's not going to be easy, you know."

"But," protested the host, "he seems very easy in his manners. Even quite amiable."

"That's all surface. Underneath he's seething with emotions which never show. Quite an actor, you know. I had plenty of chance to see under the surface during that interminable voyage. I can tell you this: he doesn't expect to stay here long. France, he believes, will realize he is being treated badly and will rise to demand his return. He never said this in so many words, but he made it clear in many ways."

"It's a forlorn hope," declared Balcombe.

"Quite. The powers of Europe will never agree to let him get away from this island. The French can demand as loud as they care—matter of fact, I don't believe they care at all—but the allies will stand firm. What chance would there be of French vessels breaking through the navy cordon we'll maintain around St. Helena? None whatever. The eagle doesn't know it yet but he's caged for life."

"I heard in town today that the other powers are sending out envoys to keep an eye on things."

The admiral nodded. "Russia, France, and Prussia. They'll bring their families and their own servants. How are we going to accommodate them?"

"It will be a problem," conceded Balcombe. "You know, my lord, the Plantation House is the only place on the island suitable for an ex-emperor. It would save us a great deal of trouble if the government would assign it for his use and let the governors make do with Longwood instead."

Cockburn chuckled. "That suggestion has been voiced in the presence of old Wilks but he pretends not to hear. Of course, he's leaving soon. I don't expect it will make any difference when the new governor arrives. The new man will be just as insistent on his own comfort."

"What's that verse about a sow's ear?"

"You mean the Peter Pindar lines? 'You cannot make, my lord, I fear, a velvet purse of a sow's ear.' Exactly, Balcombe. Longwood is a sow's ear. Not all the money in the English treasury will ever convert it into a decent residence. Certainly it won't suit a man who enjoyed so long the grandeur

37

of Versailles and the comfort of Malmaison. I watched him as we went over the place and I could read disgust in every expression of his face."

"I doubt if you can get rid of the rats up there."

"They're all over the place." The admiral gave his head a doubtful shake. "There was a hole in the floor of the room he may have to use as his bedchamber. A rat put its head through and stared at us. He was enormous and he didn't seem afraid of us at all. Napoleon looked at him and said: 'This fellow must be the king of rats. Has he many subjects?' He did not intend to be jocular. His face was white with rage. Still, he has made it clear already that he will maintain a semblance of imperial dignity, no matter where we put him. Have you heard how many people he has brought with him?"

"Quite a household, I understand."

"More than forty. Already he has made his appointments. Bertrand is to be grand marshal of the palace. He's a good enough fellow but a real stickler for form and he insists on being addressed as *m'sieur le grand maréchal.* What utter folly! Grand marshal of a cow stable!"

"I hear good things about Madame Bertrand."

"Why not? She's part English, you know. Her father was a Dillon. A descendant of the Dillon who organized the regiment of the Wild Geese in Paris."

"Oh, yes. It was made up entirely of young Irishmen, wasn't it?"

"From top to bottom. The share of Anglo-Saxon blood in the Dillons has worn pretty thin by this time. Still, it's enough to make a fine lady of her. The Comte de Montholon is to be minister of finance, external and internal affairs and prefect of the palace. Have you enjoyed a glimpse of his wife? The fair Albiné! Not at all adverse to extramarital activities, that one. It's said that Napoleon—well, I don't need to put it into words. Then there's Gourgaud, who will be chief orderly officer and have charge of the stables and carriages. And finally there's the Marquis de Las Cases who will be chamberlain and chief secretary. A different stripe from the others, this fellow. He's come for one purpose only, to get material for a life of Napoleon. He expects to make a fortune by publishing it in all European languages. Nothing of the soldier in Las Cases. The others look down on him."

The long peaceful moments while they lingered over their wine were the best that this lonely island had to offer. The sun was sinking somewhere back of the high rock walls and the light which reached them was filled with a gentle melancholy. They felt the breeze from the sea but it reached them on almost soundless wings. Only the occasional piping of birds high above them broke the silence.

"You have been here some time now, Balcombe," said the seaman, raising his glass to appraise the rich coloring. "Some people tell me this is a heaven on earth. Others say it is no more than a ghastly parody of life. Which is true?"

"I incline to favor the life here," answered the merchant after a few moments of thought. "My wife never complains, being the sweetest woman on the face of the earth, but I fancy she is on the other side. She misses her friends and the church bells and the gentle rains. I like it because it's so even. You never waken up to find snow piled up over the window sills. And you never suffer from tropical heat. I'm speaking of what we have here in this particular spot and with no consideration of the weather in town. It can get pretty bad there.

"But you know, my lord," he went on, "there are times when the longing for home becomes almost unbearable. I wish I could tell you how often I have sat on this very spot and felt that I would trade an eternity of this placid existence for one hour—one hour, mind you—in a cold house with a real old London fog making it impossible to see the railings in front."

"Of course, my dear fellow, of course, of course!" affirmed the admiral. "You wouldn't be a true Englishman if you didn't feel that way. But he"—motioning over his shoulder in the direction that Napoleon had taken—"he won't. He won't long for anything about France except the power and the glory. I don't believe there's a sentimental bone in his body. I don't indeed."

"I'm not as sure of that as you are," declared Balcombe, reflectively. "No man has lived a more romantic life."

"Are you referring to his campaigns or to the fair ladies who figured in his life?"

"A combination of both."

"I will tell you this, my dear sir. I shall be a happy man when I set foot again on the quarter-deck of my ship and sail back to England, leaving all these responsibilities behind me. It's going to be impossible to keep things on an even keel with this extraordinary man. I hope the government has the good sense to send out a diplomat, a man who knows how to tread on eggs, how to meet aggression with a properly firm hand well concealed in a velvet glove. A Talleyrand. Not an army man. No, no, that would never do! Balcombe, if the government borrowed the services of the Archangel Michael and sent him down here straight from heaven, this man would hate him on sight. He would pick quarrels and fill the air with outrageous demands. This is not guesswork, Balcombe. I know!"

5

"My lord admiral! He's gone! I can find no trace of him!"

The agitated voice of Captain Poppleton reached the ears of the two middle-aged men so casually passing the port back and forth between them. He came charging up through the gardens, his gray tails flapping behind him, his usually placid face a mask of wild-eyed dismay.

"What's wrong, Poppleton?" The admiral's voice held a chiding note. "What has happened to get you into such a state?"

"General Bonaparte, my lord! I dropped back a little distance to watch the sun sinking. When I turned around again, he was gone! My lord admiral, I assure you he was nowhere in sight. I've been everywhere—the houses, the gardens, the orchard. No trace of him have I found."

"Come, Poppleton, this is absurd. Do you think he has plunged into the sea? Do you believe he can swim all the way back to France?"

"As to that, I can't say, sir."

The loud tones of the excited officer had brought Mrs. Balcombe to the porch. In a quiet voice, she asked, "What is wrong?"

"This young donkey is convinced that General Bonaparte has made his escape already from the island," explained Admiral Cockburn.

"He's been taking a walk through the upper grounds," explained Mrs. Balcombe, smiling reassuringly at the unhappy Poppleton. "I assure you, Captain, that I caught a glimpse of him a few minutes ago. There's a path leading up to a point from which it's possible to look out to sea. I'm sure that is where he has gone."

The three men joined her on a section of the porch from which a full view was possible. As they watched, a figure with a tricornered hat emerged from a lower level.

"It's Bonaparte," declared the admiral. "Now, Poppleton, are you satisfied? There's someone with him but I expect you won't be satisfied unless you tag along at their heels."

"Quite, my lord."

Mrs. Balcombe's fingers had tightened on her husband's arm. She whispered to him in a voice filled with astonishment: "William! It's Betsy with him. Our Betsy." She waited a moment and then went on in a hushed tone. "They are strolling along together. Hand in hand!"

Chapter Three

1

Napoleon wakened the next morning at eight o'clock. He had slept well. The cool breeze which came in at one window and left by another was in pleasant contrast to the heat of the room he had occupied at the inn. A vague thought took possession of his mind. Would those busy officials of the stubborn English Government allow him to remain here permanently and forget all about the possibility of converting that rat-infested rookery on the crest into a residence for him?

After a few moments of such speculation, he sat up in bed and called, "Marchand!" There was an instant squeak of leather soles outside the door and his head valet entered.

"Yes, Your Imperial Highness," said Marchand, bowing.

"I shall get up now."

"That is good, Your Imperial Highness," declared the valet, opening the toilet case he had carried in with him. "There is a breakfast ready for you. Monsieur Lepage has not yet been able to set up an oven but the cook from the other house brought over a loaf. It is too much, Your Imperial Highness, to hope for anything eatable from a servant trained in English ways. But it must be allowed that the bread smells most appetizing."

Marchand was right. The loaf had been spreading an enticing odor all through the small rooms of the pavilion. Napoleon seldom had much appetite in the morning but for once the thought of bread hot from the oven was an invitation.

"The shaving may wait, Marchand," he said.

The table was set out with flowers fresh from the gardens and practically dripping with dew. There was a pot of chocolate, the loaf on a plate of brightly colored crockery, a large pat of butter, and a jar of jelly made from Cape gooseberries. The Man of Destiny took a bite of bread and said in

42

audible tones: "Ah! It is good. What miracle is this, Marchand?"

"The miracle, Your Highness, if you think it such, is the work of a colored woman, wearing a purple ribbon around her head."

"That would be the one they call Sarah," said Napoleon to himself. "She is *ma petite* Betsee's best friend in the household. I perceived that much at the meal last night."

After breakfast he bathed in a special tub of India rubber, which had been brought out with his other belongings, was shaved by the skilled fingers of Marchand, and dressed in his invariable costume. Then he strolled out into the garden.

The first evidence he had of life at the Briars was the prompt appearance of two small round heads above the fence which separated the two houses. "These must be the sons of the family," he thought. He walked down the path and said, "Good morning." This exhausted his supply of English for the moment and he waited for developments. There were none immediately. The two round faces seemed very young and quite devoid of expression. He pointed to the larger and said, "You are Will-yum."

This elicited a response. The larger face nodded. "Sir, some call me Billy and some Will."

Napoleon looked at the smaller face. "And you?" he asked, pointing.

"I, sir, am Alex," said the small boy.

"Alex," repeated Napoleon. "You are named after the emperor of Russia, then?"

Somehow the smaller boy grasped the sense of this and shook his head. "No, sir. I'm named after my grandfather. My mother's father. They say he was a nice old man but I never saw him. I was too young. But," proudly, "he left me his watch. In his will. It's gold."

The visitor could not think at the moment of anything to say beyond this question of names. He tapped his chest and then raised his forefinger. "Who am I?"

They responded to this at once. "Boney!" they exclaimed, in unison.

At this moment a sound of shrill and angry barking reached their ears. Apparently a crisis of some kind had arisen at the rear of the Briars. The two faces vanished from sight and Napoleon could hear the scrambling of feet through the gardens as the boys raced to discover what was happening in the kingdom of their pets.

"The small boy is exactly the size of the King of Rome," the prisoner said to himself as he retraced his steps.

2

The Marquis de Las Cases was waiting for him on the un-roofed porch. He also had fallen under the spell of Sarah's bread and was brushing crumbs from his waistcoat with a chubby hand. The marquis could be described as a tubby man; in stature an inch shorter than Napoleon, his neck thick, his waistline prodigious; a careless and indifferent dresser, moreover. There was a hint of the scorbutic in his ample cheeks and his layers of chin.

"M'sieur le marquis," said Napoleon, regarding the sky, which was without a cloud, "this will be an excellent day for work."

"As you say, sire, most excellent. It occurred to me that a table might be placed for us under that clump of tamarinds, and I asked Gentelini to see to it. Ah, here he is. I,—er, took it on myself to have Gentelini lock the gate. To avoid inter-ruptions, sire."

"Then let us proceed."

Napoleon's attitude while dictating, when not pacing up and down, was to lean so far back in his chair that his face would be turned up to the sky, and to keep his eyes closed. The first sentences would come slowly like the preliminary pacing of cavalry but would soon develop into a tumult of words which resembled the headlong charge of his horse brigades on a downslope. He had no mercy on the hand which strove to get his words on paper. Sometimes he would pause and make some such remark as, "Wait! Go back to—oh, you know where I mean, the place where I talked to some-one—found it yet? *Ma foi*, how slow you are, my dear Marquis! Well, this is how I want it worded." And he would be off on another rampage of rhetoric, some of it well consid-ered and clear but a great deal turgid and impossible to fol-low.

For an hour he went along at his fastest gait and the pudgy hands and arms of Las Cases seemed ready to give up in sheer exhaustion.

"We are going well today, my dear Marquis," said Napoleon, nodding with self-satisfaction. "I think I am making the conception of the campaign entirely clear."

"Yes, sire, I pray that my notes will be equally clear."

At this moment the sound of light footsteps sounded on the path from the other side of the fence. A quick tap on the gate was followed by a girlish voice, crying: "It's me! Let me in."

A gratified smile spread across the features of the Great Man. "It's *la petite* Betsee," he said. "Unlock the gate for her, Las Cases."

"But, sire, we had decided not to allow interruptions—"

Napoleon rang a bell on the table and ordered Gentelini, a footman who had followed him from his first exile at Elba, to bring a third chair. The titled amanuensis seemed about to argue about this but decided, after a second glance at the Napoleonic countenance, that it would be of no avail. Betsy came in, smiling over an armful of flowers.

"Oh, sire," she exclaimed, "you have laid a spell on Toby. He actually cut these for me to bring. If it had been for any of the family, he would have shaken his head and said, 'No flowahs to be cut!' Toby is a tyrant."

"Do you mean the very black little fellow who was working in the gardens all last evening?"

"Yes, sire. He was brought here on a slave ship from Africa."

Napoleon got to his feet and walked over to a spot in front of the porch where part of the sod had been cut away in the form of a crown. "He was here early this morning, I am told, and paid me this very pleasant tribute."

"How clever of Toby! But please, sire, don't let anyone else know. He would get into trouble."

"Your wishes in the matter, mam'selle, will be scrupulously observed. The honest Toby must be spared trouble. And now, will you stay a while with us?"

"Will I be in the way?"

"Not at all. Your presence will lend some amelioration to a difficult task. I have had a chair brought out especially for you. But you must promise not to talk."

She did not take the chair immediately. Instead she stood up very straight and patted her skirts into place with a self-conscious air.

"Do you like this dress," she asked.

"I like the color . . . What have you done to your hair?"

"I wanted to look my best. So I brushed and brushed and brushed!" Then abruptly she asked, "Who's that?" She had caught sight of a young and sober face pressed against the glass in the attic window. The face disappeared at once.

"That is my son Emmanuel," said Las Cases shortly.

"But, m'sieur, what is he doing up there?" She obviously was disturbed. "It gets *awfully* hot in that attic room in the daytime. I never go there in summer any more."

"He is working," explained the marquis, addressing himself to Napoleon. "Last evening he did no work at all and so I told him he must make up the lost ground."

"Is it necessary, my dear Marquis, to have these copies made of your notes? Why can't you put them down legibly in the first place?"

"Sire! have you any idea how fast you talk? No human being could get it all down correctly. I have found it necessary to develop a kind of shorthand which Emmanuel understands. He goes over all my notes and makes a fair copy of them."

"All unnecessary! When Berthier was with me, and we went driving over the face of Europe day and night in that remarkable coach of mine—which I designed—I never stopped dictating orders and letters, hour after hour. Berthier got everything down perfectly. He never made a mistake. Ah, how much I missed the fellow in my last campaign. But he lacked the courage to come out for me after I left Elba." Napoleon paused and glanced up at the window above them. "Aren't you working him too hard? The boy doesn't look very healthy."

"The boy is healthy enough. He's growing, you know, and that makes him look lean."

Betsy had thought the owner of the face at the window looked lonely and unhappy. "Are all French boys as dark and homely as that?" she wondered. She felt sorry for him but this did not seriously disturb her satisfaction in the role she was now to be allowed. She seated herself in the third chair and patted her skirts into place. "I'll not say a word, sire," she promised.

So the work was resumed and after a few moments Napoleon was as much absorbed in his task as he had been before her arrival. For half an hour he continued to talk about the turning point in his military career which had come when he

46

was appointed to the command of the French armies in Italy. Betsy sat as still as a bird on a twig and did not speak a word. The pen of Las Cases raced and sputtered in his frantic haste and left many blots on the paper. He did not dare stop long enough to take a pinch of snuff, although the condition of his neckcloth and waistcoat attested the fact that he was an addict. "What a very unpleasant-looking man," thought Betsy.

Finally the voice of the great conqueror came to a halt. He paused, changed his position, and, after a luxuriant stretch of his arms and legs, addressed himself to Betsy.

"Well, my child. Did you find it interesting?"

Betsy fidgeted uneasily in her chair. Should she temporize? Or would it be better to say what she thought?

"No, sire," she said, finally.

"No! I am surprised. I thought it was all most exciting."

"It was"—she hesitated again—"it was rather dull."

"Dull!" Napoleon's voice carried an incredulous note.

"Dull!" echoed the marquis.

"Well, it was all about cannon and ammunition and supplies. You didn't tell any of the kind of stories I read in other books."

"Other books? What other books?"

"Books about you, sire. Have you any idea how many have been written about you? Every ship that puts in has a great load of them. Everybody reads them because we have no other way on this island of keeping up with events. Of course I only see the proper ones, because Mamma picks them out herself. Sometimes she takes a pen and inks out parts. Sometimes, too, she tears out whole pages before letting us have the book."

"Does that happen often?"

"Oh, yes, sire, all the time. I can't help wondering what is said on the pages which get torn out and burned. I do my reading at nights. I put a screen around my bed so the light won't disturb Jane, who likes to sleep. Sometimes I read for three or four hours. Often Mamma comes up and puts out the candle."

"And what," he demanded, "is there in these books which you miss in what I'm dictating?"

"Oh, they always have a lot of stories. Mostly about you but sometimes about other people. Sometimes the stories are very amusing and sometimes they are—well, sort of gossipy. And they always give a lot of details. About how the ladies at the court dressed, and the talks you had with them, and all that."

"Don't you ever read about my campaigns? About the great battles?"

"Of course! I think I like the description of battles better than anything else. But I—I skip the details about cannon and ammunition."

"You mean that you skip the kind of things I've been dictating today."

"Yes, sire. I'm afraid you think me very stupid."

Napoleon moved his chair around so that he was facing her. He studied her face intently. Suddenly he pounded his hands down on his knees. "Las Cases, she's right!" he exclaimed. "It *is* dull. I was finding it dull myself and that was why I went so slowly."

"Slowly!" said the marquis to himself, flexing his numbed fingers.

"Tear these notes up!" commanded Napoleon. "Tear them into shreds and burn them. This afternoon we'll start again and I shall put in some personal information as well. Many incidents occurred to me this morning but I brushed them aside, thinking them trivial or immaterial. Now I am sure I was wrong. I remembered what Augureau called me when I arrived in camp. *Le petit bougre!* The remark was heard and soon even the men in the ranks were calling me that. But my men found that I knew more about warfare than all the rest of the generals put together—and, when they called me that, it was a term of endearment." He checked himself and looked with a guilty air at Betsy. "Did you understand what I was saying?"

"N-no, sire."

"That is good. I must be more careful when you are around." He got slowly to his feet. "There is still an hour before lunch. What do you propose to do with all that time, *ma petite?*"

"I have an errand to do. I must ride over to one of our neighbors. The Veiled Lady. I left some fresh peaches there yesterday afternoon and I must go back for the basket."

"I shall go with you," decided Napoleon. He raised his

voice. "Archambault! I am going to ride. Saddle Mameluke."

Betsy sprang to her feet also. "I'll have to hurry and change, sire. This is my best dress and Mamma would be furious with me if I rode in it. I'll only be a few minutes."

what I was and they treated me in the end made them
hate the French, whom I... Corsica make him choose
...together as a race and kind.

Chapter Four

1

After turning out from the green paths about the Briars and the cool solace of its shade trees, they found themselves on the rocky and twisted Longwood Road. The change to the scrubby brown growth which barely covered the hard surface of the earth and the stunted trees of strange patterns was as abrupt as it was unwelcome. The handsome Mameluke stirred up yellowish dust with his majestic hoofs, and the barricades of bush and undergrowth made it necessary for even the diminutive Tom to detour around them.

Across the granite shelvings of Rupert's Valley they caught glimpses of the sullen Atlantic rolling into Flagstaff Bay. It was not a pleasant prospect even to Betsy, who knew every foot of the road. It inspired in Napoleon a bitter train of thought.

"Islands!" he said. "The seas are full of them, these useless patches of land, vomited up by the sea—all of them harsh and unfriendly and lonely. I'm sure this one is going to prove the worst of all."

His downward glance as he indulged in this opinion crossed an upward look from Betsy. She seemed disturbed at what he said. Perhaps she had been hoping he would come to like St. Helena.

"Mon Dieu!" continued the onetime Man of Destiny. "All the misfortunes of my life, I verily believe, can be traced back to islands."

"I must make it clear in my recollections," he went on, "that my life has been conditioned, restricted, and thwarted by nature's inconvenient habit of dividing the earth between continents and islands. To begin with, I was born in Corsica. On an island such as that the people become different from all others—in habit, in speech, in looks, and in dress. When I was sent to a French school, all the other boys knew me for what I was and they looked down on me and made things hard for me in every way. Because Corsica raises fine sheep, my fellows at school would get together in groups and bleat at me as I passed. 'Mouflon!' they would shout after me. I was not happy at school but perhaps it was just as well because I had nothing else to do but study and read." He glanced down a second time at his companion, jogging along sidesaddle on her stocky pony. "Do you find this dull also, Mam'selle Betsee?"

"No, no, sire. I am listening to every word you say."

"You will find my next point more interesting, *ma petite*. It concerns England. That large and wealthy island stood in my way at every stage of my life. The English refused to make peace with me and kept all Europe in arms by supplying the funds. Never was I given a moment's rest by those stubborn shopkeepers. Why did I not lead my armies across the Sleeve and beat them to their knees? I had my plans made, and once, at Boulogne, I had an army of invasion drawn up and ready. But I held back. Why? Because England is an island. The English Navy was so strong I could not hope to defeat it.

"All through the centuries the English have known how to reap the advantage of that narrow twenty miles of water between them and the continent. Europe has been torn by wars while the English have sat in their seclusion, in peace and comfort, and reaped all the profits. I loathe these people of yours, my child. But I also admire them.

"Yes, Betsee, it is not because of the snows of Russia or the huge armies of the allies that I am now a prisoner. It is because England is an island!

"When my generals betrayed me and I had to abdicate the first time," he went on, "they sent me to an island. Elba. It was pleasant enough. Some day I will tell you about it, and some of the strange things that happened while I was there. But when a man has been the ruler of most of Europe, can he be content with a cluster of little hills and a few thousand yokels to govern? Elba, the island of peace, drove me mad!

"I should have remained there, of course. The waters of the Tyrrhenian Sea provided a barricade between me and a continent swarming with my enemies. I should have realized that France was exhausted. But I had complete faith in my power to ride any whirlwind they might stir up. As I fled

51

from this sanctuary, I said to myself, 'I shall never set foot on an island again!'

"And now I am on another island, the smallest, the hottest, the most remote they could find. Trust the perfidious English to select a natural prison house!" He paused as his eye ranged along the line of the hills, the black and tortured masses of rock which volcanic action had raised above the level of the ocean. When he resumed, it was in a low tone, as though he had forgotten his listener. "The English believe in islands and they think I can be kept here until I die. Perhaps they are right. But if I must remain here, it will not be for long. Can an eagle survive if chained to the mouth of Hades?"

2

The barrenness of the soil and the stunted trees came to an abrupt ending. Ahead of them stretched a pleasant elevation of land somewhat similar to the Briars. Betsy said, "Whoa, Tom!" and slipped to the ground.

"This is where she lives, sire."

In a clump of green trees stood a low frame house built around an interior courtyard. The windows were all closely shuttered and it looked deserted. The paint was peeling from the boards and the high-pitched roof was in need of repairs.

"A secluded place, certainly," commented Napoleon.

"That was why she selected it. She never sees anyone and it's impossible to find the servant most of the time. I can't help feeling very sorry for them."

"I am not sure, Betsee, you should waste your sympathies on people like these. The woman has some desperate need to hide herself away. She may be a criminal or a political refugee."

Betsy gave her head a shake. "I can't believe that, sire. I've seen the servant a few times and she always smiles. She has a most pleasant smile. But she never speaks."

"Do you come this way often?"

"Every morning. I make a point of coming home this way when I'm finishing my ride before breakfast. I always whistle to let them know I'm coming and then I call, 'Good morning, lady' as I ride by."

"And they don't answer?"

"No, sire. But I know she hears me, and somehow I am sure she doesn't mind. Really, I've an idea it pleases her."

"Do your parents know about this?"

Betsy hesitated. "N-no," she said. "I've told Jane. And Toby knows because he helped me get the peaches to take over to them. Look! The basket is hanging on the outside of the gate. It looks empty." She glanced up at him and smiled. "You might have been served fresh peaches last night if I hadn't robbed the trees. I expect Mamma was upset when she found there were none to be had."

Betsy walked over to the wide wooden gate which stretched between the two wings of the house and seemed to be the only means of entrance. The small basket, hanging above the iron lock, was empty, as she had expected. As she reached up to take it, a door at the rear of the courtyard opened and a serving girl in a gaily colored dress appeared. She was, as Betsy had previously observed, rather attractive in a decidedly buxom way; her chief asset being a pair of blond braids hanging down on each side of her shoulders.

The girl smiled broadly as she crossed the cobblestoned yard and peered at them through the pickets.

"Pitches—good!" she said.

"Oh, I'm so glad you liked them," said Betsy. "I'll bring some more one of these days. Did your mistress like them?"

The servant sensed what had been asked but her stock of words was so limited that it took some time for her to say, "Ma'am—enjoy."

Betsy's attention at this point was drawn to the activities of a lonely and scrawny chicken, scratching between the cobblestones with the most meager results. She pointed at the bird and then indulged in a pantomime to express the opening of an egg with a spoon. "Would you like some eggs?" she asked.

The servant's smile grew wider as she grasped the meaning. Then she shook her head. "Hen, no. Roost' " she said.

"Then you must need fresh eggs. Perhaps I'll be able to bring you some."

The girl's broad cheeks broke into a smile which expressed real delight. "Aches?" she said. "Ah, aches good."

Before reaching the house they had been aware of a small black speck in the sky, somewhat larger than a man's hand but certainly not in excess of a human head. As they talked it had grown considerably and was approaching with alarming speed. Betsy looked up and gave vent to an exclamation of dismay. She sprang back into the saddle.

"We're in for a heavy shower, sire," she said. "I'm afraid we'll have to gallop all the way back if we want to escape a good drenching."

But Napoleon's eyes were fixed on the figure of a horseman a short distance down the road. They began to glitter with malicious amusement.

"There he is, the great simpleton," he said. "The spy they have set on me. What is his name?"

"Captain Poppleton."

"A typical English name. Well, *ma petite*, it occurs to me that if we were to loiter a little this—what is your word for it?—Ah, yes, ubiquitous. This ubiquitous captain, this English *fathead*, would have to ride a long way behind us and he would get soaked to the skin." He had a tendency to play tricks on those about him as his new friends would soon discover. "Betsee, let's teach him a lesson."

Betsy looked down the road and saw the Captain Poppleton was wearing the rather elaborate parade uniform of the 53rd, a long-tailed gray coat buttoned back by loops of gold lace, a scarlet collar and cuffs, the skirts of the coat showing a white lining. "Poor Captain Poppleton!" she thought. "It's not his fault. He's here on orders. That beautiful uniform would be *terribly* damaged by a heavy rain." To Napoleon, she said: "But, sire, we have ourselves to think of. It would ruin my dress if we were caught in the rain and you can imagine what Mamma would say to that. Besides, sire, what about that wonderful coat of yours?"

Napoleon gave in instantly. "Of course, Betsee, I must not get you into trouble. But"—the malicious light still showing in his eyes—"we must plan between us to play some tricks on this fellow. When the weather is better."

Betsy tapped the flank of her pony with a suddenly insistent heel. "Up, you slow fellow Tom! We're going to catch it if we don't ride hard." Then she called, turning her head in the direction of the shuttered windows, "Good-by, lady!"

As they galloped back with the black cloud becoming alarmingly close by the moment, Napoleon leaned down from his high saddle. "My hearing is rather acute. When we stopped in front of that house, I heard a slight click. It was like the space between shutters being cautiously enlarged from the inside. It must have been your mysterious lady. Betsee, I'm certain she saw and heard everything."

Chapter Five

1

Work on the improvements at Longwood proceeded slowly. The only mechanics available were slipshod and slow. The rotting floors were replaced by unseasoned wood and no efforts were made to provide proper foundations. It seemed impossible to do away with the rats. The sharp faces of inquisitive rodents peered out from holes on every side. It seemed equally impossible to vanquish the stable odors which clung to the old timbers and even filled the new rooms with an all-pervading reek.

For this and other reasons, Napoleon showed no desire to leave the Briars. He had become absorbed into the home life of the Balcombe family and, to the amazement of everyone, he seemed to be quite happy. The two boys paid him daily visits and the younger one, little Alex, would climb up on his knees and play with the glittering decorations he sometimes wore. They called him "Boney" and even made him the victim of boyish tricks. In the evenings there were games of hide-and-seek and blindman's buff in which everyone joined although the results had a certain monotony; Napoleon caught Betsy or she caught him. Not a morning passed without her "It's me!" reaching his ears from the garden gate. She was always welcome and she would listen to his dictation with absorbed attention. She never failed to make comments, sometimes devastatingly unfavorable, on what he was setting down. They would fall into bitter arguments, some of which the girl won.

The Captive had brought a number of horses and three coaches. In addition a *calèche* had been purchased for him at Cape Town, a light and open carriage. One of his daily recreations was to go for rides along the narrow and winding mountain roads. He seemed devoid of fear and would sit back in complete relaxation while calling to the coachman for speed and more speed. This was dangerous in the extreme for the roads along the rocky sides of the hills had been constructed for the most careful and sedate of travel. Often the carriage wheels would be within inches of the edge. It was perhaps not so much an evidence of courage that he could sit with folded arms and calmly look down into the abyss yawning beneath but as of belief in his own destiny. He was convinced it was not in the stars that he could be involved in the kind of mishaps which snuffed out the lives of ordinary men.

He took Betsy on one of the first of these daredevil adventures along the mountain roads. She cringed in a corner of the carriage with her hands covering her face. Napoleon watched her out of a corner of his eye but made no move to check the mad speed at which they were going. When they returned to the Briars, safe and sound but badly shaken up, Betsy stepped down slowly to the ground. Her face was white, and she seemed to be trembling.

"Did you enjoy the ride?" asked Napoleon.

She found it hard to answer at first but finally managed to say, "It was—it was quite exciting, wasn't it?"

"Are you ill?"

"Oh, no, sire, I am not ill."

"You look pale, *ma petite*. I am concerned about you."

"There is no need for that, sire."

The next time he sent her an invitation to join him, there was some small delay but she finally arrived and took her place in the opposite corner of the rear seat. She was wearing a poke bonnet, tied with a blue ribbon under her chin. It was most becoming but its purpose, clearly, was to serve as a "blinder."

"*Eh bien!* It is a compliment for you to wear such a very fine bonnet. Shall I tell Archambault to go somewhat slower today?" asked Napoleon.

Betsy replied without any hesitation. "Please, sire, you must not consider anything but your own desires."

The drive was, therefore, a repetition of the first one. At the end Betsy thanked him politely but vanished quickly into the house. "A brave little creature, that one," Napoleon said to Las Cases who was waiting in the garden for the incessant dictation to begin. "There is a word for it in the English. I think it is 'game.'"

"Your Imperial Highness," said Las Cases, speaking with

the utmost formality, "I trust you will pardon my frankness. I am finding the intrusions of this child very difficult to endure. She interrupts our work all the time. Do you realize, sire, how little progress we are making?"

"Have no fear, Marquis, we will provide you with plenty of material for that *very* profitable publishing venture you have in mind. Has it not occurred to you that the intrusions of Betsee offer you an amusing sidelight for the book you intend to write?"

2

There was a sequel to these disturbing rides which came about through the presence in the garden of the Las Cases' son. He had been summoned to check in his notes on statements Napoleon had made the previous day. His manner became more diffident than usual when he saw Betsy sitting completely at her ease beside the chair of the once dreaded conqueror. Napoleon observed this and he smiled with something of the air of a tomcat which sees a rat's whiskers twitching in the shrubbery.

"Mon enfant," he said to the son and heir of the Las Cases family, "have you nothing to say to Mam'selle Betsee?"

The boy stammered, keeping his eyes on the ground, "Good morning, mam'selle."

"Good morning, M'sieur Emmanuel," said Betsy.

"Allons donc, how very formal." The Napoleonic smile was broadening. "It is much too formal. It seems to me quite within the bounds of probability, Betsee, that this young man will some day be your husband. I cannot see a better prospect for either of you."

Betsy was shocked into crying: *"That boy!* Oh, no, sire, never that!"

The senior Las Cases was heard expostulating indignantly over the idea. As for the boy, he turned scarlet and an expression took possession of his face which could only be described as stricken. He gave one unhappy glance at Betsy and then turned and ran from the garden. They could hear him stumbling up the wooden steps which led to the hot little garret where he spent most of his time.

"I must protest, Your Imperial Highness," said the marquis. "When arrangements are made for Emmanuel's marriage, it will be with full regard for his illustrious descent. There has never been a *mésalliance* in our family for over seven hundred years."

Napoleon seemed to be enjoying himself. *"Mésalliance?"* he repeated the word with a certain relish. "Come, my dear Marquis, is that not a little strong? Have you not heard there is a certain, shall we say, secret, about Mam'selle Betsee's descent?"

"Please, sire," protested Betsy, "I would rather not have that discussed."

Las Cases sat in a sprawling attitude in his chair, his face black with offended dignity. With an angry hand he brushed grains of snuff from the knees of his nankeen trousers.

"I have arrangements in mind for my son," he declared.

"It seems to me I have detected in the manner of our youthful Emmanuel," said Napoleon, "a definite trace of admiration for our charming Betsee."

"My son will be guided in such matters solely by my wishes and commands. We are in concurrence on all points."

Smiling broadly, the great man rose to his feet. He was looking more than usually distinguished and commanding, the Eagle as he had appeared in his heyday. For the first time he had discarded the white piqué breeches and had donned a a pair made of swanskin which fitted him perfectly. His coat was equally new, a handsomely fitted garment of chestnut brown with silver buttons. Reaching for his snuffbox on the deal table, he turned to Betsy.

"Come, *ma petite*," he said. "I feel the need of a stroll through the gardens. The work," nodding to Las Cases, "will resume at the usual time tomorrow."

Napoleon had nothing to say for several moments, as they slowly climbed the winding path through the shady banyan trees, the tall lacos, the myrtles. "If you belonged to a French family," he remarked, finally "your future would have been settled long ago. Ah, what a precise people the French are, particularly in the upper-middle classes. The vaunted aristocracy of our friend back there places him at the very bottom of the hereditary titled class and so no more than a fraction above the middle. How bitterly offended he would be if he heard me say that! *Eh bien*, for you the papers would have been drawn up, the marriage settlements and the dowry down in full detail. Every contingency provided for." He glanced with an amused pucker of his lips at his companion.

"I get the impression, little baggage, that you have a lack of esteem for the scion of this titled family about which the good marquis boasts so much. Have you thoughts of your own on the subject?"

Betsy indulged in a low laugh. "*No*, sire! Of course not. That may be the French way but it's not the English. Why even our Jane is not considered old enough yet for any serious matrimonial plans. Of course," she added, after a quick glance in his direction, "I know when men are looking at me with what one might call *interest*. There is, for instance, one of the officers of the 53rd. He's a widower but he's young and he's really rather handsome."

"A widower! And quite handsome!" The cheeks of the former emperor flamed with one of his frequent rages. "You, Mam'selle Impudence, are saying this to annoy me. You know I would never consent to have you marry an English officer! Any English officer. They are not soldiers. Now in the French Army an officer serves in the ranks and is promoted when he shows courage and merit. But the English!—the officers have rich fathers who buy commissions for them. Consider, *ma petite*. Buying the right to take command of soldiers!"

"Sire," asked Betsy, who knew that he had stepped from his military academy into a junior commission, "how long did you serve in the ranks?"

There was a moment of silence while Napoleon watched her with suspicious eyes. "I am trying to explain that the French system is a good one. But the English way! Bah, those officers know no more about war than an army mule."

"According to all reports," commented Betsy, "they did rather well at Waterloo."

There was a long silence and then Napoleon began to speak in ominous tones. "Betsee, I have given the strictest orders that no one is to mention in my hearing the name of that battle—that fatal last battle."

He began to speak then in an almost oratorical tone, gesturing with both hands. It sounded as though he were reciting the account of the battle as it was to appear in his reminiscences. "That badly bungled battle where my staff men failed to carry out orders. Where they doddered and delayed. Where everything went wrong. Where even my luck in weather failed me. Before that the heavens opened when I needed rain to prevent armies from combining against me. When I wanted fair weather so I could attack, the skies smiled. But on this day of all days, this terrible, fateful day, it rained all morning, soaking the ground so I could not move my artillery until nearly noon. With good weather, I could have beaten Wellington," pronouncing the name as though it were spelled Vilainton, "before the Prussians arrived. Ah, that sluggard, that slow-footed misinterpreter of orders, that Grouchy! And that sunken Ohain Road which my scouts had not noticed, cutting right across the English front where it checked the charge of the guards which would have won the battle for me!

"That battle is always in my mind! Waterloo, Waterloo! Where I was beaten by that fat-witted Wellington—no, that is not fair. He was a stouter and stronger general than the others I had faced. But only by such a combination of catastrophes could he have beaten me." He paused and glared at Betsy. "Have you not been aware that I forbid any mention of that day?"

"Yes, sire."

"You knew?" angrily.

"Yes, sire, I knew."

"And yet you speak to me in this way?"

"Yes, sire." The girl paused for a moment. "I'm too young to understand about things of this kind but I am finding that when I like someone very much—and I like you very much, sire—there are times when I want to say things or do things to hurt them. Perhaps you feel the same way when you take me on those dreadful drives and then try to make me confess I am frightened."

"Ah, ah!" said Napoleon, with a nod.

"I *am* frightened when we drive so near the edge. I want to scream. You see, I'm afraid of heights. I get dizzy and ill. Do you enjoy torturing me in that way?"

"No, Betsee, I feel sorry for you. Perhaps it is as you say. Although I am unable to understand how a child of your years can discover such things for herself." He was speaking in a puzzled tone. "I believe now I have always been hardest on those I like best. I loved Josephine very much and yet I would get into furious rages with her. My oldest friend in the army was Junot and I had a great affection for the blockhead. But I enjoyed finding fault with him. I never made him a marshal although he wanted it more than anything in the world. Then there was Lucien, the best of my brothers—he

61

was an orator, at any rate, and a wise politician—I could hardly bring myself to be civil to him. He was the only one of my brothers that I refused to make a king!"

"I am delivering an oration, it seems," he went on, leaning over to give her cheek a most affectionate pat. "But what you said started me thinking. We had better reach an agreement, you and I. I want you always with me when I go for drives but they will be at a sensible pace. I will give Archambault orders to keep away from the edges. How pleased he will be about that! And you, my *bambine*, will never again distress me by bringing up memories of that dreadful day."

Betsy looked up with a trace of tears in her eyes. "No, sire, oh, no! Never, never will I mention it again."

3

They returned from their afternoon walk in the most companionable of moods. Betsy had been asking questions about everything that came into her head—except the battle of Waterloo!—and he had answered with long introspective speeches. Finally she found the courage to raise a point which had been most often in her mind. "Sire, you are very unhappy about this separation from your wife and son."

His mood, which had been pleasant and chatty, changed immediately. He seemed unwilling to make any response. Then, with his usual habit of raising his eyes under lowered brows, he said: "It is the separation from my son which I feel the most. When I was sent to Elba, it was promised me that my wife and son would go too. This pledge was broken. The boy was sent to his grandparents in Vienna. My wife made no efforts to see me. She did not answer my letters. At first I thought they were being kept from her but afterward I did not allow myself that consolation. I became convinced she wanted to have nothing more to do with me. I, who had raised her so high! But my little son! How I longed for him! When my possessions are unpacked, I shall show you a portrait of him. Never in this world has there been a more handsome and manly boy."

"Have you portraits of the empress?"

He nodded indifferently. "If I display them, it will be for reasons of policy. I cannot show hostility while my son is in their hands." He was beginning to find it easier to discuss the breach, even to experience some satisfaction in telling about it. "I was quite enamored of the empress when we were first married. She was obedient and good-natured. And attractive in a Germanic way—healthy and bright and with that fine clearness of complexion. But since my misfortunes started, she has not been loyal. I have tried to convince myself it's due to pressure from her parents but lately the reports on her conduct at Parma are most disturbing. There's a German count who controls her household who—well, I can't discuss that with you, my child. My son, fortunately, is still in Vienna where they call him the Duke of Reichstadt. Such effrontery! I suppose he will be raised to believe himself a Hapsburg and to consider his father an upstart! And through it all my once obedient and loving wife misbehaves herself in Italy with this Count Neipperg—a stiff-necked nonentity with a blind eye!"

"No, Betsee," he concluded, "I conceal my feelings about her and pretend to know nothing. But I can tell you, as we are such good friends, that I no longer have any affection or respect for her."

"How old was she when you were married, sire?"

"Eighteen years."

Betsy drew a deep sigh. "Eighteen! What a *wonderful* age. I can hardly wait to be eighteen. You know, sire, it is *awful* to be as young as I am."

"*Ma petite*, the years will pass quickly. You will reach this age you think so idyllic before you are aware of it."

"It's dreadful to be fourteen, sire. Everyone treats you like a child. You have to obey the rules the grownups make. You musn't do this or that. You mustn't say what's in your mind. You must go to bed early."

Napoleon was now smiling again. "Yes, my poor one, I can see how hard your life is. But be of good cheer, Betsee, the years will fly. And you have it in you to make life meet you with gifts in both hands. You happen to have a good brain. And you have courage. As for marriage, you will have plenty of suitors to choose from. There will be a fine young man with a title and great estates who will curl up in your path like a pet dog and beg you to trample on him."

"But, please, sire, he must not be too young. I won't be content with any husband unless he's much older than I am."

"Now, that is very sensible. A woman's chief purpose in life is to be a good wife and bring plenty of children into the world. And so husbands should have more experience of life." He leaned over and tweaked her ear. "But get out of your head all these foolish notions about English colonels who happen to be widowers or, for that matter, young English officers with titles and plenty of money but no brains. You know, I mean to have something to say about your future, little baggage. I will have plans for you."

He came to a halt and patted Betsy on the cheek. "It has been a most pleasant afternoon." He turned then and made his way up the steps of the pavilion with a gait which suggested a certain degree of fatigue. Betsy had passed through the gate and was well on her way back through the outer gardens to the main house when she heard his voice, raised to a pitch which suggested excitement.

"Betsee! Betsee!"

She turned and saw that he had come out on the porch and was holding a sheet of paper in one hand. This he waved in her direction.

"I have something to show you. Something most strange."

She went in through the gate, wondering what could have happened.

"See! I found this envelope under a book on the shelves in my room. It is addressed to a Sir Arthur Wellesley. Was not that the name of the Duke of Wellington?"

"Yes, sire. Weren't you told that he occupied this house for a few days many years ago?"

Napoleon's face displayed some disbelief over this information. "Here? In this house? What a coincidence! What a very strange coincidence!" He walked to the table under the banyan trees and took his usual chair. "Betsee, this passes belief. How did it come about?"

"It was many years ago," explained the girl. "It was in— now, let me see. I was four years old at the time. It must have been 1805. He was returning from India. There was trouble over the drowning of some sailors and his ship was held over. He was sent to stay with us."

Napoleon fell into a silence, his face a picture of intense preoccupation. It was some time before he turned his head again in the direction of his companion. "Betsee, this is one of the curious twists in life which fate provides. I have encountered so many of them in my time. Do you remember anything about what happened?"

"Very little, sire. I remember how kind he was. And I remember his nose above everything. It was one of the kind that my friend Private Knock would call a conky nose."

Napoleon smiled. "A conky nose? Now why? And who is your friend Private Knock?"

"An English soldier. He was, on sentry go at our gate on the morning you rode over to Longwood. We had a talk."

"How long was Wellington here?"

"Only three days, I think."

Napoleon lapsed again into an introspective mood. "Sir Arthur Wellesley! How quickly they loaded him with honors after that. Looking back, it could be said that his real career was just beginning when he was your guest. Strange, strange!"

After a further silence he turned to the girl. His eyes, which had reflected nothing but melancholy over this sudden contact with the past, had lighted up. They seemed to glow. "*Mon Dieu*, is the hand of fate to be seen in this? He left this island to enter on a new phase of his career. His greatest work was ahead of him. Is history going to repeat itself? Will a new life begin here for me? Why not? Why not, indeed, my child? The people of France are not happy without kings. Strong kings. This huge specimen of degeneration they have now will not satisfy them. This Bourbon monstrosity! Do you know that he weighs something like three hundred pounds? Do you know that he eats and drinks enough for a whole company of hussars? No, this Louis the Eighteenth is not capable of reviving the French spirit. The Russian armies will retire, the Prussians and Austrians will disband their forces. And then France, with only England to contend with, will demand my release. Am I wrong in reading some such turn of fate in the finding of this envelope?"

But after a further spell of silence, this exhilaration of mood left him. He frowned and sighed deeply. Finally he began to speak in a low voice, as though he had forgotten her presence.

"No! I must not expect such miracles. This curious tie between the Englishman and me has no favorable significance. It was at the beginning of his career that Wellington stayed

65

in this little house. But it's at the end of mine that I come here. I am a prisoner on a forgotten island, with nothing ahead of me but death, and nothing left but the lees of glory in the wine glass!"

Chapter Six

1

At the junction of three small roads not far from the Briars there was a depression at one side. Water collected there after rains and during the autumn and winter months it became filled with leaves. No footmarks were ever found on the surface and all drivers of vehicles were careful to take the far side.

One afternoon, while accompanying the emperor on a walk, Betsy sighed deeply while passing this spot. "Poor Old Huff!" she said.

"Old 'Uff? I seem to have heard that name mentioned. But why should your tone denote so much sorrow?"

"Because he's buried there," explained Betsy. "He was tutor to my brothers for a short time. A very nice old man and *very learned*. We were all so fond of him. But," laying a forefinger on her temple, "a little touched here."

"Ah, demented. But why is he buried on the road? Are there no graveyards?"

Betsy hesitated. "Well, sire, there was an inquest after he died and it was decided he had committed suicide. So he could not be buried in the churchyard."

"No?" with a puzzled frown. "And why not?"

"I am sure no one would have objected. But we have a curate who is very set in his ideas. He said it could not be allowed." She raised her voice to a high pitch in imitation of the Rev. Mr. Stodgkin, " 'I cannot condone any deviation from the hallowed rules of the past.' So poor Old Huff, who did not know what he was doing, had to be buried here. The servants never walk this way at night unless there are several of them together. They say his ghost comes out and hides in the bushes, ready to pounce on them."

"I am sure you do not believe in ghosts yourself, Betsee."

"Oh, no, sire. Certainly not."

"That is good. It shows you have a sensible head on your shoulders."

"I have noticed," said Betsy, "that we always turn back here. I was beginning to wonder if you had heard the story. But now I'm forced to believe it's because you are getting a little lazy, as Mr. O'Meara says."

"Not at all! It's because my breath is a little short. I seem to tire easily."

"Mr. O'Meara says—"

"Do not speak of that busybody! Sometimes I am sorry I brought him with me. He claims to be a surgeon but I suspect he knows very little about the human body."

"But I thought you liked walking, sire."

"In moderation, Betsee. The real difficulty is that I must give so much time to the notes. If that scion of an ancient family, our illustrious friend the marquis, had more nimble fingers, I would have more time for walking."

"Then why don't you get one of the others to help? With two of them taking turns, you would get the work done so much faster."

"Now that seems a good idea." Napoleon halted to think it over. "Gourgaud, of course. He has nothing to do. He even complains that I favor the others and keep him at a distance. An excellent solution. I will speak to Gourgaud at once." He began to walk again. "I trust you like Gourgaud."

"Sire," said the candid Betsy, "it's a little like your feeling about daily walks. I like Baron Gourgaud—in moderation."

2

That evening Napoleon and Las Cases came over for a game of whist with Mr. and Mrs. Balcombe. Betsy, who was quite keen at cards, was sauntering around the table and keeping a watchful eye on the game; sometimes drawing in her breath sharply when she detected the Great Man cheating, a habit of his. Suddenly a violent noise broke out in the kitchen wing of the house. It was customary for all members of the staff to assemble there in the evenings, with the exception of William Pitt, who spent his hours of leisure in silent contemplation. For several moments there was an unbroken pandemonium of shrieks and groans. Mrs. Balcombe rang the bell to summon Sarah.

No Sarah appeared. In fact there was no response to her repeated ringing until they heard a reluctant footstep approaching through the long and dark passage from the kitchen. The door opened and the head of Mantee Timms appeared.

"I didn't ring for you," said the mistress. "I rang for Sarah."

"Yes, Mis'tuss. But dat Sarah, she 'fraid come. She say I mus' come."

They got the story from him with considerable difficulty. Sarah had gone out into the garden and there she had seen the ghost of Old Huff. He was hobbling along among the trees behind the house and seemed to be searching for something. Her shrieks, as she ran in and slammed the door after her, had thrown all of the staff into a panic. They were now huddled closely together in a corner of the kitchen.

William Balcombe was smiling broadly. "Tee," he asked, "did you see Old Huff yourself?"

"Yes, suh! I see de ghos'. Dat Ole Huff him tryin' get in house. I see him lookin' in windus and tryin' all the do'hs."

"Is the work in the kitchen done?"

"Yas, suh. W'ok done."

"Then go back and tell Sarah and the rest of them to go to bed. There's to be no more noise. There's nothing to be afraid of, Tee. There's no such thing as ghosts."

But Mantee showed no willingness to leave the lighted room. He kept a hand on the doorknob and he shuffled his feet and he did not raise his eyes.

"Tee," said the merchant finally, "are you afraid to go back alone?"

"Das' it, suh. I'se 'fraid to go back alone."

Balcombe was a man of very considerable good nature. He lifted a candle from the table and motioned the servant to follow him. "I'll escort you as far as the kitchen door, Tee. Come along. You needn't be afraid of ghosts if I'm with you."

"No, suh. Not 'fraid with you."

The game was resumed and no further noise was heard from the kitchen quarters. The episode was almost forgotten by the time the visitors rose to return to the pavilion. Napoleon chose this juncture, however, to give rein to a mischief-making turn. Looking back as he opened the gate, he saw that Betsy had come out on the lawn and was waving good night to him. He threw his arms in the air and shouted to her.

"Betsee, Betsee! Old 'Uff! He's behind you!"

Betsy gave a squeal of terror and started to run toward the house. Then, with obvious effort, she stopped and looked back. When she realized how easily she had been deceived, she became angry and walked into the garden with indignant strides. Napoleon, his sides shaking with laughter, was still within hearing. She called out to him:

"Waterloo! Waterloo! Waterloo!"

3

A canvas marquee had been raised beside the pavilion to give additional accommodation for the emperor's staff and to allow for a kitchen. His chief chef seemed, however, to prefer the Briars and prepared many of the meals there. It followed that there were frequent community meals which were most pleasant. For perhaps the first time in his life, Napoleon began to display a weakness for rich foods. His color began to improve almost from the day of his arrival but his waistline showed at the same time a tendency to expand.

When the emperor decided to have more assistance in the preparation of his notes, he summoned Gourgaud at once. The latter was happy to accept and moved from town. Somewhat to his dismay, he found himself installed in a corner of the marquee. Doubtless he had expected to be given the rooms occupied by Las Cases and his son.

From the first Gourgand made it clear that he resented even more than Las Cases the way the younger daughter of the Balcombe family monopolized the time of Napoleon. A lean, dark figure, he stalked disapprovingly about the gardens, his lathlike legs encased in the tightest of breeches.

Once Napoleon whispered a question in Betsy's ear. "What do you think of the gallant Gourgaud?"

"The gallant Gourgaud," she whispered back, "makes me think of black spiders."

"Come, come, *ma petite*. Surely he is not as bad as that!"

"Well you see, sire, I have a friend in the 53rd Regiment—"

"Ah, ha!" cried Napoleon. "The truth is coming out. You have a friend in the regiment. One of these brainless young asses with long yellow mustaches. I knew it would come to this sooner or later!"

"No, sire, no! He's not an officer. He's just a private."

"Don't you know, mam'selle, that young ladies should not speak to privates?"

"But this one is different. He's nice. And he says such odd things. He says there are only two kinds of people—those for you and those *agin you*. I saw right from the start that Baron Gourgaud was *agin us*."

"This is a form of English humor—allowing that there is such a thing—that I don't profess to understand," declared Napoleon. A moment later, however, he indulged in a fleeting grin. "*Certes*, he is partly right, this great friend of yours. There was a saying in my armies that Gourgaud hated everyone. Even, at times, himself. Now *that* is good, is it not? That is civilized French humor. He hated himself!"

"There have been Englishmen like that too," commented Betsy. "They seemed to hate themselves. And it *has* been talked about. Even in England, sire." After a moment, she asked, "Is he a good soldier?"

"Um-m, yes. But perhaps not as good as he thinks himself."

"Does he never smile?"

"Never! He is *lugubre, triste*. Even *affreux*."

"Then why did you select him to come with you? Wouldn't cheerful people be better? *Ma foi*—"

"*Ma foi, ma foi!*" cried Napoleon, bursting into loud laughter. "You are coming to our ways, *ma petite*. Even to our ways of speech."

"But it seems strange to me that you brought this very gloomy officer with you."

"Listen, and never repeat what I tell you. I did not select him. He selected himself and nothing could discourage him from coming. I did my best." He indulged in even louder laughter. "*Ma foi*, yes!"

"Is he a woman hater, this *lugubre* young man?"

"Betsee, you should know better than that. He is a soldier, is he not? Soldiers are never woman haters. On the contrary."

Gourgaud was taciturn but on occasions he indulged in spells of boasting. On one occasion he was talking to Napoleon in the marquee and was interrupted by the appearance of Betsy's face between the canvas covers at the entrance. He frowned angrily and drew the rapier which dangled always against his lean shanks.

"You again!" he said. He held up the weapon, to display a red stain on the blade. "Do you see that, mam'selle? The blood of an Englishman. He intruded on me once and we had words. I called him out, mam'selle, and I ran my blade through his heart."

"Was he a soldier, this Englishman?"

"No, a civilian. A glum fellow, like all the English."

"So!" said Betsy. "He was a civilian and not used to weapons. It could not have been very hard for you to run him through the heart, my brave soldier!"

Betsy had observed that one of the emperor's ceremonial swords was lying on the table. Afterward she declared that Napoleon looked at it and winked; and it is not on record that he ever denied either the glance or the wink. At any rate, Betsy intruded herself further into the marquee. When she saw that Gourgaud had replaced his honorably stained sword into the scabbard with a sharp blow of his fist as though to say, "Now you know what I think of the English!" she seized Napoleon's sword and began to brandish it over her head.

"Put it down!" cried Gourgaud. "You'll be hurting someone. Perhaps even the emperor!"

Betsy contended later that she glanced at Napoleon and that he, in a quite surreptitious manner, winked again.

"No, gallant Gourgaud!" she cried. "It's not the emperor I'll hurt. *You!*" She began to stalk across the room, swinging the blade above her head with increasing carelessness. "So, M'sieur Eater-of-Frogs, you killed an Englishman, did you? I am going to even the score. I am going to kill you!"

Gourgaud found himself in a serious dilemma. He knew he would become the butt of jokes if he drew his own sword to defend himself against a mere girl. On the other hand he was thoroughly alarmed by the wildness of the passes she was making at him. He began to skip from one side to the other, crying, *"Se désister!"* Finally he found himself pressed into a corner of the canvas walls and in desperation he made an effort to draw his blade again.

At this point Napoleon winked quite openly. "That's enough, Betsee. I know you don't want to hurt my brave officer but your handling of a sword leaves much to be desired. It cannot be called skillful at all. You may do him a mischief

72

without intent. Or—and this we would all deplore—you may wound yourself."

Gourgaud emerged from his corner with a scowling countenance.

"Sire, have you any further instructions for me?" he demanded in brusque tones.

"None, my dear Gourgaud, none. Except this, perhaps: no more duels, if you please, with Englishmen."

"Then," stiffly, "I have your permission to retire?"

"You may retire. Mam'selle Betsee is returning home. You will kindly act as her escort."

If Gourgaud heard this, he gave no sign. The canvas closed behind him.

Napoleon frowned. "Perhaps we made a mistake in selecting that one for the dictation."

Chapter Seven

1

The morning after the episode of the swords, Betsy did not put in an appearance. Napoleon kept an ear open for her customary and cheerful "It's me!" at the gate and seemed disappointed that nothing happened to break the monotony of dictation. Finally he said to Las Cases, *"Ou est Mam'selle Betsee?"*

The marquis grunted. "I do not know, sire. But I do know it is a great relief not to have her here."

As the morning wore on, it occurred to the emperor that an unnatural silence reigned in the gardens of the Briars. He had been fully aware that the Balcombe family possessed among other pets a newborn family of pups. From the first he had heard shrill barking as they followed Betsy about the grounds. Often he had encountered her with one of the pups in her arms; always the same one, he believed.

"What do you call that animal?" he had asked her on one such encounter.

"I call him Snooky, sire."

"Hmm! An odd name."

"But it suits him. You see, in London—"

"That dreadful city!"

"It's a *wonderful* city, sire. You've never been there."

Napoleon happened to be in a grumpy mood. "The world," he declared, "is full of splendid cities—Paris, Rome, Vienna, Venice, Cairo, Moscow. They are all quite different, and they are all greater than London. When I was planning to invade England, back in 1808, I made no provision for the safeguarding of London. If it had been neecssary to destroy it for military reasons, it would have been wiped out. It's a dismal place, full of fog and smoke."

"Just as you say, sire," commented Betsy cheerfully. "And now that you've disposed of London, may I point out that the people of that city are very lively and amusing and have unusual names for things? They call your head a 'snook.' When the pups were born, this little fellow had a much larger head than the others, and so I called him Snooky."

Napoleon studied the dog with a critical eye. "He has a rueful countenance, like Don Quixote."

"But you must make allowances for the poor little fellow. After all, he's just an English dog."

"I dislike him intensely. He bears a strong resemblance to one the empress had when we were married."

"The Empress Josephine?"

Napoleon nodded. "She called the noisy beast Fortuné. I told her once she seemed to care more for the little pest than she did for me."

At eleven o'clock on this particular morning, when Betsy had so unaccountably absented herself, one of the pups began to bark mournfully from the direction of the house, a steady *Moo-roo! Moo'roo!* Napoleon said to himself: "It's that lugubrious one. Now I am sure there is something wrong." He got to his feet, motioned to Las Cases to indicate that dictation was ended for the time being, and walked over to the main house. The dog doing the howling, he found, was Betsy's special pet. Seated beside one of the cellar windows, with head pointing up toward the skies, the pup was venting his unhappiness in sound.

"Betsee!" called Napoleon.

Her face appeared promptly at the cellar window. She attempted to smile, but it was a complete failure.

"*Ma petite*, what are you doing down there?"

With some difficulty, she managed to open the window. In the better light thus provided, he saw that she had been crying.

"I am being punished, sire."

"For what? Have you been guilty of some serious offense?"

"It's because of what I did last night," she replied, blinking back her tears. "Someone told Papa I tried to kill you and Baron Gourgaud with your sword. Papa was very angry and wouldn't pay any attention to what I said. I must stay here all day."

The almost habitual sternness of Napoleon's face was replaced by an expression of compassion. "My poor child!" he said. "This is all wrong. It was a joke and I was more at

75

fault than you." He nodded his head with a return to his accustomed severity. "I suspect the hand of the good marquis in this. Last evening I gave him an account of the way you dealt with that great swashbuckler. I am sure he could not wait to tell your father. It must be most uncomfortable down there."

"Yes, sire. All the wine is stored here and the sweet smell of it is making me sick."

"Are you not being allowed any light?"

The child's woebegone face was shaken in denial. "No, sire. And it's terribly dark. I'm afraid to move." She strove to get closer to the wall. "I think Old Huff must stay here during the daytime. I hear sounds of rustling."

Napoleon knelt down on one knee and stared into the dark recesses of the cellar.

"Betsee, you told me you didn't believe in ghosts?"

"No, sire," she responded, with a catch in her voice. "I don't believe in them. But just the same, I'm afraid of them!"

"Come, come, you are too brave to have such ideas. But I don't think you should be kept in this damp place. It will make you ill. Have you anything to sit on?"

She shook her head. "There's a three-legged stool somewhere. But I'm afraid to look for it."

"Has your father gone into town?"

Betsy nodded. "I must stay here until he comes back."

"Then I shall speak to Madame your mother. It will be hard for me to make myself understood. I have not been improving in my English, have I? Still something must be done. Please be brave while I am gone. And stay where you are."

He was back in a short time, followed by Mantee carrying a chair. This was placed at the window and Napoleon seated himself in it.

"Have you had any trouble? Has Old 'Uff been up to any tricks?" He gave a short laugh. "Madame your mother is as sensible as she is charming. She grasped what I was attempting to tell her. She feels, *ma petite,* that you must have been partly at fault and so must be punished. She does not think she should countermand your father's decision but she is reducing your term of detention to one more hour. So, my small one, we must make the best of it, you and I. I shall sit here and keep you company. Old 'Uff will be on his best behavior. It stands to reason that the spirit of a crazy old schoolteacher won't stand up to the winner of sixty battles."

"No. Oh, no. I won't be afraid with you here."

"To keep your mind off your troubles, we must talk. What would you like to talk about?"

"Something *very* interesting, sire."

"Of course. You select the topic."

"Then tell me how you met your wife. Your first wife, sire. The Empress Josephine. I have thought about her so much."

"It is known to all," began Napoleon, "that a man cannot achieve great and unusual things without have a perspective on himself. Everyone has faults, even the greatest of men; and if they are truly great they realize their faults. It is as though a man is able to watch himself and say, *Ma foi*, this thing I am doing is wrong. I must correct this habit. I must be as hard on myself as on others.

"In this respect, my Betsee, I have been a great man. I have always been able to watch myself in action and to decide when I am right and when I am wrong. It is not a pleasant thing to have the gift for seeing oneself. It is so often hurtful to the pride.

"Conceive of me, Betsee, when I first emerged from obscurity. To others I seemed an insignificant fellow. In the first place, I am not of commanding stature. You would not say I was tall, would you?"

"No, sire. You are not *exactly* tall."

There was a brief pause.

"When one is not exactly tall," he resumed finally, "it is unfortunate if he is at the same time thin. I was thin. I was dark and sallow and my hair was lank. I looked undernourished. No one knew this better than I did myself—"

Chapter Eight

1

The story that Napoleon told proceeded along some such lines as this.

It was on the great day of 13 Vendemiaire (October 4, 1795) that the fortunes of Napoleon Bonaparte took a turn for the better. By a grim and free use of grapeshot he scattered the rabble of Paris and freed the Convention from the tyranny of the mob. This won him the favorable notice of Barras, the leading figure in the Directory.

These were strange and wild days in Paris. The Terror and the roll of the tumbrils had become a memory. A degree of freedom mounting to license had gone to the heads of the people. Unscrupulous men like Barras, intent on power and wealth, were in control of administration. At the top of the social life of the city was a group of beautiful and immoral women. Napoleon had heard the story, generally believed, that three of the most strikingly lovely of them had been confined together in one cell in the prison of the Carmelites during the final days of the Terror and that they had escaped the guillotine by the narrowest of margins. One was Madame d'Aiguillon, a patrician, and coldly lovely. The second was Theresa Cabarrus, who had been the mistress of Tallien and inspired him to the bold move which overthrew Robespierre and brought the Terror to an end. This made her the heroine of the people of France who called her Our Lady of Thermidor. She was a softly beautiful creature with no morals but, also, no meanness or malice. The third was the widow of an aristocrat from Martinique, the Vicomte de Beauharnais, who had perished under the knife. Her name was Marie Josephine Rose Tascher de la Pagerie.

It was said that even the most gross and cruel of the guards at the Carmelites would peer through the slit in their door and say, "What a pity it is that these beautiful heads must roll in the basket!"

The young Corsican, who was now being called General Vendemiaire by the public, knew there was no truth in this story. All three had been in the Carmelites but in different cells. He had then, as always, an ardent eye for feminine beauty and he knew also that advancement in the service could most easily be won by feminine support. There can be no doubt that he had often thought of Our Lady of Thermidor and the Fair Creole, as the widow Beauharnais was called. He would gladly have married either one of them. But these fair and giddy ladies, alas, were barely aware of the existence of the sallow and still somewhat obscure Corsican.

Napoleon met Josephine at the table of Barras. He went there knowing she had been the mistress of General Hoche but was now enjoying the protection of the great man of the Directory. "Barras listens to this mad coquette," he said to himself, as he brushed his somewhat threadbare uniform. "I must strive to make a good impression."

On his way to the Rue Basse-Pierre, he called at the War Office to have a word with Carnot, the Minister of War. An underling required him to repeat his name and none of the officers in the anteroom gave him as much as a nod. "These are not soldiers," he said to himself. "They are cheap imitations. Why should I worry because they think me of small consequence? Some day—ah, some day—things will be different!"

Carnot, the very efficient and overworked head of military affairs, smiled and laid a hand on a roll of manuscript. "This is excellent," he said. "I think it would succeed. I said so to the directors yesterday. Of course, they will take some time to make up their minds. Mine is already made up."

Bonaparte was not surprised. He knew the plan he had drawn up for a fresh campaign in the north of Italy was novel as well as brilliant and practical. How could they fail to approve? He was disappointed that Carnot said nothing about appointing him to command the operations. But that, surely, must come later. As he returned through the crowded outer office, he must have allowed a spark of triumph to light up his dark and usually sombre eyes, for the nonentities who made up the whispering groups sensed a change in him. There was even a lightness in his step which had been lacking before. They watched him with what seemed a new curiosity, even envy.

The Fair Creole was acting as hostess for Barras and Napoleon approached her on different feet. But the warm brown eyes of Rose (she was known everywhere as Rose at that time) smiled at him with an unexpected friendliness.

"Ah, General Bonaparte, this is a great honor," she said. "Do you know that we are all secretly afraid of you? How daringly you dealt with that mob! I wonder—are you as brave and ruthless in all things?"

Napoleon found that his tongue had loosened. Looking straight into her eyes, he said, "Dear lady, I stand in a peril at this moment to which I can bring neither bravery nor ruthlessness."

He said this with a fervor which was real. He was seeing this beautiful woman, who had scattered her favors so lavishly, in a new light. There was no hint of the wanton in her, no suggestion of calculation in the glance with which she favored him. She was gentle and graceful and, in his eyes, indescribably lovely. Once he had thought of her in terms of the help she might lend him in his advancement; now he was swept away by her charms. He had been in love often enough but never before had he felt such an overwhelming surge of emotion.

He never could tell afterward what manner of dress she wore on this epic occasion. One detail alone remained in his memory. A pair of lions' heads, wrought beautifully in enamel, served to hold her dress on her shoulders. He thought them in the most pleasant of taste. Afterward, when they had been married for some time, he asked her why she never wore these clips. She seemed at a loss about them, in fact she found it hard to recall them at all. They had, no doubt, been lost, she said. As he was soon to learn, she was very careless about her possessions. Jewelry vanished, money flowed through her hands and dissolved into thin air, nothing was important enough to command a conscientious custody. Josephine could always get what she wanted. Why, then, make a wardrobe mistress of herself?

Josephine had a gift for setting men at their ease, of saying the right things. The young Corsican found other compliments to pay her. He talked of himself, he even boasted a little. Finally he commented on her name.

"I always hear you spoken of as Rose," he said. "As a name it is not suited to you."

This came as a surprise to her and she regarded him with a half smile, half frown. He was soon to discern that she had a way of contracting her eyes so that her smiles carried with them the hint of a frown while her frowns were equally suggestive of a palliating approval.

"But, m'sieur le général," she said, "I have always liked my name. Is it that you think I bear no resemblance to that flower?"

"No, madame," he responded. "You are more lovely than any flower. But there are so many who bear it. In France it has become almost a fixed habit for parents to name a daughter Rose. And you—ah, madame, you should be called by something more distinctive. You have another name which seems to me more fitting. Josephine."

She repeated the name in a low tone, almost to herself. "Josephine. Well, m'sieur le général, it is possible you are right, although I must say I have never been fond of it. Josephine!" Suddenly her eyes lost their quizzical half frown. They opened in a wide smile under their dark lashes and she touched his arm with a hint of approval. "Perhaps you *are* right. It has *some*—distinction, as you say."

"I shall always think of you as Josephine," he said, "even though you may never allow me the privilege of addressing you that way."

"Consider, M'sieur Vendemiaire, that the privilege is already yours."

They talked for as long a time as she dared allow him. The guests kept pouring in, mostly men, and she had to greet them all. Napoleon watched her, standing silently at one side and paying no attention to other guests. He saw that she was tall and slender and he thought her graceful beyond compare. "I have fallen in love for the first time," he said to himself. "What need I care about her past? The present and the future shall be mine."

She did not look again in his direction and he began to fear he had failed to make a good impression. Before they went in, however, his fears were relieved somewhat. He heard her say to one of the other guests: "No, no, m'sieur, I do not agree with you. General Vendemiaire is not lacking in personality. He has a strange and compelling face. It makes me think of the profile of a Roman emperor."

"Ha, my lovely lady!" he thought, triumphantly. "Some day, perhaps, this profile of mine will be seen on medals cast in the French mints. An emperor of France! And if this comes to pass, you, my sweet and gentle Josephine, shall be empress!"

She stood at the wide doorway to bid farewell to the guests when the meal came to an end. There had been many wines and the talk at table had been brilliant and exciting; and these causes had combined to bring a slightly pink flush into her usually pale cheeks. She touched his arm again as he filed slowly past her.

"Perhaps the hero who saved the Convention," she whispered, "will condescend to have luncheon with me tomorrow. At my place on the Rue Chantereine."

2

Paris is not only the city of beauty and romance, it is also the home of the unexpected. It is full of strange little corners which only a people of great imagination could have created. Every part of it has its own particular color, its own distinctive atmosphere. You walk down one of its famous avenues and suddenly you perceive something you have never seen before; an opening, perhaps, between familiar buildings which you have never explored.

The opening is narrow and it leads you into a thoroughly strange backwater. It may be a small square with a fountain in the center, or a statue long since turned green with age, or even no more than a stand for carriages. You say to yourself, perhaps Bussy d'Amboise strolled through here; it may have been here that Dunois had modest quarters. You think the air still holds a faint whisper of old conspiracies. Sometimes it proves to be the center of curious trades and businesses—where skilled dressmakers have the ground floors, or doctors who deal in questionable practices and drugs. You feel calculating eyes on you as you pass and you realize there are peepholes beside the doorbells.

Most often it will be a select area of the greatest beauty, given over to the small *pied-à-terre*, not designed for family use. The houses are much too small for children and much too intimate and discreet for open social activities.

Napoleon had never set foot in the Rue Chantereine but

he felt sure of his ground with the first glimpse he had of it. No one but Josephine, he said to himself, could have found and adapted to her use so perfect a hideaway from the madnesses of Paris. The street was no more than a hundred yards in length and No. 6 stood across the ending, behind a stone wall covered with vines. The walls of the house were white, the window-frames green, the door had a hint of the medieval about it.

He was ushered in through a vestibule from which opened three doors. The butler led the way into an apartment which was serving the double purpose of drawing room and dining room. Behind the second door, as he learned later, was a bedroom. The third opened the way into the most interesting corner of this small jewel of a house. It had been planned originally as the drawing room, but, as it was semicircular in shape, Josephine had introduced into it mirrors for all the walls and couches of curious shape, thus turning it into a luxurious dressing room and boudoir.

The chateleine was down to receive him and so Napoleon gained little impression of the drawing room. She had a warm smile for him but there was no time for her to say more than, "Ah, my brave general!" when two other guests arrived. The table was set with four places, so the company was now complete. The others were introduced as the Marquis de Caulaincourt (Napoleon would have given him close inspection if he had realized that this suave man of obviously good breeding would some day serve as his Minister of Foreign Affairs) and a General de Segur who would become one of his officers. De Segur would not hesitate later to pull strings to get promotions (unsuccessfully, as he was an indifferent officer) but on this occasion he showed no vestige of respect for Napoleon and even stared at him resentfully out of arrogant eyes.

Napoleon had little to say during the meal and so took advantage of the opportunity to study the room which Josephine had created for herself. It was sparely furnished but everything was in the best of taste. A small fire crackled in a very small fireplace and on the mantelpiece stood an excellently executed bust of Socrates. During the afternoon he asked her the reason for the bust and found she had not known it was of the Greek philosopher. In fact, she had never heard of Socrates. She had selected it because it had about it something of Danton; of whom she knew a very great deal.

When the two other guests glanced at their watches and said it was time to go, Josephine gave Napoleon's hand a surreptitious touch and whispered, "Please stay." He remained, therefore, in an intoxication of happiness, more aware every moment of her grace and charm.

They went back into her boudoir where they seated themselves on adjoining chairs and conversed at considerable length. The dog Fortuné was there and quite resentful of the visitor. If Napoleon shifted his position or raised a hand to emphasize a point, the indignant pet would bristle and growl. Josephine found this amusing but explained that she kept the dog out of gratitude.

"He is an unfriendly fellow," she said, "and has often bitten my guests. Have a care, m'sieur le général, I think he may have selected you for some such attention. But I am deeply in his debt! You see, when I was in prison and fearing that each day would be my last, my children were sometimes allowed to visit me. They would always bring Fortuné with them. He wore a special kind of collar and in it notes were concealed for me. It was the only way I could be kept aware of what was happening outside those dreadful walls. And so I feel the little creature is entitled to as much affection as I can feel for him. He has one very bad fault. Jealousy! If you were to lay your hand on mine, he would spring at your throat."

"I think," said Napoleon, with a smile, "that it would be well worth taking that risk."

They talked for more than two hours and Napoleon, as he realized later, had much more to say than his hostess. It was not until he rose to go that he told her something he had been reserving for the last.

"Madame," he said, "I have a secret to divulge."

Her eyes opened very wide at this. "A secret? Ah, a most delightful word. But are you sufficiently certain of my discretion and friendliness? Paris is full of eager ears to hear everything, every rumor or whisper. Beware of telling secrets, even to the closest of friends."

"I must tell you because it concerns both of us."

"But—but how can it? We are so newly acquainted."

"It is this, I am to have command of the three armies in

Italy. It has been officially decided. I was informed this morning by General Carnot himself."

"My dear general, this is wonderful!" Her voice indicated a genuine delight with his news. "I am sure you will cover yourself with glory. I am sure all Paris will rock with excitement when this become known."

"For various reasons, no public announcement will be made at once. I am telling you because of what it means to us. I must leave in three weeks. And that leaves us with so little time."

"Time?" she asked, smiling into his eyes. "Time to become better friends?"

"Time," he said, "for us to be married."

3

The days passed rapidly. Napoleon spent interminable hours in the war offices, perfecting his plan of campaign and settling the most important points of supply and equipment. It had been agreed that he could take his own staff of aides and he had already selected a group including Junot, Murat, Marmont, Desaix—thus introducing for the first time names which will resound as long as the Napoleonic saga is remembered.

Each day he managed somehow to have a few minutes with Josephine, and each day he proposed to her again. Her answer was always the same, No, No, No!

"But, *ma foi!*" he would protest. "You cannot mean it. I love you so much. It is inconceivable that I can lose you."

"Marriage, my brave general," Josephine would respond, "is a matter of mutual consent. The determination of one is not enough. *Tiens!* M'sieur Vendemiaire, am I not to have a say in this?"

"You do not love me, then?"

This question would inevitably lead to much discussion. She loved him, yes, she would say. But did she love him enough? She was disposed to think not.

Napoleon was aware there was a story all over Paris that he had been given his appointment for taking Josephine off the hands of Barras. The latter was planning to move into the Luxembourg Palace from his relatively small house in the Rue Basse-Pierre and would then begin to entertain on a lavish scale. As titular head of the nation, he could no longer permit the widow Beauharnais to serve as his official hostess. And so, ran the rumor, he was providing a husband for her.

This did not shake Napoleon's resolution. In the first place, he knew the story to be untrue. There had been no "deal." At the same time he realized that a less suitable match could not have been found for either of them. His only income was the enhanced salary he would receive in his new post, and so, in all common sense, he should marry a woman of property. It had not taken him long to discover that the Fair Creole was living in desperate though genteel poverty. Her lease on the house in the Rue Chantereine had more than a year to run and would be taken care of by Barras. Her two children were at fashionable schools which meant a heavy drain on a purse as frail as its owner's morals. Hortense, her daughter, was actually at Madame Cambon's, perhaps the most exclusive and expensive on the continent. The money to send them, however, was provided by Josephine's mother who still lived in some degree of comfort in Martinique.

The household on the Rue Chantereine resembled nothing so much as a slack-wire walker keeping half a dozen balls in the air at once. Josephine did not hesitate to borrow from her servants and they seemed happy to comply. Gonthier, the butler, was a diplomat of rare parts. Each morning he took a basket to the markets, where he argued, bullied, beseeched, and cajoled what he needed from the grumbling merchants. There were never any bills at the butcher's because her friends sent in large baskets of food to her every week. Josephine's only source of income came through her influence at the offices of the Customs. She was allowed to bring in duty-free large quantities of silk stockings and fine lingerie, which she sold to friends.

Napoleon was fully aware that she was running up bills with a charming prodigality which inevitably would lead to a resounding crash.

Finally, he knew that she was thirty-two years old to his twenty-six. A most unsuitable match indeed!

For her part Josephine was giving some consideration to the possibility of accepting this persistent young man. The time had come when she must find a husband to assume the burden of her butterfly existence. But almost without exception her friends protested that Napoleon was the least suitable of the many suitors who had presented themselves. This

Corsican *nullité!* If he lost his first battle—and it was generally anticipated that he would—he would be demoted at once. Her children were shrill in their opposition. "That one, that skin-and-bones!" stormed Hortense. "*Maman*, he will never do!" Both Hortense and Eugene, the son, contrasted the sallow Napoleon with General Hoche who was handsome in a Herculean way.

Still, her stock was dwindling on the matrimonial exchange. Perhaps this determined young officer would be a great success and be able to keep her in luxury. A point in his favor was that none of the other men who desired her had ever spoken in terms of love. Every sentence he spoke, every note he sent her, was filled with burning words of devotion. Surely his love for her was such that she would be able to keep him in subjection by the twiddling of a finger.

One morning Napoleon rose early, shaved with great care, and left his headquarters in the Rue Neuve-des-Capucines, humming to himself (off key as always) a recent popular song:

> *When you always know how to please*
> *You are never more than twenty.*

He knew that Josephine would still be in bed and entertaining callers, a curious custom which had persisted throughout the century. This proved to be the case. When Gonthier admitted him, he heard many voices and much restrained laughter from the direction of the bedroom. There were several canes and male hats in the vestibule as well as expensive feminine cloaks, lined or trimmed with fur. This was to be expected, for outside a brisk March wind was blowing and enough snow had fallen to conceal the early flowers.

When Gonthier announced him, the company grouped about the bed went suddenly silent. He heard a male voice mutter, "That one!" in a disgusted tone.

"An unexpected honor, m'sieur le général," said Josephine, with a welcoming smile.

Despite the earliness of the hour, it was evident that she had not neglected the long rites with which she began her days. She had been in the hands of her maids for a full hour, undergoing the *faire sa tête*. This consisted first of the massaging of her face and neck and shoulders and the skillful application of rouge to conceal the ravages of time. The chemise she had worn while sleeping had been replaced by a camisole of the most delicate percale with trimmings of Valenciennes at the neck and sleeves. Her nightcap had given way to a fresh one of embroidered muslin, delicately trimmed with lace. It was apparent that her coiffure had been completed, for her thick and slightly auburn hair (which remained thick and became increasingly auburn all the years of her life) was in perfect order. A cup containing the remains of an *infusion*, her inevitable first meal of the day, stood on a chair at her right hand.

"I regret this interruption," said Napoleon. "But it happens I have something for your ears which I feel should not be delayed in the telling."

Josephine waved a white hand in the direction of her dressing room. "Do you mind?" she asked the half dozen visitors who sat about the room or lounged on the foot of her bed. "I am sure it is a matter of urgency or m'sieur le général would not have come at so early an hour."

The other visitors quickly dissolved from view. Napoleon removed the half-emptied cup from the chair and sat down himself.

"Sweet and incomparable Josephine," he said, using a phrase which often appeared in his letters to her, "I received my final orders this morning. I must leave for the front in three days. Do you appreciate what this means, my fair one?"

"It means," said Josephine, with her warmest smile, "that I shall be deprived of your company much sooner than I had expected. It is a great misfortune, my dear general."

The smile which Napoleon had worn into the room left his face and was replaced by an expression of stern determination. "It means much more, *mio dolce amor*. It means that for us it is a case of now or never. And permit me to point out that *now* means today."

"Napoleoni!" exclaimed the slender occupant of the bed, using for the first time a name he had often begged her to employ. "Today? Truly, that is nonsense. It is impossible. Even if I had decided to marry you, which I have not done— No, no, my Napoleoni, I have not indeed—it would be out of the question to make the necessary arrangements. Today? Every minute of the time is filled with engagements!"

"Break them!" commanded Napoleon. "They cannot be of

sufficient consequence to delay our union, dearest Josephine. I shall leave here at once to make the necessary arrangements for the ceremony. It is a simple one, as you know." He stooped to pick up a gown which had fallen by the side of the bed, a trifling thing of India *mousseline de soie.* "Is this what you were planning to wear today? It will do perfectly for the ceremony. Dismiss your friends and begin to pack what you must take."

"But, my impetuous one!" cried Josephine, "you cannot compel me to do what you wish!"

At this juncture Gonthier rapped discreetly and then entered the room. "Madame," he said, "M. Raguideau is here. He says he has an appointment with you."

Josephine grasped at this opportune interruption. She said to the butler: "Have him wait five minutes. Then show him in." To Napoleon she explained in a whisper: "I had forgotten he was coming. But truly it is a matter of great importance. He is my man of affairs, my lawyer. Please go now and come back later."

"I know who he is and I've heard him well spoken of." Napoleon was frowning still more ominously. "I will go. As far as that window. He won't see me, this excellent man of affairs, but I will see him. And I will hear what he has to say."

There was no time for expostulation. Josephine bit her lips as Napoleon stepped to the window embrasure and concealed himself behind the curtains. The notary, a middle-aged man with a heavy beard, bowed himself as far into the room as the foot of the bed behind which he paused.

"Good morning, madame," he said. "It is a beautiful morning."

"Is it, m'sieur?" Josephine's voice had taken on a plaintive note. "I have been hoping it would prove a day of heavy rain with perhaps thunder and some quaking of the earth. The kind of weather which would prevent me from leaving the house *under any circumstances.*"

The notary looked much surprised. "Indeed, madame? I am surprised in view of the matters I have come to discuss with you."

The lady glanced apprehensively in the direction of the curtains behind which Napoleon had placed himself. "You have brought the papers I asked for? Particularly the statement of my financial standing?"

The whiskers of M. Raguideau seemed to curl with a sense of amusement. "You are well aware, of course, of the far from substantial nature of what we might call your estate?"

"Quite, m'sieur. I am quite aware that I have no assets. And that in addition I am much in debt."

The notary nodded his head. "Yes, dear madame, you are much in debt. But you *have* assets. True they are in the nature of intangibles. The affection of your many friends. The—the ties which exist. The possibilities which the future may hold for you."

"If I were to marry now," pursued Josephine, deciding to let the eavesdropper learn everything about her affairs, "I would have little to contribute to the union."

M. Raguideau drew down the corners of his mouth and gestured with both hands. "Nothing. Your beauty, madame, your great charms, the esteem of people in high places. But nothing else!"

"Have you any advice then to give me as to the suitability of a certain soldier who must go unnamed?"

There was a moment of silence. The man of business then raised his hands in another gesture, this time to denote uncertainty. "This is what I must say to you. Inasmuch as you have no property of your own, the young man in question, who is also penniless, is utterly unsuitable. He may be destined for great things. But this is a matter of the future. At the moment he has only his cloak and sword."

"You feel, then, it would be a mistake to marry him?"

"A mistake? Madame, a catastrophe! What you need, with your beautiful children, is a husband of substance. A man with investments in the funds, land, fine estates. A banker, perhaps. Or an industrialist."

"Thank you, M. Raguideau. You have been very honest."

"But wait, madame la vicomtesse! I owe it to myself to speak as I have done. But I owe it to you to add something. This young general is a man of strange caliber. It is conceivable that he may become in time a very great man indeed. Perhaps the gamble is one which after all should be taken. As your notary, I advise against the match. As one who sincerely desires the best for you, I am not as sure you should say no to him."

The curtains parted and Napoleon stepped out from the embrasure. He was wearing a pleased and confident smile. "I have heard this discussion," he declared. "You have spoken like a man of honor, m'sieur le notary. I thank you. Madame de Beauharnais and I had made up our minds to be married today. I will consider it an honor if you will personally draw up the marriage papers. At once, for we must take the vows tonight. May I add that I am certain we can put our trust in you and that I desire you to continue as our adviser. It may be that some day it will be of very considerable importance." He raised Josephine's hand to his lips. "I must leave you now, my precious one. But I shall keep in constant contact with you during the day. Junot, one of my aides, will be assigned to post back and forth between us. Even"—with a side smile for the benefit of the man of affairs—"if we have torrential rains and earthquakes."

Josephine had not missed the byplay and there was a hint of petulance in her voice when she addressed the notary. "Are you deserting me, M. Raguideau? You must see that we are facing a man of great determination. What am I to do?"

"Marry him, madame. That is the best thing for you to do."

4

Napoleon was late in arriving for the ceremony that evening at No. 3 Rue d'Antin. He was so late, in fact, that all of those present were beginning to wonder. What had happened to this man of infallible punctuality? Had he changed his mind? Had his appointment been unexpectedly revoked at the War Department?

The mayor of Paris was there, fast asleep in a comfortable chair in the reception room, his muffled snores rising to a ceiling of gold with a frieze on which the heroes of mythology disported themselves in the broadest of colors. Josephine had been prompt in her arrival. One witness later stated that she was wearing a semi-transparent tunic but the others represented her as attired in charming taste. A. M. Camelot was there to assist M. Raguideau in acting for her. Barras and Tallien had come to sign as witnesses for the young general and, as the time passed, both men displayed much impatience over the tardiness of the groom. Barras smiled as he placed a consolatory hand on Josephine's arm but he frowned angrily as he whispered in Tallien's ear.

They had assembled at eight o'clock but it was not until

ten that the bridegroom put in an appearance. His brow wore a frown, his hair was awry. Under one arm he carried a large sheaf of loose documents. Junot, who accompanied him, carried papers under both arms.

"My humblest apologies," said Napoleon, addressing himself to the bride.

"What reason can you give for this extraordinary delay?" demanded Barras.

"The stupidity of officers in the War Department, M'sieur Director," explained Napoleon. "I have been delayed and bedeviled by stupid little place holders who have no conception of the supplies needed. We have been debating matters at bitter length which could have been settled in a few minutes."

"If the debates had lasted five minutes longer, m'sieur le général," declared Josephine, "you would not have found a bride waiting for you."

"That you endured this delay, my gracious one, will remain in my memory forever."

The papers were ready for their signature. Perhaps never before had such lack of worldly goods been mutually affirmed. Napoleon had only his uniforms and his books to declare. Josephine had her clothes and nothing else. Despite this proof of poverty, the usual clauses had been included to cover eventualities, such as the death of either contracting party.

"Who is getting the worst of this?" whispered Barras in Tallien's ear.

The notary Raguideau seemed thoroughly unhappy about one point. His brows drew together in disapproval as he pointed to the ages set down. Napoleon had added two years to his age and Josephine had subtracted four from hers. This had brought them to a parity at twenty-eight.

"This," he said in a whisper to the contracting parties, "is a very great mistake. A very great mistake indeed. It invalidates the marriage. Do you realize that?"

The mayor had wakened up and was listening with both ears, so Napoleon replied in equally low tones. "My birth is recorded in Corsica. My wife's can be obtained only in Martinique. A long distance separates them, m'sieur le notary. No one will ever be in a position to discover the error."

M. Raguideau shook his head impatiently. "It may seem a

small matter but it could place you in jeopardy later. Suppose, for instance, that you attain a high post in the state, high enough so that everything about you will be subject to curiosity and scrutiny? Suppose that some busybody discovers the mistake in the figures and runs all over Paris with it? My dear general, and you, madame, you must be wise and allow me to correct them."

Napoleon brushed the matter aside. He knew that Josephine felt a deep reluctance to avow her real age. Perhaps if he had known that on a memorable day in the future he would sit on a throne and be crowned emperor of France, and that Josephine would be beside him, he would have realized the wisdom of what the lawyer proposed. It would prove no light matter then to cover up the discrepancy in the dates. Much diplomatic chicanery would be required.

That was something for the future and nothing to bother about on this wonderful evening when his Josephine was placing her future in his hands. He laughed and whispered to her, "Do you see any need to worry about this?" She smiled as she answered: "Is there a mistake? I am certain my age is correctly stated."

So they joined hands and swore to their desire to be made man and wife. Nothing else was necessary under the new laws recently enacted. Napoleon scratched his signature on the document in an illegible hand.

An immediate problem now had to be faced. "Dearest wife," said the young general, "my quarters are filled with officers and clerks. Not to mention piles of correspondence and maps. And saddles. I am afraid I cannot ask you to accompany me there."

"My dear Napoleoni," said Josephine. "I have seen your rooms. It never entered my head that we might go there. Have you any objections to my little place on the Rue Chantereine?"

"None!" he declared fervently.

"We will have no officers or clerks there. Not a single document or map. And certainly no saddles. The only one to dispute possession with you will be—Fortuné!"

"Ah!" said Napoleon. "I begin to foresee certain difficulties!"

No supper was served. Barras kissed the bride's hand, bowed ironically to Napoleon, and took his departure in an imposing state coach. A barouche had been provided for the newly married pair in which they rode to the Rue Chantereine.

5

Gonthier served them with a well-cooled bottle and then tactfully disappeared. Josephine raised her glass and sipped worn the *mousse-line de soie*. Her wedding dress was of beige gratefully. She had not followed her husband's suggestion and satin and, when she gracefully crossed one knee over the other, she accented what was called a *gros de Tours*, a ribbed band of heavy material carrying wreaths of flowers. It was somewhat ornate but well suited to her unusual type of beauty.

"I don't understand this," she said, frowning. "How did it come about? When I said 'no' to you so often, I meant it every time. I didn't intend to marry you."

"What you thought and said had no bearing on the case," declared Napoleon. "It was destined that you were to marry me. There was nothing you could do to influence the result."

"Destined?" Her frown deepened. "Do you mean by God? Or the fates?"

"By me," said Napoleon.

He had emptied his glass quickly and had placed it back on the tray. It was clear he did not desire more.

Josephine laughed. "Really, I cannot concede that I am a mere pawn in your hands."

Napoleon's eyes seemed to grow in size and to glow with an increased intensity. "Josephine, I am afraid to put into words the things for which we are destined. You and I are going to scale great heights together. Are you prepared for the climb?"

"You frighten me! I don't think I am suited for such great heights. I don't want to be the wife of a Director or the commander of all the armies. Or a—a king!"

He relaxed sufficiently to allow a fleeting smile to cross his face. "What kind of life do you want, *mio dolce amor?*"

"A life of ease. An *affluent* life. I want to be able to buy anything I see without giving a thought to the cost. I want to have wardrobes full of expensive clothes. Oh, how I want dainty and beautiful things! Gowns to make all other women green with envy, sweet little hats, shoes that I will never wear more than once, jewelry! Yes, and fine beds to sleep in and gorgeous cabinets and wonderful paintings on the walls. I don't care to have money in my purse, because it's really a nuisance. I want it to be something that appears by magic when the need to pay bills arises—but which I need not see. I want gardens full of flowers and the finest harp ever strung. And I want good marriages for my children. That is what I want—and I don't care for titles. Oh, well, not enough to struggle for them. And I'm quite willing to let others sit in the tall chairs of the great."

"All these things, my frivolous but adorable wife, you shall have. I intend to make you the most pampered consort in the world. But this life of luxury will be obtained only by climbing the heights of which I spoke."

She asked plaintively, "Must I always be with you when you are doing the climbing?"

"Of course. I will lead the way but you must come behind, clutching my coattails if you find it necessary, and shutting your eyes so you won't see the frightful abyss on each side. You won't need to know the risks we are taking."

"I am more frightened now! Could it not be arranged for me to follow later? By comfortable, level roads? In a closed carriage, perhaps?"

"Sometimes that way may be possible and even advisable. But when it comes to the important moments, my Josephine, you must be either by my side or immediately behind."

Napoleon was thinking, while they talked: "What an absurd and selfish little creature! But she is Josephine and I love her with all her faults. I wouldn't have her changed!" There can be no doubt that the new bride found a share of the fascination in all these grandiose plans and claims but it was equally certain that she considered them a form of boasting. At any rate, she suddenly realized that she was very tired. She concealed a yawn with the back of one hand.

"It has been a long day," she said. "I feel ready for bed."

"I," exclaimed Napoleon, "am filled with unquenchable energy and with ambitions quite different from what we have been discussing."

Josephine had helped herself to a second glass of wine and she smiled archly over the rim. "In that case—" She motioned toward the door of the bedroom which stood ajar. "Everything is ready. There is a warm fire in the grate and another

95

bottle, if we want it, on a serving table. I think there are biscuits. The bed has been turned down." She paused. "I must explain. It is a most comfortable bed but it is not large. It will hold two. But three, no."

"Three? I don't understand."

"Fortuné! She always sleeps with me."

Napoleon's indignation at this point passed all bounds. "That incredible dog! Are you hinting that I must be content with a hard couch in some miserable corner, or perhaps even a chair?"

"No, no. Not, that is, if you can manage to persuade Fortuné to relinquish her place."

Napoleon got to his feet. "That," he declared, "will not be hard."

"You must be gentle with the poor little thing!" protested Josephine.

He was as gentle as possible under the circumstances. Finding the small dog curled up comfortably at the foot of the beautifully appointed bed, and snoring loudly, he lifted it up and clamped it firmly under one arm. Locating the room where Gonthier slept, he received sleepy directions which led him to a harness room, opening off the stables at the rear of the premises. Here he placed his wife's pet on an old blanket, which he was pleased to see was quite ragged and moldy, and closed the door carefully. He returned to find Josephine seated before a mirror and doing something to her hair.

Napoleon did not like heavy perfumes but he had been conscious of a pleasant aroma in the room which did not offend his critical sense. It came, he now saw, from a bathtub of a rather fantastic design in one corner. He peered over the screens which partly obscured it. Josephine had been quick to enjoy a brief bath while he was finding a bed for the dog. Several intimate articles of clothing lay on the floor.

He then became aware that another tub had been placed behind screens in an opposite corner. This, obviously, was for his use. He felt very much relieved because he was becoming embarrassingly aware of his heavy uniform and knee-length army boots, and also of the fact that he had worked unceasingly all day. The tub was not substantial enough to bear his weight while he undressed, so he had to squat on the floor while tugging at the boots. The water proved quite warm and he felt a certain reluctance about splashing loudly. His bath, although thorough, was quickly finished, therefore.

Josephine was in bed when he emerged from behind the screen, her dark long lashes veiling her eyes. She was, he thought, more lovely than any of the expensive possessions she hoped to have showered upon her. He blew out the candles before approaching the bed.

Perhaps he had not closed the door of the harness room as securely as he thought or it may have been that Fortuné discovered some other means of exit. At any rate she found herself free after an hour of embittered barking, of which only the faintest echoes had reached the nuptial couch. Her small frame shook with indignation when she discovered that all the space in the bed was in use and that the occupants were still awake.

Napoleon had not heard her arrive and his first intimation that there were were now three in the bed was when he experienced a very sharp pain.

Fortuné had bitten him on the shin!

6

The two days which followed were busy ones for the new commander of the French armies of Italy. He had dinner on the first night with Josephine and luncheon on the second; and the time was spent on his part in efforts to persuade her to accompany him. Josephine professed to be willing, even anxious, to go but she kept pointing out a difficulty: How could she get ready in time?

Napoleon scoffed at this. "An army can be made ready, equipped, rationed, and even marched into battle in two days. How long does one woman need to prepare for a journey?"

"A week," was the answer.

At regular intervals during the two days, Junot arrived in the Rue Chantereine with notes for her. In them the new bridegroom voiced the intensity of his love. She was his adorable wife and he worshiped her. He would be intensely unhappy if he had to leave her after so brief a taste of the sweetness of her company. How could he devote himself to his new duties if he would think of nothing but her absence from him? Come, lovely Josephine, come with the man who adores you.

She would read the notes, while Junot waited for the answers. Then she would fold them up into neat squares and place them in a belt worn at her waist, and smile at the ambassador. Junot was as sleekly dark as a young seal; and Josephine always had a smile for handsome young men.

"And do *you* think I should pack in this insane hurry and go with him?"

"Undoubtedly, madame. His peace of mind depends on it."

"Is it not a very long journey? I have no sense of distance whatever but it seems to me certain I would not survive it."

"Yes, madame, it must be conceded that the journey is a long one."

"Would we ride all day long?"

"But, yes, madame. And sometimes part of the night."

"I would arrive in a dying condition. Unless I expired on the way and had to be buried by the side of the dusty and lonely road."

"I don't think the hardships of the trip would be as great as that."

"Would I have time to dress properly, to bathe, and to refresh myself? You must give me the truth."

"Madame Bonaparte, I—I want to be honest. You are certain to find the journey exhausting. How much time would be required for these intervals of rest?"

"A few hours only."

"Madame!" in horrified tones. "Ten minutes might be allowed perhaps. But certainly not more."

"Please tell my unfeeling husband that I do not wish to kill myself. Tell him I have decided not to accompany him but that I will join him later. That is my final answer."

"Would you be kind enough to explain in a note which I will carry back to him?"

"No, my brave colonel. Even though I am not engaged in the fatigues of packing, every instant of my time is in demand. I have so many appointments and so many insistent friends. There is no time to sit down and write him a note. You, my kind new friend, will convey my answer in suitable terms."

At ten o'clock on the evening of the second day, Napoleon arrived in the Rue Chantereine in a carriage with four horses and three of his aides, Junot, Marmont, and Berthier. They had been working all day in the mad haste imposed on them by the iron-willed Corsican. Junot was nodding with sleep, the others had already succumed and were in a collapsed condition on the back seat.

All the windows of the house were lighted up. Gonthier was obviously taken by surprise when he opened the door and saw the carriage, the uniformed driver and the horses jingling with equipment.

"Is it that m'sieur the general is leaving so soon?" he asked.

"Yes, Gonthier. I have come to say farewell to Madame Bonaparte."

The sound of the closing door had the effect of wakening Marmont. His father had been a member of the small nobility and an officer in the royal army. The son knew something, therefore, of the pleasures of ease and luxury.

"Why am I starting out on an adventure of interminable fatigue, in which I shall undoubtedly be killed? There are times," he said, "when I think that war is an insanity."

Berthier struggled to a sitting position. His hair was tousled and he was badly in need of a shave. Thinking of what Marmont had said, he fell into his usual practice of biting his fingernails while he considered it.

"But the rewards, Marmont," he muttered finally. "Think of the rewards."

"We are more likely to get a bullet in the throat as our reward than a title and a fat grant of land."

"Have you not heard Napoleon say that greatness is in the grasp of all of us? I put my faith in him." Berthier sighed. "Still, it is true that great hardships are ahead of us."

"Let's be honest about this," declared Junot, who was as vain as a peacock in full feather. "What is our chief reward? The uniform we wear! True, we risk our lives. But when we strut out in all our grandeur, the women throw themselves at our feet. Pouf! all their resistance melts away. Isn't that better than living in peace at a desk or mucking about in plowed fields? I never want to be seen again in baggy gray clothes and hats as flat as a cow's compliments."

"You speak of honesty," grumbled Marmont. "Is there such a thing as real honesty any more? Consider our brave Napoleon and his Fair Creole. He has been pleading with her to accompany him to the front. Does he want her to come? He does not!"

"Sapristi!" cried Junot, the bearer of all those pleading

notes. "This is positively absurd, Marmont. I tell you, the man has been in a frenzy."

"Listen to me, Junot. If the fair Josephine had decided to come, what would have been the result? We would have had to hang around for at least two more days while she got herself ready. We would lose a week on the road because she would get too fatigued for long stretches. At a time when every hour counts, we would have this complaining female on our hands, holding back and whimpering for more sleep."

"Then why did he try so hard to persuade her?" demanded Junot.

"He is a wily one, this little Napoleon. He wanted to make her think he would be heartbroken without her. Why? Well, he was thinking of the future."

"But what if she had decided to come?"

"In the first place, he knew her too well to think she would give in. If she had—"

"*Sapristi!*" cried Junot, making use again of this favorite expression. "That is the point. What if she had agreed?"

"Our ingenious little leader would have found it necessary to move quickly and find some way to make her change her mind again. I'm sure he had it all thought out."

At this point Napoleon emerged from the stout oaken door of his wife's charming home. Even in the darkness, which was intensified by the shadow of the trees under which the house stood, it could be seen that his eyes were filled with tears. But his gait was brisk, even cheerful.

"Observe him!" whispered Marmont. "Was I not right? This is the way he wanted it."

"Well, comrades-at-arms!" cried Napoleon, as he took his place in the carriage. "We are off at last! I begrudged every second we lost arguing with those blockheads at the War Office. In a few days now we will be with our brave troops along the Apennines. And then we'll break the back of Austrian pride on the anvil of French genius!"

The driver cried, "Up!" and curled his whip over the backs of the horses.

It was from this train of events, still so vivid in his mind, that Napoleon drew in spinning a story for Betsy's benefit. The version she heard was, of course, much shorter. At many points he was careful to wield a mental blue pencil, even to

100

tiptoe discreetly around many episodes which he realized were not for her ears.

At the finish Betsy sighed deeply and said, "You loved her very much, sire."

"Yes, Betsee, I loved her very much."

"More than any of the—the Others?"

"Yes, more than any of the Others."

Chapter Nine

1

They heard at this point a sound of footsteps on the stairs leading down to the cellar. The opening of a door admitted a bar of light across the stone-paved floor. It became immediately apparent that Betsy's half fears had been ill founded; there was nothing to hint of the presence of Old Huff.

It was Mrs. Balcombe and she called out in affectionate tones: "Come, Betsy, you have been punished enough. Dear me, what a winey smell there is down here. It's enough to make a person ill. I wish I could clean the place right out. But your father *insists* on having a gentleman's cellar."

"I'm coming, Mamma," said Betsy, turning away from the window. "I haven't minded it so much because His Imperial Highness has been telling me a story about himself. Wasn't that kind of him?"

"He is always very kind," asserted Mrs. Balcombe, becoming aware of the awkward fact that she was still wearing a very plain household dress. "Up you come, my child. You must go straight to the bathroom. You'll need a good scrubbing to get rid of this terrible smell of wine. I think I must have some words with your father, my dear."

Napoleon uncrossed his knees, causing an ominous creaking sound. He winced slightly and wondered if the aches of a quarter century of campaigning were finally taking possession of his bones.

"If I had followed my first ambition and made a novelist of myself, I would be living today in the comfort and security of a booklined house and not a prisoner on this barren island. Still," with a wry smile, "it would have been a dull, closed-in, and liverish kind of existence."

102

Late that afternoon Betsy was sitting at her ease on the lawn between the two houses and trying to find some way to keep her active mind busy. There was a new book in the house which her father had brought from town the day before. It was entitled *The Usurper's Barber Tells All He Knows* and she had been inclined to dip into it but she decided now it would be trashy. She devoted some thought to the Veiled Lady and wondered what explanation there could be for her presence on the island. This topic exhausted itself almost immediately, for no one on St. Helena had any idea of the truth.

Betsy was wearing a comparatively new dress of light brown with a few touches of gold here and there which matched her hair. She realized that she looked well in it and was hoping that Napoleon would finish his everlasting afternoon nap in time to notice it.

When she had reached a decision to walk to the other side of the house and see if the family of pups were having more success than she at amusing themselves, there was an interruption. Emmanuel Las Cases arrived on the scene, walking down from the high-perched pavilion with reluctant steps. He was wearing fawn nankeen trousers so widely cut that his thin shanks seemed swallowed up in them, and his collar was so stiff and high that he could barely look over it. He approached her very, very slowly.

"Mam'selle," he said, in a tone which he kept purposely low, "I have come to tender you an apology. I have heard that you were punished today for something my father told your parents."

This was news to Betsy. It had not entered her head that Las Cases *père* had any part at all in the incident.

"It wasn't your father, M'sieur Emmanuel," she said, with a friendly smile. "I think it was that bold killer of helpless civilians, the brave Gourgaud."

The boy shook his head sadly. "No, Mam'selle Betsy. It was my father who repeated the story to M'sieur Balcombe. He will be very angry if he should learn about this. But—I had to come and express my regrets."

Betsy was thinking: "This poor Emmanuel! He feels so badly about it. And he's got himself, oh, so dressed up!"

"I know, mam'selle, that you do not like me," went on the

boy, "and so I do not know what to say. I am"—he gulped—"at a loss for words."

"Emmanuel!" exclaimed Betsy. "I *do* like you. At least, I'm sure I would if I could know you a little better. You keep so much to yourself. Why do you stay up in that hot little attic? Why don't you come down and join in our games?"

"Mam'selle," explained the boy, "I am not good at games. You would all laugh at me. There is only one game I have ever played. Catch."

"Catch?" Betsy frowned. "I've never heard of that one."

"It is a fine game," exclaimed the boy, displaying a sudden degree of enthusiasm. "You have a rubber ball and you throw it up against a wall. When it bounces back, you try to catch it."

"Is that all there is to it? How many play the game?"

"Oh, just one."

"You mean to say there aren't others trying to catch it? That there isn't someone swoshing away at the ball with a bat?"

"Oh, no. You play alone. And when you catch the ball, it is *very*—exciting."

Betsy suddenly developed a sense of the need to be tactful with this strange foreign boy. Instead of blasting him with a "You mollycoddle!" or some such expression, she said, "Yes, I guess it is exciting." Then she had an idea. "Emmanuel, why don't you let us give you one of our family of pups? We have more than we need. It would be company for you. They're all such nice little fellows. I think I could part with Victor. He's a bossy one."

The French boy shook his head sadly. "I can't have a pet," he said. "My father says it is a sign of weakness, of—of insufficiency in oneself. He says there has never been any such sign of weakness in our family for seven centuries."

"You mean to say," cried Betsy, "there has never been a dog in your family for all that time?"

"That is the truth. We—we are a proud family. We boast of our self-sufficiency. That is my father's word for it." He paused before adding, with a partially suppressed eagerness: "I have heard the emperor speak of all the pets you have. It must be very nice, Mam'selle Betsy, to have so many."

"Well, we have the dogs. And two cats. Nice little cuddly ones. Maltesers. And a parrot. You must have heard him squawking. Then Mamma has a pair of lovebirds in her room."

"But—but you haven't mentioned the crocodile."

"Crocodile?" Betsy was very much perplexed. "Where did you get that idea?"

"His Imperial Highness spoke about it one night at dinner when the others were with us."

"The Berthiers and the Montholons? And that—that Gourgaud?"

"Yes, mam'selle. The emperor said you had a small one and that it came crawling across the floor at dinnertime and that all the guests had to lift their feet up under them to escape being bitten on the heels. He said it was very amusing. I wish I could see it sometime." Then he added hurriedly, "At a safe distance, of course."

"So," said Betsy, in a tone which might be described as both reflective and grim. "The emperor said it was very amusing, did he? I suppose everyone laughed."

"Oh, yes. Everyone laughed. My father laughed so much he did not frown at me when I joined in."

"I am so glad you told me about it. Perhaps, some day, M'sieur Emmanuel, you will have a chance to see this crocodile. Perhaps I'll be able to arrange it."

Emmanuel had lost his timidity in the course of this long conversation. But now his customary shyness suddenly returned. He dropped his eyes and he began to scrape some pebbles around with his feet. "I—I—" he began. Then he turned abruptly and started to walk back toward the pavilion, slowly at first and then with an accelerating speed, his baggy trousers flapping ludicrously about him.

William Balcombe returned home at an earlier hour than usual on the afternoon of the second day thereafter. He called, "Betsy!" in a loud voice when he reached the porch. The second daughter of the family answered, "Gracious, Papa! What's wrong?" as she came running from somewhere in the rear of the house.

"Betsy," said her father, "there's a man here, a sailor. He stopped me to say he has something for you. Whatever it is, it's in a long box. Now what in thunderation—"

"Oh, Papa!" cried Betsy. "It must be! It must be! I asked around when I was in town last with Mamma as to where we could get a young crocodile—Mamma didn't know I was doing it, of course—and I heard there was a sailor off one of the ships who had one. A very young one, Papa. I told him we— I—would like to borrow it for a few hours. I said we would pay—well, I said half a crown."

"Your sailor is outside now." William Balcombe's voice was grim. "Betsy, this is really the most incredible thing! *Goggins*, child, have you taken leave of your senses? A crocodile—!"

"Well, you see, it was this way. I heard how the emperor told about our pets at a dinner for his proud French guests. He said we had a crocodile which came slithering in at meals, and came up behind our guests, and took nips at their heels. He made it very funny and those French people—weren't they all raised up from the gutter by Napoleon himself?—laughed and laughed about it. Do you think, Papa, the emperor should have done that? I don't! He was making fun of us." Betsy seemed reluctant to tell what she had planned to do. "Well, Papa, this was my idea. The emperor—please don't frown at me, I always speak of him as General Bonaparte to strangers, though I hate to—is coming over for dinner tonight. I thought if I could get this young crocodile for an hour, I could let it loose and have it come right into the dining room. It would give him a scare! And, Papa, I think he deserves it."

"Betsy!" cried her scandalized father. "You can't do a thing like that! Don't you realize he might be injured?"

"Oh, no. I would keep an eye on it to be sure it didn't get close enough."

"Can you imagine how indignant he would be? I don't suppose he would ever come back here."

"You're wrong, Papa. I've come to understand him pretty well, I think. He enjoys practical jokes. Mostly, of course, when he's playing them himself. He might be startled at first. But then he would throw back his head and laugh. I can see him doing it." She smiled expectantly. "May I bring it in? Just for you to see?"

"I'll do the bringing in," said her father angrily.

The box had no sooner been deposited on the floor of the porch than Mrs. Balcombe appeared from the hall of the house. She always dressed well when Napoleon was due to visit them and on this occasion, because there was a chill in the air, she was wearing a heavy skirt with a brown velvet waist. Her cheeks were pleasantly flushed.

"My dear," said William Balcombe, "our daughter has planned a surprise for our distinguished guest. It's in that box."

Mrs. Balcombe looked at the box and gave an exclamation of surprise. "It moved!" she cried. "Betsy, is there something alive in that box?"

"Yes, Mamma."

"A crocodile," said the head of the house.

"A young one, Mamma. A very young one. It's quite small."

"Do you want to see it, my dear?" asked William Balcombe.

"No, no! I don't want to see it." Then curiosity got the upper hand and Mrs. Balcombe took a cautious step toward the box. "I've seen pictures of crocodiles. Ugly creatures! Perhaps—if you just raised the lid a second—!"

Betsy obliged cautiously. Mrs. Balcombe emitted a loud cry of horror. Seizing her skirts with both hands, and thereby revealing a very neat pair of ankles, she ran into the house. "Ugh! that terrible thing! William Balcombe, get it away! Get it away at once!" By this time she was running for the stairs at the back of the hall. "I won't come down until I know this dreadful creature is miles away."

William Balcombe looked at his daughter with raised eyebrows. "Well, there you are. Do you realize now the—the enormity of what you intended to do? I'll take the box back and I'll talk to your sailor. I'll give him his half crown and I'll tell him to get a mile away from this house as fast as his legs will carry him. As for you, Betsy, you watch outside and let me know when he has turned onto the Jamestown road, so we can tell your mother it is safe for her to come down. You and I will have a serious talk about this later this evening."

It happened that Napoleon was strolling in the gardens which surrounded the pavilion and heard Mrs. Balcombe's horrified scream when she set eyes on the young crocodile. He came over at once.

"Betsee, what is wrong?" he asked. "I heard Madame your mother cry out. Has she been hurt?"

"No, sire. She was upset by something. I—I think I might as well tell you because you'll hear anyway. I was planning, sire, to—to play a joke on you this evening."

"Is it some new game?"

"No, sire. You told all those people a story which amused them very much. About our pets and especially our crocodile."

Napoleon smiled broadly. "Yes, Betsee, I acknowledge it. I did make up a story for them."

"I was upset when I heard about it because it seemed that you were making fun of us."

"No, no, *ma petite*. I would never do that. You have all been so kind to me that I would not repay you with ridicule. Come, come, Betsee, do not look at me with such an expression. I do not want you to be angry. But consider the position I was in. There I sat with those faces around me, no one saying much and just eating, never a smile, never a quip, never an amusing remark. I give you my opinion of them in confidence; they are a dull lot. So I had to do something to enliven things and I invented this story about a crocodile."

Betsy looked relieved. "I hoped, sire, it was something like that. And not—well, not an unfriendliness. We all like you so very much."

Napoleon also displayed some relief. "There, that is better. You have smiled, my little Betsee. We are still friends. And now let me, what was this joke you were going to play on me?"

Betsy proceeded to explain. She had made inquiries and had heard of a sailor, on a ship which had put into port, who had a small crocodile as a pet. His name—the sailor's, not the crocodile's—was Jeremy Tripper; and the crocodile's name was Sam Creepy. The sailor was very fond of Sam Creepy but had agreed to loan him to her for one evening for half a crown. He had arrived a short time before and her mother, after one look at it, had given the shriek which had brought him over to inquire.

The emperor's expression as he listened was rather set and stern. "I feel as Madame your mother did. I saw some crocodiles on my Egyptian campaign and they horrified me. Did you plan to have this"—with a shudder—"this terrible object come behind my chair and surprise me? Would you have laughed if it bit me on the feet?"

"No, no, sire! I intended to watch it carefully. I wasn't afraid of it and I would have stopped it from getting near you. It was—please, sire, it was just to be a joke."

Napoleon perhaps found it difficult to condone such an affront to his dignity. At any rate, there was silence for several moments. Then his expression changed as another train of thought took possession of his mind. He even began to smile. Finally, he slapped one knee and gave vent to a laugh.

"You are *une petite drôlesse!* But you and I, we understand one each other, do we not? I am glad you thought of this joke at my expense because it gives me an idea, an exquisite idea. I will invite all these same people for dinner, even Gourgaud, who has no sense of humor and will be outraged, *le gros baudet!* You will contrive to get your crocodile into the room without anyone seeing it." He paused and indulged in a still louder laugh. "What a delicious jest, *ma petite!* Perhaps this ugly creature will close its jaws at the point where the enormous ankles of that great scholar Las Cases settle into his shoes. Or perhaps it will be the little white ankles of Madame Montholon!"

Betsy was seeing this picture as clearly as he and her eyes were sparkling. But she was compelled to enter objections.

"I can't arrange to keep the crocodile that long, sire."

"Then we will buy it."

Betsy shook her head. "The owner is very fond of Sam Creepy. He said he wouldn't sell him for all the slats in a moneylender's till."

"Slats?"

"Money, sire. But even if he did sell, what could we do with Sam Creepy afterward?"

"Get rid of it. Throw it into the nearest creek."

"We wouldn't be able to do that, sire. It's against the law. Would you keep it? Or would you expect us to give it a home?"

"*Mon Dieu*, no! Is there a law against knocking it on the head?"

"Oh, sire, I would never forgive myself if the poor thing had to be killed!"

Napoleon was still unwilling to relinquish his plan. "Well, there seems to be just one way left. I will invite my guests for tomorrow night. We can return the miserable animal to its owner afterward."

"But the ship sails at dawn tomorrow."

Napoleon gave up. "This seems to be a lost battle," he said in a tone of deep disappointment.

Chapter Ten

1

Betsy never failed to pass the house of the Veiled Lady on her early morning rides. For some reason the spot where it stood was unusually cool. But the real reason, of course, was the mystery surrounding the occupant which drew the fourteen-year-old girl like a magnet.

On a number of occasions she took along her basket, filled with offerings for the solitary women in the silent house, generally of fruit but sometimes fresh eggs. She would attach it to the inside of the gate and the next morning would find it empty and hanging on the outside. On perhaps the sixth occasion, as she came riding down the road and whistling as usual, she saw no signs of the basket. Nevertheless she called out her cheerful "Good morning!" and was turning to ride away when the servant came into the courtyard through one of the interior doors. The girl cried hurriedly, "Wait! Pliss!" She was carrying the basket. For the first time it was not empty.

"Take home. Pliss," said the girl, smiling in the most friendly manner and handing the basket over the gate.

Betsy leaned down from her seat on the pony and took the handle. A quick glance told her that the container held a letter and a small box, neatly tied with ribbon.

"Thank you." She took the letter in one hand and saw that it was addressed to MY KIND FRIEND AND HER PARENTS. She studied it for a moment and then turned to smile at the serving girl.

"Do you mind telling me your name?"

The girl did not grasp the meaning at first. In fact, it took some pantomime on Betsy's part to make her understand the question. Then she nodded her head several times and said: "Me, Margette. Margette."

"Well, Margette, my mother and I will read the note when

110

I reach home. I expect to be along as usual tomorrow morning. Good-by." She tapped the flank of the pony with her heel and called out, as she rode away, "Good-by, lady."

For the first time she received an answer. A cultured voice spoke from behind one of the shuttered windows. "Good-by, my young friend." There was no trace of accent and Betsy felt sure that the owner of the voice was English. She was so excited that she cut her ride short and came up to the stables at a gallop. Springing from the saddle, she called out: "William Pitt! William Pitt!"

The old man's head appeared above the hatch. He had not been well for some time, and even in her haste Betsy noticed that his back was more stooped than usual and that his head showed a tendency to droop.

"Please look after Tom," she directed. "Give him a drink but not much of a rubdown. We didn't go far this morning. I'm in a *very* great hurry, William Pitt."

The old man bowed with his usual show of dignity. "Yes, Mees Bet'," he said. "Come, you Tom. You be good fella now."

Mr. and Mrs. Balcombe were already at the breakfast table when Betsy burst into the room in a state of the greatest excitement, holding the basket out in front of her.

"The mysterious lady has come to life!" she announced. "She spoke to me. Yes, actually. And the maid gave me back the basket with this note and a box in it. I'm sure it's a present."

Mrs. Balcombe took the note. "I was beginning to think it time for some acknowledgment. This is for us as well as Betsy. I'll open it."

William Balcombe cracked the head off a brown egg and dipped a strip of toast into it. This was a habit he had acquired as a boy and to which he was still addicted. "By all means, my dear."

Mrs. Balcombe began to read to herself. "A very nice note," she said, at the finish. "I'm sure she must be English. And she shows good breeding. I'll read it to you."

My kind friends:

Having no knowledge of my neighbors, and not even knowing your name, I am not able to address you in a more formal way. I assume that the pretty girl, who rides past my house each morning and calls a greeting to me (this has become the most pleasant moment of my day) has parents and lives in the house I can glimpse rather briefly through the trees. This is to thank her, and you, for your very great kindnesses.

I do not go out and so depend on my serving maid to do all the shopping. She goes into town at intervals but her knowledge of English is almost non-existent and she is not very successful in keeping the household well supplied. The little brown basket that Margette finds so often attached to my gate has been, I assure you, a great boon. The fruit is always delicious. But those fresh eggs! Ah, what a treat and a blessing I find them!

It is time I let you know how much I appreciate your kindnesses. The box contains a small gift for my daily visitor and I beg you will allow her to accept it.

I must not reveal my identity and, as it would be absurd to use a fictitious name, I am sending you this note unsigned. It goes to you with my warmest thanks.

"May I open the box now?" asked Betsy, fairly dancing with curiosity.

Mrs. Balcombe nodded and the girl eagerly stripped off the ribbon and paper. It contained an oblong piece of jewelry, consisting of a stone of the deepest red, about an inch and a half in length. It was set in a plain strip of gold, on the outside of which were minute garnets.

"Isn't it beautiful!" cried Betsy, holding it up for her parents to see. "Oh, what a rich color! I am going to love it."

Mrs. Balcombe took the stone and examined it carefully. "It could be used either as a brooch or a drop on a chain. I think it would be more effective as a drop. It's the color of a garnet but I've never seen one as large. It really is most unusual."

The firm of Balcombe, Fowler and Chase imported a little jewelry into the island and the head of the household recognized the stone without the need of a closer look. "Yes, it's a garnet. A rather rare variety and I agree that it's really handsome. This variety is sometimes called a Cape ruby. But that's an erroneous term. It doesn't belong in the ruby family. Perhaps I had better examine it."

After several moments he nodded his head. "Yes, that's what it is. It's most exceptional in size. A really fine stone."

"Is it valuable?"

"Well, my dear, I'm a bit at a loss about it. Garnets are not too expensive but this one is such a big specimen that I would hesitate to set a value on it. Oh, yes, it's a good piece. Perhaps much more valuable than any figure I would dare to name."

"May I keep it?" Betsy by this time was fairly bursting with excitement.

Mrs. Balcombe hesitated. "It's a gift rather out of proportion to what we've done for her. And yet I'm sure she would be much hurt if we sent it back. I think we should allow Betsy to keep it. Do you agree, William?"

"I think so. Yes, by all means. Let the child keep it."

Betsy, her eyes sparkling with delight, held up the stone at her throat. "This is really wonderful, Mamma. I will write her a note of thanks and leave it at the gate this afternoon."

"It's too large and striking for a girl of your age to wear," said Mrs. Balcombe. "I think, Betsy, we'll have to lay it away until you grow a little older. Then you can blossom out in it."

William rubbed the end of his nose with a forefinger, the usual sign that he was engaged in serious thought. "This adds to the mystery about our neighbor," he said, finally. "I've been wondering about her lately because I've been informed the money she receives each quarter is fairly considerable. Now we find she can afford to give away something as valuable as this stone. Who can she be? And why, in tarnation is she living in such complete isolation? Do 'ye know, my dear, I think this lady may even be of some rank and consequence."

A thought came into Betsy's head and, as was her habit, she put it into words. "Do you mean—she might even be a connection of the royal family?"

Her father gave her a quick and decidedly severe look. "Now what put that into your mind?"

Betsy wished she had kept this supposition to herself. "I don't know, Papa. It just popped into my head. I'm sorry I spoke." At the back of her mind she was thinking: "But why should it be this island? And why does she live like this?"

The matter was not discussed further. William Balcombe, having finished his breakfast, left the room, and they could hear him calling instructions to Mantee Timms to saddle his horse. Betsy and her mother bent their heads over the gift, and exchanged almost rapturous opinions, an occupation in which Jane, coming down a little late as usual for breakfast, joined them.

2

The midafternoon sun was beating down on the neighbor's house when Betsy rode over to deliver her note of thanks. Everything seemed unusually still. Not a sound came from any part, and if there were birds perching under the eaves or the cover of the inner gallery, they gave no sign. Nor was a leaf stirring on any of the trees.

Betsy pulled up at the gate and called, "Margette!" The maid appeared almost immediately at one of the doors. She was wearing a dress of many colors and of rather fantastic design, for both of which reasons it smacked of the southeastern part of Europe. "She's really quite pretty," was the thought which ran through the visitor's mind.

"Margette," said Betsy, leaning over the gate in order to hand her the note. "Will you give this to your mistress?"

Margette crossed the courtyard with a clumping sound which attested the solid quality of her flat shoes. She took the envelope and then proceeded to lower the bars of the gate. This done, she drew a piece of paper from a pocket in her voluminous apron and handed it to Betsy. It read:

Will you spare me a few minutes?
There is a question I would like to ask.

Betsy nodded to the maid and slipped down out of the saddle. When the gate swung open, she led her pony into the courtyard. At the far end there was a stone hitching post and here she tied him up. Then she produced a carrot from a pocket and held it on the palm of her hand under his muzzle.

"I tell," said Margette, and vanished into the house.

Betsy had enjoyed no more than passing glimpses of the courtyard and she proceeded to take quick note of everything. She knew that the house had been built by an Englishman who had thought the island would prove an ideal place in which to spend his declining years. He had been a man of considerable means, obviously, for the agent he employed to supervise the building did everything with a free and liberal hand. Fine wrought-iron grillwork was sent out for the projecting roof on the inside. A mantel had arrived which caused approving shakes of the head and much informed talk in which the word "Adam" was freely used. There had even been some articles of furniture, all with the patina of age and high excellence. But something had happened to change the owner's mind. The valuable extras ceased to come and the work of construction had ceased finally. For the first few years there had been a positive refusal to sell or rent. The Veiled Lady had become the first occupant.

Betsy studied the narrow inside roof with its delicate iron tracery and the iron posts which held it up with great interest. "Rather like a cloister," she thought.

Margette appeared again and called, "Pliss!" Betsy followed the maid inside. She found herself in a dark and pleasantly cool inner corridor with a tiled floor which impelled her to step cautiously and with little noise. This led into a large square room with shuttered windows on two sides. Margette lighted some candles on a corner table, dropped a curtsy, and left.

Betsy looked about her curiously. The light from the candles brought the furnishings of the room into shadowy relief. It must be said that the whole effect was haphazard. There was a secretary-desk of obvious age on one wall but all about it were rather shoddy pieces of no value or interest. The mantel filled a large part of one wall; and over it there was the portrait of a handsome man in a powdered wig and a high black stock.

"I am happy to see you, my dear."

The voice, a pleasantly modulated one, came from an open space in one wall, over which a curtain had been draped. Betsy looked quickly in that direction but could not see anything behind the curtain.

"Please sit down."

The young visitor seated herself on a divan which was so well upholstered that she sank deeply into the cushions.

"Your note was a sweet one," continued the voice. "I am glad you liked the gift. It was given to me by my father when I returned from school. As I liked it then, I thought you would like it now."

"But, ma'am," said Betsy, "you are being too kind. Should I have something you have liked so much?"

"My dear, when you grow older you will realize that a real

115

gift must be something you have valued and enjoyed yourself. To purchase one in a shop and send it to an address is lacking in the quality of true generosity."

It occurred to Betsy, as she listened, that she had felt a little guilty when she offered Emmanuel Las Cases the pup she valued least of all. She should have been prepared to part with her own particular pet. She thought, "This is something I must always remember."

"How old are you, my dear?"

"I've turned fourteen, ma'am."

"I always know when you are coming down the road. By your whistling. It is quite extraordinary—for a girl. It is so high and clear. I think it is like some new type of songbird. One with the strongest and most melodious of notes. Where did you learn?"

"I've always been able to whistle, and I suppose I keep on improving. I think it's to compensate me for being such a poor singer. Now my sister Jane—she's two years older—has a lovely singing voice. It's very clear and sweet."

"How strange this is! I seem to feel that I know you very well. But I don't know your name. The signature on your note was—well, a little hard to make out."

Betsy laughed at this. She was beginning to feel very much at home. "My writing is *terrible!* Oh, the wiggings I got at school about it! My name is Elizabeth Balcombe. But everyone calls me Betsy."

"And may I? Well, Betsy, I am sure, after seeing you this close, that you are going to grow up to be a tall young lady. And while you are at this growing a miracle may happen." The voice paused. "I am very glad to see that you are so tanned. It's clear you don't just sit around the house and primp as most pretty girls of your age do, and think of nothing but clothes and parties. Of course I could have expected you to be like this because you always seem to be so busy, riding and running about and so very much concerned with your pony and your dogs." There was a longer pause. "There is a question I would like to ask you."

"Yes, ma'am."

"A few years ago something happened which changed the whole course of my life. When I came to this island I had lost interest in everything. I have never ventured a step outside this gate. Sometimes in the dark of evening I take a walk but I never leave the courtyard. I have not heard a whisper from outside; and I have not cared. But suddenly I find my curiosity aroused."

"Before the—the incident occurred," the voice continued, "I was in Vienna once with my father who had gone on a mission for the British Government. There was a need to keep our presence a secret and so I saw little of that city. But one afternoon the place became alive with excitement. The French emperor was making an unexpected visit. I went out on the balcony of the house where we stayed. I saw him ride by. Yes, I saw Napoleon Bonaparte with my own eyes. He was the archenemy of England, the terrible ogre, the unbeatable general—but I was deeply impressed with his appearance as he passed below in an open carriage.

"Betsy, I have seen you riding twice with a man who resembles Napoleon Bonaparte very much, so much it is hard to believe it is not the emperor. Though, of course, I know that is utterly impossible. He even affects the same style in his clothes, particularly in his hats. I am curious enough to ask, Who is this man? And what is he doing on this island, so far removed from the rest of the world?"

"He *is* Napoleon Bonaparte," said Betsy.

She heard a gasp from behind the curtain. And then a silence settled over the house, a silence which had a note of finality; as though all life had stopped and would never start again. Betsy thought, "This is the strangest place I've ever been in." She was not frightened, because the voice had been friendly and reassuring, but she felt better when she heard the clash of a pan in what she supposed was the kitchen wing.

"My dear child," resumed the voice, "I know you are telling me the truth. But—but it is hard to believe. What has happened? Has the world been turned upside down?"

"We all wondered when the news reached us that he was being sent here."

"The last I heard of him, he had retreated from Russia. The great powers were planning a coalition against him. Did they succeed in driving him from his throne?"

"Yes, ma'am. He abdicated and was sent to the island of Elba."

"I've been there. Once. It was quite pleasant."

"He didn't think so. He escaped, got back to France and raised another army. He was finally defeated at a place in Belgium called Waterloo. By the Duke of Wellington."

117

"Wellington? That must have been our general, Sir Arthur Wellesley who was doing so well in the peninsula."

"Yes. He had been made a duke. Once he stayed for a few days in the same room where Napoleon is living now."

"What an extraordinary coincidence! But—but why is Napoleon here?"

"This island," explained Betsy, "was selected as the safest place to keep him in, being so far away from everywhere."

"The same reasons which occurred to—to some other people." There was a brief pause. "Then he's a prisoner?"

"Yes, in a way. He's staying in a summer pavilion we have until a permanent home can be made for him. They are enlarging a place called Longwood. It will be different then: I'm afraid he will be a real prisoner."

"You speak as though you like him."

"I do. Oh, I like him very much. You see, I speak French well enough to act as interpreter for him. We are together much of the time."

"When I heard you talking outside my window, I knew from the tone of his voice that he was fond of you. How long will he be kept here?"

Betsy found a lump in her throat and did not answer at once. "Ma'am," she said, "he will be a prisoner here as long as he lives!"

Now that she had broken her rule and established a contact with the outside world, the mysterious occupant of the square house found other questions to ask, having to do mostly with the conditions which had resulted in the exiling of Napoleon. "When I saw him in Vienna," she said finally, "he looked much younger. I think he has become heavier."

"Yes," said Betsy. "He kept thin by working so hard. Since coming here, he sits around most of his time and dictates his reminiscences. He rides a little and I can sometimes talk him into going for a walk. Everyone notices that he had been putting on weight."

"Hasn't he been told about it?"

"He brought quite a household with him but they're all afraid to say anything. All *they* do is sit around and drink bottles and bottles of wine every day. If he didn't have these selfish people to provide for, he might be allowed to remain with us instead of being sent up to that dreadful Longwood."

"And you would like that?"

"Oh, yes, ma'am. Very much."

As Betsy untethered the pony, she cast an eye around the line of darkened rooms opening on the courtyard. "Big," she said to Margette. The maid seemed to understand that word but she shook her head to express a negative opinion. "See," she said.

Betsy followed her to the arm of the house opposite the wing where the mistress had her quarters. Margette threw open a door and Betsy saw that the interior was in an unfinished state. Plasterers had been at work when the order to stop had come from England and the gantry they had been using was still there. The visitor looked through each of the four rooms which constituted this wing and found the same condition prevailing in all of them. The windows were covered by shutters but there was no trace of glass.

"Why don't they take this place for the emperor instead of Longwood?" was the thought in the girl's mind as she climbed into the saddle. On second thought, however, she realized the selfishness of this. In that event where would the Veiled Lady go?

3

Betsy did not cross into the pavilion gardens until late the next morning. Napoleon had finished his dictation and was sitting alone with a pot of chocolate on the table beside him and two cups. He was slumping in his chair. Although the weather was cool and pleasant, he seemed quite exhausted. The usual wisp of hair lay dank and lifeless on his forehead.

She called, "May I come in?"

The great man was surprised. "Of course you must come in. The gate's not locked. And I have a cup of chocolate here for you."

Betsy took her usual chair so meekly that he looked at her with surprise. "*Mon Dieu*, is there trouble?" he asked. "Have there been more punishments?"

She shook her head. "No, sire. No trouble. It's just that there's something I must say to you. And I know you are going to be very angry."

"*Ma foi*, what is it then you must tell me?"

Betsy swallowed hard. "I've noticed, sire, that when you sit in a chair it begins to creak."

"Must I accept the blame when chairs are in need of repair?"

He had been dictating notes about the Hundred Days, and his feelings about England and the English had become so aroused that he could not speak with any civility. He began on a tirade about furniture.

"Don't you realize that English furniture is abysmally inferior? It is cheap, uncomfortable, unattractive. Now in France—ah, there you find the best of everything. The French *fauteuil* is a thing of perfection! Everything we make is superior. Those marvelous provincial sideboards, the graceful consoles, the delightful divans. Do you realize, child, that you find better furniture everywhere than in England? I took home from Egypt an Arabian musnud that was worth all the Chippendale chairs in existence."

If Betsy had felt in her usual spirits, she probably would have retorted that Georgian furniture was dignified and strong and that all French pieces were overly decorated and trumpery. As it was, she simply shook her head. "It was not the chair that was at fault. Don't you realize, sire, that you are—*gaining in weight?*"

A flush spread across the Jovian brow. "Are you telling me that I am becomming *gros?*"

"No, no, sire! Not gross. It's simply that you—well, we have a word in English which expresses it. You are getting a little—er, portly."

Apparently the word was new to him. "Portly?" he said. "A typical English word. It expresses nothing. I deny that I am becoming *portly. Ma foi*, it is a wonder you did not use another English word which I *do* know. *Fat!* The most vulgar word, I believe, in a language universally known for its vulgarity."

Betsy had sunk back into her chair and was looking quite small and distressed. "Please, sire. It is a matter of your health."

"It is true," he conceded, "that I have been leading a sedentary life. For the first time. I was always active. I was out all night before a battle, looking over the ground for myself. I drove pell-mell all over Europe in planning the movements of my armies. Do you know about the special coach I had built for me? It had the strongest steel springs ever made and I could ride at top speed without any jolting or swaying. Well, with very little. The interior was fitted out with all manner of drawers and storage cases for maps. Berthier, my chief of staff, rode with me and I would dictate orders to him all night long. Then I would curl up for a short nap and, when I wakened, Berthier might still be busy, writing out the full details of roads and timetables. *Mon Dieu*, that fellow never made a mistake!"

"Aren't we getting away from the subject, sire?"

"What subject? Nothing, child, is as important as what I have been telling you. Do you know that I often went a whole day without food? That chefs had to keep half a dozen chickens on the spits, so there would always be one ready when I could find the time to eat?"

"Yes, sire, I know all that—"

"Even in times of peace I worked at least sixteen hours every day. I was always in my cabinet, laboring hard, with scores of inferior officers lolling about and doing nothing."

"Yes, sire. But we are now far away from the subject. The question of your weight."

Napoleon looked at her sternly. "Proceed, then!"

"Everyone is noticing it. They talk about it a great deal. They are worried."

"It is true," he conceded reluctantly, "that I notice a slight difference in the fit of my clothes. But it has never occurred to me that it was something people could observe! If it is true, why haven't they spoken of it?"

"Because, sire, they are afraid of you. When you frown, they are all ready to curl up in corners or run away and hide."

This, apparently, pleased him. He indulged in a smile. "But not *ma petite* Betsee! She's not afraid of me."

"Oh, yes I am, sire. I am trembling this very minute. But—but someone had to speak about it."

Napoleon took the matter under consideration and for several moments nothing more was said.

"Well," he said finally, "what do *you* think should be done in the face of this great crisis?"

"I think you should ride every morning early. Before you have breakfast. And at least once a day you should go for a long walk. Not the kind you take when you are thinking something out. Like this." His hat was lying on the table. She took it and placed it on her head and then started to pace about slowly, her arms behind her back, her feet splayed stiffly. Then she came back and resumed her chair, after replacing the hat. "Not that way, sire. That may be the way to work out knotty problems but it does nothing to lessen your waistline."

"It is clear, Betsee, that you are going to make a shrewish, nagging wife for some stupid Englishman with a long mustache and no chin. You are not being fair about this. Don't you know I waken up every morning at six o'clock?"

"How would I know? You never get up then."

"I hear you running about in—in *appalling* activity. And I hear you whistling. There is one tune you seem to like—"

"Is it this?" Betsy began to whistle a favorite air, which was catching and gay. Napoleon nodded his head. "That's 'Lillibulero,'" she said. "It's an air that helped to drive an English king off his throne."

"Betsee! You are underestimating me. I have been a close student of English history and I know all about this 'Lillibulero.' Your James the Second was one of the most stupid kings in England, where practically all kings have been stupid. I'm sure the music was imported from Europe."

"No! It was written by an English composer. A great composer. We have them, you know, even in poor benighted England."

Napoleon's mood changed suddenly. He sat up in his chair, which creaked most suspiciously, and began to laugh.

"You mean well," he said. "And, egad, you've had the courage to speak about it. Perhaps you are right. And so, *ma petite*, I will see what can be done about it. I will eat less. You did not mention food but I could see disapproval in your eye. I will go for brisk walks and I will take morning rides. We will ride together. If I am not up and about, come to the gate and whistle your 'Lillibulero'.* Then I'll come down and we'll ride off madly like a pair of young cavalry officers. Will that satisfy you?"

*This is the air of "Lillibulero," which Betsy whistled every morning at the garden gate.

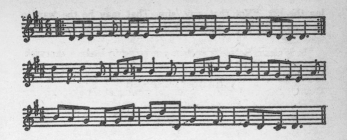

Chapter Eleven

1

Longwood is ready (said Admiral Cockburn), Longwood is in a state of complete unreadiness (said Napoleon), it will be a comfortable residence even for an ex-emperor, it is a converted cow stable and fit only for the rats which infest it, it has some of the charm of Malmaison, it is a cheap villa at which a bumbailiff would scoff, it stands on a high plateau and will be cool in summer and warm in winter, it is on a bleak and arid moor and will be stiflingly hot in summer and exposed to the raw trade winds in winter.

So the discussion went while unskilled workmen ran up wooden partitions and drove in crooked nails. Napoleon would have to go there finally, and he knew it. There was no other place on the island save the handsome manor where the governors dwelt; and when had a governor, with royal papers in pocket and ermine on his cloak, allowed his comfort to be infringed by the merest jot? There was the Briars, of course, and Napoleon would have been ready to stay there indefinitely, for he had found much content in the easy atmosphere of the Balcombe ménage. But that could not be a permanent solution. Longwood had been renovated for him and to Longwood he must go.

The admiral came to the Briars one morning and said to the man who had lost an empire in one day of bloody struggle at Waterloo: "In my judgment, General Bonaparte, the place is now complete. There can be no further delay."

The face of Napoleon darkened with furious dissent. "I am to be treated as a criminal, then? I am a prisoner and must go to my jail!"

"This is the best arrangement we can make. We think you will live there in comfort and dignity."

"I alone am the judge of that."

"Then," declared the admiral, who was an amiable man

and found it hard to be firm, "you must visit Longwood and see for yourself how we have improved it."

To that Napoleon had been compelled to agree.

Half an hour later his carriage drew up on the rutted road between the two houses. Archambault was driving, and Admiral Cockburn, ready to efface himself, was seated beside the coachman, leaving the back seat for Napoleon. The latter looked about him and asked a familiar question, "Where is Betsee?"

Betsy was never far away on such occasions. She came around almost immediately to the front porch and said, "Here I am."

Napoleon began to talk to her in hurried whispers. "Betsee, this is going to be unpleasant. I know I am going to be very unhappy. Come with me and divert my mind from this official indignity that I must suffer, this"—he stammered in his white-faced rage—"this brazen disregard of honesty and ethics! We will talk and, as usual, we will find something to quarrel about. That will occupy my mind and, perhaps, amuse me."

"Yes, sire," said Betsy. "But I must get Mamma's consent."

The consent was given and the girl was installed on the back seat, wearing a pink dress and a broad-brimmed hat with a pink silk band encircling the crown and falling at the back to her shoulders. With one foot on the step, the ex-emperor sternly admonished his coachman. "Now, Archambault, there must be none of your rashness today. Remember, you must go slowly on the narrow roads and take the curves gently. It makes Mam'selle Betsee ill when you indulge in your mad impulses. So, no more nonsense."

The coachman goggled at his master with obvious surprise. Then he nodded his head. "Yes, Your Imperial Highness, I will drive slowly."

2

The afternoon was drawing to a close when the carriage returned. Napoleon stepped down to the ground and stalked with grim face up the path to the pavilion. Betsy joined her parents who were drinking sherry under the trees.

"Child, what is wrong?" asked Mrs. Balcombe, when she saw that her daughter's eyes were filled with tears.

"Oh, Papa and Mamma, it is going to be dreadful! It is so ugly and uncomfortable. And it reeks of paint."

William Balcombe nodded his head. "We have so few good artisans on the island. I have been hearing about the slapdash way they are going at it up there."

"The rooms are so small! The floors creak. The fireplaces will smoke, I'm sure. And the rats! I counted a dozen of them!"

"It will look better when the furniture is moved in," opined her father, who was of an optimistic turn of mind. "After all, those palaces in France are drafty old barns."

"We've become so accustomed to having him here." Besty was now unable to restrain her tears. "It will be very dull without him."

"We'll get accustomed to it, child," asserted her mother. "We were getting along very nicely before he came."

"I'm not really thinking of *us*. I'm thinking of *him*." Betsy was trying to locate her handkerchief. "He's going to be treated like a thief or a murderer. There will be sentries around the grounds day and night and he won't be permitted to cross the line without a consent of the governor. He won't be allowed any visitors unless they have permits too. They're actually building some kind of a signal machine—"

"A semaphore."

"Yes, Papa, that's what it's called. It will be used to let the governor know what's happening at Longwood. Fancy! One arm will mean he's riding or walking in the grounds. Another will tell them he's in the house. A third will mean he's sleeping. There is even one to give the alarm—*if Napoleon escapes!*"

"We'll never see that one go up," said her father, refilling his glass. "And I am reminded to tell you that word reached port today of the appointment. Sir Hudson Lowe has been chosen to succeed old Wilks. He'll arrive in the spring."

"And who," asked his wife, "is Sir Hudson Lowe?"

William Balcombe frowned as he considered his answer. "Sir Hudson Lowe," he said, finally, "is perhaps the worst possible choice they could have made for governor of St. Helena."

"Is he from the Foreign Office?"

"No, my dear. He's a soldier. He's been rather more on the

administrative side than the fighting side. Oh, he's figured in a brush or two. But what he likes is to handle detail. Sit him down at a desk, pile it up with papers and reports, and he's happy. When the horse guards tried to stir up a rising against Napoleon on Corsica, they put Sir Hudson Lowe in charge of the Corsicans who enlisted. Think how that will endear him to Napoleon!"

He was clearly very much disturbed. "He was married recently to a widow with grown-up children and a pot of money. She will come out with him. They say he has no sense of humor. None at all. There *are* people who claim they've seen him smile but no one really believes it. The Duke of Wellington called him an ass in a London club." The head of the family gestured hopelessly. "How could a Cabinet, made up of the soundest men in the kingdom, presumably, have agreed on such a man? Well, it's official. He's coming." He concluded with a solemn shake of his head. "I'm afraid we're going to see a lot of trouble."

Betsy, looking very woebegone, left them and went inside. They then began to discuss the arrangements which were being made for the members of Napoleon's train. The Bertrands were to have a small house called Hutt's Gate which stood at the point where the main road turned in to Longwood. There were several small structures back of the main building and here the Montholons, Gourgaud, and Las Cases and son would be lodged.

Mrs. Balcombe who had been visiting back and forth with the families in Jamestown had become quite attached to Madame Bertrand. "I feel so sorry for her," she said. "She's a lady and she doesn't keep nagging about things as the rest do. The other day she said, 'The only thing that has kept me alive is the fear that I would be buried here and that everyone would finally return home and leave me here alone.' "

"You like her better than the fair Albiné then?"

"Madame Montholon? I dislike the creature. She's common and immoral. The color of her hair seems to me quite vulgar. It is dyed, of course."

"No doubt, my dear."

"William," asked Mrs. Balcombe, in an abrupt tone, "do you think she has been Napoleon's—?"

"I am firmly convinced she has not been Napoleon's—"

"You may be right but—well, it's becoming clear that she's

127

going to do her small share in adding to the population of the island."

The man of the house was still thinking of the situation which would face them later. "I know what will happen when Lowe arrives. He'll send a note to Napoleon, addressing it to General Bonaparte. It will not be opened. He will keep on sending them and they will all be burned or returned. Finally there will be a great uproar, an earthquake, an avalanche. From what I hear, Lowe will not hesitate to put him in a prison cell. And won't that be a pretty kettle of fish? The whole world will be upset about it, one way or another. As I must supply the household with everything, I shall be right in the midst of it. My dear," he went on, "can you spare a dozen eggs?"

His wife stared at him as though she feared the prospect of so much trouble had unhinged him. "Eggs? Of course. The hens are laying quite well. But, really, why do you want a dozen eggs?"

The head of the house indulged in a rueful smile, "I must practice treading on them."

3

On the thirteenth of December which, quite fittingly, was cloudy, raw, and threatening, the rumble of oxcarts reached the ears of the occupants of the Briars. William Balcombe had already left for his office, so his wife went out to see what was afoot, accompanied by her daughters. They saw a string of crude vehicles, drawn by wide-horned oxen, moving slowly up the Longwood Road. They were loaded high with furniture, clothing, and household supplies of all kinds.

At the same time there were sounds of activity about the pavilion. Voices were raised in admonishment and restraint. Furniture was being moved, hammers were hammering, saws were sawing.

"I am afraid," said Mrs. Balcombe, with a sigh, "that our guests are leaving us."

"He's being taken to prison," said Betsy, with a catch in her voice.

Napoleon came out and stood for a few moments on the porch. In his attitude there was nothing of the conqueror, no hint of the commander of troops surveying a battlefield. He was looking tired and, apparently, had not slept well. Finally he raised his arms in a gesture of recognition, placed his tricorne hat on his head and came slowly down the path.

"My dear benefactress," he said to Mrs. Balcombe, "I am leaving you today. Under the strictest of orders. It has been reported to me that the odor of paint has gone. *Mon Dieu!* They do not realize it was not the smell of paint we detected about the place. It was the smell of infamy!" He drew closer and took both of Mrs. Balcombes' hands in his. "Ah, madame, how much you look like my beloved Josephine! I cannot pay you a higher compliment, for Josephine had a charm which set her apart. I shall never forget you, dear Madame Balcombe."

The chateleine of the Briars was afraid she would break into tears and hastily applied a frilly handkerchief to her eyes. "It has been such an honor and a pleasure to have you here. We are going to miss you very much."

"I have a premonition, madame. I shall never come back." Betsy, who was standing by to translate, seemed ready at this point to break into tears also. He paused and looked about him. "Misfortune is making a sentimentalist of me. I want to walk about the grounds for the last time so that I'll forget nothing." He nodded to Betsy. "Come, *ma petite*, come with me. We will make this tour together."

They started off in silence.

Several more oxcarts drew up close to the pavilion and were soon piled high with the emperor's effects. The Marquis de Las Cases came out and took a quick glance over the gardens, studiously avoiding any notice of Mrs. Balcombe. He took a pinch of snuff and then flapped a handkerchief carelessly over his cravat.

"Emmanuel!" he called.

The attic window opened. "Yes, my father."

"Are you not finished with the packing? You have been an interminable time at it."

"It is finished, my father. All I have to do now is change my clothes."

"What absurdity is this?" demanded Las Cases. "You will accompany me in the clothes you have been wearing."

"But—my father!" protested the boy. "These clothes are—very much the worse for wear."

"You have only one other coat and I will not permit you to take this dusty ride in it. Come as you are!"

When Emmanuel reached the front door he glanced out cautiously, and it was not until he had seen the figures of Napoleon and Betsy at a distance that he allowed himself to come any further. Well aware of the poor figure he was cutting, he seated himself behind a tall piece of furniture and all that anyone saw of him was a long pair of very thin legs dangling over the back of the vehicle as it began its creaking progress.

While the packing had been underway, Mrs. Balcombe had been aware of unusual activities in her kitchen. There was a continual din of voices, most of which she recognized but some of which, clearly, were French. The talk was punctuated by much loud laughter. She was on the point of going back to investigate when the very dignified figure of Cipriani, the emperor's maître d'hôtel, came strutting pompously down the kitchen path. He had a rubicund tint of nose and a Santa Claus smile, and in build he resembled a tun of his native wine.

"Madame!" he intoned. "It is our—our desire to—" His supply of English deserted him at this point and he began to indulge in a long and excited barrage of which not one word could be identified by his listeners.

Then he turned and waved an arm. A procession came forward to the accompaniment of loud cheers. Lepage, the chief imperial cook, held one end of a large platter and Perron, the butler, had a firm grip on the other. They were a morose-looking pair. For thirteen years Lepage had watched the long spit on which the daily relay of Napoleonic dinners had turned; and this was enough to poison the disposition of any conscientious chef. The duties of Perron had included the weeding out of callers who had come in droves to see the emperor on every conceivable pretext, and, naturally enough, a deep suspicion of the human race had taken possession of his mind. On this occasion, however, each was striving to smile.

On the platter between them reposed the most remarkable specimen of the cake-making art which perhaps had ever greeted human eyes. It was considerably more than three feet high and its circumference could not have been determined by any ordinary tape measure. It was iced in enticing pink and bespangled with bonbons, lozenges, candy figures, and
130

cinnamon strips; and on top it boasted a glittering crown made of spun sugar.

The two bearers of this gustatory masterpiece carried it to the table under the trees and deposited it there.

"Kind madame," said Cipriani, "a small token, this. Of—of our—er—ah, *oui—esteem.*"

The three officials bowed in concert at this. The Balcombe household staff, which had followed somewhat cautiously in the rear, burst into excited cheers. Mantee Timms, in fact, indulged in a quick caper like the first steps of a dance. The two sons of the family, escaping from their studies, came bounding out. They began to circle the table and to eye the cake with the keenest anticipation.

Mrs. Balcombe, with a trace of moisture in her eyes, assured the donors of the gift they had made her very happy. She had never seen the equal of the cake and was certain that nothing like it would ever be produced again. Then she added, "We are sorry indeed, messieurs, that you are leaving us."

After another deep bow, the three Frenchmen retired. The household staff melted back in the direction of the kitchen. The sons of the family reluctantly obeyed a peremptory demand from their tutor to resume their studies.

Jane, staring with open-eyed wonder at the confection, asked, "Is it to be eaten?"

"Every crumb will disappear. It won't last long."

At this point the gallant Gourgaud emerged from the marquee, trussed up almost to the bursting point in a dark blue uniform. He paused and raised one arm in the air. His equerry, who had been standing about, did not require any further instruction. A horse was led forward and the baron sprang as nimbly into the saddle as the tight fit of his uniform permitted.

Although his eyes opened a trifle when they rested on the monumental pink cake, he rode by Mrs. Balcombe and her daughter without any sign of recognition. Reaching the main road, he started his charger at a gallop and disappeared in a cloud of dust.

"Well!" said Mrs. Balcombe. "What very bad manners! He didn't even look at you, Jane, and I thought he—well, he seemed to be very much interested in you."

"He was," said Jane. "But I wasn't interested in him at all and I let him see it. I expect his pride was hurt. These officers think they are quite irresistible. I hear he's been looking else-where since."

All the carts had departed and the squeak of wheels was no longer heard when Napoleon and Betsy returned from their tour of the gardens. The emperor walked up the path to the pavilion with a sombre air. Besty, without giving a glance at the cake, vanished into the house. Jane looked questioningly at her mother and then followed her. She came back in a few minutes, looking somewhat disturbed.

Archambault drove up with the imperial carriage and took his stand at the step. There was some delay and then Napoleon appeared. He was in full uniform and his breast blazed with orders.

"These, dear madame," he said, indicating the various ribbons which sparkled with gems, "are worn in your honor." He kissed her hand before going on in his halting English. "How can I thank you for all you have done? I have had more of happiness here than I ever thought to enjoy again."

"But surely we are to see you often?"

"That will not depend on me. My movements will be restricted. There will be a jailyard about this place to which I go." He turned to Jane who was standing beside her mother. "And you, Mam'selle Jane. You have been so kind also. I shall miss seeing you very much." He looked about him. "Where has Betsee gone? Is she not going to say farewell to me?"

"No, General Bonaparte," said Jane. "She can't come down. She's lying on her bed—and crying her eyes out."

BOOK TWO
Betsy Grows Up

Chapter One

1

Admiral Cockburn took a copy of an English newspaper with him on a visit he paid the Bertrand family in their tawdry little house called Hutt's Gate. He laid it on a table, folded back to a long story on an inside page.

When he left, Bertrand pounced on the newspaper. He could read just enough English to absorb the substance of the story. For a full hour he sat in a deep silence, the print lying on his knee.

Later the grand marshal summoned up courage to carry the information to Napoleon. The latter was in the hands of his barber (having loafed about all day in a dressing gown) but he gave permission with a wave of his hand for Bertrand to enter.

"News?" he asked, shifting his body in the chair. "Good news? *Ma foi*, no! How could it be good? I do not expect to live long enough to receive any word which can be considered good. It's bad, then?"

"Bad, Your Imperial Highness."

"Someone has died?"

"Yes, sire. A brave man. I have heard you call him the bravest of the brave."

"Ney?"

"Yes, sire. Two months ago."

"In his bed? No, no, surely not. I can't conceive of the gallant Ney dying in his bed."

"Not in his bed, sire. He died before a firing squad."

There was a long silence in the room, broken only by the scraping of the razor and the shuffling steps of the valet. Suddenly Napoleon said, gruffly: "Enough. Wipe off the lather, Marchand. Let me get up." In a sitting position, he stared with solemn eyes at Bertrand.

"This is the very worst of news. Not only because a brave

man has been killed. Thousands of brave men died in all our campaigns. But because it is proof of the state of mind in France. Marshal, have you read the whole article?"

"No, sire. My understanding of English is still meager, I fear."

"We must send for Betsee. She will read it all to me. Get her at once, Bertrand. I must know everything.".

"M'sieur and Madame Balcombe are coming for dinner tonight. I can send a messenger, asking that their two daughters accompany them."

"Yes, yes," said Napoleon eagerly. He had been missing his daily rides and walks with the young English girl since the removal to Longwood. The long miles of rough road between the two houses was an obstacle which made visits infrequent. "I must hear every word. Is it a long report?"

"Quite long, sire. I gathered that the execution was demanded by the people about the king. The members of the royal family."

"Sycophants! Cowards! They lived abroad in peace and comfort and did nothing to bring about the restoration of their effete line. Bertrand, Bertrand, this is evil news. There was no demonstration in favor of Ney? No mass efforts to save a national hero?"

"I detected nothing of the kind, sire."

The Balcombe family dined at Hutt's Gate and were then escorted to Longwood by two soldiers of the regiment. Napoleon greeted them at the portico, with smiling warmth. He bowed to Jane and tweaked Betsy's ear.

"I have missed my young friends," he said. "Is it to be a game of whist this evening? But first there is a report in an English newspaper which I desire Betsee to translate for me." He glanced at Mrs. Balcombe. "May this be the first order of the evening?"

Mrs. Balcombe did not grasp the meaning of this, so Betsy replied for her. "Yes, sire. It is understood. We discussed it at dinner."

Napoleon led the way into one of the suite of small rooms where a billiard table had been installed. It was not quite large enough for the purpose and the hideous yellow wallpaper which had been pasted on the rough plank walls made it seem even smaller. This had ceased to give cause for complaint. The Captive was an indifferent player but had the same savage determination to win which entered into everything he did, and it had become hard for his more skilled assistants to make enough mistakes to allow this to happen. On that account, the games had become increasingly listless. The table was now piled high with books and sheafs of reports and notes.

As he led the way in, he pointed to the volumes and said with a rather grim smile: "I get more pleasure out of them than by knocking little ivory balls about. Still, I shall teach you to play, Betsee. I think you'll make a better player than these stupid people who really think they can beat me at it. Such impudence!"

He gestured to Betsy to seat herself in one of the two chairs in the room, an ugly, overpadded affair in which she almost disappeared. "Don't blame me, Betsee, if you find it uncomfortable," he said. "It is an English chair. Here, child, translate this for me. I tried to get some sense out of it but my command of the vile language does not seem to improve."

He seated himself on a corner of the billiard table and listened with complete absorption, asking few questions. At the finish he shook his head and sighed deeply.

"Poor Ney, poor Ney!" he said. "I hoped for a better ending for him. Of course, it was his own fault. Why did he not get out of the country in time? He might have known those raddled spinsters of the royal family would demand his head." There was a long pause. "I made the same mistake, Betsee. I should have slipped away like Joseph and made my escape to America. But I stayed on until it was too late. I could not bring myself to believe my sun could sink. I was sure it would remain forever in the sky." He shook his head despondently. "It would be a kindness if the English would treat me as the French have treated Ney. A word of command, a flash, and all would be over. How much better that way!"

He slipped down to the floor and began to pace about the room. "This is the most dismal of news. If the people of Paris made no effort to support Ney, or to demand clemency for me? Certainly nothing can be hoped for until they grow tired of this monstrous Bourbon king. How long will that take? Too long, *ma petite*. This dreadful climate will be the death of me before honor raises its bludgeoned head in France."

His strides became more vigorous. The books were piled so high on the table that he had only occasional glimpses of the girl's face. Betsy knew that a new mood had taken possession of him because his forehead was flushed, a sign of anger.

"You can have no conception how dismal the life here has become. This is a prison, a run-down country jail which I share with rats. That horrible odor of paint still hangs over the dark hole they call a dining room. I have nothing to do and so time hangs heavily on my shoulders. And"—pausing to stare across the barrier of books with a frown for her benefit—"you are to blame. I don't hear you whistling in the mornings and so I stay in bed. I am gaining in weight again. I don't go for walks. I seldom ride, and when I do it is like going around and around and around in a sawdust ring. Yes, it is all your fault."

"But, sire!" cried Betsy, very much disturbed, "it isn't my fault. I can't come here without a permit and they refuse to give me one. Oh, I've asked. It's only when we're invited to the Bertrands' that I can cross the line. You know that."

"Yes, *ma petite*. I know. Pay no attention to what I say, for I am in a bitter mood. I know this can all be blamed on that one conceited fool. He was so sure of himself, so certain he was right. *He* advised me to stay."

"Who, sire?" asked Betsy, on the point of tears.

"My brother Lucien. He was so convinced he could persuade the deputies that I should retain the throne. And I—I listened to him!" He raised a hand in a gesture of resignation. "But why should I disturb you with my sorrows? It is pleasant to have you here, Betsee, and I must make the most of it. I think you have grown some."

"Yes, sire. Nearly half an inch. I know, because I measure myself. It's a great relief. I don't want to be a small woman."

"And why not? I prefer them to the long, loping, gawky kind you see so often in England."

"Never having been in England you are in such a good position to judge. No, I shouldn't speak that way to you, sire. Please forgive me. And I know that most men prefer little women. They certainly marry them."

Napoleon was smiling. "*Ma foi*, how you rush in to defend that miserable little island. And what do you do now that I'm not with you but with my train of sad refugees?"

"I read much of the time."

"What about?"

"Often about you, sire. But I also read novels and histories and books about horses and dogs. I'm going to become really educated. But it gets very dull. We all miss you so much."

"Do you miss me more than the others?"

Betsy looked up at him and smiled. "Yes, sire, I think I miss you more than the others do. Sometimes I go over to see the Veiled Lady and I tell her about you."

Napoleon indulged in a frown. "I am not sure, Betsee, it is wise for you to go there."

"But why not? She's a great comfort to me. It's like talking to an older sister. But she's much younger than I expected. I don't believe she's thirty yet."

"Do Papa and Mamma Balcombe know you go to see her?"

Betsy nodded. "I don't always tell them when I go. But generally I do. They are sure now there's nothing wrong in visiting her." She had been glancing about the room as they talked. "This place still looks so shabby and down-at-heels. If we could only lay a picture of it before those fine gentlemen of the government! It might open their eyes."

"No good can come of appeals to them. They have put me in the power of the most unrelenting of jailers."

"Do you mean this man on his way out?"

The Captive shook his head and pointed through a window in the direction of the sea. "No, no. The British Navy. Even on the dullest of days I can see their sails out there. How can I expect to escape from them?"

2

It was several weeks after the visit of the Balcombe family. It had been decided that the evening would be spent at the whist table and all members of the once imperial train had gathered in the small drawing room, waiting for Napoleon to appear. It would be a distasteful evening for all of them. Although, oddly enough, he had no card sense, Napoleon insisted on winning. He would bluster, argue, and cheat openly; anything, in fact, to win, although at the finish he would refuse to accept the winnings. Yes, it would be two long hours of unpleasantness.

Bertrand and Las Cases settled down to a game of chess in

one corner and the rest sat around and waited listlessly for the Great Man to put in an appearance. But the door of the imperial bedroom did not open. Napoleon's bedroom was a dowdy chamber, fifteen feet by twelve, the windows covered by muslin curtains and the walls colored by nankeen which had once been brown but now presented a scrofulous effect. The carpet was so faded that the original color was lost and gone forever. The furniture was secondhand and shabby, the discards of others houses on the island. The bed was a small iron field cot which he had used on many of his campaigns and which he had preferred to any more luxurious couch. There was a sofa which established a record for disreputability, being so very rickety that it creaked and expostulated when subjected to any weight. A small round table was his pet aversion because it was of the drum variety and had come originally from England. He seemed to take a pleasure in spilling ink on its once glossy surface and in scratching the sides. The room, in fact, had all the lack of comfort and decency which might be expected in the third floor back of a London rooming house.

While his court waited for him, the emperor was seated on the sofa which meant that he faced the windows opening on the gardens. He was looking in a different direction, however, toward his left hand where a small fireplace had been installed. On the wall above it he had hung the best of the portraits of his young son, who was still called the King of Rome. How alert and intelligent the boy seemed, and how handsome! The mind of the Captive was filled with speculations as to what would have happened if he had not destroyed his son's chance of succeeding to the French throne.

"He would not have been a soldier," was one thought which predominated over all others. "There is too much of the artist in his eyes. He may lack the drive, the will, the willingness to gamble so many lives. But what of that? There has been enough of soldiering in the family. Perhaps my handsome little son would succeed in consolidating our hold on the throne. What more could I ask of him?"

He heard a sharp sound like something striking the glass of the window directly facing him. The trade winds swept so continuously over the high broad lands on which Longwood stood that this was nothing new. He paid no attention to it. But the sound was repeated, a sharp and unmistakable *ping*, and he turned his eyes in that direction. It was dark outside but he saw faintly a human face.

Napoleon had been sitting in partial gloom with only one candle on the small drum table. Rising cautiously, he blew out the candle and then walked to the window. He drew up the sash with difficulty because nothing fitted at Longwood. Then he had to prop it with a long volume of maps. A small dark figure was standing on the edge of the terrace where a gum tree provided some concealment.

"Sire!"

"Betsee! Is it you?"

"Yes, sire. I came to tell you something."

"Yes? What is it? More bad news?"

"No, I don't think so. It's because I thought you would be pleased that I came tonight. I couldn't be sure when I would see you again."

"Is it concerned in any way with politics? If so, *ma petite*, you should not tell me. It might get you into serious trouble. And that must not be allowed to happen."

Besty answered in such careful whispers that he found it hard to follow what she was saying. "It is a personal matter. About one of the Others. I thought you would like to hear."

"Ah, the ladies in my life. You seem to take a great interest in them, Betsee. More than you should. Which one is it?"

"I've forgotten her name. Except that she was generally called La Bellilote."

"That one. Pauline Fourès. What has happened to her?"

"You heard the gun two days ago? It meant the arrival of a ship in the Roadstead. There was a Frenchman aboard who had gone ashore at Rio de Janeiro. I heard my parents talking at dinner tonight about what he saw. Sire, he saw La Bellilote at Rio."

"Nonsense, Betsee. She is in Paris and living well, I am certain, on the settlements I made on her. She is married again."

"But it's true, sire. This Frenchman was certain he saw her. He went to a theater one evening. All the people in the house were staring up at one of the boxes. There was a woman sitting there all alone. They were looking at her because she was so beautiful. He recognized her at once. It was La Bellilote."

Napoleon fell into deep thought at this point. Could it be true? Was La Bellilote really in Rio? Why was she there? She had always been adverse to travel, having no stomach for the sea. Only on an errand of the greatest importance would she have left the beloved Paris. Then a possible reason occurred to him.

"Betsee, how far away is Rio?"

"It's the closest port to St. Helena, sire. All American ships for the east stop there first."

"In what direction does it lie?"

"Almost due west. This island is on the Tropic of Capricorn, and Rio is just south of it."

"Ah!" Napoleon indulged in a new train of speculation as a result of this information. If a conspiracy were afoot to rescue him from the island, the port of Rio would play an important part in it. Had La Bellilote been sent there to find a temporary hiding place for him? It seemed unlikely—and yet he remembered that the Abbé Force had spoken of her on several occasions and had seemed to think well of her. He had been convinced she still felt a deep attachment and loyalty for him, Napoleon. The abbé was never wrong about people.

"Betsee! Listen to me, child. I am not going to ask you any more questions about this. If she's really in Rio it is a coincidence. But promise me you will not tell anyone you came here tonight, not even your parents. It could be misunderstood so easily and you would find yourself in trouble. How did you manage to get here?"

There was a hint of amusement in the girl's low-pitched voice when she answered. "I had a *time* of it. I rode over and tethered my pony off the road some distance from the sentry lines. I hope the little beggar doesn't start neighing for me to come back or I will be in trouble! It was hard getting over the wall because two sentries were marching up and down and they never seemed to pause. Finally they turned in opposite directions and I took a chance at getting over. I fell into some underbrush but the ground was so soft with the rains that I made no sound. I had to crawl after that on my hands and knees." She laughed lightly. "I am a sight! I'm soaked from my head to foot because the ground is so damp, and my hands are covered with mud. I must get back before Papa and Mamma return from church. *They* mustn't see me. I know I'll get a dressing down from Sarah Timms."

"There is one question I must ask after all. By what name is she called in Rio?"

"I think this man said she had been married again and that she was using her second husband's name. Ran—something or other."

Napoleon's manner took on a sharp note. "Betsee, you must return quickly. Be most careful, child. Don't let the sentries hear you. And make sure Sarah doesn't tell M'sieur and Madame, your parents. This adventure of yours must be kept a strict secret. And will you also promise never to do anything so foolish again?"

"Yes, sire. I promise."

There was a pause and then the Captive said in a low and gentle voice, "Betsee?"

"Yes, sire."

"Good night. And thank you, *ma petite.*"

3

Napoleon stood at the window, listening intently, for a long time after she had disappeared in the thickening darkness. At first no sounds reached his ears other than the gruff exchanges of the sentries. Then, from some distance, he detected the beat of hoofs. A smile of relief flitted across his face.

"She is safely away," he said to himself.

It was time to join the company in the drawing room but he found himself in no mood for either conversation or whist. He returned to the sofa after relighting the candle, and stretched himself out at full length.

He realized now that he had been roused and even excited by the news Betsy had brought him. It might all be a mistake, of course. La Bellilote almost certainly would have been adverse to stirring her tiny feet to such an unpleasant necessity as leaving her beloved Paris. But on the other hand, if she were in Rio, it meant that something of the greatest importance was afoot.

The Abbé Force would be behind any plan to effect his escape from St. Helena and that astute churchman had always held a favorable opinion of Madame Fourès, although he himself had considered her something of a flutter-brain. Certainly, also, any escape scheme would be predicated on the possibility of reaching Rio before the British ships could throw a net about them. The picture began to come into focus in his mind.

Pauline Fourès! She had been one of the most beautiful of the ladies who were now designated by Betsy as the Others. She had come into his life at a time when he had finally become convinced of Josephine's lack of fidelity. Perhaps he would have been infatuated with her even if Josephine had not provided such provocation. She, that pretty Pauline, had a most unusual combination of charms: her ash-blond hair, her soft slate-blue eyes under the longest and darkest of lashes, her daintiness of figure. How could anyone resist her?

He reached for a bellpull close at hand on the wall. A footman materialized as promptly as might have been expected at the Luxembourg or the Tuileries.

"Inform the grand marshal I desire his presence."

Bertrand, who always wore a court uniform in the evenings, responded with equal promptitude. He remained in the doorway, however, waiting for a gesture from Napoleon to enter. He then advanced a few additional feet and took his stand near the foot of the sofa.

"Were you acquainted with the Countess de Ranchoup?" asked Napoleon.

"Slightly, sire."

"What did you think of her?"

"She was most attractive, sire."

"What did you think of her, apart from the question of her beauty?"

"I had small respect for her."

"Does she still use the name of her second husband, that dotard of a Ranchoup?"

Bertrand thought for a moment and then nodded his head. "There was another husband after him but I can't recall his name. The third marriage did not last much longer than the first two. I am quite certain she had been living in Paris under the name of Ranchoup."

"M'sieur the grand marshal," said Napoleon, with a trace of a smile, "you are a man of few likes and many dislikes. I seem to recall that you have little regard for the Abbé Force."

"That is true, sire. I could never understand why you made so much use of him. I think he might well be called the greatest glutton in France. His habits unfortunately do not include a regular use of the bathtub."

"But his mind, Bertrand, his shrewd mind! He is as wise as a fox. Because of the shortcomings you point out, I was un-

144

able to use him in the upper branches of diplomacy but I depended on his advice to a greater degree than you know. He warned me that Tallyrand was false to me, and I would have been wise had I accepted his view. I should have hanged Fouché and put the abbé in his place. Bertrand, I am not in a frame of mind to play whist tonight. Will you inform them and convey my regrets."

"Yes, sire." It was clear that Bertrand was pleased. He bowed and retreated backward to the door. "I trust you will sleep well, Your Imperial Highness."

"I will not need Marchand for another half hour."

Ranchoup! That was the name Betsy had failed to remember. He had been somewhat unsure of it himself, for his memory was no longer to be depended upon when it came to names. Well, the story was beginning to take on definite form. It seemed certain that La Bellilote really was in Rio, although he must not begin to read too much significance into that. He must wait for some word from the Abbé Force.

His mind began to go back over the past, to the time when he first saw Pauline Fourès. How beautiful she had been, how gay and enchanting!

Yes, she had been one of the Others. In fact, the first.

Chapter Two

1

History does not give any completely acceptable explanation for the sending of an army of forty thousand Frenchmen to conquer Egypt. Napoleon was undoubtedly the chief sponsor of the plan and it may have been an urge to outdo the exploits of Alexander the Great which led him to the East. Most certainly the invasion was an ill-fated and ill-timed adventure; an opinion openly and bitterly expressed by practically every one of the forty thousand. Forty centuries might be looking down on the army from the lofty tops of the Pyramids (as Napoleon rhetorically pointed out) but the unhappy troops were much more concerned with the heat which reached them from the deserts and caused so many of them to die in madness. To make matters worse, a little snippet of an Englishman whose name was Horatio Nelson took an English fleet to the Nile and destroyed the French ships which Napoleon was depending on to convey his men back to France. And there they were, these victorious troops of the Little Corporal, caged under the blazing sun with nowhere to go.

Napoleon did the best he could for the grumbling soldiers under his command. He led them farther into Egypt and captured the city of Cairo. Here, to provide them with entertainment, he established a pleasure park which he called the Tivoli Egyptien.

It was there that he first saw La Bellilote.

One of the orders issued before sailing was that no officer should take his wife along. Little heed had been paid to this command, apparently, for many wives were on board when the ships sailed, most of them, as they thought, suitably disguised in the uniform of the drummer corps. But it was not in tight-fitting blue trousers and cutaway coat and pillbox cap which could not conceal her abundant blond curls that the Napoleonic eye first saw Pauline Fourès. She was attired in *very* close-fitting white vest and trousers and green coat. On her head she wore the tricorne hat peculiar to Napoleon himself and she was giving a very good imitation of his voice and mannerisms for the benefit of a large company of French officers. Standing at the darkened entrance to the gardens, where his arrival had not been noted, the commander of the expedition watched this impudent performance without any trace of a smile. It happened that in one of his pockets he was carrying a letter which had almost destroyed his pride and had certainly reduced him to feelings of humiliation such as he had never known before.

This letter, in brief, made it clear that his beloved Josephine was living openly (not expecting him to come back alive or not caring) on an expensive estate a few miles from Paris with a man named Hippolyte Charles. The estate, moreover, was none other than Malmaison which she had purchased on his, Napoleon's, credit. The letter was from Joseph Bonaparte and had been sent to Junot who was to use his judgment as to whether the infatuated Napoleon should be told. Junot at this point was Napoleon's closest friend and he had decided the general should know the truth.

"I cannot believe it!" said the heartbroken Napoleon, as the two of them found chairs in the dark shade of the thick palm trees. "Has any other soldier ever been as faithful as I have, Junot?"

"Never, my general."

"How I have loved that woman! I have beggared myself to let her live in luxury. I have had no eyes for other women. What have I done to deserve such treatment as this?"

"Nothing. Nothing, my general."

"Have I looked around for a dusky mistress, as the rest of you have?"

Junot made a casual gesture. "One does the best one can. Yes, it is true. My Jaunette—I call her that because her real name, Xraxarne, is too hard to pronounce—is not an Egyptian girl. She's an Abyssinian slave. But she's young and willing. What more can one ask?"

"*Ma foi*, Junot, I am told she is enormous."

"Well, my general, yes. But her supply of flesh—and there is a great deal of it, it is true—is arranged on her bones in a pleasing way. 'Arranged' is perhaps not the right word but I

147

am sure you understand what I mean. *Sapristi*, she would not do for you, my general. In the first place, she uses very strong perfumes—"

"No more, if you please, Junot. You are making my flesh crawl."

"Ah, well, as I said, one does the best one can."

The commander's mind had gone back to the news contained in the letter. He was so disturbed that he neglected to dry the dampness of his brow. "This fellow, Hippolyte Charles," he said, finally. "Is he the great simpleton I had to cashier out of the Army?"

Junot nodded. "He has gone into business. A grocer or poulterer or something of the kind. He's quite a dandy, I hear."

Napoleon's face became suffused with rage. "If I called him out, would he have the choice of weapons? Might I find myself forced to fight him with an iron spit or a larding spoon? Junot, Junot, this passes all belief! When has a trusting husband been treated as basely as this?"

Suddenly the mood of the army commander changed. "Junot," he whispered, when the imitations came to an end amid a burst of enthusiastic hand-clapping and loud cries of *Brava!* "This is a game at which two can play, I am of a mind to make her regret her loose conduct."

"*Oui, oui, mon général!*" Junot burst into laughter. "Yes, it is a game at which two have been playing for hundreds and thousands and millions of years. Ever since the seventh day, or thereabouts. And I don't need to tell you, my general, that it's a form of retaliation which carries its own reward."

Napoleon plucked at the sleeve of his subordinate. "Who is this little baggage who has been aping me up there?"

"She is Pauline Fourès, wife of a lieutenant in the line."

"Ah, that fellow! He has no future in the Army. A stupid, conceited donkey. Junot, I've taken a fancy to her. Could you arrange to have me meet her?"

"Nothing easier, my general. Leave it in my hands. I think," he added, "it would prove a sure cure for—for what you have learned in that letter."

2

The meeting did not take place at once. Junot soon had all the arrangements made but Napoleon himself was too busy with matters which seemed to him of much more importance. The shrewdness of the lawmaker, which came out later in his remarkable Napoleonic Code, was beginning to manifest itself. If he was to have idle time on his hands, he must find ways of using it profitably.

One of the leading scientists of France, Gaspard Monge, a practical scholar who had simplified many military problems by the application of mathematical rules, had been sent with the expedition. Napoleon took advantage of this by organizing an Institute of Egypt for scientific research, naming Monge president and contenting himself with the title of vice-president. There were other scientists with him and he set them all to work on problems such as the deciphering of the Rosetta Stone. This puzzle would continue to baffle scholarship for many years but it may have been that the stimulus of the conquering general's interest led to quickened results.

Most of the questions propounded, however, were eminently practical. He was not satisfied with the army baking ovens. How could they be improved? And could a factory be established in Egypt for the manufacture of gunpowder?

It was some time, therefore, before he felt free to proceed with Junot's plan. The latter intended to have a little group of high-ranking officers entertain the French women in Cairo. No husbands were to be invited.

"*Ma foi*, Junot," said Napoleon. "You know I am striving to put an end to dueling among my officers. Won't these husbands come charging in and issue challenges right and left?"

Junot now displayed how much experience he had in the ways of philandering. "No, my general. The husbands are all in a vulnerable position. If they acknowledge these ladies as their wives, they are confessing to a serious breach of army orders. I know they won't want to get themselves court-martialed."

Accordingly the plan was set in motion. Napoleon received an invitation to dine with General Dupuy, the commandant of Cairo. He replied that he was very busy but would put in an appearance for a few moments only. When he arrived coffee was being served. As he had anticipated, the company was made up almost exclusively of ladies. He looked about

149

him and had no difficulty in singling out Madame Fourès. Attired in a gown of beige silk, she was unquestionably the most attractive one there. Sitting down beside his host, he began to sip a cup of coffee, saying little but watching the beautiful Pauline with fascinated interest. In a few moments he rose, excused himself to his host, bowed to the company, and departed.

The next step was for the officers present to circulate among the charming guests. Junot joined Madame Fourès and contrived to spill coffee over her skirt. It was an expensive as well as becoming costume and the poor lady was very much disturbed.

"Madam, my abject apologies!" said Junot. "How could I be so clumsy! But the stain can be removed if it's attended to at once. Dupuy, there will be a maid on the floor above, will there not? Who will see to repairing the damage I have done?"

"Of course."

So the unhappy Madame Fourès withdrew and found a room on the floor above where an open door seemed to welcome her. But it was not a maid she found inside. It was Napoleon Bonaparte, wearing the most ingratiating of smiles.

"You need assistance, madame," he said. "Ah, what a catastrophe! What a beautiful dress! The damage must be seen to at once. But it will be necessary for the skirt to be removed."

The lady sat down in a chair he had drawn forward for her. Her beautiful slate-blue eyes studied the general with an intentness which suggested she was blessed with a certain degree of sagacity as well as all the qualities which make women desirable. There was also, perhaps, a mere hint of calculation.

"Yes, my general," she said.

It had not been difficult. Napoleon did not find his admiration diminished by what might have seemed a too hasty surrender. Nor was he inclined to think of her solely as the instrument of retaliation he had been seeking against Josephine. He found her charming and gay and, in fact, the most pleasing of companions. She had confided to him that in the little circle of French husbands and wives, thrown into one another's company by the centripetal conditions in an alien city, she was called La Bellilote.

150

"La Bellilote," he had thought. "Very apt for so vivacious a lady. I must command the undivided company of La Bellilote."

The busy commander turned to his friend and confidant in this situation. "Junot," he said, "do you recall the story of David?"

"Which David?"

"The king of Israel."

"Oh, that one. He wouldn't climb very high in this Army. Too much given to singing and twanging of harps."

"Make no mistake, he was a great king, a fighting king. You must recall the story of Bathsheba, the beautiful young wife he saw taking a bath on a housetop. There was some stiff fighting going forward in the desert so he had her husband Uriah put in the front ranks where, of course, he was killed."

"Yes, I remember that story. Do you mean to say that this lieutenant, who is such a stupid and conceited donkey, is to be placed somewhere so a bullet or the point of a Bedouin spear can put him out of the way?"

"*Mon Dieu*, no!" cried Napoleon. "What I propose is to single him out for honors. I want to send him home with dispatches. Of course, he won't be able to run the gamut of the English ships and they'll put him in a prison camp for the duration of the war."

Junot looked somewhat distressed. "But won't that be giving away secrets?"

"Not the kind of dispatches I intend to entrust him with. He will carry only papers that I will be glad to see in the hands of those stupid English."

"Ha, a decoy! Do you want me to arrange this?"

"He's in your division but all I want you to do is to send him to Berthier for instructions."

Berthier, the chief-of-staff, who as a result of the heat was existing in a condition which suggested a fish in aspic, actually envied Lieutenant Fourès his honor. "How lucky you are to be leaving this furnace for a fine sea voyage and an honorable mission in Paris. You must have attracted favor in high places."

Fourès was not aware that he had done anything to attract the notice of his superiors, but he should have had a faint stirring of suspicion when he learned his wife was not to accompany him. "My brave young man," protested Berthier when the point was raised, "after all there is danger in this mission. We can't subject a woman to it."

It happened that the commander of the English ship which promptly swooped down on the little vessel conveying the carrier of dispatches, had a quality which Napoleon had not expected to find in English. He had a sense of humor.

"By my word," he exclaimed after looking over the stale and unimportant papers in the Fourès dispatch case, "there is an odor about this of dead fish on shaol sands. Why has this poor dupe been sent out with information which was stale weeks ago? Clearly someone high up wanted to get rid of him. Why should we not return the compliment by sending him back?"

In the meantime Napoleon had established his headquarters in the Elfi Bey palace and had assigned a very pleasant house next to it for Madame Fourès. She dined with him every night. Very soon in the army they were calling her by a new name, Cleopatra. Sometimes she appeared on parade, wearing a military cloak and a plumed hat. Once at least she was seen riding an Arab horse with a tail which almost touched the ground, and handling herself very well indeed. It was soon apparent that the soldiers liked her. When they cried "Vive Clioupatre!" they meant it. Apparently her vivacity and charm were not surface qualities, assumed for the intimate moments alone with the man whose favor she had won. They were a part of her and were appreciated by everyone.

La Bellilote provided Napoleon with relief from the heavy grind of his days. Her habitual mood was one of gaiety. She called him "Boney" and "Nappy" and sometimes "m'sieur, the great and illustrious general." There was just one point of issue between them: the future. What did Napoleon propose to do about Josephine? He assured her positively that he intended to get a divorce as soon as he returned to France. And what then? Another wife, of course; one, however, who would present him with a son. The tempo of the discussion would be retarded at this point. What could the vivacious Pauline say? It was whispered about that she had said to him on one occasion, "Is it not that I am doing my very best?"

Napoleon was declared to have answered with what might be described as an affectionate snort: "You little *sotte!* Are you implying it is my fault?"

152

Naploeon was proud of her. Even Josephine's son, Eugene, who rode behind the coach as an aide-de-camp, did not object at first. He had achieved at an early age the viewpoint of the soldier. War was war and men who might die the next day found solace in the present. But in a very short time he felt unable to acquiesce in his stepfather's conduct. He begged to be relieved of the duty of attendance.

This was the situation to which the now aroused husband returned. There were violent scenes. But the lady refused to leave her cushiony nest and the outraged Fourès found it impossible to gain an audience with the commander of the Army who had robbed him of his wife. Finally it was suggested to him that he should get a divorce, an army divorce. So he made his application and was immediately given his freedom. For the next six months he suffered the humiliation of seeing his beautiful Pauline riding out with Napoleon in the cool of the evening, with a full military escort.

But Napoleon never allowed affairs of the heart to stand in the way of advancement. Advices began to reach him from France which showed how incompetent and blind the Directory had become. It was clear that the people were dissatisfied with the men governing them and wanted a change. Napoleon decided that the hour had struck. He must return to France.

It was a daring decision. He had no way of determining to what extent the lack of success in Egypt had rubbed the gloss from his once resplendent reputation. To make matters worse, the sails of the English fleet were thick in the Mediterranean and he might be captured if he ventured out into the area they controlled. But Bonaparte never hesitated to take risks. He left his headquarters at Cairo in the dead of night, saying a fond farewell to a sadly weeping mistress who had begged to go with him. The best he could do for her was to instruct General Kleber, who was assuming his place, to send her home as soon as possible. It is said that Kleber took rather too good care of her but there is no evidence to prove this.

Napoleon's boldness paid him the usual rich reward. The ship in which he embarked crept slowly along the North African coast from one small port to another. It was not until they encountered the glassy glare of Tyrhennian waters that they ventured out. A successful dash around the western end of Sicily brought them to Corsica without interference. From the island of Napoleon's birth it was not difficult to reach France.

Here two climactic events followed one another. He forgave Josephine (who from that time remained faithful to him and became intensely jealous of his interest in other women) and he struck suddenly at the Council of Five Hundred, the elective body of France. The House was dispersed at the point of bayonets and a new government was set up with Napoleon as its head with the title of First Consul. This bold move, called in history the *coup d'état* of Brumaire, placed the young general firmly at the head of the state.

This was the condition of things when La Bellilote finally reached France. She had expected to be received with open arms but instead she met with silence and neglect. Finally the truth was broken to her. Napoleon, as head of the administration, had to be above reproach in his private life. He could not allow himself to see her. It may be said for Napoleon that he was always generous with the ladies who shared his favors. It was his intention to provide for the little charmer whose family life he had wrecked so completely. But in the activities of his own new life he neglected to do anything about it. It was not until Junot and Duroc, the Grand Marshal of the Household (Bertrand's predecessor in that somewhat ornamental post) came to him that he learned she had fallen into serious financial straits. He took immediate steps to repair this oversight. A generous settlement was made on her (so generous that she was never in serious want thereafter) and she was instructed to marry again. When told that she preferred not to take another husband, he became quite indignant.

"The little *sotte!*" he exclaimed. "Make it clear to her, Duroc, that she has no option. She must take a husband."

A second mate was chosen for her, one Henri de Ranchoup. He was, according to La Bellilote herself, old and dull; but marry him she must, marry him she did. It was Napoleon's plan to send her as far from France as possible and the first move was to appoint her husband vice-consul in Spain. Later he was sent to Sweden in a similar capacity.

The great years in Napoleon's life seemed to pass quickly, but not for the discarded Pauline. She secured a divorce from Ranchoup and married again. She was in Paris through the years of the Empire, that spectacular period when Napoleon's sun was so high in the heavens. She saw him once only.

There was a masquerade ball at which the emperor had agreed grudgingly to appear. He took no pleasure in such events and he was standing at one side of the great room, still wearing his mask, when a familiar voice said from close beside him, "Sire?"

The emperor had a clear memory for voices and he knew at once who it was. Despite his firmness in refusing to receive her, he seems to have experienced a quick pleasure in encountering her so unexpectedly.

"Pauline! It is you?"

"Yes, sire. You are not angry?"

"I have never been able to feel anger where you are concerned. Is there anything you need?"

There was a moment's silence. "No, Your Majesty. You have been generous to me and I am living in comfort."

"I am very glad of that."

"I am keeping very busy, sire. I am writing. Each day I am at my desk."

A feeling of alarm took possession of him. "There must be no writing of memoirs," he said, sharply. "I will not consent to any use being made of the past."

She hastened to reassure him. "Oh, no, sire. I am writing a novel. I have your letters still and I cherish them. But I give my solemn promise never to let other eyes see them. They will be destroyed before I die."

The emperor felt a distinct relief on receiving this reassurance. He was to become the most written about man in all history but he always had an intense dislike for the free use by others of intimate detail.

"And," she went on, "I am beginning to paint. I think I am a better painter than novelist. I have just finished a self-portrait which my friends say is a good likeness. Also I am beginning to sing."

"I had no idea you were so talented. I hope you will be successful in all these branches of the arts."

His interest seemed to give her real pleasure. "I won't accomplish much, sire. You will never hear a whisper of me again. "Sire," she whispered after a long pause, "I have been standing at the gates many mornings when the young empress goes out to ride. Once she had your son with her. Ah, sire, what a bright and handsome boy! I felt very happy for your sake. You wanted a son so much and she—the empress, I mean—has done her duty. It seems," with a sigh, "that you were right. I have been married three times and I still have no children. So it *must* have been my fault." After another moment of silence, "If there was only something I could do, some sacrifice I could make. I would like to show that I am still—much devoted."

It must have seemed to Napoleon that this was a pointless protestation. What indeed could a somewhat déclassée widow, no matter how well liked she might be, and how beautiful, do for one who held all power in his hands and the peace of Europe as well? Nevertheless he felt a certain curiosity about her.

"Pauline," he said, "I would like a glimpse of you. When the time for unmasking comes."

"Yes, sire. I will be close at hand. It will be a great honor to see you again. And I won't attempt to speak to you. Or give you any reason for—for being displeased with me."

At unmasking time, therefore, he had a final glimpse of her; and it seems certain that for a moment at least his heart must have stood still. La Bellilote, still in her twenties, was even more beautiful than his memory of her.

Chapter Three

1

The next morning there was an unusual coolness in the air.
As was his custom Napoleon did not dress on first rising.
Without summoning his valet, he slipped into a pair of white
cotton trousers and then donned a quilted dressing gown of
dimity. Departing from his general rule, however, he removed
the red bandana he wore on his head while sleeping, and his
hair appeared somewhat comically tousled and rather thin.

Generally he would have coffee or tea served to him on the
round table in his bedroom, after which he would sit about
for a good part of the morning, skimming through the books
which kept arriving for him. This morning he felt more ener-
getic than usual and so decided to step out for a look over
what the English press, seeking to make a case for the governmental policy toward the prisoner, called a "park." There
had been a heavy downpour during the night and the ground
was wet. Stepping cautiously into the gardens immediately
outside his bedroom, he saw Count Bertrand approaching
with books under his arm. In accordance with the etiquette
they had evolved, Bertrand came to a stop and waited for an
invitation to speak.

"More books?" said Napoleon, in a disinterested tone.
"Anything very interesting in the lot?"

"No, Your Imperial Highness. A small package from London. I fear you won't find them of much use. But the English
Government has not neglected to send a bill for them. They
should be very rare and bound in gold, judging from the
amount."

Napoleon was too full of the matters which had brought
him out so much earlier than usual to express any annoyance
over the penny-pinching policy of the London Cabinet.

"In what direction is Rio de Janeiro, my dear count?" he
asked.

There was an alertness about him this morning which had been lacking ever since they landed on the island, and most particularly since they had been moved to Longwood. The grand marshal believed for a moment that some word from the outside had been received to account for his new attitude. This possibility he dismissed quickly, however. It was impossible for Napoleon to have any communications from the faraway world save through his hands.

Bertrand led the way to the monotonously level ground on the western side of the house and pointed directly through a gap in the high stone walls.

"It lies over there, sire," he said. "Almost due west."

Napoleon thanked him with a nod and then turned to stare in the direction indicated. The marshal expected to be asked other questions and stayed close at hand. Napoleon at first remained silent. There was a rigidity about the stocky figure in white and in the set of the bare head. It was fully a quarter of an hour before Napoleon turned.

"Bertrand," he said, "we have been waiting a long time for some word. Five months we've squatted here on this God-forgotten pile of rocks and sometimes I think my friends no longer care. Not a discreet word, not a hint in the newspapers—at least, not in the copies we are allowed to see. Nothing has reached us in the way of a gift of special wine."

"No, sire. But I have been watching closely. Many different varieties of wine have come, but nothing from the source in question. None, that is, from Spain. Or is it the Balearic Islands?"

"From Spain. From Barcelona but shipped out of the country through Cadiz. You see, Bertrand, I'm not one of your experts where wine is concerned. To me wine is something to drink, not to taste and sip and nod your head over knowingly. Some kinds I like and some I don't—and, as you know, I generally pour a little water into my glass before I drink. That, in the opinion of these connoisseurs, these bibbers, these *buveurs* who can take one sip and then tell you the year when the stuff was bottled and the hillside where the vines grew—to them my way of drinking is a cardinal sin.

"This wine I am expecting will taste very much like all other wines, even if it does come from an obscure corner of Spain or one of those islands. But the man who will send it thinks it the finest in the world and, if he uses it to get in-

158

formation to me, I will agree with him about his precious vintage with the utmost willingness."

As he talked Napoleon had been aware of a face at one of the windows in the small outbuilding which was serving as a home for the Montholon family. He now looked back over his shoulder and saw that it was the countess herself. She stepped away from the window as soon as she saw he was aware of her presence there.

"This constant curiosity!" he said, in a tone of deep annoyance. "Do you realize, Bertrand, that I cannot step outside without having eyes follow me at some of the windows? The first sound of my step brings them even to those little ventilating slits in the attics. Eyes, eyes, eyes!"

"Sire, can you blame them? They have so little to do. And there are so many of them crowded into these tiny rooms. To watch you stroll in the gardens gives them something to think about."

Napoleon was not in a mood to be pacified easily. He was thinking: "She is always at that window. What does she expect? That we can resume the familiarity we fell into during the voyage down? Perhaps I should have a frank talk with her."

He said to Bertrand in a grumbling tone: "Walls and sentries everywhere and semaphores to report my movements! Isn't that enough without my own people spying on me as well? I suppose their tongues wag in the kitchens over the smallest things. *Ma foi*, can I be blamed for feeling weary of it?"

"No, sire. But I'm afraid it is inevitable and that nothing can be done about it."

This brought the Captive's mind back to the train of thought which had occupied him as he stared out over the gray sea in the direction of Rio. "Bertrand," he said, in a low tone, "let us go back to the gardens where we can't be overheard. I have much to say."

They retraced their steps and took possession of two very old and very rusty chairs. The gardens had been so hastily planned that they did not drain off at once after a rainfall. There were pools around the chairs and the surface was so soft that the metal feet sank deeply into the grass. The sun was struggling through a small break in the clouds but there was no promise yet of sufficient warmth to dry the ground.

Only the windows in the emperor's private suite faced on

this portion of the gardens so they were free from observation for the time being. Napoleon began to speak in low tones.

"Before I let my great optimistic lunatic of a brother—it is to Lucien I refer—convince me I should stay in France, I had given serious thought to taking ship for America. Great things are going to happen there. I could have made a new life for myself if I had gone with Joseph. My mind was made up that war and thrones were to be forgotten. I intended to become what they call a leader of industry, a millionaire. *Ma foi*, I would have been in my element! Several of these United Staters had been to see me in Paris. Builders of ships. Men with long chins and firm lips and cool gray eyes. They all agreed on one thing: that the time had come for a new kind of merchant ship. The word 'clipper' was always on their lips. This new kind was to be narrow so they could cut through the waves, and they would carry incredibly high masts and huge sails. They would be hard to handle and they wouldn't carry as much cargo. But they would outsail the ponderous English square-riggers and get to the Orient and back in half the time. They had no doubt that they were going to revolutionize world trade. I should have kept them in France and turned over to them the control of our Navy and our merchant marine. But I was too busy with raising armies to give any time to maritime problems and so I missed a great opportunity.

"If the English and the European powers had left me alone when I escaped from Elba," he went on, "I would have been completely willing to keep the peace. It was in my mind to make France a great maritime nation and build a fleet of those fantastic clippers my American callers described. I thought I would send for some of them to come over into my service. But England and Austria and Russia wanted to punish me. So I had to raise armies again and fight them.

"It was in my mind also, when I put myself in English hands, that I was still emperor of France and father of the future emperor. If they forced me to abdicate, I must consider myself above any scheming or planning to get free. I must demand deference and never do anything to cheapen myself in the eyes of the world. No running away in the darkness of night, no resort to disguises or any form of subterfuge.

"But, Bertrand, it is always necessary before making a ma-

160

jor decision to consider every possible course of action. I realized the English might behave badly and so I—I kept a line of retreat open. Now you see how abominably they are treating me—compelling me to exist in this rat-infested pest-house, and keeping me a prisoner thousands of miles from civilization. I must now take advantage of the arrangements I made. I am going to tell you everything in the strictest confidence. These others—*eh, bien,* I can be sure of their loyalty but what of their intelligence? And, which is more important, what of their discretion? This much I shall explain now. The letters I am expecting will come from the Abbé Force. Don't frown and shake your head. He is the best intelligence agent I ever had. If anything can be done to get me out of this *feu d'enfer*, he is the only man I can count upon.

"He writes a curious hand. Very small and cramped and hard to decipher. But to receive a letter now in that odd script of his would arouse in me again the hopes I have ceased to feel for a long time. He and he alone, that slovenly old churchman you think so poorly of, is capable of conceiving and carrying out plans for my release."

He rose from his chair and they started to walk back to the huddle of low roofs and the blotched walls, resisting the influence of paint, which was called Longwood. Bertrand perceived the alertness in his master's eye and realized that there was even a hint of spring and jauntiness in his step.

"One little grain of truth has been dropped most innocently and unexpectedly on my path," whispered Napoleon. "Bertrand, I think it won't be long now before that case of wine reaches us."

2

In Jamestown the heat was excessive. The unfortunate residents left their desks and their shops and haunted the quay in the hope of benefiting from any vagrant breeze the sea might send them. There was no amelioration at night and the people carried out blankets to spread on the baked earth in the small squares of open space which passed as gardens. The taverns were crowded in the hope that the tepid beer for sale would bring some slight relief. It was, everyone agreed, the worst stretch of weather the town had ever experienced.

"This," men said to each other, "is a punishment intended for that ruddy Corsican butcher. It's our bad luck to share it with him."

"Can't the Old Poger wait until Boney's dead before turning on the heat like this?" was another speculation.

William Balcombe had taken Mantee Timms into town with him to operate the fan in the main office. He was sitting there silently, without enough energy to notice that Mantee's shirt was making no pretence at all of joining his trousers, when Count Bertrand was announced.

Bertrand had been picking up a little English and Balcombe rather less of French but they managed to carry on a conversation between them which was as full of knots and snarls as an amateur's efforts with a rope.

"Sit here, Count," said the head of the firm, placing a chair where the full benefit of the fan would be felt.

He was surprised at the coolness and composure shown by the head of the Napoleonic household. Everyone in St. Helena had heard the story that Fanny Dillon (the maiden name of the countess) had said to Napoleon when he proposed that she marry Bertrand, "Why not marry me to the pope's monkey?" The thought ran now through Balcombe's mind that she could not have seen the prospective groom before she made that remark. Bertrand's clean-shaven face was full and quite handsome in a rather solemn and bland way. It was generally believed that the union had been a happy one.

"The *Peveril* came in two days ago," said Balcombe. "We have most of the special supplies we ordered for you. The people over there," motioning in the direction of the castle where the government offices were located, "are still looking everything over. They've run rods down into each keg of sugar and been sifting around in the flour. Each length of cloth has been examined under telescopes. What do they expect to find?"

"Letters, no doubt," answered Bertrand coolly.

"So far all they've reported is a case of wine which was put on at Cadiz, addressed to the general personally."

"Ah, yes," said Bertrand, showing no concern. "He has been asking about it. It seems to be a favorite wine of his and an old acquaintance at Barcelona promised to send some on to him at intervals."

"Something in the port line?" asked Balcombe, with immediate interest.

Bertrand shook his head. "No, m'sieur. I believe it's a rather thin wine and more on the sour side. I don't recall having tasted it." He paused. "I hope there are the dates and figs that Madame Montholon has been wanting. She acts as though she suspects me of having countermanded them."

"They're in the order. The zealous young men at the castle went through them from top to bottom. They found plenty of worms but no letters."

"Ah, too bad. She's most fastidious, so I must warn her what to expect."

The next morning Bertrand carried to Longwood a basket from which protruded the necks of bottles. The Captive saw him coming and was standing on the portico to greet him.

"Ha!" he said. "It has arrived."

Bertrand bowed. "Yes, sire. I would suggest, as we are under observation, that you pay no attention to this basket. I will turn it over to one of the staff."

They remained outside for a considerable time, engaged in conversation for the benefit of the military observers at Alarm-House. When they finally went inside, they found the basket on the table in the dining room.

"Have all the doors locked," instructed Napoleon eagerly. "Ask Gourgaud to stand guard at the glass door. With a pistol loaded and ready."

"He won't like that, sire. He will feel he should be inside with us."

"*Mon Dieu*, Bertrand, this is no time for his stiff-necked nonsense."

Bertrand was wondering why the dining room had been selected for this purpose. Napoleon had such an aversion for this particular chamber that he seldom allowed himself more than a half hour for dinner, making his way through soup, fish, a *relevé* (a highly seasoned appetizer), two entrees, a joint, and two desserts in that time in his anxiety to be out of the place. In planning the suite (a high-flown term for this clutter of tiny and dismal rooms) the need for light and ventilation in the dining salon had been overlooked. The only light was admitted through a glass panel in the door leading to the library and as a result candles burned there all day long, and the air was heavy with the odors of food and cookery.

It was, moreover, a badly decorated and furnished room.

163

The walls were painted a hideous bright blue. The carpet, which had been picked up somewhere in the town, was of a gloomy red and was much worn. The table was a mean and prosaic oval, the chairs secondhand and most unsafe. There was also a cupboard and a sideboard. Ugliness seems to be a common fault with sideboards and this one had never been surpassed in that respect, a lumpy affair of dismally dark wood. At a later period the table would be pushed back and Mass would be celebrated on the sideboard. The ceremonial candles, guttered down to the wicks, would often remain there all day and sometimes had been overlooked when Cipriani opened the door to announce, "His Majesty's dinner is served."

What a contrast to the state banquet halls to which he had become accustomed: the great chandelieres hanging in glittering magnificence from the elaborate plaster angels and saints of the ceilings and holding hundreds of candles winking like stars, the walls gorgeously paneled with murals by famous artists, the table which seemed to have no end with its gold and silver and glass; the stately processions, two by two, the uniforms and orders of the men, the costly gowns of the ladies, the jewels, the powdered hair, the gay music of stringed instruments!

This dank and ghastly room was a caricature which quelled the spirit and prevented any enjoyment of the food or any sprightliness of talk. The first time he took his place at the head of the table, Napoleon had looked about him and said, "Here we can dine in all the vulgarity of a bourgeois Sunday."

This morning, however, he walked in briskly and seated himself in his usual place.

"Look them over, Bertrand," he said. "There should be one bottle with a flick of tallow on the label."

The grand marshal found it at once and drew the cork with the greatest care. Then, on instructions from the emperor, he began to whittle the cork with the point of a sharp knife. Halfway through an obstacle was encountered.

"Ha!" said Bertrand, triumphantly. "Sire, a letter."

A few sheets of thinnest paper had been curled up inside the cork. Napoleon smoothed them out on the table and ran a quick eye over the contents.

"It is important," he whispered. "From the abbé, as I expected."

"It comes, then, from America?"

"Yes. My brother, the king of Spain, is bestirring himself already. Under the name of the Count de Survilliers, he has purchased a stretch of park land along the Delaware River near a place called Bordentown. Here he intends to build a manor house of considerable size. It will be large enough to accommodate us if we can make our escape. Under the house he will have secret rooms, with underground passages leading to exits on the banks of the river and at an artificial lake he proposes to dig in the grounds. A wise precaution against assassination. And to allow for escape if necessary."

"It seems a good start, sire."

Napoleon read through the last pages of the communication. "There is a plan suggested for our escape from here. Clearly of my amiable brother's concocting. It is wildly lacking in practicality. The good Joseph has no imagination or ingenuity, although he considers himself abundantly endowed with both. I am sure the abbé has sent it on only because of Joseph's insistence. It's possible to read that between the lines."

Napoleon sat in silence for several moments, his brow wrinkled with thought. Then he took the letter in both hands and proceeded to tear it into small pieces.

"Everything in it is stamped idelibly on my memory," he declared. "And so it seems advisable to destroy the letter itself. You will pardon me, my good Bertrand, if this seems to hint at any fear of your discretion. I have the most complete confidence in you. Later I shall tell you what else was contained. But," and he let his voice fall to a whisper, "I cannot be sure they haven't a spy or two among my people. Any hint that a communication had been received could completely destroy our chance of success. You agree with me, I am sure."

"Most decidedly, sire."

The Captive filled one of his pockets with the pieces of paper and the fragments of cork. "Order two glasses to be brought us, so we can test the wine. We must sit here over this bottle like a pair of addlepated Englishmen, who, I am told, will drink their port at any hour of the day. Have a fire lighted in my bedroom." He patted the pocket containing the fragments. "When I retire later, I shall burn all this to the finest powder."

When Bertrand returned, he found that Napoleon had risen

in the meantime and was pacing up and down the chamber, so deeply sunk in thought that he did not desist immediately. Finally he came to a halt and seated himself again, motioning to the grand marshal to join him at the table.

"There were other specific pieces of information which I must mention. The abbé tells me he has attended to matters A and B. Come, we must drink while we talk. Pour me a glass and then help yourself. *Pfui!* I do not admire the good abbé's taste. However, drink it we must for it may be that many such consignments will be reaching us in the future. Now, there are points A and B to be explained. Were you aware, Bertrand, that when I sat on the imperial throne, it was necessary for me to make use of doubles?"

"I heard whispers of it, sire."

"There were four in all. I used them to take drives during the day in the imperial carriage when I did not want my real activities to be known. One of the four even reviewed troops for me on certain occasions. That one was an intelligent fellow and a most loyal subject; and we were as much alike physically as identical twins. He was a Frenchman and I could never see him without thinking of the legend of the Man in the Iron Mask. His name was Roberaud. When they first brought him in to my cabinet to display him I decided immediately that he could be used to great advantage. Often we had visitors who wanted to see me at my desk; people of high rank from other countries, the families of diplomats, the kind we did not want to displease. They would be taken to a post from which it was possible to look down into a room of some size. Here they would see Roberaud busily at work, crouched over letters at a desk which resembled the one I used or even pacing up and down with his arms folded behind him. He had a touch of the actor in him and they would go away convinced."

"Two of the four are dead," continued Napoleon. "One has disappeared but we have had a piece of great good fortune in connection with the fourth—none other than Roberaud himself. The abbé has been in contact with him and has persuaded him to take my place here, if the transfer can be arranged."

The grand marshal showed the astonishment he felt. "You mean, sire, that this man is willing to commit himself to imprisonment, perhaps for life, so you can go free?"

"I told you of his great loyalty. Still, his plight could not

166

prove as bad as you picture it. If I get away from this island, the whole world will soon know it. I am sure the heads of the allied governments in whose hands the fate of Roberaud would rest, could not fly in the face of world opinion by punishing this splendid fellow too severely."

"Well," he continued, "so far so good. Now the point B has a bearing on the same problem. You must remember Henri Ratafie in Paris."

"The man who trained candidates for the stage and the opera?"

"The greatest coach in all history. My plump little Mam'selle George owed a great deal to him. He had another profitable accomplishment. He was a master artificer of wigs and beards for use on the stage. The abbé has kept in touch with him, and he is now engaged, most confidentially of course, in the making of necessary aids for my disguise. Roberaud has a heavy head of dark hair which he will allow to grow much longer than the way I wear mine and he is growing a beard."

"That leaves us," said the Captive, "with the most difficult problem to solve. Our escape from here."

Bertrand sighed and gave his head a shake. "I don't believe you are aware of all the restrictions they have imposed."

"*Ma foi*, no! It is bad enough to face my jailers without having to hear of their silly contrivances. As you know, I have refused to discuss them. But perhaps I should now have a full description of what they've done."

"In the first place, sire, they have a patrol of warships around the island. No vessel, no matter how small, is allowed to approach. A drunken woman in a bumboat, according to Admiral Cockburn, would be ordered off. No shore leaves are allowed the crews of the warships. Merchantmen from England carrying supplies are allowed to remain in the outer roadstead but no one may go ashore. The supplies are taken off by cutters from shore. Under no circumstances is anyone allowed to depart on these supply ships except those returning to London under instructions from the governor."

"It is a matter of extreme regret to me," declared Napoleon, with a wry smile, "that I am the cause of upsetting the life of the island in this way."

"There are troops at all points on the shore where even a rowboat could land. They keep watch at the mouths of all streams pouring down through the rocks. They have nets to snare any bottles which are washed down."

"But they would hardly expect to find me doubled up in a bottle like a genie."

"For letters, sire. There is a guard day and night on the wharves at Jamestown. You know, of course, of the signaling system they have set up?"

"I know the semaphore at Alarm-House reports my whereabouts."

"That is only part of it. The signals from Alarm-House are picked up at six other points and the messages are duplicated. On every spot on the island it is possible to see a semaphore sending out these messages."

"What signal would they give if I were missing?"

"A blue flag, following three cannon shots. If that should ever happen, sire, all the troops on the island—there are nearly fifteen hundred of them—would be assembled at once, to inspect every foot of ground until you were found."

Napoleon sat in silence for many moments, turning these facts over in his mind. "I grant you, Bertrand," he then said, "that there seems no solution to this problem."

"Perhaps in all the schemes we've discussed since coming here," said Bertrand, "there may be one with the germ of a practical idea."

Napoleon snorted. "Sheer lunacy, all of them. *Ma foi,* would you have me doubled up in one of the stinking barrels which they send here filled with fish, and then rolled aboard some sailing vessel? Don't you suppose the sentries would insist on examining the barrel before they let it be taken aboard? And that other masterpiece of idiocy, that I should disguise myself as an old man and go hobbling on a crutch all the way down to the harbor! I seem to remember that was Gourgaud's contribution—and he couldn't see a flaw in it!"

"There was the plan about a submarine," said Bertrand, frowning thoughtfully. "That still seems a possibility to me."

"My dear Bertrand, that submarine hasn't progressed beyond the inventor's charts. Some day there will be ships under the surface of the sea but it will take endless experimentation before it can be made perfect. And even if it could be built now, do you realize what an escape in it would entail? I would have to climb down the face of one of those rocky cliffs in the dead of night. What chance would I have of reaching the bottom in safety? And if I did, I would have to be taken off in an experimental ship under the surface of the sea. The ship would need to stay submerged until we had gone hundreds of miles so none of the patrol vessels would sight us. Would any sane man take such risks?"

"No, sire. I'm afraid the idea is not to be considered after all."

They remained in a deep silence for some minutes. Napoleon, bending low over the table, was sunk in thought.

"We must find a way," he declared finally. "If we don't, they will keep me here until I die. Bertrand, every battle I fought had special problems, all of which I had to find an answer. Will I fail now in the hardest test of all?"

He raised his head and the marshal recognized the expression he wore; everyone in the armies of France had spoken of it as his "fighting face." He said in low tones: "There *must* be a way. *Mon Dieu,* I cannot face life imprisonment for lack of a little ingenuity in planning. There is always a way. I must find it."

It had been Bertrand's intention to return to his own house after delivering the wine. Now, however, he remained at Longwood, busying himself with details of household administration. For six hours he heard steady footsteps from the bedroom to which Napoleon had retired. Up, and down they went, at a steady, undeviating pace. Only once was there an interruption and this of brief duration. Had he paused to consult a document? Time and again the marshal shook his head dubiously with a thought which could not be banished from his mind: "It is an impossibility. He can find no way out of this trap."

The Great Man was late in coming to the drawing room before dinner. For the first time he seemed untidy and his hair was uncombed. The full company had assembled there, the men in dress uniform, each wearing his orders, the women in their best frocks. Madame Bertrand, looking quite queenly in black silk, kept to one corner of the room while Madame Montholon, in a rather daring red which set off her trimness and the vivacity of her eyes, was in another. There was no cordiality between them and they spoke only when circumstances demanded.

Napoleon did not take any part in the conversation at dinner until the finish. He kept his head down and was satisfied with a few mouthfuls of food. He drank a glass of the

169

new wine and did not forget to give a nod of approval for the benefit of the company. One course followed another with a rapidity which was especially disconcerting to Las Cases who was enjoying each dish and so had to resort to gobbling. Gourgaud, who had not forgiven the command which had set him on sentry duty, frowned blackly. He found the *relevé*, which consisted of shellfish with a highly flavored sauce, to his liking, and the speed with which it was removed added to his discontent. He did not say a word until the finish when, with a loud "Good!" he evidenced his satisfaction that the meal had come to an end.

The one topic which had drawn Napoleon into the conversation was introduced in the course of some discussion of a recent book. What were the underlying causes of romance? The men seemed to lack interest in the matter and the talk became a debate between the two ladies. Madame Bertrand thought it was a question of spiritual values, a meeting of minds, a sharing of interests. Madame Montholon took a more mundane view. Romance, she was sure, developed from a sparkle in the eye, a lilt in the voice, even perhaps the neat turn of an ankle.

"You are both overlooking the real reason," declared Napoleon, who was finding the topic tiresome. "Proximity."

"Proximity, sire?" said Madame Montholon, giving him the full benefit of the sparkle in her own dark eyes.

"Of course. Most men marry the nearest woman and think they find in her the enticements you mention, my dear Albiné. If I had remained in Marseilles, I would undoubtedly have married my sweet little Désirée Clary, and perhaps have been happy enough with her, although at no time was I carried away. Duty led me elsewhere and she then took a fancy for that simpleton she finally married. How lucky for her! Now she will become queen of Sweden when Bernadotte succeeds to the throne, instead of sharing a cow stable with me."

Madame Montholon gave this point a moment's thought. "I think, sire, you are right," she said. Madame Bertrand contributed nothing more but she indulged in a guarded glance, first at the emperor and then at the fair Albiné, as though to say, "We have already observed some of the results of proximity."

When Napoleon rose from the table, he dropped a hand on

Bertrand's shoulder. The pressure of his fingers was sharp and sudden.

"I have it!" he whispered. "The final details occurred to me as I sat here. Yes, Bertrand, I have it!" His eyes were glowing with an inner excitement. "I am going to my study and will not be with the company tonight. Join me in half an hour."

As the rest of the party filed into the drawing room, he became aware that Madame Montholon had lingered behind. Her eyes beseeched his attention.

"You have something to say, madame?"

"Yes, sire. It is a long time, six days indeed, since you have spoken to me. Have I done anything to offend you?"

"Certainly not. I have been immersed in work."

"But did you not see me this afternoon?"

Napoleon seemed puzzled. "This afternoon? No. I saw no one."

"But, sire, I took the liberty of entering the study. The door was open and I saw you pacing up and down in your bedroom." Her mouth, which was small and of the kind often described as a rosebud, began to quiver. "I was certain, sire, that you looked at me several times. But you gave no sign and so I—I realized you did not intend to let me speak. Finally I left."

"I apologize. I was aware of a figure in the study but I did not know it was you."

Madame Montholon seemed on the verge of tears. "Sire, I am most unhappy. In what way have I offended you? Have you forgotten so soon what we have been to each other?"

It was clear that Napoleon resented the necessity of continuing the conversation. "This is no time to ask explanations. Are any necessary? You have not offended me and I have *not* forgotten. There! Does that suffice?"

"Can't you see, sire, why I am so unhappy? It is a blow to the pride when one is not recognized. Who did you think it was? One of the servants? A ghost? I am sure if it had been that talkative little girl, you would have recognized her."

"Ah! If it had been Betsee, things might have been different. She probably would have walked in."

"I am sure she would. And I don't think you would have minded."

"She is a mere child."

"In years only." She leaned forward and placed a hand on

171

his sleeve. "Don't you see? If it had been this mere child, you would have stopped your pacing up and down. You probably would have talked with her the rest of the afternoon. I know I am breaking the rules by detaining you now but surely this situation must be discussed. If you are tired of me, please, please, tell me so. In that case I could persuade my husband to ask permission to go home to France. That would relieve you of my presence."

Napoleon studied her face which remained quite pretty in spite of the varied emotions which were disturbing her. Finally he smiled.

"We cannot talk tonight," he said. "I expect to work until daylight. But later, yes. Tomorrow afternoon, perhaps? My dear Albiné, you are making too much of this. You must not think of going back to France. I need you and your husband here. Do you believe me?"

He smiled again and, taking her by the arm, began to urge her toward the door into the drawing room. "Come," he said. "Smile. They must not suspect there has been a scene between us. They are all too ready and eager to gossip as it is."

The lady leaned her head over to touch his hand with her cheek. "Ah, sire! Did you mean it when you spoke tonight of—of proximity? When you said that, I thought it offered me a chance after all."

Napoleon, freeing his hand, allowed it to drop behind her. In doing so, he gave her a quick pinch.

"We were speaking of enticements," he said. "Have no fear. You do not lack them."

Chapter Four

1

Napoleon had prepared himself for the task which lay ahead of him by the time Bertrand appeared in the doorway. He had two candles burning and half a dozen in reserve. A pile of paper and a row of pens had been lined up on the table in front of him. From a box of sweet biscuits he had selected a large assortment and had placed them within reach of his hand.

"Sit down, Marshal," he said. "As I told you, I have my plan." I expect to work all night. I can leave nothing to them"—he motioned largely—"at the other end. Joseph would dawdle interminably. Every decision he made would be wrong; so there must be no decisions left for him to make. The abbé has a sharp mind but everything he suggested would be vetoed by that brother of mine. So—I must decide things now. I must solve each problem in advance. It will be necessary to explain every detail in full. But before I begin, I think I should explain the plan to you. There must be one here who knows what I am doing."

Bertrand bowed his head. "I am honored, sire."

"First. You know I have large funds in the hands of various bankers in Europe. I shall send authorization so the abbé can get into his hands as much money as will be needed. A very large amount.

"This will be spent in launching and financing a new shipping company in America, to operate between New York and the Orient. I shall suggest the name of the New York and Bombay. Do you approve?"

"It is a good name, sire."

"This island lies exactly halfway between these two great ports. If an active trade between New York and the East were established, St. Helena would be the crossroad port for the line. That, however, is a matter for the future."

"This company," he went on, "will be completely American in control and personnel—on the surface. There will not be a single European connected with it openly. There will be no whisper of French co-operation. They will begin by building a ship in New York where there are yards on the East River. The world will be told that this ship will be constructed on the most advanced lines, that it will be the model for the future. The masts will be the tallest ever constructed and they will carry the heaviest head of sail. In other words, a thing of beauty and of speed. Yes, speed, my dear Bertrand, enough to sail the New York-Bombay route in record time. The building of it, needless to state, will attract world attention. The first ship might be christened *The Flying Yankee*. Do you approve?"

"Yes, sire. A name to stay in the mind. But, sire, I must point out that this first great American ship will not be permitted to stop here."

"That, of course, occurred to me. I was going to explain that the ship will be too extreme. The masts will be too high, the sails too heavy. On its maiden trip it will suffer a serious mishap just off St. Helena. With some assistance from those on board who are aware of the plan, the main mast will break and will carry overboard much of the rigging. The ship, with the broken mast trailing behind it, will limp as far as the outer roadstead and it will be reported to the admiral in command here—I don't know who it will be, but Cockburn will have returned to England by that time—that her condition will not permit her to proceed. Metal supports must be forged for the mast and the rigging must be largely replaced.

"This, as you must see, will present a difficult problem. The British will not dare to refuse help. There is no other port within a thousand miles and the vessel would founder if it ventured further for aid. I am certain the solution arrived at will be to keep the damaged ship as far from shore as possible while the necessary repairs are made. None of the crew will be allowed to land save those who must superintend the arrangements, all of them under the closest watch. No one will be permitted to board the ship after the port authorities have searched it from top to bottom.

"The captain and head carpenter will go ashore, of course, and there should be a third man, a supernumerary whose duties have to do with the advanced structure of the vessel—a man with a heavy shock of dark hair and a black beard,
174

which would prevent anyone from detecting in him a resemblance to me. The name he will go under will be far different from his real one, which will be François Eugene Roberaud."

Bertrand's face had lighted up as he began to sense the possibilities of the plan. "Yes, sire, yes!" he said.

Napoleon continued in brisk tones. "Now. The repairs to *The Flying Yankee* have been completed. It will sail with the next turn of the tide, early the next day. The three officers spend the preceding evening on shore, attending to final arrangements.

"Early in the morning one of the people here—Montholon, perhaps—comes out from the house in a state of great alarm. He cries out to the sentries that Napoleon has disappeared, that his bed has not been slept in. Other members of the household follow him in great excitement. It's clear they think there has been foul play."

Napoleon paused at this point. "Bertrand," he asked, "what do you think would happen then?"

"Bedlam would ensue," declared the marshal. "The sentries would signal to Alarm-House. The blue flag would be hoisted, followed by the three cannon shots. In a matter of seconds a blue flag would be fluttering from every signal station on the island."

"Yes," affirmed Napoleon. "And what then?"

"You have over fifty people here now, sire, and every one of them would be outside. People living in this vicinity will be arriving—from Robinson's, from Legges, from the Orange Grove. From what we have learned of Sir Hudson Lowe, he will gallop up in mad haste, shouting orders as he comes. He will have half a dozen aides with him. At least a thousand of the troops will be alerted and ready to begin the search."

"You have pictured the scene accurately," said Napoleon, "and realistically, my dear Bertrand. Now, would anyone be likely to pay attention to the presence in this milling crowd of the American officers? Two of them, at least."

"It would be noted. But those in authority would be too busy in organizing the search parties to do anything about it. When you *are* found, it will seem unnecessary to do anything at once beyond restoring the sentry lines around the house."

"Inevitably," continued Napoleon, "one of the searchers will catch a glimpse of the familiar green coat. The figure of a man is lying prone on a ledge of rock beneath the road

175

where it runs through Geranium Valley. You must know the spot. There is a cover of trees there."

Bertrand nodded. "The explanation will be, no doubt, that you had gone out for a late walk and had stumbled over the edge. I know the exact spot for it. It isn't seen easily from above."

"Observe, Bertrand," declared Napoleon, with a satisfied smile, "how all their unnecessary precautions combine to help us. Everybody is so busy carrying out the instructions provided for such an emergency, that they are unable to notice more vital things. The body on the ledge is hauled to the surface by ropes, in an unconscious condition. He is carried to Longwood and in course of time recovers consciousness.

"Is it necessary for me to explain that the body recovered in this way is not that of Napoleon? It is, of course, Roberaud, his hair cut, his beard shaved, and dressed in one of my uniforms. He will have an unpleasant wait, I am afraid, for it will be necessary to lower him to the ledge at some time during the night."

There was a pause while Napoleon, his head resting in his hands, seemed to be sunk deep in thought. Then he looked up and smiled. "Now there is the other part of the plan. How am I to pass myself off as Roberaud and go aboard the ship?"

"I was wondering about that, sire."

"A discreet rumor will be spread through the house that evening that my life has been threatened. This will set the servants to talking and will serve to increase the excitement they display when I am reported gone the next morning. I will not go to bed and when the household is sleeping I will put on the wig and the beard and dress myself in Roberaud's clothes. Before dawn I will climb up through the hole in the ceiling in the library and conceal myself in the attic above, which is not occupied. Soon after dawn you will arrive and have Montholon wakened. You will tell him you haven't been able to sleep because of the story about the threats. The pair of you will knock on my bedroom door. When there is no answer, you will go in and find the room empty. The bed has not been slept in. Marchand will be summoned and will go through my clothes. He will find that one uniform is missing. All the servants are then aroused while Montholon goes out to tell the sentries that I am missing. You, Bertrand, will continue to wander about in the house and the gardens in a

176

distracted state of mind. If any of the servants remain, you will demand that they go out to aid in the search. Finally you will come in and let me know that the body has been sighted in the ravine and that everyone has rushed there to be as close as possible when the rescue is accomplished. I will then climb down from the attic and will slip out into the gardens. From there I will go outside and linger on the edge of the excited crowds. While the body is being carried up the road, I will join the two officers from the ship.

"By the time the blue flags fluttering all over the island have been furled up as a signal that Napoleon has been found, wounded but alive, the *three* American officers have taken to horse. They have just enough time left to ride to Jamestown and get aboard. Their belongings are on the wharf after having been thoroughly searched. Each of them is then subjected to a personal search. They then take the tender out to *The Flying Yankee*. They go aboard and so make their departure on *the fastest ship sailing the seven seas.*"

"It is my hope that Joseph has completed the building of his ingenious manor house," concluded Napoleon, "when we arrive in America. We must be safely located there before any serious suspicions arise as to the real identity of the prisoner at Longwood."

"Sire," said Bertrand, "I can foresee one difficulty only in the carrying out of this magnificent plan. There must be no difference in weight between you and the double."

"Trust the wily abbé to foresee that point. In the letter I have destroyed, he gave me Roberaud's weight and promised to see that he stays at the same size until we need him."

Bertrand gave an appraising glance at the figure of the exiled monarch. "Sire, it will be necessary to reduce your weight."

Napoleon nodded glumly. "I am aware of that. I must take off something in the neighborhood of twenty pounds."

"*Mais certes*, I shall miss Berthier tonight," said Napoleon, with a shake of his head. "I could dictate to him for hours and then go to sleep. When I wakened up, the writing of all the orders would be finished, the copies made, and dispatch riders would be posting in all directions. Never a wrong word, never a comma out of place. The man was a wonder. Of

177

course," he added, after a pause, "he was a simpleton in all other ways."

Bertrand had taken a small case from a pocket under his belt while they talked. He opened it now to reveal the presence inside of three small cigars. One of these he selected. Then, with a deep sigh, he replaced it, closed the case, and returned it to the pocket.

"There are no more on the island," he said dolefully.

"One of the most absurd things in life," declared Napoleon, "is a man smoking tobacco. In a year and a half you will be back in Paris. Surely by that time you will be cured of this silly habit."

"Never, sire, never! But—a year and a half! Will it take that long?"

"It is impossible to organize a new shipping line and build a ship on such revolutionary lines in less time. Yes, it will be a full year and a half before I can thumb my nose a second time at my English jailers. But now, to work. Make the whist game short this evening. I will need quiet in the house and security from prying eyes. Draw the curtains, Bertrand. I want no sentries staring in at me and wondering what is keeping me up so late."

"I will remain outside your door in the study until you are finished," declared the grand marshal.

"Is O'Meara still here?"

"No, the doctor left late this afternoon."

"Then have a glass of wine sent in with one of those abominable pills of his."

When he was alone Napoleon picked up a pen. "Ah, Berthier, Berthier!" he said to himself. "How much I need you tonight!"

2

Bertrand awakened with a sense of guilt. He had been sleeping on a lumpy sofa, his head on a backboard of elaborately carved wood, his feet stretched out in front of him. He rose stiffly and went to a window to raise the curtain. The sun was up and climbing above the eastern ridges.

"It must be seven or even later," he muttered.

A glance at a small clock on the wall confirmed the guess. Bertrand, who had intended to remain awake all night, went

178

on cautious feet to the door leading into the bedroom. A sound of rustling paper reassured him. Napoleon was awake. He rapped with his knuckles on the door.

"Come in."

Apparently Napoleon had just completed his task. A pile of paper sheets, covered with small handwriting, lay on the table in front of him. The last of the candles was on the point of guttering out. All the biscuits were gone.

The emperor had discarded his shoes. His face was the gray of complete exhaustion.

"Bertrand," he said, in a tone little above a whisper. "I am finished. The plan is without a flaw. I have gone over it a dozen times, and see nothing wrong in it."

A feeling of confidence took possession of the marshal and he nodded his head eagerly.

"Of course, sire."

"The question now faces us of getting these notes into the hands of the abbé. I know you are finding it easy enough to get letters out but that won't do now. The only safe means is to have one of our company return to France and take the notes with him."

"Yes, sire. We can't trust to the easy ways with this." He paused in thought. "Gourgaud?"

"No!" said Napoleon emphatically. "His jealousies have warped his mind. I don't trust him any more. He would make some outrageous mistake. No, Bertrand, I have the man. Piontkowski."

"Piontkowski! No, sire. I don't believe we can trust him. Where did he come from? What is he doing on this island? Where does he get his money from and why do the English give him a free hand? All of us are convinced he's an English spy."

Napoleon brushed this side. "I know where he comes from. I know what he's doing on this island. I know where he gets his money. The English give him a free hand because they think he's acting as a spy for them."

"What you say astonishes me, sire. I had no idea you were responsible for his coming here."

"Piontkowski is a dedicated man. He has been spreading the word that his father is dying in Brussels. That is sufficient reason for him to ask permission to leave. All this, Bertrand, is according to the plan we made."

"You relieve my mind, sire. I have been much concerned about his presence here."

"When I have had some sleep and my mind is fresh, I will devise some way in which he can conceal these sheets in his belongings so they won't be found." Napoleon yawned. "That will not be hard."

"I will take the papers, Your Imperial Majesty, while you get some rest."

Napoleon nodded. He rose and stumbled across the room on stockinged feet. He fell on the bed and in a matter of seconds was sound asleep.

Without raising the curtains, Bertrand gathered up the papers. Footsteps could now be heard from the direction of the kitchen, and a low murmur of talk. An English voice, raised in sharp interrogation, made it clear that a sentry was close at hand. The marshal buttoned his tunic over the papers before proceeding out through the pillared portico.

Chapter Five

1

Under a heavy head of sail, H.M.S. *Phaeton* came majestically into the roadstead, to be welcomed with a salvo from Alarm-House. It was on an afternoon in mid-May and the quay was black with spectators. The yamstocks (as the native-born were called) nodded their heads with satisfaction and said among themselves that the cargo would be a heavy one and there would be pay for all of them in the handling of it. The merchants, the officials of the port, and the officers of the garrison, who were wedged in the crowd, spoke of the man who was arriving.

"I don't look forward to what's going to happen, Betsy," said William Balcombe to his daughter, who was holding his arm. "We've been getting hints from many sources about this man. He'll be difficult to get along with. Especially for me. I'll be between two fires."

"The emperor will be watching through his army glasses," said Besty. "Through the shutters. I'm afraid, Papa, it's going to be *very* difficult for him."

"I hear this man advised the government to pass a law, making it a criminal offence for anyone on the island to hold communication with Napoleon. That gives you an idea of him."

The winter season was setting in and the eastern trades were providing a taste of the bitterness which later would turn noses blue and send shivers down thinly covered spines. The sea, gray and menacing, was rolling in with rumbling hostility against the rocky shores. Betsy covered her face for a moment with the stylish little muff she wore on one wrist and said to her father, "Papa, it's *terribly* cold."

She stood on the tips of her toes to watch the longboat come slowly in to shore. The new governor was now plain to be seen, with feathers in his hat and orders blazing on his uniform. When his party fell into line behind him, he led the way up to the landing and with a wave of his arm demanded that a path be cleared for him. He then walked straight ahead, two full paces ahead of his rather buxom wife.

"He has bad manners, Papa," whispered Betsy.

Sir Hudson Lowe passed within a few yards of where she stood, and so Betsy had a good look at him, noting his proud air and the aloof expression in his eyes. His hair was a light red and his eyelashes were almost white. The severity of his features was accentuated by a large and dark blemish on one cheek.

His strutting figure was followed, first, by Lady Lowe. She was not a handsome woman but her figure was good in a somewhat large way. She glanced about her cheerfully and seemed interested in everything. Betsy heard her say to her husband, "Please, Huddy, not so fast."

"She uses rouge," thought Betsy, considering it a foolish thing for a woman of her age, and even rather sinful for young women. The half dozen officers who came next were all alike, young and stiff-backed and with set expressions. Even their mustaches seemed to bristle with inner austerity. They made Betsy think of a set of wooden soldiers she had possessed once. She began to smile.

Admiral Cockburn met the newcomers at the end of the dock and there was much bowing and shaking of hands. Betsy kept her eyes on the new governor and she observed with inner qualms that he never smiled. He was, clearly enough, carried away by the importance of his new post.

"M'sieur Balcombe," said Count Bertrand, coming up through the press of spectators. "This is—er, fortunate. Mam'selle Betsy, how well you look."

The two men faced each other for several moments in silence. It was easy for them to exchange the thoughts aroused by this first glimpse of the new controller of the island without either uttering another word. Both had been appalled by the stiffness of the governor's manner, the bleakness of his eyes.

Bertrand then spoke to Betsy in a whisper and she translated what he had said for her father. "He asks, Papa, if there would be any objection if he took me home for tonight. Madame Bertrand is not feeling well and he thinks it would rouse her spirits if she had someone to talk with. He will drive me back in the morning."

William Balcombe smiled and nodded. "Of course, Betsy. I guess we can spare you that long."

A few minutes later she climbed into the small carriage which served to convey the Bertrand family about the island. She ensconced herself on the back seat beside the count, grateful that her mother had permitted her to dress in her best for this occasion. The months which had elapsed were reflected in her costume. Gone were the obnoxious pantalettes which Napoleon had derided, and gone also was the almost styleless simplicity which Mrs. Balcombe had so rigidly decreed for her. Over a blue dress, raising its ruffles above the collar, she was wearing a gray redingote with the largest and handsomest of buttons and even some trim blue frogs which were positively gay. The muff on her wrist was almost adult.

"I'm so glad you want me, Count Bertrand," she said, cheerfully. "We're having company for dinner tonight. The ladies talk all the time, and the men are mild-looking old coots with big, limp mustaches and they never say anything but, 'We can't be too severe with Bonaparte.' They'll be singing the praises of the new governor. Then, of course, the Rev. Curate Stodgkin will be there and he can cast a shadow over any evening. Did you ever feel when you were young that it was pleasant sometimes not to stay at home?"

Bertrand nodded. "Many times, mam'selle."

2

Hutt's Gate was a frame house with something of the compactness of a sentry box, and the room in which Betsy spent the night was under a slanted roof which made it almost triangular in shape. It had room for a bed and practically nothing else. The conversation during the evening had been concerned almost entirely with Napoleon, and Betsy's interest had been so deeply engaged that her dreams, when she fell asleep, were exclusively of battles and sieges and fast marches. She dreamed finally that a French army was advancing into some strange and hostile country and that Napoleon rode in the van while she was beating a drum in the band which followed at his heels. It was an exciting experience and she brought forth a loud tattoo which served to drown out all the other drummers. Finally the army came to a halt and the sound of approaching horsemen could be heard. They were riding at full speed and it was clear they were bringing important information. They arrived quickly, the horses lathered and the riders breathless. Napoleon listened to them with a deep frown and then turned in her direction. "Mam'selle Balcombe, step forward!" When she obeyed, the emperor said to her, "Betsee, I have received disturbing news and I want your opinion as to what I should do under the circumstances." At that point she wakened up.

At first she could not be sure she was fully awake because the sound of horses' hoofs still filled her ears. In the light which entered the room through a small dormer window, she could make out the arm of a chair over which she had hung her dress and other articles of clothing. Thus she realized she was in bed and that the army of her dream had vanished, Napoleon and all. She sat up and listened, the blankets drawn up close around her neck.

"Someone," she thought, "is riding up the Longwood Road. This is very strange. Why are they coming here at this time of night?" A disturbing thought took possession of her. "Are they coming to take Napoleon away?"

It was contrary to Betsy's nature to remain quiescent in the face of a situation such as this. She sprang from bed and with shuddering haste stepped into her slippers. Then she wrapped the redingote about her, grateful for the warmth it afforded. It was only a step to the window and she peered down at the road.

It was a clear night and the moon, almost directly overhead, stared down at her with unfriendly and cold scrutiny. "This is no concern of yours, silly child," it seemed to say. "But it is," she said to herself, still under the spell of her dream. The riders were quite close now and were covering the ground at a full gallop.

The next moment Betsy recognized the man who rode in the lead. It was Sir Hudson Lowe! "I *am* asleep," she said aloud. "What would he be doing out here?"

But the moon was making everything as clear as day and there was no mistaking the stern outline of the man's features nor the intentness with which he was gazing straight ahead. This, without any doubt, was the proud and solemn general who had come ashore that afternoon with so much state. He had dressed himself in a great hurry, for the military tunic on his back had been pulled on over what clearly were civilian trousers. The young officer who followed two lengths behind

184

was fully dressed and his mustaches protruded from his cheeks like yellow spikes. Betsy gained the impression that the attendant had no idea where he was going or why.

Hearing footsteps below, Betsy lighted a candle and made her way down a narrow stairway which squeaked and shook with every step. The count was standing at a window. He had donned an elaborate black and orange dressing gown but he had neglected to spread what hair remained to him over the round bald spot on the top of his head.

"So, they've wakened you also," he commented, turning around. "I hoped you wouldn't hear and would sleep right through like my wife."

Looking at her in the dim light of the candles, he indulged in a frown of surprise. The redingote was buttoned up snugly under her chin and this gave her face the clear-cut delicacy of a cameo. It was her hair, however, which drew his attention. It was a mop of golden curls which lost nothing from the unruliness of the pillow. "Egad, I've never seen a handsomer head of hair in my life," he thought.

"M'sieur, what is going on?" asked Betsy.

"I have no inkling. I managed to get a glimpse of the semaphore. It gives no hint of anything wrong."

"I know who it is," said Betsy.

"Ah," said the marshal in a relieved tone. "Then it's just some of the islanders out on a midnight spree?"

"No, m'sieur. It's Sir Hudson Lowe. He has an officer with him."

The jaw of the grand marshal fell open at this announcement. "Really, mam'selle, I'm certain you are mistaken." He held up the candle so the light fell on the clock over the toy-sized mantelpiece. The hands pointed to three-thirty. "Why would he be riding to Longwood at this hour of the night?"

"But I saw him so plainly!"

Loud voices now reached them from the direction of Longwood. After much vehement talk, the voices began to diminish in volume, leaving the impression that the two riders had started a tour of the grounds.

Bertrand sighed at the duty which his position thrust upon him. "Sir Hudson Lowe or not, I shall have to dress and go over at once," he said. "You must get back to bed, mam'selle, or you'll catch a very bad cold. If Madame Bertrand wakens, please tell her where I have gone."

So Betsy turned and retraced her steps. The count's doubts

had not disturbed her certainty that it was the new governor of the island who had ridden by. In a few minutes she heard footsteps below and the slam of a door. She looked out and saw Count Bertrand emerge, fully dressed. He turned in the direction of Longwood at a run.

It was so cold in her room that she had to snuggle down under the robes and nature quickly asserted itself. She went back to sleep.

At breakfast she was greeted by a grave host. Madame Bertrand, behind a steaming coffeepot, smiled cordially at the young guest; but it was clear she had not taken in the full purport of the night's happenings. The Bertrand children had not roused yet, but their dog, who was called Tom Pipes, sat on the floor at Betsy's corner of the table and wagged an expectant tail.

"Well, Betsy, you were right," said the count. "It *was* Sir Hudson Lowe. We've had a demonstration which makes me fear what the future holds for us. This man is incredible! It seems he went to sleep and dreamed that Napoleon had escaped. He wakened with a start and was convinced it was more than a dream, that Napoleon *had* escaped. So he threw on some clothes and rushed out, bellowing for a horse. They brought horses around and he rode off like a madman with one attendant to see if what he had dreamed could be true."

"How very strange of him to do that," commented the countess.

"I am glad you can take it so calmly," said the count. "The pair of them rode through the sentry lines and the governor knocked on one of the doors loud enough to waken the dead. A footman came to the door finally. 'I must see your master,' said the governor. 'I must see him with my own eyes. I must be convinced he has not escaped. And I'll have no excuses or subterfuges or denials.'"

Bertrand went on: "Ah, that good Montholon, he is a great sleeper! He came out, rubbing his eyes. 'Now, then, what in the name of Tophet is all this?' He was informed that it was Sir Hudson Lowe. *'Sapristi!'* he said, 'So it is.'"

The count replaced the hot roll on which he had been munching. It was apparent he had lost all appetite. "It must have been a strange scene. Montholon blocked the door and the governor flew into a furious rage. I verily believe he has a mad streak in him. Montholon says he rolled his eyes and waved his arms and gestured wildly when told the emperor was asleep and could not be disturbed. 'But I am Sir Hudson Lowe!' he kept repeating. 'If I am not admitted at once, I shall call up the sentries and force my way in!' Montholon told him there were fifteen armed men in the house and they were under orders to shoot anyone who tried to invade the emperor's suite. 'I must be convinced he is inside!' cried the governor. 'I can't sleep until my mind is at rest. If he isn't here, I must rouse the whole island and run him to earth!'"

"What did our poor Montholon say to that?" asked the countess.

"He showed good presence of mind. Did the governor, he asked, want to create an international scandal by the violent measures he proposed? That cooled the English general off a little and he then asked to know if the emperor had received a notification that he was calling there this morning? The letter had been received but it was addressed to General Bonaparte, so Montholon said, No, the letter had not come to hand. 'Inform him then,' said the Englishman through gritted teeth, 'that I shall be on hand for the appointment.'"

Countess Bertrand seemed very much disturbed at this recital. "I find it hard to believe," she said. "Henri, you will need the tact of a Talleyrand, in dealing with this man."

Betsy was making no pretence of eating her breakfast. "What time is the call to be made?" she asked.

"At nine."

The girl looked up at the clock. Twenty minutes to nine! "Please, madame, may I be excused?" she asked.

Betsy ran up to her room and hastily donned her cloak and hat. The beat of raindrops on the windowpanes announced that a fitful shower was beginning. It seemed to her that Longwood, with its shoddy additions and streaked walls, had never looked more dismal. Then she caught a glimpse of a distant sentry pacing a beat in front of the house. There was a familiarity about the lines of his back and the way he carried a musket over his shoulder.

"I think it's Private Knock," she said to herself. "How very lucky!"

The countess looked up when the girl came down the stairs. "I don't believe, Betsy, you can be driven home as early as this," she said.

"I am going to Longwood. And I can walk."

The fine dark eyes of the countess showed real concern at

this. "But, child, do you think that wise? The emperor won't see anyone. He will be in one of his tempers, you know."

"Yes, I understand that. It's why I want to go."

"You mean"—the countess was really disturbed now—"you mean you intend to *speak* to him?"

"Yes, madame. He should be warned about the kind of man he's dealing with. If he refuses to see him a second time— and in a rain like this—there will be serious trouble. Don't you agree?"

"I do indeed. My husband and I talked about it and he told me he was very much worried."

"May I ask if he has spoken to the emperor?"

The countess glanced anxiously over her shoulder at the door through which the count had disappeared a few minutes before. "No, he said nothing. You see, the emperor has refused to speak. He has been sitting in his studio and he has that—that look in his eyes."

Betsy said to herself: "They are all afraid of him." Aloud she asked, "Hasn't anyone urged him to—to be sensible and see the governor?"

"I don't think so."

Betsy turned toward the door. "Then I must try. Please don't tell the count. He would probably refuse to let me go."

"He most certainly would. Now, Betsy, remember this: this is all your idea and you have *not* spoken to me."

It was not difficult to get through the sentry lines. Betsy had been right in believing she recognized Private Knock. He whistled in surprise when he saw her running toward him through the rain.

"Gal-go-rarily!" he said. "Nah, then, miss, what are ye up to here?"

"It *is* Private Knock isn't it?" asked Betsy, stopping to peer in his direction. "I thought I recognized you but I couldn't be sure in this light. In fact, I can't see much of anything."

He looked at her in surprise for a moment. Then his face took on a broad grin and he winked at her.

"Comin' to think on it, miss, it *is* hard to see anythin' in this banging weather." He wheeled about in readiness to return down the stretch of ground he was patrolling. "I didn't see ye, miss. I didn't see nobuddy. I didn't hear nuffink!"

this, first child, do you think that wise? The emperor will
see anyone. He will be in one of his tempers, you know."

Napoleon was in his study and sitting in doubtful ease in a
chair with a broken back and creaking legs when Cipriani announced a visitor.

"Mam'selle Balcombe, Your Highness. She insisted on having me say she wants to see you."

The emperor hastily removed the red flannel cap which he
sometimes wore on his head at night and secreted it under
some books. He shoved his feet into carpet slippers.

"Show Mam'selle Balcombe in, Cipriani."

The chief usher looked very much surprised. "Show her in,
Your Highness?"

"That is what I said. But, Cipriani, the prohibition stands
as far as all members of the household are concerned. I shall
see no one else!"

Betsy hesitated at the threshold, suddenly uncertain as to
what she should say. Napoleon straightened up in his chair
and smiled on her.

"Ah, Betsee. Is it that you were at Hutt's Gate last night
and they told you I was not seeing anyone?"

"Yes, sire."

"That was unfortunate. If you had come to see me, it would
have relieved the tedium of a very solemn evening. Madame
Montholon tried to sing some gay songs from her youth but
her voice is much better suited to dirges. The eminent and
erudite Las Cases talked interminably about the fifteenth-
century poets, a subject on which his ignorance is appalling.
It got so trying I even regretted the absence of Gourgaud."
He gazed at her with an expression halfway between a squint
and a frown. "You have come, of course, to give me some
advice."

Betsy smiled in turn. "Sire, I am a very great nuisance."

"You are going to tell me I must see this leader of Corsican renegades when he calls this morning. Am I right? You
are going to say also that I should be polite to him."

"Yes, sire. You always know what I am going to say, don't
you?"

This pleased him. "Certes, Betsee, don't you think I know
what is going on in that little head of yours? You have a notion these people of mine are afraid to speak up and tell me
things."

"Yes, sire. You put on your grimmest look—and oh, how

189

forbidding it is!—and they curl up when it comes to telling you some truth for your own good. Just as I am now."

"You were right once. About my weight. But this time, *ma petite*, you are wrong. I must not make the mistake of unbending at the start. This fellow has the instincts of a mongrel pup. He snaps and snarl and whines. I must treat him as the poor-souled underling that he is in reality."

"But, sire—"

"Say nothing more, Betsee. My mind is made up. I do not intend to receive him today."

He reached for an envelope on the table beside him. "Observe. This is the letter he sent me. It is addressed to 'General Bonaparte.' When your absurd Englishman comes it will be handed back to him. He will be told there is no longer a General Bonaparte. He ceased to exist eighteen years ago when I became First Consul; but the glory he won for France will never be forgotten."

He reached up and pulled a bell cord on the wall. When the usher appeared he was handed the letter. "For the Count Montholon, Cipriani. Inform him I have not changed my mind. He is to use the *exact words* I gave him in returning it to the sender."

Napoleon then gave his attention to Besty with an air that was almost bland. "So, *ma petite*, it is settled. Don't disturb yourself about it any more."

"But, sire, everyone is afraid of what may happen if you refuse to receive him. They say he will turn quarrelsome and domineering. He will cause you pain and inconvenience."

The contour of the emperor's face seemed to change. A deep wrinkle showed in his forehead and his jaw seemed to project itself at a belligerent angle. "Have you any idea how quarrelsome and domineering I can be? Betsee, I can be unpleasant enough to make a puny fellow like this shrivel up and crawl back into his shell."

His manner reverted almost immediately. He even smiled at her.

"You are a foolish child. There you sit and I swear there are tears in your eyes. You are not true to the English breed, my Betsee, because you are sentimental and the English have no sentiment in them at all. They are grasping and hard." He studied her for a moment. "How old are you now?"

"I am fifteen, sire."

"And yet you remind me of Madame Mère, my mother.

She was always worrying about me. A dozen times she came to me and protested that I was going too far, that I would pull down the whole international house of cards about my ears. I would laugh at her—and then proceed to show her she was wrong. She was right just once and that was about Russia. She begged me not to lead the Grand Army into that country of swamps and snowstorms and human savages." He indulged in a short laugh. "And now I have a mentor and critic of fifteen to tell me I am wrong. I swear you remind me of her, sitting there in such a state. And yet she was old and wrinkled and you are young and not at all unattractive."

There was a sound of horses' hoofs on the road leading to the Longwood boundaries. Napoleon got to his feet abruptly.

"Here they are, Betsee. Now we shall have a first test of wills between us. Do not look so worried. *Ma foi*, I know what I am doing."

The blinds were drawn over the two windows which looked out on the garden. He went to one of them and raised the edge a cautious inch. After several moments of observation, he said. "He rides in state, your brave Sir Hudson Lowe. Six, seven, no, eight, officers are with him. All in full uniform. The rain is beginning to give them a bedraggled look." There was a long pause. "He has a most disagreeable face. A man of little capacity and understanding who doesn't know his own limitations. The hardest kind of all to handle. I can see from the look of him that he's mean, driveling, spiteful, and conceited. Yes, I shall have trouble with this weakling."

The riders had turned in and had pulled up at the portico. The listeners in the study heard Count Montholon at the door and then a declaration delivered in a high and rasping voice. Other voices joined in but through all the talk which followed the one strident voice seemed never to stop. "I am Sir Hudson Lowe!" it said. "And I have come to speak with General Bonaparte!"

The emperor turned and smiled grimly at Betsy. "Am I supposed to run out and abase myself before this absurd fellow? *Mon Dieu*, I have never in all my life disliked anyone so much at first glance. I do not intend to recede an inch."

The debate on the portico came to an end and the emperor watched the party start on foot on a tour of the grounds about the sprawling house. The rain was falling heavily now. The feathers which had stood up so proudly on cocked hats began to droop. Cloaks had been donned to protect the well-ironed uniforms. All the faces showed bad temper and a suppressed desire to indulge in some retaliatory violence.

Napoleon left his post behind the window blind and returned to his chair, with a suggestion of a dance step in his gait. He looked at Betsy and said, "Well, my policy of firmness seems to have been effective." Then he sprang to his feet again and produced a bottle of wine from under the table. Without summoning help, he found two glasses and filled them halfway. Into one he poured water from a carafe.

"Do you like water in your wine, as I do?"

"Yes, sire."

"You are a sensible child. Is this wine to your taste?"

The girl, after taking a sip, found herself under the necessity of returning a frank answer. "Not much, sire. It seems to me rather sour."

"It *is* sour. I don't like it myself. But this, *ma petite*, is a special wine that a friend sends me from Spain. This is the second lot I have had from him. I think we should drink a toast. To the Future which may not be as bleak as the Present! Do you believe that possible, Betsee,"

"Yes, sire, yes!"

"You must not underestimate me, my little friend. I am still Napoleon. I have it here," touching his brow, "and here," his hand moving to his heart, "to reverse the situation in which an unkind fate has placed me. A world filled with bumptious nonentities like your Sir Hudson Lowe will not be able to keep me here."

The visiting party, more damp and belligerent than before, returned to the portico where they sought shelter from the steady downpour. Napoleon returned to his watching post. A bristling argument began among the members of the governor's party. Fists were shaken at the unseen occupants of the locked house.

"They are walking back to their horses," reported the emperor, after several moments. "They will be half drowned before they reach shelter again."

He stepped back from the window and this time he did execute a not too expert imitation of a ballet step.

"The first battle has been fought and won!" he said, jubilantly. "Come, take that gloomy look off your face. Are you still frightened?"

"But, sire," said Betsy, "because you have won this battle, you may have to fight a great many more."

192

"Then I shall win them all."

The rain stopped with an unexpectedness which the most experienced of the yamstock could not have foreseen. Even in the dark, shuttered rooms of Longwood, it was clear that the sun was winning its struggle to appear.

"You must go now," said the emperor. "Will there be any difficulty in getting back through the sentry lines?"

"I think not, sire. I am rather good at playing Indian."

"Come back soon, Betsee. I miss you when you stay away. And I must begin your lessons in the honorable game of billiards."

When Betsy came out from the study a feminine figure appeared through the door at the other end of the darkened dining room. It took a moment or two to identify Madame Montholon, dressed in a short-waisted dress of green bombazine. This was a most fashionable material but rather thin for the chilly interior of the house. It had been necessary to wrap a shawl of silvery sheen over her shoulders.

"You have been speaking to His Highness?" asked the countess. "You are honored above all of us. He refused to see me, and even my husband and the impatient Count Bertrand are waiting for a word with him. Did he ask your opinion as to what he should do?"

"Certainly not, madame. His mind was made up."

"He took the course I would have urged," declared the countess. "But, I expect he would not have listened to me. I would have told him that the less we have to do with the English, the better off we will be." She paused and regarded the girl with sharp hostility. "From what we hear, no one will be allowed to visit us much in future. If at all. I suspect you won't like that."

"No, madame. I won't like it."

The countess turned back toward the door through which she had entered. She gave her skirts a flounce.

"I will, " she declared.

Chapter Six

1

William Balcombe turned into the extensive grounds which surrounded Plantation House. He was in a far from cheerful mood. The note he had received from a secretary of Sir Hudson Lowe, summoning him to a discussion, had been curt and even unfriendly.

He was so certain that a difficult interview lay ahead of him that he had no eyes for the beauty of the home of the governors of St. Helena. Plantation House was a large white building of two stories with wings on each side. At this period of the year, late autumn in the island, the extensive beds of flowers were not at their most prolific, but the trees, which had been intelligently spaced about the house, seemed to be in full leaf and bloom. He had always been impressed by the remarkable way in which trees imported from England had grown in close proximity to those indigenous to the island. There were actually oaks, rearing their noble heads far above everything else save a few pines whose green peaks stood three hundred feet in the air. There were rows of chestnuts, and splendid cedars and poplars, as well as a few beeches and birch trees. Nature's instinct for color and design had never before been displayed so remarkably; for these trees, as rugged as the men of the island from which they came, had blended in both design and color with the more florid exhibits of the East—the banyans, the tamarinds, the cocoa trees, the sassafras. When he had taken possession of the Briars, he had striven to emulate this mingling of the nobility of the North with the flamboyance of the East. And in a minor way he had succeeded.

But on this occasion he saw everything with a preoccupied eye. He did not even pause to observe the line of tall black men who made their way in a line across the wide green lawns in front of the house, plying their scythes in skillful

194

and unceasing unison. He was barely aware that their number had been increased. Had he counted, he would have found that there were twenty-eight.

The offices of the governor were in one of the wings and so Balcombe took a side entrance. The heels of the footman who admitted him clicked sharply on the hardwood floor. The man carried himself with swaggering self-importance.

"Bulkum?" he said, in peculiarly thickened tones, "His Excellency will see you soon." He pointed to a hard wooden bench. "Sit down, Bulkum."

"Thank you," said William Balcombe. "I wish to point out there's a word in the English language, one which everyone uses all the time, but with which nevertheless you seem to be unfamiliar. I refer to the word 'mister.' "

The footman stared at him with an air which made it certain the point of the remark had been lost on him. "Uh," he said.

Balcombe (for authors must make free with proper names) knew there were five footmen in the household and an infinity of other servants. The rest, he hoped, were more intelligent and polite than this one; but it hardly seemed likely in this house of forty rooms.

The anteroom had walls paneled in oak and a red-brick fireplace just a little murky in shade from years of use. Here he sat and waited, catching glimpses through converging halls of the long white-walled concert room at the other end of the house. A prophetic sense would have told him that within a few years, a ship sailing from London to Australia, where he would fill the post of treasurer of the province of New South Wales, would put ashore at St. Helena, and that he would be given a suite of rooms on the floor immediately above this most imposing of reception rooms.

As he sat there he said to himself, "While at Plantation House one should give no thought to the conditions at Longwood."

Sir Hudson Lowe, who had succeeded by this time in confronting Napoleon twice and been exposed on both occasions to furious blasts of complaint, was seated at an expansive and beautiful walnut desk. It may have been that his face had a drawn look about the eyes and there could be no doubt that his manner had become more abrupt and testy.

"Bring Balcombe in," he said to one of his minor secretaries. The top of his desk was a model of neatness but he nervously rearranged some piles of papers while waiting for his visitor to appear.

"Follow me, Balcombe," said the secretary when he reached the anteroom. "His Excellency will see you now."

Their footsteps as they walked to the governor's office were echoed by other heels at the main entrance. Lady Lowe had returned from a drive with her two children by a former marriage and a bevy of nieces and nephews. They had been to the Devil's Punch Bowl and were still exclaiming about the awesomeness of it.

Lowe had selected a pen and was engaged in a pretence of industry which made it impossible for him to look up at once. A full two minutes elapsed before he raised his eyes.

"Ah, Balcombe," he said. "I think perhaps you had better sit down. We have many matters to discuss."

"Yes, Your Excellency," said the visitor, taking a chair.

The governor looked at him sharply from under his reddish brows. "Balcombe," he said, "you have been in close contact with Bonaparte from the first day of his arrival."

"Necessarily. It had been arranged that the firm I represent would supply his household with what was needed."

"It has been reported to me that you have been on a most friendly basis with him. You and your family."

"He was a guest in my house for over two months," was Balcombe's quiet response.

"This must stop! From now on, Balcombe, things must be kept on a purely business basis—prompt, precise, and to the point. Is that understood?"

"It will be difficult to replace friendliness with incivility. If that is what you want."

"I said nothing about incivility. But it may come to that. Are you aware that a law will be passed making it illegal, perhaps even an indictable offense, to have any relationship with Bonaparte and his train beyond the bounds of commercial exchange?"

William Balcombe glanced up. "Has this become law, Your Excellency?"

"Not yet. But it will. I have recommended it. Most emphatically. If you are to continue as purveyor, you must be prepared to place all dealings on a strictly business basis."

A silence ensued which Sir Hudson Lowe filled by a nervous turning over of the documents in front of him. Finally he produced a sheet and spread it out with an air which carried a hint of intimidation.

"I have here," he said, "your latest report on the goods supplied to Longwood and the total cost. I find it preposterous. A total of four thousand pounds for a half year. Which the British Government must pay. Eight thousand pounds a year! Something must be done about this absurd state of affairs."

"He has a large household. There are twenty-three attendants and servants from France. Then there are a number of Italians, Elbans, Poles, and Swiss. About forty people in all."

"Preposterous!" repeated the governor.

Balcombe would have liked to ask how many servants were employed at Plantation House and if it were true that his personal salary was twelve thousand pounds a year but a sense of caution restrained him. He contented himself with pointing out that living costs had been climbing steadily on the island, due in part to the few ships now stopping there.

Lowe did not discuss this point. He placed the tip of a stubby forefinger on one item. "The wine!" he exclaimed. "The amount they consume daily is incredible."

"The French, sir, are great wine drinkers."

"Must the merest valet or kitchen helper have more than one bottle a day?"

"Surely that is not excessive. We have in England, sir, many three-, four-, and even five-bottle men."

"Sir," exclaimed Sir Hudson Lowe, his face becoming suffused with anger, "I will not permit any mention in this discussion of the habits of English gentlemen! A subject, may I say, on which you are in no position to speak."

All suggestion of amiability deserted in turn the face of William Balcombe. He answered in an angry voice. "You compel me to point out that I spent some years of my youth at Carleton House and I then became an officer in the Royal Navy. I have had more opportunity than anyone at present on this island—*anyone, Your Excellency*—to learn at first hand and to participate in the habits of English gentlemen!"

The governor was too angry at first to make any response. His eyes emitted sparks of rage and his lips were more tightly clamped than before.

"There is no point to such discussion between us," he said, finally. "I summoned you here to consider the extravagance which is being shown in the provisioning of this household.

The yearly cost must not exceed six thousand pounds from this time on."

"Have you suggestions to make as to how these economies are to be effected?"

"There is no need for him to have so many people about him. The first step will be to send some of them back to France, or wherever they come from. But that is no concern of yours. You are the grocer, and on that head I have some definite ideas. We will reduce the number of bottles of wine provided daily. Less expensive brands must be sleected." His forefinger progressed down the page. "And this item. Butter. Their food must positively swim in butter. Supply them with less and buy only butter of poorer quality. And now this about bread. Is it necessary to build costly ovens so fancy kinds of French bread can be baked every day?"

"They are very particular about bread, sir."

Lowe tossed his pen in the air and jumped to his feet. He began to pace about the room.

"Let them eat English bread!" he cried.

2

The discussion of supplies for Longwood continued for half an hour or more. The lips of the governor remained firmly clamped throughout the long debate and his eyes glinted, glowered or blazed in accordance with the various antagonistic moods which gripped him in turn. He seemed to hold William Balcombe responsible for the eating habits of the emperor's people. "You must restrain yourself," he said, in discussing the consumption of beef. "Clearly you are the worst kind of spendthrift, Balcombe," he declared more than once. "I shall have to put restraints on you."

Finally a temporary solution was arrived at. The governor himself would discuss with Count Bertrand the selection of members of the Bonapartist staff to be sent back to Europe. Balcombe would contrive somehow to inject economies into the purchase of supplies.

While the talk progressed, the visitor had allowed his eyes to observe certain changes in the room which had been made since the new governor arrived. The large portrait of King George III remained in the place of honor over the fireplace and his gaze lingered there for some time with a display of feeling it would be hard to define. A rather good portrait of Clive had been moved to an obscure corner to make room for a member of the present Cabinet. Balcombe decided it must be Lord Bathurst who now served as Minister for the Colonies and who, he knew, was Sir Hudson Lowe's chief sponsor. There was also a picture, a recent one, of the Duke of Wellington; and he found it hard not to smile as he wondered if it would remain when word reached the governor of the great general's description of him.

Everything about the room, the furnishings, the hangings on the long windows, the silver candles in wall sconces, the thick-piled carpet which prevented any sound, bespoke elegance.

The visitor could not prevent himself from indulging in a reflection arising from this show of grandeur. "If all the furnishings at Longwood were put up for sale, they would be lucky to get twenty pounds for the lot."

He rose to his feet, having no desire to prolong the discussion but Lowe motioned him with a hint of impatience to resume his chair.

"There is another matter, Balcombe. A most important one in my opinion. You, of course, have not seen this." He handed across the desk a clipping from an English newspaper.

William Balcombe took it and, with the first sentence he read, his figure stiffened and his face reflected incredulity and an intense dismay. He read it all slowly. Then he laid the clipping back on the desk with a hand which trembled.

"This is an outrage!" he exclaimed. "Montchenu has been here as the representative of France for a few months only. He has never been in my house. He has never spoken to either of my daughters. I believe Napoleon has refused to see him. This is viciously false from beginning to end. General Bonaparte's attitude to my two daughters has been that of—well, perhaps of an affectionate uncle. To say he has been carrying on an affair with my youngest daughter, who is no more than fifteen years, is the blackest of lies!"

He got to his feet. The flush with which he had read the printed story had been replaced by the pallor of deep anger. "I intend to call him out. Two friends of mine will see him at once and deliver my challenge."

"You will do nothing of the kind," declared Lowe. "If you had exercised the proper control over the conduct of your

199

daughters, this could not have happened. But since it has happened, I do not intend to let you spread the story in the press of the world by fighting a duel with the Marquis de Montchenu. I want the story to subside. It must not appear to the outside world that there is a sentiment in the island favorable to Bonaparte. The only course to pursue is to say nothing."

Balcombe looked him steadily in the eye. "My daughter's honor has been besmirched by this lying Frenchman. I, and I alone, must be the judge of what is to be done."

"You do not understand—" began Sir Hudson Lowe, in a tone denoting intense annoyance.

"It is you who do not understand," declared Betsy's father. "It is my daughter who has suffered at the hands of this miserable scribbler. The decision rests with me."

"Sir!" cried the governor, now aroused to a degree of intense passion. "I represent the Crown. I want to hear nothing more from you. And I want obedience to my decision."

"This is a matter of personal honor. What anyone else thinks is a matter of no consequence to me."

"You dare say this to my face?"

"Yes, Your Excellency. I intend to call the man out unless he retracts publicly the lies he has put in print."

Lowe snorted loudly. "He will refuse to meet you. He is a member of the French aristocracy and he has had military training. What chance would a grocer have against him?"

"I also had military training and it may interest you to know that I'm a good hand with the pistol."

"Well, he will refuse to meet you."

"If he does, I'll horsewhip him publicly. If we do meet, it will give me great pleasure to place a bullet between the eyes of this French cur." He bowed stiffly and turned to leave the room. "I bid you good day, Mr. Governor."

Balcombe disappeared as a great clock in the hall with musical chimes began to strike the hour of eleven. It was not until silence settled down again that Lowe called across the room to his adjutant who sat at a desk slightly less imposing than his own.

"I shall have to get rid of that fellow."

Mantee Timms had received his instructions once only. And so at five o'clock he stood at the mounting post at Plantation House with his master's latest equine favorite, Monmouth. The footman who has already been alluded to came out and scowled.

"Who for?" he asked.

"Mist' Ba'come."

"Bulkum? He's gone. He left at eleven this morning."

At this moment William Balcombe was standiing in front of his office in town, and looking about in vain for his horse and his man. He was inexpressibly weary and the prospect of walking home did not appeal to him at all. It did not take him long to realize that he had no alternative. While beginning stiffly to exercise shanks' mare, he saw the governmental carriage turn into the main street and the occupant spring out in front of the castle. The carriage had the latest in steel springs and was most comfortably upholstered and padded. It was clear to the weary pedestrian that the governor had come to learn what had happened. He said to himself, "It will not improve his temper."

The mile-and-a-half walk left him exhausted and for a few moments he leaned against the stone pillar at the foot of his drive. His eyes turned in the direction of the pavilion, which was showing little more than the top gable and two windows above the thick cover of trees.

"If Napoleon had not passed here that first morning," thought the owner, "and seen how peaceful and aloof it was, the Balcombe family would have been saved much trouble and grief."

Mrs. Balcombe was on the steps when he reached the house. "William, you *didn't* walk!" she cried. "Where was Mantee?"

"I don't know, my dear. I only know where he wasn't."

"Oh, if Sarah were not such a jewel! But we can't get rid of him without losing her also."

The head of the house sighed. "I have something to tell you, and you must prepare yourself for a shock. Can we use that sitting room of yours?"

His wife looked at him with augmented concern. "Of course," she said, leading the way into the house.

The sitting room in question was on the first floor up, a

tiny cubicle opening into the main bedroom. It was largely devoted to sewing but it did contain a tall bookcase, packed with much used volumes, and it had bright chintz curtains which gave the room an atmosphere of charm.

Mrs. Balcombe insisted on the best chair for her husband and then stood beside one of the arms, looking down anxiously at him. "What is wrong?" she asked. "Not—not the business?"

"No," he said. "The business is reasonably prosperous. But this morning I had to speak my mind to that charming gentleman at Plantation House. I don't know what the outcome of *that* will be. And, my dear, look at this."

He handed her the clipping. On reading the first few sentences, she cried out, "Oh, no!" and placed one hand over her mouth. After a few more sentences she could bear no more of it and let the paper flutter from her nerveless hands.

"William! Oh, William! What dreadful thing is this?"

"Have you met this miserable scandalmonger?"

"Once. I disliked him at sight."

There was a moment's silence. "Well, my dear, I took the necessary steps. I called him out. Dr. O'Meara and Arthur Princey delivered my challenge. They saw him early this afternoon."

Mrs. Balcombe was almost beside herself at this point. "Oh, my dear husband, you are not going to fight him! He has been a soldier. You may be killed."

"What the outcome might have been will never be known now. The fellow proved himself a miserable coward. He told my friends it was all a mistake, that he had been given wrong information. They said his face was as white as chalk and his hands trembled. He promised them to retract everything in a statement to be sent to the papers where the story had been printed. I am to see what he writes and it must have my approval." Balcombe patted his wife's hand which she had placed protectingly on his shoulder. "So there will be no duel. And, do you know, I'm a little disappointed. My hands are still itching with a desire to sight my pistol on him or, at the least, to lay a horsewhip over his shoulders."

Mrs. Balcombe sank into a chair beside his. "How relieved I am! If they had arranged for you to meet him at dawn, I wouldn't have been able to survive the night. I know I would have died of fright."

"But now," said Balcombe, "we have a problem to face

quite as serious as the duel I am not to fight." He pointed to the clipping on the floor. "What are we to do about our daughters?"

Mrs. Balcombe shook off her emotions. "There does not seem any reason to interfere with Jane's plans. He says nothing much about her. She's a young lady now and she hasn't much interest in Longwood. But it's a different thing with Betsy. She must not see General Bonaparte again." She was speaking with sudden decision. "Some might think we should let things go on as before and in that way express our conviction that this is all a pack of lies. But I don't look at it that way. Besty must go back to her old habits and never see any of them at Longwood. Until she grows older, I mean. For one thing, we can't impose any restraints on Napoleon's conduct. No, I think the proper course is the obvious one. Betsy must be kept at home."

"I think, my dear, you are right."

The talk between them went on for some time longer. The husband had little to say, although he gave sufficient attention to his wife's remarks to feel sure he was in accord with her. He was thinking of something which had happened before they left England; before their youngest son had been born and Betsy was four years old.

In answer to a note, a quite brief one, and written in the fine script of official tradition, William Balcombe had taken his youngest daughter (Jane being ill at the time) to a castle which covered a wide stretch of low hillside with time-honored stone. They entered through a high arched gate and were escorted along a cold hall to one of the minor drawing rooms. It was a gloomy apartment with dark portraits on all the walls. The fireplace was enormous but it was empty and black.

Betsy burrowed her nose down into the collar of her coat and said, "U-h-h, Papa, how cold it is in here!"

An old man came to greet them, with his hands tucked into the capacious pockets of a tweed surtout. Even now, thinking back to this scene of so many years before, William Balcombe did not give the old man a name in his mind; in spite of the intensity of emotion with which he had studied him at the time.

Although he had once been of good height, the stoop of the old man's shoulders now detracted from his stature. His wrinkled face still showed some remnants of a florid complexion. It was clear that he was ill. A black-coated attendant, who held his arm as they entered the room, tried to guide his steps to a chair. But the old man would have none of that. He walked over with dragging step to face his visitors.

"Well, Will-yum," he said. "Well, well! It has been a long time. A very long time. Why? Why has it been so long?" He drew one hand from its pocket and rubbed it across his brow as though to clear his powers of recollection. "What is this about you? Oh, yes, you are going away. To the colonies. To St. Helena, is it? The smallest colony of all but one which deserves much praise because it never causes trouble. You will have a double satisfaction there, Will-yum. You will be standing on your own legs and will enjoy knowing that in the colonies commerce is mostly in the hands of gentlemen."

William Balcombe bowed and would have made some response if the stooped old man had not turned his attention to Betsy.

"And this is one of the daughters! She has never been to see me. Jane, eh, what? Ah, not Jane. Then it is—" A long pause followed, during which an effort was being made, clearly to discipline a fading memory. "—Ah yes, Elizabeth. You are Elizabeth?"

The small girl curtsied as her mother had taught her. But a hat of such wide brim had been selected for her that her face was completely hidden. The old man reached out and raised the brim.

"Well, well, well," he said, with an increase of geniality. "A very nice little girl. And a very pretty girl, eh, eh? Will-yum, how happy I would be to have a daughter like this—or a granddaughter—what, what!—now that all my own have deserted me and are married and gone here and there, leaving me with such a long and monotonous array of sons." His face, above the tightly buttoned collar of the surtout, lightened up with a twinkle. "There are so many boys around here. I don't know where they come from. I would trade you the pick of any two or three of them for this nice little girl."

Their breaths hung on the air like long wisps of vapor. The black-coated attendant, who was wearing warm gloves, tried to lead his charge away, presumably to more comfortable quarters where there would be crackling fires to warm them. The old man shook him off impatiently.

"My small one," he said, smiling down at Betsy. "You haven't told me if your name is Elizabeth."

"I am always called Betsy, sir," piped up the child.

"Betsy? Good, splendid. It has such a real English ring to it. Now, then. Would you like to live here with me? You would find it very fine, I think. Rooms to yourself, and all the clothes and toys you want, and servants to wait on you, what, what?"

Betsy had been instructed in what she should do but not in what she should say. It had been taken for granted, no doubt, that she would have nothing to say. So she fell back on a denying shake of the head.

"What, what!" he exclaimed. "You do not, then, like me?"

"Oh, yes, I *do* like you. You are kind, even though you don't have fires." Her teeth were beginning to chatter. "B-b-but I like my own papa best."

"When you come again I shall have a roaring fire for you and a splendid tea." He leaned over and tapped Balcombe on the arm. "No hypocrisy about this daughter of yours, Will-yum. I like her very much. Some day I must do something for her. Something handsome. You are so stiff-necked you won't let me do anything for you, even though you are off to the ends of the earth. I hardly think, Will-yum, I shall ever see you again."

As the old man showed signs at this point of an inability to stand by himself, the attendant took him peremptorily by the sleeve. Smiling back at them over his shoulder, he waved his free arm to them, rather feebly, and vanished from sight.

They had entered by one of the public gates but now they were escorted out through an interior door which opened on a great enclosed court. There was an enormous round tower in the center which must have been as old as Methuselah because the stones were gray with age, and about them in all directions were towers and walls with turrets and heavy arched doorways. Betsy looked about her with the roundness of wonder in her eyes.

"Papa," she whispered. "Does he, that nice old man, live here always?"

"Most of the time, Tot."

"Is all of this his house?"

"Yes. But he needs it all. You see, he has hundreds of people with him all the time."

"But, Papa, if he's so poor he can't afford fires, why does he have such a large house"

"He's not poor. His income is quite enormous but he has to pay salaries to all these people. And he has about a dozen sons who have the knack of accumulating debts which their father has to pay off every now and then. That makes him think he's poor and he tries to save money in small ways. Like not having fires in all the rooms, and being very hard on other people who—well, would have a claim on him if they cared to do anything about it."

"Do you mean he has fires in some of the rooms? Is it only visitors who are very poor and are having to go out to the colonies that they send to rooms where there are no fires?"

He said to himself: "Now how did she come to think of that? Some day, of course, I'll tell them all about it."

There was a long pause while the four-year-old studied the aging grandeur about them.

"Papa, are you very ill?" she asked, finally.

"Of course not. I am in perfect health. What put that in your head?"

"Well, he, that old man, said you had a stiff neck."

Her father exploded with laughter. "Betsy," he said, "that doesn't mean I actually have a stiff neck. It's just an expression. It means that, when I get an idea in my head, I never change. You see, he has sometimes asked me to agree to certain things but I've always said 'no' to him. Are you still cold?"

"Yes, Papa. I'm freezing."

"Then I think we had better get out of here as fast as our feet will take us and find a nice warm shop where we can have tea and buns with sugar on top."

Betsy nodded enthusiastically. "Yes, Papa. But if you don't mind I would rather have chocolate. Both Jane and I prefer chocolate to tea."

"Well, then, we'll make it chocolate for once."

When they were seated in a comfortable teashop and Besty had been applying herself with a splendid appetite to the sugar buns, she suddenly stopped eating to ask a question.

"Papa, does Mamma like the idea of taking this big ship out to that island?"

"Of course, my dear. She will be more comfortable there. We'll have a fine big house and large gardens and horses. And

206

there will be servants to do most of the work." He considered her intently. "Why do you ask, Betsy?"

"Because," said the girl, "I wakened up once when it was very late and dark. And I heard her crying."

When his mind reached this point, it did not return at once to the problems of the moment. He said aloud, with a sigh: "He meant it. He intended to do something for her. But now it's too late."

Mrs. Balcombe looked at him with a puzzled frown. "William, whatever are you talking about?"

He explained in apologetic tones. "My dear, I was thinking about something which happened many years ago. Before the old king got into his mental difficulties. Please forgive me."

4

At this point a clatter of pony hoofs announced the return of the daughters of the house. Dogs barked, the voices of servants were raised, and Betsy whistled a lively catch as they came through the front door and up the stairs. They had been to a party and had enjoyed themselves; as was attested by the tin horns in their hands and the fancy tissue-paper caps on their heads. Jane's cap was a high-peaked witch's headgear. Betsy's was wide and tricorne-shaped in the familiar Napoleonic pattern.

William Balcombe was startled into saying sharply: "Take it off! Betsy, you must never wear such a thing again."

The girl looked so surprised that he immediately regretted yielding to the impulse which, of course, could be traced to the clipping in his hand.

"I'm sorry I spoke so hastily, Betsy," he said. "But there's a reason which—well, which makes it unwise for you to display your sympathies this way. Put it away among your souvenirs if you like. But remember this: you must never wear it again."

The girl removed the cap and stared at him with a puzzled frown. Then she walked over close to him and asked in a grave tone, "Papa, what has gone wrong?"

"Well, Tot," he said, using that term for the first time in more than ten years, "at this exact moment, most everything seems to have gone wrong."

"But, Papa, what is it?"

William glanced beseechingly at his wife. "My dear, you will tell them? It's a matter of such delicacy, that it calls for a mother's explanation. I will—I will go downstairs. And I think I shall break my rule and have a whiskey-and-water before dinner."

"Yes, William, I think it will do you good. I'll explain to Jane and Betsy."

William Balcombe sipped his whiskey-and-water slowly as his mind dwelt on the events of the day. Was that martinet at Plantation House right? Was there anything he could have done to prevent this from happening? Had he been remiss in his share of the responsibility of bringing up two such charming daughters? He was certain there had been nothing wrong in their behavior to the distinguished guest in the house. It was all a pack of lies, conjured up by Montchenu in his anxiety to find ways of blacking Napoleon's character.

He knew there had been nothing in Betsy's familiarity with Napoleon to warrant criticism. She still seemed to her father the little child he had taken with him on his visit to that castle on the eve of their departure. After thinking the situation over with the greatest care, he could not see any reason for feeling a sense of personal guilt.

He got to his feet and walked to a window. Off to the west Plantation House was a blaze of lights. During the afternoon he had learned that the governor was giving a dinner and that Montchenu would be among the guests. He stared with gloomy intensity at the official residence and wondered what kind of reception the French representative would be accorded. "If Lowe makes any mention of this tonight—if there is any talk at table about it or snickering—I'll call *him* out!"

He then made his way to a window on the southern wall and studied the semaphore at Alarm-House which was lighted up to show the position of the arms. They indicated that Napoleon was safely inside his domicile. Several other lights, blinking in the distance, carried, no doubt, the same message. Balcombe had heard that the governor had acquired the habit of going to a window half a dozen times in the course of an evening to assure himself that the prisoner had not escaped. "Such childishness!" he thought. "Why all these silly precautions here on shore when the Navy is keeping such a close patrol? The man's mind must be unsettled!"

When he came back to the table he saw that he had placed

the clipping on the tablecloth at his own place. He picked it up again and discovered that the other side of the paper contained a news article under a heading in bold type. The words arrested his attention: NEW SHIPPING LINE.

As a means of diverting his mind from the distressing topic which his wife was discussing upstairs (he could tell from the pitch of the voices that the two girls had already been told the worst), he began to read about the new maritime venture. After the first few sentences, he became immersed in the information imparted.

A group of wealthy Americans had organized to launch a new line of sailing ships for trade with the Orient, under the name of the New York and Bombay. He recognized many of the names from the list of officers and directors, which convinced him that this was a major undertaking. The ships were to be revolutionary and of the type already called clippers; an American innovation, including the narrowing of the hulls and a great elongation of the masts and rigging. The first vessel was already under construction in a naval yard on the East River in the city of New York. It was to be christened *The Flying Yankee*.

It was explained that owing to the prohibition on calling at St. Helena, the new line would send its ships into Rio de Janeiro and from there sail direct to Cape Town. When the restriction was raised, St. Helena would be a port of call, lying as it did directly halfway between the two terminal points.

"This is very interesting," thought Balcombe. "If it becomes advisable, or necessary, for me to find another way of making a living, I would enjoy having some part in a venture like this. It's clear these Americans have a shrewd eye to the future." It occurred to him then that he would not enjoy life in New York, not because he had anything against that city or the American people but through a shrinking from living under any other flag. "Perhaps," he thought, "there would be something in the way of an agency in London. Or even here, later on."

He was still giving this consideration some thought when the sound of footsteps on the stairs warned him that the discussion between his wife and their two daughters had come to an end. Walking into the hall, he met them at the foot of the staircase. Mrs. Balcombe was in the lead and a trace of tears still showing in her eyes made it clear that she had found the task a painful one. The two girls were walking together behind her, with their eyes lowered.

"Well, we've talked it over," said Mrs. Balcombe, applying a handkerchief to her face. "Both Jane and Betsy agree that our decision is wise. They—they are very much upset, of course."

Betsy walked over to her father. "My brave papa!" she said. "I'm very proud that you were willing to fight a duel over me. And I'm sure you would have given that horrible man the worst of it."

"I'm afraid, Betsy, this is going to upset things for you," he said. "And you also, Jane. Though in a less degree."

Betsy took his arm and gave it an affectionate and confiding squeeze. "Oh, I'll keep myself busy," she said. She was striving to make her voice sound casual but was not succeeding. "I won't mind not going to parties for a while. You know I'm beginning to find them tiresome. After all, Papa, I *am* growing up. There's so much I ought to learn. I know nothing about sewing and dressmaking."

"That's my brave girl."

"I'm going to see a lot more of you and Mamma. Will you be able to stand it? I'll try not to be too troublesome."

Chapter Seven

1

Madame Montholon's last child, a girl who had been named Napoleone, was now two months old. The mother, it was clear, had regained her health. When she appeared in the doorway leading from the dining room into the emperor's study, she was wearing a handsome lace berthe over a low-necked black dress. Her hair, done in the most recent fashion, was parted in the middle and combed back on each side; and all of this was very effective indeed. She caught his eye and waited for the signal to enter.

Napoleon was busy with a pile of his most recent dictation and did not want to be disturbed. When it became apparent, however, that she had no intention of going away, he frowned and then motioned her to enter. The new mother did not wait to be invited to seat herself. She chose a chair opposite him and took pains to settle her skirts about her in such a way that he could not overlook the trimness of her ankle and the smallness of her feet.

When he waited for her to speak, she took an extreme liberty. Lifting one of his hands and saying, "They are more beautiful than a woman's," she placed the thumb between her small white teeth and bit down sharply.

"Ha, my dear Albiné," said Napoleon. "You seem to be yourself again."

"Yes, my good lord and master."

"And how is the infant?"

"In excellent health, sire. There is much discussion as to whom she resembles most."

"Her father, from what I hear. Which must make my good Montholon a very proud man."

Madame Montholon smiled as she lowered her eyes. "Indeed?"

"The child will be your last?"

The countess raised her eyes quickly. "Well—as to that—"

"Your health will not stand more childbearing," declared Napoleon. "I am quoting O'Meara, who is very much concerned about you."

"How good of him." After a pause, she added, "You are more solicitous of my health than you used to be."

The Captive had nothing more to say on that point. Lifting his pen again, he leaned forward to the table to resume his labors. "What is your object in coming to see me at this hour?" he demanded to know.

"This," said the countess, laying a printed slip of paper in front of him. "A copy of an article which appeared in Paris a short time ago. A friend sent it on to me, thinking I would be interested. She was correct. I am very much interested."

Napoleon glanced at the paper and then read the print with quickened concern. His face became dark with anger.

"Montchenu!" he exclaimed. "That tattler, that malicious spreader of gossip, that black trifler with the truth!" He got to his feet. "You have read this, madame?"

"Of course, sire."

"And what do you think about it?"

"I think the girl is much to be blamed, sire. She has laid herself open to such speculation."

"*Mon Dieu!* This is not speculation. It is an open charge. Do you believe it?"

Madame Montholon hesitated and then, reluctantly, shook her head. "No, sire."

Napoleon tucked the offending sheet of paper under his belt and strode to the door. "You have my permission to retire, Countess," he said. "I must speak to Bertrand at once."

Passing out through the study door, he said to himself: "There was a sly glint in her eye. She is delighted, that is clear. If Montholon were not so useful to me, I would send him back to France, to rid myself of this woman."

Bertrand did not need to read the story. He had already seen the copy in Balcombe's possession, and had been informed of the decision reached by Betsy's parents. "It was to see you about this that I came over so early. M'sieur Balcombe informs me that he and Madame Balcombe have decided it will be wise for their daughter to go into seclusion for a time. She is not to be allowed, at any rate, to see you again until—well, until she is closer to years of discretion.

212

She is not to visit any of us until the story has blown over. He asked me to acquaint you with their decision."

Napoleon's face had assumed a grim expression. "Has Balcombe taken any other action?"

"Naturally. Being a man of spirit, he called Montchenu out. That troublemaking fool is an arrant coward, it seems. He was stricken to the core of his timorous soul and has agreed to retract everything. All he wants now is to have the matter forgotten."

Napoleon remained silent for several moments. Then his face flushed with sudden anger and he cried: "No! *Ma foi*, Bertrand, my life in this miserable hole is bad enough without further restrictions being laid on me. The only thing that served to make life bearable when I first came was the kindness of the Balcombe family, and particularly the understanding of little Betsee. Isn't it enough that her visits have been restricted since they sent me to this pesthouse? Because this *bavard*, this sponger with the desires of a Don Juan and a body like an overstuffed sausage, has seen fit to print lies about me, am I to be treated like an adolescent? Tell Balcombe I refuse to agree with this sanctimonious decision they have reached!"

He stamped from the reception room, where the discussion was being held, and slammed after him the door of his bedroom. Almost immediately, however, the door opened a few inches and he asked through the gap. "Is Balcombe a good shot?"

"Fair, I believe, sire. Better than Montchenu, from what I hear."

"Then it's too bad they didn't meet. It would have brought the attention of all Europe to the way I am being treated."

For a good quarter of an hour there was silence in the bedroom. Then, slowly, as though it shared the reluctance of the hand on the knob, the door opened.

"I have been thinking about this situation, Bertrand," said Napoleon. "I am most unhappy about it. Those people were all most kind to me. It would be a poor return for all they did, if I thought only of my own wishes and acted solely on my personal reactions. Bertrand, I have changed my mind. Tell Balcombe I agree with their decision."

He slammed the door a second time as though annoyed by his own amiability.

For a year and a half Besty remained in partial seclusion. She was too active, both of body and mind, to find time heavy on her hands. In fact, she kept herself so busy that often the days seemed too short for all the things she wanted to do. And often, also, she found herself playing a part, although a small one, in the drama being enacted on the island.

There was, for instance, a morning half spent while she curled up in a chair in her bedroom and became deeply engrossed in a book which had arrived from England. It was a novel entitled *Pride and Prejudice*, published anonymously early in the year and written by a woman (or so Betsy believed). Having been given a room all to herself (the sewing room had been converted to her use), she had now an imposing list of books on open shelves along one side of the rather diminutive chamber. None of them had compelled her interest as deeply as this. She was so concerned over the romance of Elizabeth Bennet and her not too impetuous lover Darcy that her father had to call her twice from the foot of the stairs before she became aware that he wanted her.

"I'm sorry, Papa," she said, hurrying down with the book in one hand and a finger holding her place. "I was reading and didn't hear you."

Count Bertrand was sitting on the porch and it was apparent from the flush on his usually placid brow that he was in a disturbed state of mind. He smiled warmly, however, and stood up to offer her his chair.

"Thank you, m'sieur," she said. "But I'll sit on the steps."

"We need you," explained her father. "The count's English is improving—a little—but my French remains as bad as ever. I thought, as you were in the house, we would ask you to interpret for us."

A situation had developed with reference to the cost of upkeep at Longwood. The eight thousand pounds which had seemed the probable yearly figure when William Balcombe first discussed it with Sir Hudson Lowe was not proving enough. It seemed certain, in fact, that the costs would stretch beyond the twelve thousand mark.

"Papa says," began Betsy, after listening to her father's slightly embarrassed explanation, "that this embargo," she paused until the visitor nodded to indicate that she had chosen the right word, "is raising costs on the island. He says he had a report of food prices from London which disturbs him very much. The prices for food here in St. Helena are three times as much as they are in Paris."

Bertrand frowned anxiously. "That seems absurd, mam'-selle."

"It's what the report said. They are four times higher than in Vienna and Berlin. And so, m'sieur, he is finding it hard to make both ends meet. But he's very much afraid that the emperor is displeased with him."

"The emperor," said Bertrand, with a sigh, "is displeased with everyone at the moment. He complains of the quality of the food. The beef! He says it's the poorest grade and refuses to eat it. Then there's the butter. Rancid! It's the same with everything. And so he has decided to proceed with the plan I proposed to your father a short time ago. He must contribute what he can to the household costs. He is now willing to offer his silver service for sale and to apply what it brings to meeting these rising costs."

"Oh, m'sieur!" exclaimed Betsy. "Those beautiful plates! It seems a great shame, doesn't it?"

"Yes, mam'selle. Your father was to discuss the suggestion with the governor. My main object in coming today was to find how the idea was received."

It had been received badly, it seemed. William Balcombe had been subjected by the governor to a torrent of abuse. Did he, Balcombe, realize the effect this would have on world opinion? Did he not see that by offering the plate for sale the impression would be created that England was starving General Bonaparte?

"Well," Balcombe had responded, "that is the charge he hurls at me when I try to explain why there is no better beef and mutton and the wine is of such poor quality."

Lowe had resorted to his usual habit on such occasions. He had jumped to his feet and had started to pace about the room while continuing to talk in angry tones. He had even asserted that the firm Balcombe represented was making too large a profit. "My father says," Betsy explained, "that his firm is making no profit at all and that he sometimes thinks it would be wise if they withdrew."

"I see no objection to General Bonaparte's contributing to the cost of his ridiculously large household," Lowe had said, finally. "But I'm convinced he is doing this to create sympathy for himself. I am sure there would be quite a scramble for the service if it were offered for sale and so there would be a great deal of talk."

"Yes, Your Excellency, it can be taken for granted that the sum realized would be sufficient to meet the deficit we are facing now."

"Understand this, Balcombe!" cried the governor, shaking a fist in the air. "There is only one way of disposing of the plate to which I would agree. It can't be offered complete. That would cause talk in every capital of Europe."

"But to sell it piecemeal," protested Balcombe, "would take some time and the return would be much smaller."

"Under no circumstance," cried the governor, "would I agree to sell each piece separately. In England. In Europe. Or even here in St. Helena. No, Balcombe, there is only one way it can be done without stirring up talk. The plate will have to be melted down and sold as silver *without identification*."

Nothing Balcombe said could move him from this position. When Betsy conveyed the substance of it to Bertrand, the count at first was unable to believe it. "Melt the service down!" he exclaimed. "Mam'selle, are you certain your father heard him correctly? Why, as silver it would not bring in a twentieth of its value."

There had been no mistake, Betsy assured the count. The governor had shouted, "Melt it down!" at least half a dozen times, getting redder in the face with each repetition.

"Then," said Bertrand, "I shall convey this information to the emperor."

He rose to his feet and bowed to William Balcombe. "Tell your father," he said to Betsy, "that although the emperor gets angry at times and blames him for the insufficiency in the supplies, he knows it has not been his fault. In fact, he made it clear to me that he would not allow anyone else to dispose of the plate, so convinced is he of your father's integrity. As for you, mam'selle," lowering his voice, "he asked me to say that he misses you very much."

The suggestion of a tear appeared in the corner of each eye. "It makes me very unhappy that I can't visit him any more," said the girl.

Betsy began to find the evenings long and dull because Jane was now old enough to be launched into the social life of the island. She managed to keep in touch, of course, with what was going on and was one of the first to learn of the

216

melting down of the silver service and of the purchase by Napoleon of a cheap set of china in a Jamestown shop. "What is the need for silver plate when you have no food to eat from it?" he had said. The remark was repeated all over the island and in time reached London and the continent; thereby creating the impression that Napoleon had anticipated.

It was perhaps a week after the silver had been shipped to London to be offered for sale that Count Bertrand stopped at the Briars on his way to town, carrying a bundle under his arm. Betsy greeted him at the door. He touched the tip of a finger to his lips.

"Mam'selle," he whispered, "this is for you. From the emperor. But you must be very careful and tell no one save your parents. Who knows what that fair and honorable man at Plantation House would do if he heard about it?"

When she opened the parcel in her bedroom, she found that it contained a piece of the original service, a large plate with a delicately chased border circling to the imperial eagle at the top.

"Oh, oh!" she said to herself. "How beautiful! And it's for me. Now what can I do to keep it safe and untarnished?"

A short time before her father had given each of the sisters a handsome length of silk material from the east. It had been Betsy's intention to use hers as a shawl to be worn over the shoulders with formal dress. "If I'm ever thought old enough for formal wear," she had said to herself. Now she took this silk of many colors (as beautiful, she was sure, as Joseph's coat) and wrapped the piece of plate in it. Then she placed it on a shelf behind a line of large and formidable-looking books, none of which she had opened.

"No one," she said to herself, "will ever move *these*. My lovely plate will be safe here."

Jane was out most evenings, and becoming very popular with the young officers of the regiment, and so Betsy fell back on books to pass the time. One night she was so deeply engrossed in what she was reading that she placed a screen about her bed to conceal the fact from her parents that she was still awake. Thus protected from interruption, she read on and on, unaware of the passing of time until she heard the voices of her father and mother who had retired to their bedroom.

217

They were talking about the melting down of the silver and Betsy heard her father say: "Yes, Lowe has been incredibly stupid and yet I am beginning to feel sorry for him. Do you know, my dear, that Napoleon has money he could draw upon and so didn't need to sacrifice the silver service? He did it for a purpose. He wanted the whole world to know how badly treated he has been. The trap was neatly laid for the governor. It was his idea that the silver must be melted down, not realizing that this was what Napoleon wanted."

"What plans he spins behind that magnificent forehead," went on the head of the family. "Lowe, who follows out the orders from London without using any judgment and always lets his black temper get the better of him, is a mere pawn. Napoleon moves him around the board with a mere touch of his fine white hands."

"In spite of the way he treats us," he concluded, "I still feel that Lowe is to be pitied."

"You are always too kind about people, William," said gentle Mrs. Balcombe, who could be completely realistic in such matters. "Sir Hudson Lowe treats you like dirt under his feet and I won't be happy until it's known what a conceited and irritable little man he is and they pack him on a boat for home!"

Betsy came out from behind the screen and walked to the open doorway into the parental room.

"I couldn't help hearing what you were saying, Mamma. I think you are right."

"Well!" said Mrs. Balcombe. "Mamma is right. For once."

"He's a horrid man," declared Betsy. "And Pappa is too kind and easy. He should be more like Napoleon, who isn't kind at all."

"Dear, dear," said her mother. "Have we discovered a fault in the great man?"

"Napoleon is a great man. Really great men always have faults and they are sure to be great faults. I read that somewhere. It seems to fit the case, doesn't it?"

"I'm more interested in knowing what you are doing up so late, young lady."

"I'm waiting for Jane to come in."

"It may interest you to know that Jane came in long ago. She's in bed and sound asleep."

"Oh." Betsy turned to go back to her own room. Then she paused and indulged in a light laugh. "That *was* a cute trick,

218

wasn't it? I mean making that horrid man so angry that he demanded the silver be melted down, because he thought that was the only way to keep it a secret. And now it's known all over the world, and everyone is feeling sorry for Napoleon."

3

It had been agreed that Betsy should learn to ride one of the horses and she had selected Monmouth. Having risen one morning at an unusually early hour, she proceeded at once to the stables. William Pitt was nowhere to be seen but Mantee Timms was on hand and seemed to have assumed the old man's duties.

"Where is William Pitt?" she asked.

"Will'p he sick," said Timms. "He not get up."

Betsy made her way to the rear of the stables where the old servant had converted an unused stall into a bed for himself. He was lying there with his eyes closed and Betsy was much disturbed to see how thin he had become. In a matter of a few days, it seemed, the bones of his forehead had become a high arch above the rest of his face and the skin had a drumlike tautness.

"William Pitt!" she exclaimed. "Why didn't you let us know?"

The old man's eyes opened and he strove to sit up; but without success.

"Mis' Bet'," he said, in a whisper. "No med'sin help. I go home now." Then his eyes, moving slowly, became aware of the riding costume she was wearing. "You ride Tom?"

Betsy shook her head. "No, not Tom. I'm getting too heavy for him. I'm going to have a lesson on Monmouth."

"You Papa with you?"

"No. He's not up yet. But it's all right. I'm just going to amble around the grounds."

"That Monty," whispered the old man, using the name that all the servants had for Mr. Balcombe's favorite mount. "That Monty go like wind. Doan let him off walk, Mis' Bet'."

But she had not reckoned on the impetuosity of the big roan. As soon as she was ensconced in the saddle and had the reins securely in her hands, he started off like a bolt from a bowstring. She felt a moment of panic when she realized the

219

length of his stride but, as she seemed capable of maintaining her seat in spite of this, the sense of alarm passed quickly. Instead she even began to have a feeling of confidence and to enjoy the way the wind whipped past her ears. By the time they had circled High Knoll and had come out on the road to Plantation House, she felt that the situation was well in hand.

"Easy now, Monty!" she called. "Easy, boy. We mustn't give the little man who lives up there a scare."

They crossed the road to the governor's house almost in one stride and were going so fast that Betsy caught no more than a glimpse of the wide white walls of the mansion and of a single servant ambling across the lawn. He was wearing black dungarees and he came to a stop as he watched the mad progress of the horse and his diminutive rider. Betsy would have waved to him to let him know there was nothing wrong but found she needed both hands on the taut reins.

They went by the house of the Veiled Lady with a thunder of hoofs and Betsy made no effort to call a greeting. They took to the fields again and found themselves on an upward climb so steep that the horse was forced to abate his speed. This gave the girl a chance to gather in more of the reins and so to hold him to a more sensible gait as they swung around Alarm-House. Getting back to the main road the roan was content to pass Hutt's Gate at an easy enough rate of travel.

"Now, then, Monty," said Betsy, beginning to catch her breath. "You and I must come to an understanding. No more of this kind of thing, if you please. If Mantee Timms tells my father, I'll be put back on the pony brigade. You don't want that to happen to me, do you?"

The horse, content apparently with his first splurge of speed, turned in at the Briars and came to a stop at the entrance to the stables. Mantee Timms, his eyes distended by the fright he had had, came forward and extended a gingerly hand for the bridle.

"Mis' Bet'," he said, in a frightened whisper. "You all right?"

"Of course, I'm all right," said Betsy. "My, but we were going it, weren't we?"

"This fella Monty, he gits so he needs to use he legs. Whew, but you was a kickin' up dirt! Me, I scared plumb to death."

Betsy slipped out of the saddle. She would not have acknowledged it to anyone but she was happy to feel the good earth under her feet. Her knees seemed to tremble a little. Laying a hand on the horse's mane, she said to the servant, "He and I are going to be good friends, Mantee."

"Is that what you think?" asked her father, coming up from the house and wearing a stern and serious face. "It may be that your friendship with Monty ends right here."

"Why, Papa, you're up early."

"Not early enough, it seems," said William Balcombe, grimly. "Betsy, I didn't give you permission to ride this fellow without me along. I heard you start off and it gave me a scare, I can tell you. By the time I reached a window, you were well on your way to the Plantation road. I reached for my binocle and watched you as long as you were within sight, expecting you to be tossed from the saddle. We'll have no more of this, young lady! Will you please get that through your head?"

"But, Papa, I was never in any danger. Any *real* danger."

William Balcombe was a just man and he had to acknowledge that his daughter had given a good account of herself during the time he had watched her. "Betsy," he said, "I was frightened but I was proud also. You were riding like a veteran. Were you afraid?"

"N-no. Not really afraid, Papa. At least, I wasn't after the first few minutes. I soon became sure I could stay in the saddle no matter how fast we went."

"You must have been born with the knack of it," he conceded. "You have a fine pair of hands. Well, I think, you meant to obey me but were taken by surprise when he took his head so unexpectedly. Was that the way of it?"

Betsy nodded. "But please, Papa, don't be angry with Monty. He's such a wonderful fellow."

"You must make me a very solemn promise. Don't take him out again unless I'm with you."

"I promise. And, Papa, poor old William Pitt is very ill. Shouldn't we have a doctor?"

"I'll go down and have a look at him."

On the way to the stables Betsy put her head in at the kitchen door and received from Sarah Timms a plate covered with a napkin.

"Sarah never forgets a promise," she said, rejoining her father. "I asked her yesterday to make some of those scones and to put raisins in them, because William Pitt likes raisins.

Here's some for him. I hope he'll be well enough to eat them."

The old stableman's eyes indicated interest when he saw the cakes in Betsy's hands. He even succeeded in raising an arm for them.

"They've got raisins in them."

She turned away for a moment to speak to her father and, when her eyes came back, the scones had disappeared. This did not surprise her. She knew the old man had hiding places for any possessions which the other servants might want to pilfer. The cakes were now safely hidden away.

"William Pitt," said the master, looking at the sick man with anxious eyes, "I'm going to get a doctor for you. You look like a very ill man to me."

"Med'sin man?" The old chief shook his head feebly from side to side. "Too late, med'sin man. Suh, you kind to me but now I go home. My spirit wear plumes and I be called great chief again."

William Balcombe shook his head soberly when they emerged from the stable. "He looks in a bad way. I'll get Dr. O'Meara up to see what can be done."

It was late in the afternoon, however, before Napoleon's physician put in an appearance. He looked very tall in a double-breasted coat with exaggerated shoulders and buttons down the front in rows of three. Betsy's anxiety had mounted so high that she met him on the drive.

"I hear," said the doctor, in a heavy voice, "that you've got a sick fellow here who thinks he's the lord of all he surveys—but who's likely to meet the real owner of that title very soon."

"Yes. It's William Pitt. He's seven feet tall and he comes from the Mountain of the Moon."

The doctor studied her for a moment. He seemed to be looking down from a great distance. "Which are you, Jane or Betsy?"

"I'm Betsy."

"I suspected so. Well, Betsy, show the way."

His legs were so long that the girl had to go at a half trot to keep up with him. When they reached the stables, she did not go in. The doctor came out soon afterward, shaking his head.

"Can't do anything for him," he announced. "There's nothing wrong with him except he's lived too long. His body is ready to give up the ghost."

"Poor old William Pitt!" Betsy drew out a handkerchief and wiped some tears away from her eyes. "I don't know what I'll do without him. He's always been so kind to me. There aren't many people in the world I like better. Just about six or seven."

Walking back to the road, Dr. O'Meara drew a pipe from one of his pockets and began to fill it with tobacco. "This is my first chance all day to have a smoke. That's how busy I've been. Does your father smoke?"

"No, sir. But, please, do you mind telling me if you call him General Bonaparte or emperor?"

"You have me there. I'm compelled to confess I'm occupying a position in which no Irishman should ever be caught. I'm sitting right on top of the picket fence. I don't say either 'General Bonaparte' or 'emperor.' I simply say—he."

"Well," said Betsy, "he says that smoking is a bad habit."

"Does he now. Well, if you give any serious thought to it, you're likely to say that all habits are bad. But, ah, the grandeur and glory of the first pipe of the day! I have it generally before I get out of bed. All the emperors and all the kings and sultans in the world couldn't break me of this habit."

He took a bottle from another pocket in his shaggy arsenal of a coat and drew from it a small strip of wood which was thicker than a toothpick but less substantial than a ramrod. There was some material on the end of it which ignited as soon as it contacted the air.

"Splendid!" cried the doctor. "Not often I get it the first time. It generally takes four or five draws. These matches are poor things."

Betsy's curiosity had been aroused to such an extent that for the moment she forgot her sorrow over the report the doctor had made on William Pitt's condition. "What *is* that?" she asked.

"They call it a pocket luminary. Fellow in London invented it a few years ago. The matches don't have enough sulphur on the tip. But this thing is better than tinderboxes or priming pins and much better than fire pistols. Ever seen one of them?"

"No, Doctor."

The pipe was now drawing handsomely and he was puffing

out clouds of smoke with the greatest gusto. "Ah!" he remarked. "Life is worth living after all."

Betsy's interest reverted to the condition of the old man in the stable. "How old do you think he is?" she asked.

"Now as to that, I can only guess. But I would say the old codger is one hundred years old. Or getting mighty close to it."

"My, that *is* a great age. What can we do for him?"

"Nothing at all. Just see that he's looked after and kept as comfortable as possible. Oh, you might see that he has a spoonful of brandy each night. It will warm up his ancient insides and not do him any harm."

They had reached the end of the drive where Dr. O'Meara had tethered his horse. After untying the knot, he glanced up at the girl.

"I'm a curious fellow. Guess most Irishmen are. But do you mind telling me who the six or seven are you put ahead of that bronze statesman back there?"

"Well," said Betsy," "there are my father and mother. And I have an older sister and two young brothers. That makes five, doesn't it. Then He comes next. And then there's Sarah Timms. And there's a lady I've only recently met and whose name I can't mention. Coming to think of it, I don't know her name. That makes eight."

"What? You have no young beaux on the list?"

"No, Doctor O'Meara. No young beaux."

Three nights later, after going to the stables to see that William Pitt had his spoonful of brandy—a luxury which had gratified the old man very much—Betsy emerged in great haste and ran to the house with her head held down. Her father was sitting alone at the dining table with a bottle of port at his elbow. He was in a dreamy mood and his eyes seemed fixed on some distant scene. Perhaps he was recalling the days in England when his evenings were always spent with a group of his friends, good fellows without exception, who kept the port circulating at an almost giddy speed. Perhaps he was recalling the pleasant sound of logs crackling on the hearth and the beat of cold winds on frosted windowpanes.

"Papa!" she cried. "William Pitt is dead!"

Her father shoved the bottle to one side and got to his feet, with a faint trace of unsteadiness.

"Are you sure?"

Betsy nodded her head. "I could see he wasn't breathing. So I touched my hand to his cheek and it was quite cold."

"I'll go out and make sure and then I'll see that Sarah and Mantee take things in hand. They have their own ways."

Soon afterward he returned to the house and nodded to Betsy who had seated herself at the table and, with her head leaning on one hand, was looking very sad and woebegone.

"You were right, Betsy," he said. He sat down and reached for the port. Then he changed his mind and shoved it away. "He looked quite contented," he said.

"Oh, yes, of course he was contented. He talked to me about it many times. You see, he was quite sure of where he was going and what he would find when he got there."

Her father looked up with a puzzled air. "That's strange. He refused to go to church. He paid no attention at all when that eloquent and convincing exhorter, the Rev. Godefroi Stodgkin, tried to make a Christian of him. Where could he have learned about heaven?"

"His people have their own ideas about heaven. Their country is at the base of a very high mountain. There are two ledges around it and the chiefs go to the top ledge after they die, and the ordinary tribesmen go to the lower. William Pitt said it was a wonderful place to be because the chief's ledge was high enough up so they could talk with the gods but not so high that they couldn't keep an eye on the second ledge and even watch what was going on at the foot. He said it was their duty to send messages down when the people living at the base did anything wrong or to warn them of danger from other tribes or when there was to be an earthquake or a flood. When he was acting as chief, he used to get these messages all the time. It was like a whispering in the ear. I asked him if it was like the Lord speaking to Moses—but he had never heard of Moses. Each one of the chiefs on the ledge had turbans as yellow as the sun, with diamonds in front as big as eggs. Each one carried a golden spear. When one of them gets hungry, he raises his spear and right away there's a pot beside him filled with sizzling meat."

William Balcombe replaced the cork in the port bottle. "Do you suppose they can see as far as this from the ledge?" he asked. "Well, I hope he is already wearing his yellow turban and carrying his golden spear. What an unusual conception of what a heaven might be!"

Betsy gave an almost hysterical laugh. "Papa!" she admonished. "You must never let the Rev. Mr. Sodgkin hear you say anything like that. I'm sure he wouldn't condone such a heresy."

4

It seemed to Betsy that the weather was being deliberately controlled to add to the discontent she had begun to feel after six months of her term. Through one period in the winter months, it rained continuously for two weeks, during which time the sun never succeeded in finding a break in the clouds. The bitter trades bombarded the island unmercifully, whistling through the trees and setting up dismal echoes in the rocky declivities. The girl sat unhappily at a window when she was not striving against the mounting monotony of books. The most ancient of the yamstocks declared it was the worst spell of "they winds" they had ever suffered.

Napoleon was equally dispirited. On the high flatness of Longwood the walls of rock looked more grim and forbidding and the dampness came through the walls, creating a sour atmosphere in the small rooms. The fastidious imperial nose was grievously offended.

"I hate rain," he said to Bertrand. "Do you remember how it poured all morning at Waterloo?"

Finally a morning came when early risers saw signs of a break in the grayness of the skies. When Napoleon shook off the evil dreams which made his nights an ordeal, and sat up in bed, there were slender bars of unmistakable sunshine coming through the shutters and making cheerful patterns on the dun-colored carpet. He sat up and shouted, "Santini!"

The household usher, an Italian with usually impeccable manners, appeared quickly from what was called the topographical room; for no proper reason, because it had been intended first as a hall and was now being used for dictation. It was clear that he had hastily donned his green tunic.

"Your Imperial Highness," he said, bowing.

"Santini!" cried Napoleon, "your tunic is unbuttoned."

"Please, Highness," explained the usher, "I was helping to clean up the mess in the study."

The ceiling in that somewhat neglected room had caved in the day before, leaving a pile of broken plaster and other rubbish on the floor. Fortunately the space above was unoccupied.

Napoleon swallowed his resentment. "We must always strive to maintain dignity and decorum, Santini," he said. "Even if ceilings fall. *Mon Dieu!* Such a climate! And such a house! Send Dr. O'Meara to me."

When the physician put in an appearance, Napoleon pointed to a pile of books on the floor at the foot of his bed. "Make a point of going into town today, my faithful malpractitioner of the science of Hippocrates. There is a small errand for you. These volumes are to be left at the Briars. For Mam'selle Betsee."

O'Meara was not surprised, having heard reports of a scene which had occurred after dinner the previous evening. Napoleon had started to read aloud some scenes from *Rodogune* by Corneille. This was one of his favorites and he had selected the same sections on several occasions. After half an hour he had caught Bertrand yawning behind a discreet hand. Glancing around the room with mounting dudgeon, he found that Madame Montholon was sound asleep while her husband was clearly sunk in a condition bordering on the comatose. The finely white and always decisive hand of the Great Man closed the book with a loud thump.

"Why," he had demanded to know, "do I cast pearls before swine? Bed is the place to sleep. You are all excused!"

Napoleon indulged in a brief explanation for O'Meara's benefit. "This child is bright but her education is being neglected," he said. "From what I hear, she is reading nothing but English novels. As you may agree—although I have small reason for thinking you are cultured in any degree—all English novels are trash. If she keeps this up, her taste inevitably will be blunted. I have here six books I have selected for her to start on."

That afternoon, with the six books tied together and hanging awkwardly over his saddle bags, Dr. O'Meara turned in at the Briars as Mrs. Balcombe and Jane were starting out to attend a reception in town. They were suitably dressed for such a pleasant occasion. Mrs. Balcombe wore a frock of black crepe with elaborate sleeves of puckered muslin under the neatest of winter jackets. Jane was wearing a light pelisse of robin's-egg blue. That they were going in the company delivery wagon was not disturbing them in the least. There were not more than half a dozen carriages on the island and the Balcombe family were accounted lucky not to be under the necessity of walking or going to town in an oxcart.

The doctor had an eye in his head for the fair sex and he said to himself as he pulled up, "Now here's what I call a neat pair of fillies." Mrs. Balcombe might have been flattered if she had heard herself classed with her daughter but in reality the appreciative glance of the physician had lingered longer on her face, which was a trifle flushed in anticipation of a pleasant afternoon, than on the trim Jane.

"You must not let me detain you, Mrs. Balcombe," he said. "I am stopping to leave these books with Miss Betsy. They are from"—gesturing over his shoulder—"a certain great judge of the finest in literature. He finds a lack of appreciation for them in what you might call loosely the social circle of Longwood."

"Dear, dear!" said Mrs. Balcombe. "How heavy they look! I'm glad they are not intended for me. Good afternoon, Dr. O'Meara."

Betsy was standing on the porch to watch the departure of her mother and sister, and seemed a little lonesome. She came down the steps, with her dog pattering dutifully at her heels.

"He," said the doctor, "will esteem it a pleasure if you will cease reading the cream of English literature—which, in his opinion, is trash—and turn instead to these French master-pieces."

"Does he think I'll enjoy them?" she asked, "or is this a part of my education?"

"Judge for yourself. I've quoted *him* word for word." The doctor untied the parcel and handed over the volumes one at a time. "Whew! Voltaire, Molière, Montaigne, Corneille, Racine! Read these and you will be saved from losing all appreciation of literature. I am happy to say that my taste in reading was everlastingly lost long ago and is safely beyond redemption!"

Betsy sat down on the steps and began to turn the pages of one volume. "I appreciate his kindness very much," she said. "But please, Dr. O'Meara, make it clear to him that I don't read French very well. It will take me a long time to get through all of this."

The physician waved an airy hand. "Take your time, little lady."

"I'm afraid I'll miss the fine points," said Betsy. She glanced up at the doctor. "You know, French is a—I suppose you would call it a subtle language. A beginner is likely not to understand much of it. Please, doctor, let the emperor know that."

"Word for word."

"Will he be ready to have me tell him frankly what I think?"

"Frankness," declared the doctor, "is not the dish on which he thrives best. Still, you seem to have a knack of your own."

Betsy was beginning to smile. "He doesn't read English and so I can't retaliate by sending him Fielding and Richardson and Smollett and some of the others. There's one English novel I think all Frenchmen would like. It's called *Tom Jones*. Our copy has vanished and I suspect my mother of keeping it away from us."

"Well," said O'Meara, with a gesture which put to one side the books and the whole great problem of literature and learning, "I was instructed to report to him on another matter. How are you getting on? Have you been gaining in weight and height? He seems to be very much interested."

"I don't think I've gained much in weight. But I *am* getting taller. Nearly two inches."

"That's fine. You can afford to go right on gaining. We want you—if you'll allow me to associate myself with him in this—to become in due course a reasonably tall and very graceful young woman. Neither of us has any doubt that you will. But it does seem to me that you're looking a little peaked. Of course, that's to be expected when you start to sprout up."

"Mamma is worried about me. She says I'm losing my complexion."

"It will come back. Your appetite is good?"

"Well, sometimes."

"Now, you're letting the doctor get a foothold in the door. If your appetite is only good sometimes, it's clear you need a tonic. I would like to provide one."

"No, doctor, I don't think I need a tonic. I can only remember once in my life when I had to take medicine. And I've forgotten why I had to take it *then*. I've always been very healthy."

"Well, so much for that. I have only one other reason for delaying my departure. Something happened yesterday which should interest you. We had a visitor. The Baroness Sturmer."

Betsy's interest was aroused at once. "Oh, I'm so glad," she said. "She's lovely, isn't she? She has come to see us here several times. She was very much interested in him and how he managed to get along as our guest. I like her so much. It wasn't just because she's so beautiful. She's just like a snow-white princess, isn't she? But besides, she's so gentle and yet so amusing."

"Well, she got in to see him. Do you know why? Because that little circle of inspired thinkers that he has about him said how beautiful she was. Finally he said, *'Ma foi*, if she's as handsome as that, I had better have a look at her.' They talked alone for half an hour and, when she was gone, he was asked for his opinion. 'She's handsome,' he said. 'But not as handsome as our Betsee.'"

The girl's face crinkled up with delight. "Did he really say that?"

Her pleasure was not due entirely to hearing this opinion of her looks. Instead it could be traced to Napoleon's use of the word 'our.' She said to herself, "Just as though we were members of one family."

It was some months later that Dr. O'Meara, who had been going back and forth constantly between the Briars and Longwood on Napoleon's orders, said to Betsy: "Dashed if I'm not getting to be like a London runner. You know—one of those red-nosed, bleary-eyed scoundrels with a breath like a whiff of corruption who stand around in the rain and are ready to carry a message anywhere for a shilling. Except that I don't get the shilling. Well, he agrees with you about his dictated notes on the three great battles. He thinks they are much better than the first draft which you said was dull. This time it is Las Cases who considers them dull. But he demands to know why I didn't have the sense to ask which one of the three was the greatest victory. Let me see, which were they now?" He glanced at a list in his hands. "Marengo, Austerlitz, the Muskowa."

Betsy answered without any hesitation, "Austerlitz."

The doctor turned the list over. "You're right. He wrote it on the back. Austerlitz."

"I wonder if it was the proudest day in his life when he won that battle?"

"I'll put that question to him and give you his answer the next time I come. It will probably be soon. He was hunting around among his books when I left to find more French masterpieces for you."

"I'm beginning to like them better," said Betsy.

"He's very much encouraged. Pretty soon, he says, you will be free of the pernicious influence of the stuff you were reading before." A broad grin spread across his countenance. "My movements are being observed. Yesterday I was summoned to Plantation House and the governor himself proceeded to cross-examine me. Why was I paying so many visits here? What messages did Napoleon send with the books? What answers did I carry back for you? He demanded to know every word that passed between us. And what conclusion do you suppose he reached after grilling me for half an hour? That I must carry the books you return to Longwood over to him so they can be examined for *secret messages*."

The next day he espied Betsy at the gate as he was riding by on his way to town. He reined in.

"No," he said, "it was not the proudest day of his life. That particular occasion is not concerned in any way with battles. He says that some day he will tell you about it."

"You have no books with you today?"

The doctor shook his head. "I told him what was said over there"—jerking a thumb in the direction of Plantation House—"and he decided he should not send any more. He doesn't want to get you into any trouble with the Grand Cham and Potentate."

One of his broadest grins (William Balcombe called them his Irish grins) spread over his face. "When I told him your opinion about the battles, I said that, if you had been born a man in France at least twenty years ago, you might have been one of his marshals. He shook his head, 'I had twenty-two marshals and four honorary marshals. On the other hand there is only one Betsee. I prefer things as they are.' "

That evening William Balcombe left the company of his bottle of port and took Betsy into a small room which he called his study.

"My dear," he said, "Sir Hudson Lowe is very angry with us. He says all this passing back and forth of books must stop. It's the opinion of that most worthy little gentleman that we are breaking the regulations that he laid down, governing relations between the people of St. Helena and the prisoner at Longwood. He informed me, in fact, that his patience was exhausted. 'Obey my rules,' he said, 'or I shall send you and your family back to England.' "

"Papa!" cried Betsy. "Did he mean it? Such trifles! Is he in his right mind?"

Mr. Balcombe smiled grimly. "All this responsibility involved in the care of a prisoner who could not under any conceivable circumstances make his escape, is proving too much for him. While we talked, I noticed that his hands twitched all the time. His voice was high and shrill. He is clearly in a state of nerves."

"And while we are at it," he went on, "I find it hard to make up my mind about your friend, Dr. O'Meara. He seems pleasant enough but you hear conflicting stories about him. Most of the people at Longwood are sure he goes to Lowe and repeats everything he hears. It seems also to work the other way. Lowe and his officers are convinced he carries everything he can learn at Plantation House straight back to Longwood. In other words, he's a sort of two-way spy. I happen to know he's demanding an increase in his salary and that Lowe is furious about it. Any man who receives twelve thousand pounds a year himself is very likely to be hard on poor devils who want a few pounds more. I must confess," he added, "that I rather like O'Meara myself."

"Papa," asked Betsy, "do you think the governor means it about sending us home to England?"

"I'm afraid so."

A stricken look took possession of Betsy's face. "That would be dreadful," she said. "I'm afraid, Papa, that we are the only real friends Napoleon has on this whole island."

Chapter Eight

1

The months continued to pass and spring began to take possession of the lands and the islands and the seas which circled the earth on or about the Tropic of Capricorn. On the upper rim the leaves were drying up and becoming brown and discouraged but already at St. Helena the trades were blowing with warm persistence. Betsy no longer saw anything of Dr. O'Meara but she noticed when he passed the Briars that he was not wearing ear muffs under his tall beaver hat but had instead a rather jaunty headpiece of felt with a brim almost as wide as his shoulders.

One evening, shortly after Sarah Timms had cleared the table, the Balcombe family were seated in quiet comfort in the drawing room. William Balcombe would return later to the solitary enjoyment of his port but for a few moments he was relaxing with his wife and daughters. The heels of the two sons of the family had just disappeared up the stairs leading to the bedrooms above.

A rap on the front door was answered by Mantee Timms.

"Doct', suh," he reported. "Jest passing, he say."

Doctor O'Meara came into the room, peering about him with an air of exaggerated vigilance. "No spies lurking hereabouts?" he asked. "No runner ready to carry the news back to Plantation House that a conspiracy is being hatched here? If my arrival has been unobserved, I should like to stay for a few minutes and gather some information."

"Sit down, Doctor," said William Balcombe. "Perhaps you will join me later at my port."

"Thanks, thanks. But no. That, I am sure, would smack of arrant treason."

He seated himself next to his hostess and proceeded to explain his errand.

"There was a little incident this evening up there in the

233

gracious halls of the cow palace. You know, I don't take my meals with the imperial circle. Captain Poppleton and I share a table in a small room between the kitchen and the dining salon. We prefer it, I may say. We can talk freely and eat slowly instead of gobbling to keep up with the rapid chomping of the imperial jaws. Well, we were enjoying filets of wild duck *au fumet de gibier*—a capital dish—when we heard a thud in the dining salon. There was much loud talking inside and then Cipriani rushed out from the kitchen and disappeared through the door. Then he came back, looking mightily disturbed. A footman hurried through with steaming hot cloths.

"The good captain and I continued with our wild duck although we were told that Napoleon had lifted the lid of a dish, which contained a red mullet with *sauce meunière*, and had been so distrubed at what he saw that he sprang to his feet and rushed from the room. Unfortunately he tipped the table in his haste and the fish was spilled down the front of Madame Montholon's gown and ended up in her lap."

Betsy, who was curled up in a chair with several books on the floor at her feet, indulged in a delighted burst of laughter. "Oh, I *am* glad it was Madame Montholon who got the benefit of the *sauce meunière*," she said.

"Betsy," reproved her mother, "you should not make such comments."

"The next thing I knew," went on the doctor, after grinning broadly at the girl, "a footman came out and said I was wanted. I was reluctant to leave the table because an *entremets*, to which I was particularly partial, had just been brought in, a coffee cream *à la française*. However, the summons was from *him*, so I followed the footman back to his bedroom.

"He was standing at one of the windows with Bertrand beside him. When he wheeled about to face me, I could see that he was in a furious rage. His face was white and his eyes were like live coals in a blazing fire. He pointed a forefinger at me. 'How much do I weigh?' he demanded to know. I told him I thought I could guess within five or six pounds and I named a figure. 'Can you only guess?' he said. 'Are you a surgeon or a grinning Irish simpleton? Why are you allowing me to destroy my health by putting on so much weight? Do you know that every dish served in there tonight is of the very richest—a *vol-au-vent*, timbales *à la milanaise* which I cannot
234

resist, *boudins* fried in butter, *quenelles* oozing in oil. I am getting heavier every day. Why haven't you warned me? Why aren't you doing something about it? Only once—*only once*—have you discussed this matter with me.'

"It happens," went on the doctor, in an affronted tone of voice, "that I could recall five separate occasions when I had talked seriously to him about his weight. I told him so and, by way of emphasis, I raised a hand with the fingers outstretched. This, apparently, was *lèse majesté* in his sight, for he seized a steel rule and struck out at me. By Gad, if I hadn't lowered my hand in time, I swear all of my fingers would have been cut off.

"Well, to get on with it. He says I must get his weight down to a normal figure in five months. For his part, he will eschew all rich food and take plenty of exercise. For some reason he has a definite schedule in his mind. Five months and not a day more, to get down to one hundred and sixty-eight pounds. In order to stick to this rigid timetable there must be a weighing machine, so he can know always where he stands. I hear there are such things for bedroom use but I confess I've never laid eyes on one."

"Do you mean a Balance de Sanctorious?" asked William Balcombe.

"I believe that's what it's called. It seems that it's possible to have a ladylike machine which can be kept in a boudoir. He," thumbing over his shoulder, "brought one in with him from France. It belonged to the Empress Josephine and it was a very dainty bit of apparatus—very feminine, made of silver, with a mirror in the top and a screen of light silk to be let down to cover the lady when she took her place on the weighing seat without—well, without benefit of clothes. When the ship was being unloaded, unfortunately, a heavy packing case fell on this delicate little machine. We have a word in Ireland for what happened, it was smashed to *smithereens*. All this brings me to my point. Do you happen to know where we could get a machine of the kind here? We can't wait three months to have one shipped in. We must have it *now*."

"I am very much afraid, Dr. O'Meara, that there isn't such a thing on the island," said Balcombe, after some moments of consideration.

"I've never seen one," declared Mrs. Balcombe. "In fact,

235

I'm compelled to confess that I had never heard of them until tonight."

"The Balance of Sanctorious," said Balcombe, thoughtfully. "There are a few in England. In fact, there was one at—well, at a place where I lived for a period in my youth. It was never used. I seem to recall that everyone was too busy adding to their weight to think about it. Doctor, how much weight must he lose?"

"Forty pounds, roughly."

Balcombe whistled softly. "That is an undertaking, doctor, a real undertaking. I wonder why he feels he must accomplish this reduction in such a short time?"

"He always wants to get things done quickly," said O'Meara.

Betsy had been listening with close attention. At this point she straightened up in her chair.

"Papa!" she said. "There *is* one on the island. I've seen it. I caught just a glimpse but I don't think it is made of silver or has a curtain. But it *was* for weighing. Now where could I have seen it?"

The rest of the company waited in silence while she strove to recall this all-important point. She shook her head several times as certain possibilities were considered and dismissed. Then, abruptly she cried out in triumph: "I remember! It's in the house of the Veiled Lady. You know there's one side of the house which wasn't finished when the owner decided not to come out. You'll think I shouldn't have been so curious but I asked if I could have a look. It was very dark but I saw there was some scaffolding which had not been taken down, and some tools of one kind and another. And there were a few pieces of furniture. I am sure I saw a weighing scale in one corner, although it was pretty well covered up with canvas. Yes, that's where it is."

Doctor O'Meara got to his feet. "My thanks, Miss Betsy, for having such a quick eye in your head. You've solved a very tough problem for me. Do you suppose there will be any difficulty in persuading this mysterious lady to sell us the machine or to give us the loan of it?"

"I am sure," said Betsy, "that she will be very glad to help."

"That brings us to another problem. Who is to arrange to get the thing? From what I hear, she would almost certainly refuse to allow me inside the gate."

Betsy nodded her head. "I'm afraid, Doctor, that she would refuse. I'm the only one she has seen and I'm ready to do what I can. First, of course, I must make sure that it is what you want."

"Well, I made my hint a pretty broad one," said O'Meara. "Miss Betsy, I leave the matter in your hands. Could you make a point of seeing the lady without delay?"

"I'll go tomorrow morning."

2

It was about the time that people were settling down in Jamestown to the glass of milk and piece of cake which were needed in midmorning to carry them through the first half of the day that Betsy rode up on a brisk but much restrained Monty to the gate of the Veiled Lady. The maid appeared almost at once, smiling a highly enthusiastic and genuine welcome.

"You—bring?" she asked.

Betsy raised the arm on which she was carrying the usual small basket and transferred it to the willing hands on the other side of the gate.

"Aches!" cried Margette. "Ah, good!"

The gate swung back and Betsy rode through into the inner court. She tied her horse to the hitching post with a quick and expert twist of the reins. Then she pointed to the unused wing and raised her eyebrows. Margette sensed her wish at once and opened the seldom used door. Betsy had to wait for a moment to accustom her eyes to the dim light before looking around her. Any doubts she may have had were immediately dissolved. In a corner, partly covered by canvas, protruded one arm of a weighing machine. She picked her way through the piles of unused building material and the long neglected pieces of furniture. Stripping back the cover, she found that the machine was about seven feet high and had on one side a seat for the weighee, revolving creakily on chains and on the other the container of the weights. The whole was rusty and it protested when she gave the seat a twirl; but, quite clearly, it was still in usable condition.

Betsy walked back across the sun-flooded courtyard and entered the opposite wing where the lady of the house spent her long tedious hours. The voice of the mysterious occupant greeted her warmly.

"Betsy!" she exclaimed. "I am so glad you've come. You've been neglecting me, you know."

"I'm afraid I have, Julia." They had reached the first name stage some time before. "I've been feeling dull and, I expect, a little unhappy lately."

"Yes, I'm sure you have. But how fortunate that you're paying me a visit on my birthday. Today I am thirty-one years old."

Betsy had reached the conclusion early that the Veiled Lady was comparatively young but this was the first confirmation she had received. "This *is* a surprise. How young you are to—to—"

"To bury myself away like this? Well, Betsy, age has nothing to do with it. The role is not of my choosing. It was forced on me. Some day I shall tell you the story but—I can't bring myself to discuss it yet." There was a pause. "You told me about your age and so I know when you became sixteen. That so, so important age! It was just a month ago. Did you have a party?"

Betsy gave her head a negative shake. "Mamma wanted to do something about it. But I—I was very much against it. You know this is a small island and everything that people say gets repeated around. All the girls we would have to invite had said things which reached my ears. I couldn't bear the thought of a room filled with so much malice and bad feeling!"

"You'll have to put all that behind you soon, my dear. Now that you're sixteen, you can't remain in seclusion much longer. We're a pair, aren't we? I can't ever come out but you—you must, and very soon. The light doesn't seem good today and I can't see you well. Do you mind stepping over closer to the candles on that side? I want to have a better look."

The girl obeyed this request and for many long moments there was silence in the room.

"You've changed a great deal," said the voice. "You are taller and so I'm sure you are going to reach a nice height. Your features are changing. I don't need to tell you that because I am sure you consult your mirror often enough."

"I don't consult it exactly," declared the girl. "I have to watch what I'm doing when I brush my hair. But I think I'm different from most girls because I don't sit there and study myself and dab at things with a comb and fuss at them with a finger. Even my sister Jane, who's so sweet and lovely, can fill in endless time in front of a mirror."

"'You'll come to it. At least, you'll begin to realize the importance of looking your best. Your voice has changed and I think you are going to sing quite well."

Betsy nodded her head happily. "Yes, I *do* sing better. My voice used to be like a crow's."

There was another pause. "I was going to express an opinion, Betsy, but on second thought I had better not. Something is happening to you. In a short time you'll become conscious of it yourself. I had better leave it at that. But to observe it gives me a great deal of pleasure."

At this point Betsy's mind reverted to the errand which had brought her. She explained about the need at Longwood for a bedroom weighing machine, and of her discovery of one in the closed-up wing of the house. Could Napoleon have the use of it? Or would she sell it to him?

"I've never been in that part of the house," said the voice. "I didn't know it was there. I had one at home and there was a time when I used it every day. I was most particular about my appearance then. But I'll never want one again. You see, I am not—I am not well. Any change in my weight is bound to be on the loss side, and I don't want a constant reminder of it. Will you send word to the emperor that he may have it, if it's still usable?"

"Oh!" The girl's tone showed how much regret she felt. "If you are as ill as that, Julia, shouldn't you have a doctor? I could bring Dr. O'Meara to see you."

"No, Betsy. There's nothing he could do for me."

Betsy sighed deeply. "I know I shouldn't pry but it's hard to think of you all alone here and needing help."

"Dear child, I won't be offended no matter what you ask me. But it's quite certain I wouldn't be able to answer you about many things. Even though we've become such very good friends. I look forward to your visits because the talks we have are my greatest pleasure now. I always feel excited when I hear you riding down the road. It's a disappointment when you don't stop. Do you remember the morning when you went by at such speed that you didn't even call out a greeting? I was sure you were riding one of the horses and it had the bit in its teeth. I was terrified. I heard the hoofbeats

239

die away. Poor Margette will never learn to talk with people, so I had no way of finding out if you had come to any harm. I could think of nothing else. Then some days later you rode by with your father and you called, 'Good-morning!' So I knew you hadn't suffered any injury.

"We are sharing the same difficulty, aren't we?" she went on. "I know I shouldn't ask you questions but I've gathered from hints you've dropped that your father is having difficulties with the new governor. How arbitrary these little colonial officials can be! I hope things have been improving."

Betsy shook her head grimly. "No. It's getting worse all the time. He has told Papa he may insist on sending us all home to England because he thinks we're too friendly with Napoleon."

"I've been afraid of that."

"But we're not worried about it, really. You see, Julia, my father has some influence at home. I want to tell you about an experience I had when I was a small girl. Papa took me on a visit to a great castle not far from London. He doesn't think I have any recollection of it because I was only four years old at the time. But I remember some things quite distinctly. There was a great round tower in the center. I think it might have been Windsor Castle."

"It probably was Windsor.'"

"There was an old man there. He called my father by his first name. They talked for a short time and I recall some of the things that were said. The old man wanted Papa to agree to something he proposed but Papa kept saying no. You see, Papa had arranged to take us out to St. Helena where he could make a good living for us."

"That would be about twelve years ago, wouldn't it?" commented the lady. "The old king was at Windsor then. But his mind was getting cloudy."

"The night before we took the coach for Southampton," went on Betsy, "a footman with legs as long as Blunderbore came to the house. He had a basket of wine for Papa and a velvet purse for Mamma with the royal crest embroidered on one side. There were ten golden sovereigns in it. Mamma never spoke of this until Jane and I were going back to England to school. She showed us the sovereigns and I counted them. They were all still there, ten. My parents were very proud of that purse."

"Then I think you have no cause to worry now."

There was a long pause. It was clear that the lady in the darkness of the inner room was trying to make up her mind about further questions.

"Betsy," she said, finally, "was your feeling about the emperor one of pride because he was staying in your house and was paying a great deal of attention to you?"

"Oh, yes. It was partly that. But it was more than pride, Julia. I liked him. I liked him very much. I still do."

"Why do you like him so much?"

Betsy paused to decide how this question might be answered. "One day," she said, "when he was living in the pavilion, we went out for a walk. He began to tell me about the Code of laws. The one he framed for France. He must have forgotten that he was talking to a young girl, for he explained everything in the greatest detail. I thought it was wonderful! I didn't understand all he was telling me but he made it clear enough that what he had done with the Code was greater than the winning of all his battles put together. It was—well, an inspiration to hear him describe it. And that, I suppose, is your answer. I think he's a great man."

"But hasn't he many unpleasant sides to him?"

Betsy laughed at this point. "Of course he has. In some ways he's a *terrible* person."

"Doesn't he trample over people and shove them aside? Doesn't he criticize all his friends?"

"Yes. He's the most critical man, I guess, that ever lived."

"Isn't he a great gossip?"

"Yes, he tells outrageous things about his friends."

"Doesn't he cheat at cards?"

"All the time. He isn't a good player but he can't bear to let other people win."

"Doesn't all this make him an impossible person?"

Betsy twined her hands around her knees and leaned forward eagerly. "Isn't there a mountain in Greece," she asked, "where the gods and goddesses and even demigods live?"

"Mount Parnassus."

"Well, that's where he belongs. He's a demigod. But instead of living up there with the rest of them, he's been dropped down on earth. He has to live with stupid, fumbling people who make blunders and spoil some of his great plans. Is it any wonder that he has such a bad temper and that he finds fault with everyone and everything? I don't blame him for wanting to box the ears of all the dull people for whose

241

mistakes he has to pay. You have to make allowances for de-migods—especially when they're forced to live on earth. And, of course, he's getting worse because he's being treated so badly here."

"Betsy, I'm sure you are patriotic. But I wonder if you aren't being won over too much to his side."

This was hard to answer. Betsy thought it over with great seriousness.

"Does it seem so to you that I am? I'm glad he was beaten at Waterloo and I talk back to him whenever he criticizes England or the English people; which is quite often. But I'm sure he can't escape from the island and so I think all these restrictions are unnecessary and even silly. It's because he resents them so much that he has become so hard to handle. Even if he did escape, he couldn't start another international war. We used to walk and ride together every day and I found that he tired easily. He hasn't much energy left. So why are they so hard on him? Is it unpatriotic to think that?"

"No. We are all entitled to our opinions. But, Betsy, it seems to me you have a bad case of hero worship. There's nothing wrong with that. It happens often. But, please, let me ask you another question. When your parents decide to let you resume your normal way of living, will you be allowed to see him often?"

"I think so. All those awful stories will be forgotten by that time."

"Let us hope so. But, my dear, you mustn't forget when this happens that you won't be a young girl any more. You will be a woman. I am disturbed because this hero worship may grow stronger and perhaps change into something much more dangerous. Into an infatuation."

Betsy smiled for the first time since they had entered on this phase of their conversation. "Don't you think we're taking too much for granted? Think how long it will be since he has seen me. How can I be sure he won't take one look at me and say to himself, 'She's turned gawky' or when he hears me speak, 'How stupid this child has become.' You see, Julia, one of his pet beliefs is that all English women are gawky and stupid. If it turns out that he feels that way, we won't have anything to worry about, will we?"

"I'm certain he won't think you are either gawky or stupid."

Betsy was still smiling. "Or suppose I'm the one to see faults. Suppose I find him old and bald, for instance?"

"That probably wouldn't make any difference. He would still be a great man. I seem to recall that most of the great men of the past were bald."

Betsy nodded her head. "I was just trying to say something bright. No, I'll never feel that way about him. Even if he turns his back on me. I'll still believe he belongs in that place up in the Greek mountains."

"Do you think it possible that your feeling for him will develop into—well, a lasting infatuation?"

The girl ceased to smile and her face took on a sober expression instead. She hesitated over her answer. "I don't know," she said, in a low tone. "It wouldn't be honest to say that I haven't thought of the possibility. Yes, I've done a lot of supposing and dreaming. I've been very silly. But I've always realized how absurd such an idea is."

"Please sit down, my dear. Bring your chair closer to me. I think I must tell you something about myself after all."

The silence in the room was so complete for several moments that the girl could hear the rustling of leaves in the courtyard and the sound of footsteps from the back of the house where Margette undoubtedly was making some special use of the "aches."

"I was in the same position as you some years ago, Betsy. It's only because of this that I feel privileged to talk so freely to you. My father had died and I was living with a witless old aunt at our home in the country. There was a rather famous man living near us. He was much older than I; in fact, there were fifteen years between us. He held a high political post and had been given a title. He was handsome and brilliant and it was certain he had a great future ahead of him. He fell in love with me and I—I reciprocated. It finally went far beyond that. I was weak enough to yield to his wishes. No—no, that is not fair. I was as much in love as he was and I was happy about it.

"It was a tragic mistake," she went on, after pausing a moment to collect herself. "It's because of this that I am here. Some day, my dear, I'll tell you the whole story but I can't force myself to say more about it now. I've told you this much because I feel you are in need of advice. Don't let yourself be carried away by his greatness and glamor. Don't drift into an impossible situation. It would be completely im-

243

possible, you know. His son is in the hands of the emperor of Austria and he can never get a divorce. Would you want to be Number Ten?"

Betsy's face became strained. "Do you mean among the Others? He said once there had been only seven of them. But I counted up and I'm sure there were twelve."

"Then I don't believe there could be any happiness for you, or even any glamor, in being Number Thirteen. Oh, I know it's natural for you to admire him. Most women do. But keep your heart under control. Be sensible, dear child. And if you don't feel like discussing things with your mother, please bring your problems to me. You will need advice and, because of my experience, I may be of help to you. Promise me that."

Betsy nodded. "I promise."

Chapter Nine

1

More months passed, long and rather dreary ones for almost everyone. The weighing machine showed a gradual decrease in the imperial girth, but Napoleon was not yet down to the stage at which he had arrived in St. Helena. The ban on Betsy's movements had not been lifted. The Captive and Sir Hudson Lowe were not meeting but the feud between them was deepening with the passing of the weeks and months.

For several days William Balcombe had been aware of an activity about his home. A table had been set up at one end of the drawing room and was now piled high with materials for feminine wear; obviously so, for he did not recognize much of the stuff. There were rolls of calendered tabby, printed muslins and chintzes, ribbons of many shades and widths, colored gauze, bands of beautiful embroidery (and this, he knew, involved much expense), satins to be converted into pelerines, and smaller matters such as *barège* notions and gay buttons and *canezou* conceits.

On several occasions he had encountered either coming or going or about the house Mrs. Christie Dimcuzzen, a youngish widow who had become the recognized seamstress of the island. He had bowed to her but had not endeavored to get any closer insight by direct questioning. No doubt he asked himself, "Now what is this all about?" or, "What will all this do to my pocketbook?" He did not open the question with his wife, however. He knew she would tell him everything in her own good time.

One evening he came back a little earlier than usual. He did not catch a glimpse of the dressmaker. The table on which all this bewildering display of materials had been heaped was empty. What was more, the dining room was already prepared for the evening meal, which caused him to think, "We must be going out after dinner."

He stood at the entrance to the dining room and called: "I say, my dear, where are you? Where are the children?"

Mrs. Balcombe answered from the head of the stairs, "I'm coming down, William." There was something about the impact of her heels on the stairs which told him she was not her usual placid self; a hint of inner excitement, perhaps of anticipation. When she arrived at the foot, he realized at once that the mysterious happenings had come to the point of climax. Her cheeks were flushed, her eyes sparkled, her hair had been done with fastidious attention. He said to himself, "By Jove, I've never seen her look better."

"Dear William," said Mrs. Balcombe, "you have been so very considerate. Have we been unfair not to let you know everything from the start? If we have, please forgive me. We wanted so much to surprise you."

"Well," he said, "I'm here. And waiting."

"Mr. Balcombe," said his wife, in a reasonable imitation of the announcements made at public affairs, "I desire to introduce you to—our daughter, Miss Lucia Elizabeth Balcombe."

Betsy had been a few steps only behind her mother. She completed her descent of the stairs with a dignity which was new and quite unexpected. Her father gasped.

He had not realized how much she had been changing. That she had been growing had been obvious to the most casual eye but it had never entered his mind that his daughter could turn so completely into a young lady in so brief a period. She was much taller but there was none of the gawkiness of the middle teens about her. With her new slenderness, she had grace and an ease of carriage. This he was to discover fully later. In the first moments he gave his full attention to her face.

Betsy's blondness, because of her continual outdoor activity, had always seemed wind-blown. Now her hair was as lustrous as polished gold. Her eyes had always been a bright blue, now they were large and vibrant; the eyes, her father thought, of a Plantagenet princess. Her nose? Too little attention is paid the nose as a factor in womanly beauty; the eyes, the hair, the mouth (how many adjectives have been coined for the feminine mouth), the complexion—but the nose had been rather passed over. Betsy's nose had become longer but the added length had given it perfection of modeling; it was, in brief, a little gay still, a trifle patrician, in every sense an enchanting nose.

246

"My little Betsy!" said her father. "How blind I've been! All this has been happening to you, and I've been in and out and grumbling around—and not aware of it! Will you ever forgive me?"

"Papa!" cried Betsy. This was all she could say. She stretched out her arms and would have gone over to kiss him if her mother had not intervened.

"Now, you know what I said. Nothing impetuous, please. We have your hair perfect and your dress just right."

The two boys, who had come down last were too awed at what was happening to say anything. It remained for Jane to make the perfect comment—Jane, who was perfect herself, in a slender, coolly brunette way, and who had no envy in her, not at least where her sister was concerned. She whispered to her father: "Isn't she beautiful? Isn't she wonderful?"

"Jane," said William Balcombe, "I'm not very much surprised. You see, I have another daughter who is also beautiful and wonderful."

"Thanks, Papa. I'm quite satisfied with my share, you know. But Betsy—oh, oh!"

Mrs. Balcombe took her husband to one side. "William," she whispered, "we're going to the Bertrands' after dinner. Do you see any objection to letting Betsy go with us?"

"Not at all! I've been thinking for some time she should be given a free run of things again. I don't think it's fair to the child to keep her out of sight any longer."

"That's what I thought. But Napoleon is going over to the Bertrands'. Does that change your mind?"

"Certainly not."

"I'm glad that's how you feel, William. I took it on myself to say we would all go. Napoleon has been told—I think this young chick of ours will soon be the reigning belle here in St. Helena."

Balcombe snorted. "Of this little island? If we were in England, she would be the belle of the London season. She would sweep society off its feet!"

When they sat down at the table, the three feminine members of the family plunged at once into talk of dress.

"William," said Mrs. Balcombe, "we've been having things made for all of us. It has tired us out—but it has been most exciting. Betsy has grown out of all her clothes so she has the major share. It was Jane who planned the dress Betsy is wearing. Perhaps she ought to tell you about it."

Jane plunged eagerly into descriptive enthusiasm. "I didn't actually plan it, Papa. I saw a description in one of the London newspapers of a frock worn by a great beauty at a ball in London, Lady Blanchefleur Whiting. She's always called Lady Blanche, even in newspapers. I made half a dozen sketches from the description and finally got it right. When I showed it to Mrs. Dimcuzzen, she fairly squeaked with approval.

"Well," went on the older daughter, "it's figured gauze over white satin. The neckline is low, as you see, and the waistline is high. As high as it can be. The waist is spanned by embroidered tulle of the lightest gold we could find. See how well it contrasts with her hair? Those are called poster-bed sleeves. At the shoulders they flare out and they are given a kind of twirl. Then they are bound in with close-fitting tulle bands. After that more flaring out and finally at the wrists there is lace in a water-lily pattern. The skirt is full and long. So long that, even when she walks, you can't see more than the tips of her toes. Now you know all about it."

"I understood all you said. In a hazy sort of way. You could become a successful society dressmaker in London, Jane, and accumulate oofs of money. Except you're certain to marry young."

"I'm not sure of that, Papa. I like dancing with the regimental officers but I don't think I could pick a husband out of the lot."

Sarah Timms was serving a steaming dish of Betsy's pet aversion, stewed veal. The younger daughter accepted a portion and proceeded to eat it. She was too much interested in the conversation to know what she was eating.

2

It was a starless night and uncomfortably warm when Napoleon sallied out for his walk to Hutt's Gate. Two of the Longwood servants were waiting for him with lighted torches which flared up and tossed wildly when the trade winds reached them. As soon as the boundary line was crossed, three sentries fell into line a few paces behind him, with bayonets drawn. An attack of anger flooded over him. He might as well be sent out with his hands shackled or his arms bound, he said to himself.

He knew that his grand marshal had invited a varied group of people to meet him, being of the belief, which he had often expressed to Napoleon, that the latter's cause would be helped if he mixed more freely and did not fall back so exclusively into the role of the recluse of Longwood. The rest of the company was assembled when he arrived. There was an English diplomat of secondary rank returning from a mission in South Africa; several officers of the garrison, some of whom he had met and had found boring in the extreme; two couples from the higher reaches of island sociability; and an East Indian officer going back into permanent retirement in England, with a new title and a fourth wife. Not a very promising lot, he concluded.

Count Bertrand had the diplomat by the arm and was leading him over to be introduced. But Napoleon had stepped to one side and was glancing quickly about the crowded room. His eyes went down the line and then came back and then repeated the inspection rather more slowly. He turned to Bertrand with a disconsolate frown.

"Where is Betsee?" he asked.

Bertrand replied that Miss Elizabeth Balcombe was present but, inasmuch as she was the youngest member of the group, she was where she might be expected to be; at the foot of the line. The guest of honor glanced in that direction. He did not immediately recognize her and so he proceeded to walk slowly toward her. Betsy curtsied, managing skillfully the bouffant skirts of her very becoming frock. Napoleon studied her at close range, a smile beginning to spread across his face.

"It *is* you," he said. "But, *ma foi*, how was I to know? I haven't seen you for so long."

He turned to a small table on which candles had been banked. Lifting one, he held it close to her face. His doubts were then entirely dissolved but he was still in need of enlightenment. How had this miracle been accomplished?

Replacing the candle, he took both of her hands in his and studied her with a delighted smile.

"Betsee, Betsee!" he said. "You were always playing tricks with me. And now you have played the greatest trick of all. You have grown up!"

BOOK THREE
The Twilight Falls

Chapter One

1

While Betsy lived in comparative seclusion, poring earnestly over books and learning to ride, and gaining in height as well as in pulchritude, the English Government had made a significant move with reference to the presence of Napoleon at St. Helena. Sir Robert Wilson, that most outspoken of English lance-splinterers, had risen in the House of Commons and denounced the Cabinet for keeping the ex-emperor in a Rat Palace, and Lord Bathhurst had found it necessary to enter a defense in the House of Lords. The Lords, needless to state, had voted to support him; but in the meantime the liberal press had seen in this issue a great round political drum and had begun to make it resound in the ears of an attentive nationwide audience. The government, in spite of Bathhurst's protests, no doubt, had announced that as much as fifty thousand pounds would be spent forthwith to provide a more suitable house for the Captive.

The architects of the ordinance had come forward with an original plan. All the materials for the new Napoleonic residence would be prepared in England. The beams for the ceilings, the paneling for the walls, the oak for the floors, the frames for the doors and windows, would be designed and measured and carved in England and then sent out over the South Atlantic in readiness for erection. Necessarily it would be a frame structure but the plans were for a decidedly handsome one; two stories in height, wide wings, fourteen windows no less across the front, the ceilings high, the drawing room thirty-eight feet by twenty instead of the meager little box at the Rat Palace. The furnishings were to be on the very verge of elegance. Antique lamps were to hang from the ceilings, the mantels to be of bronze, the halls equipped with niches for statuary. The dining room was to be capable of seating fourteen for dinner.

Every man on the island capable of lending a pair of skilled hands or a willing back had been pressed into service. Betsy watched the progress of events with wide-eyed attention. Each day she journeyed to the highest spot on the surrounding terrain from which she would catch a glimpse of the left wing setting the constructural pace for the rest of the building. Often she would ride as close as she dared to the sentry line and watch what was going on from there.

The workmen became accustomed to her presence and frequently they would join with the sentries in discussing things with her. "Nah, young lady," they would say, "this'll be something for the hull island to be proud of, this will." The soldiers, who had tramped the streets of London and glimpsed the architectural beauties of cathedral towns as well as the family glorification of baronial mansions, were less appreciative. They would shake their heads over the structure they were guarding. "Rully, miss," they would say, "you should see Blenum or cast an eye on 'Ampstead Court. Now there ye get somethin' worth while, ye do."

Her concern was due to a depth of affection which she found surprising in herself. She wanted Napoleon to be comfortable, to have a home which would offer some shreds of the dignity to which he had been accustomed in the days of his glory. "Here he will have light rooms," she would think. "The air will be fresh. There will be none of the reek of the stables. He will be able to linger over his meals instead of rushing through them because of rats running over his feet." Sometimes she speculated on the probability that the emperor would begin to entertain more guests. "He needs new people to talk to instead of that same dull lot. He may become gay again instead of being so morose most of the time." The latent instinct of the householder began to show itself. "Light hangings, I think. In most of the rooms at least. He ought to have canterburies in every room. Then he could keep his papers and books and maps in better order. He ought to have paintings, not just those portraits of his silly unfaithful wife. Why shouldn't he get rid of some of these servants who have nothing to do but stand around and gape? He could have a few musicians instead. There should always be music at his meals."

One thing bothered her seriously, the iron fence which had been put up around the new house. "He'll think it's done deliberately to remind him he's a prisoner," she thought. "What
254

other purpose can it serve? It's too low to prevent anyone from getting away or to keep intruders out. That dreadful fence may spoil everything for him."

2

A few days after the lifting of the ban, she rode over to look more closely at the mansion stretching across a substantial part of the landscape. Tying Monty to a miserable scrub tree just outside the boundary line (for the peak of the plateau where the house stood offering nothing in the way of real trees or indeed shade of any kind), she approached closer than she had ever attempted before. Her application to Plantation House for a permit had come back with a peremptory No! scratched across the face of it, but, as far as she could see, the sentries had gravitated close to Longwood and no sound came from the building itself. She looked up at the completed roof of the east wing and the tall chimneys sprouting in all parts.

"I think," she said to herself, "I'll risk a peek inside for once."

The front door was open and she walked into a handsome hall which cut the interior into even halves. With the first few steps she took, her heels created a serious clatter in the empty interior, so she made her way into the drawing room on tiptoe. Equal caution was used in her progress through the beautifully proportioned library, after which she decided to take a look as well at the main bedroom suite. She had stepped inside before she made a disconcerting discovery. The dressing room where, presumably, Napoleon would spend his future mornings in his dimity lounging robe, was occupied. Three officers in full regimentals were chatting at one of the windows, with only their backs visible. At a window on the other side, which commanded a view of Longwood, a bent figure was watching what went on there through a telescope. Her first indiscreet step caused the back of the watcher to snap up immediately into sight above the substantial stretch of blue cloth which he had been displaying below his belt. It was Sir Hudson Lowe.

At the same instant the three officers faced about. "Gad!" ejaculated one of them, twirling the ends of his mustache with both hands. The others just stared.

"What are you doing here?" demanded the governor.

"I—I wanted to see inside, Your Excellency," said Betsy.

"Have you a permit?"

"No, Your Excellency."

"Ha! You must be the Balcombe girl."

"Yes, Your Excellency."

The dark brows drew down like thunderclouds. "Did you not receive your application back? Stamped no?"

Betsy nodded. "Yes. But—but I had no intention of going to Longwood. I just wanted to have a look inside the new house."

"Are you aware," demanded the governor, "that you have broken the law?"

"Oh, no, not the law, Your Excellency. I am not carrying any communications or—or aiding and abetting. Isn't it just a regulation?"

"I don't need any interpretations from you as to what is the law and what isn't!" declared Sir Hudson Lowe, his voice rising to match the thunder note of his brows. "I am telling you that by coming here you have broken the rules I laid down to prevent improper communications with the prisoner. You must leave at once. I shall discuss this with your father later."

"But, please, you must not blame Papa—"

"I need no instructions from you as to what I must not do!" cried Lowe, losing his temper completely. "Now, go, go! Go to your home, do you hear? And never come back!"

After Betsy had left the room, the governor remained silent for several moments, his brow still red with annoyance, his eyes burning angrily. "Such impertinence!" he muttered, finally. He singled out the officer who had spoken. "Challoner, what do you think of this girl?"

"What—what do I think of her, sir?"

"Yes, that's what I asked you. What was your impression of her?"

"Well, sir, she's a bit of a beauty, isn't she?"

"Is that all you noticed? Bates-Batwick," turning to one of the others, "did you notice anything about her—beside what this idiot of a Challoner calls her good looks?"

"Well, yes, sir."

"What else?"

"Well, sir, I—I don't know just how to put it."

"You thought her beautiful too?"

"Well, yes, sir. In a sense, sir."

"Have I nothing but simpletons on my staff? Scrimpson, you don't look as much carried away as these two donkeys. Get to horse and follow the girl. I want to be sure she goes straight home. And stays there."

"Yes, sir."

The road swung in closer to Longwood before joining the Jamestown road at Hutt's Gate. Betsy, riding by, saw a familiar head above the fence with which enclosed the tiny garden. Knowing that she must not check her speed for as much as a second, she whistled the first bars of "Lillibulero." The emperor had actually been at work with a spade. He straightened up to his full height and waved to her exuberantly, expecting she would turn in. But Betsy had observed over her shoulder the oncoming Scrimpson and so she shook her head and rode off in the direction of the Briars.

3

That evening Betsy told her father what had happened and he listened gravely. "Don't think I'm afraid of anything he might do," he said. "He's waiting for a chance to get rid of us, you know. We wouldn't starve if he did and perhaps it would be better all around if we got away from this dreary island. But, please, child, don't do anything more to stir him up. We don't want to provide him with any kind of case against us."

"But did I say anything very wrong?"

"It was a mistake to say anything. Or to go there in the first place. He dislikes us because he knows we are fond of Napoleon and that Napoleon likes us. Don't provide him with any more grounds."

Later he began to ask questions, as he sipped his port, about the interior of New Longwood, not having been inside himself. When Betsy told him all she knew, he smiled rather grimly.

"It seems a fine place," he said. "Rather a pity, you know."

"Papa! What do you mean?"

"I mean it's a pity that Napoleon will never live in it."

Betsy looked deeply distrubed. "You can't mean that you think he will die before it's ready for him?"

"No, no. He's looking much better lately. Finding that Sanctorious did him a world of good. He's nicely down in weight and his color is better. No, child, there's another reason. Why do you suppose the government is spending so much for a new Longwood?"

"I suppose they've seen how wrong they were in the first place."

Balcombe shook his head. "It's all a matter of politics. The Cabinet found that sympathy for Napoleon was growing all over the country. The truth about Longwood had seeped through, in spite of all the frantic efforts of our worthy little governor. The liberal papers were full of it. So—something had to be done. A new residence was the answer. Now, don't you suppose that the man up there was hearing all about this and wondering how best he could use this sentiment in his own interests? I've never heard him say a word on the subject and no one at Longwood has whispered in my ear. But I know that he hopes the sentiment in England will grow to such an extent that the government will have to move him back from St. Helena. That won't happen if he's installed in the new house where everything will be clean and comfortable and even rather gracious. It's only the miserable conditions under which he's living which creates the feeling in his favor. So, he'll never move of his own accord. That much is certain.

"And, of course, this poor fellow Lowe walks straight into a trap. He provides Napoleon with the best reasons for refusing to move. He goes ahead and builds the house *in the worst possible location*. Napoleon wanted it here, as close to the Briars as possible." Betsy could not prevent a smile of appreciation from flitting across her face. "That didn't suit Lowe at all and he finally decided on the spot where it now stands.

"Well, there it stands on the highest part of the plateau without as much as an anemic lilac bush to give it shade! In summer it will be so hot that life will be almost intolerable. In winter the trades will find a way into every corner. It's nearly two hundred yards nearer the military camp than the present place. He will feel all those eyes on him every time he appears at a window."

Balcombe paused and shook his head in puzzlement. "Why did Lowe make such a decision? Why did he provide Napoleon with the best possible reasons for refusing to go? He might just as well have taken the government's money and heaved it over the cliff into Flagstead Bay."

"Do you think they'll try to force him to go?" asked Betsy, with the deepest anxiety in her voice.

"I doubt it. Very much. It would take four strong soldiers to carry him. Not a very edifying spectacle, what?"

"Why," asked the girl, "do you always speak of the governor with a note of pity in your voice?"

"There are quite a few reasons, Betsy. I'll give you just one. Think what history will say of him."

Betsy laughed. "And what I'll say about him in *my* book!"

Mrs. Balcombe had been sitting at one side while this conversation proceeded, with a lap full of knitting. At this point she raised her head.

"What was it you said?"

"I said, my book."

"*Your* book! What do you mean by that, Betsy Balcombe?"

"I'm going to write a book. Why shouldn't I? Everyone who has known him well is doing it. And haven't we the best reason of all right here? Didn't he come here—" she paused to find the right words, "a defeated and unhappy man? He found us kind and he enjoyed himself in our home. He didn't want to leave. In fact, he wants to come back near us. Well? Isn't that a good reason for writing about him?"

Mrs. Balcombe dropped the knitting needles into her lap and stared at her daughter with unbelieving eyes.

"Well, I declare I shall never understand you, Betsy. Write a book? A young lady like you? Is it right, is it proper? Somehow I don't think so."

"Oh, Mamma, really! What's wrong about it?"

"When are you going to write this book?" asked her father, not quite successful in concealing a twinkle in his eyes.

"Well, Papa, since you ask me, I've made a start on it. I've had nothing much to do for a long time—so, I set to work. Oh, I haven't written much. As it stands, it's just a lot of notes. Perhaps it won't amount to much. I may not be a good enough writer."

"Then why try?" demanded her mother.

"Betsy," asked William Balcombe, "what are you going to say in this book about Sir Hudson Lowe?"

"If I say anything about him, I'll make it clear that I don't like him at all. But, perhaps, I'll be sensible, Papa, and leave politics out of it."

Chapter Two

It was some weeks later (during which time the frowning eye
of the ungracious governor remained fixed on the movements
of the genial family at the Briars) that the Bertrands again
invited the Balcombes to dinner. Napoleon, it was explained,
would not be one of the guests, it was to be *en famille*. Jane
had another engagement and Betsy persuaded her mother to
let her use the most daring costume made for her during the
visits of Mrs. Christie Dimcuzzen. The choice was based on
its military note. The material was black and it buttoned up
closely at the neck while the shoulders carried a most frivolous imitation of epaulettes. The skirt, however, was entirely
feminine, flaring out with some of the abandon of a ballet
dancer's.

"Ah, mam'selle," said Bertrand, doing her the honor of kiss-
ing her hand, "it is to be hoped the emperor will visit us after dinner. He will take your charming costume as a compliment."

"He'll be over, m'sieur le comte," whispered Betsy. "As we
rode up in that *awful* delivery wagon, I felt a light on us. I
really think we were being observed by telescope."

"We are having dinner early," declared Madame Bertrand,
linking an arm in that of Mrs. Balcombe, "Just in case, you
know."

At dinner the host apologized for serving a reddish wine
with a sharp taste. "It's that favorite of the emperor's. A
fresh case came in today."

"I noticed it in the shipment," said Balcombe. "Put on at
Cadiz, I believe."

Bertrand nodded. "He welcomes it with gusto and has it
served at once. But he always sends a few bottles over to us.
How do you like it?"

The guest took a sip. "Of course, I'm a port drinker," he began.

"Quite," laughed Bertrand, speaking slowly to cover the inadequacy of his English. "No need to say anything more. There will be port with the desserts."

The port had appeared, and William Balcombe's eyes had lighted up, when a sound of activity reached them from the next room, to which the ladies had retired. There was a squeal of delight from the small Bertrand girls and a "How dramatic!" from Betsy.

Night had fallen with the suddenness of the tropics and the stars were doing very little to break the darkness between the Bertrand home and the flatness of Longwood. Three servants had walked out in the lead of a party emerging from the Longwood gardens, with torches carried overhead. Behind them walked Napoleon and back of him came Perron with something wrapped in a velvet cloth under one arm. Since the death of Cipriani, a short time before, Perron the butler had taken over most of his duties.

The Captive was wearing a frock coat, just received from the tailor's. In it he appeared taller, an effect increased by his faithful attention to the Sanctorious which had given him a new trimness. Under the light of the torches his brow seemed both wider and whiter. His pace was brisk, revealing none of the plodding heaviness with which he sometimes walked about the Longwood grounds.

Betsy was aware of a constriction of the heart. Never before had he looked so impressive and, yes, romantic. She realized fully for the first time why women had found him irresistible, and why he had fascinated even the people in conquered countries. This, she thought, was the Napoleon who had stood so still as the guard marched by, crying out to him, "We who are about to die salute thee!"

"How wonderful he looks!" she said to herself. "He doesn't seem old at all."

She remembered what her friend in the lonely house had said to her, "You have a bad case of hero worship." Her feeling for him now, she realized, was more than that. Was she reaching the stage of infatuation, about which her friend had warned her so solemnly? "I mustn't do that!" she said to herself. "I must be sensible. I must not let my feelings run away with me."

As the party turned in at the gate, Napoleon took one of

the torches from the nearest servant and gave it an exultant wave over his head. He even executed a dance step; not like the efforts of a year earlier when his bulk made him clumsy, but with lightness and even something of grace.

"What has happened?" wondered the girl, pressing her face close to the glass. "He must be in wonderful spirits. I've never seen him like this before."

Nor, for that matter, had any of the party inside the house with the possible exception of the grand marshal. If anyone had noticed, they might have seen that Bertrand's face reflected some of the same spirit which animated the emperor. But no one did. The ladies had filled the space at the window and William Balcombe had carried his glass back to the dining room to be deposited on the table. "It can't be the effect of that miserable Spanish wine," he said to himself.

Napoleon kissed his hostess' hand on entering the small drawing room. "Ah, dear madame," he said. "You are so kind and tactful. You have asked as your guests only the ones I like best."

His hand rested for several moments on the shoulder of Bertrand. It seemed to Betsy, who was watching with the closest attention, that a spark passed from eye to eye, and it needed no great degree of sentience on her part to realize that they shared some uplifting knowledge. She began to feel an excitement herself, although unaware of any reason for it. Why had the somewhat plump cheeks of Bertrand suddenly taken on a flush?

Napoleon cried, "Perron!" and took from the servant the article in the velvet cloth. It proved to be a rosewood box in which reposed a six-stringed guitar. He drew the instrument out and held it up to be admired.

"This," he announced, "belonged to my sister, the Princess Borghese. She sent it to me before I—I left Paris. *Ma foi,* how lovely she used to look when she strummed on it! But it was all for effect. My beautiful Pauline was too indolent to become a good musician. And it was the same with the empress. Josephine had a harp but she could play only one tune— and that badly!

"I'm hoping for better things tonight," he went on. "Betsy, I heard you playing on something at your house. You seemed to have some real promise. What do you think you could do with this?"

Betsy took the instrument which he passed to her. She

touched the strings and then ran her fingers over the smooth surface with an almost reverent touch. "How lovely it is!" she said. "I'm afraid it is much too fine for my poor little talent. Jane plays much better than I do."

"But Jane isn't here, and you are." He turned to Madame Bertrand. "I understand it is your purpose to play whist. There are four of you, all much keener for the game than I am. Leave me out at first. I want to hear Betsee try her hand."

It *was* the purpose of the rest of the company to play whist, or so they affirmed, and Betsy found herself directed into the gloom of the small garden by a possessive hand on her elbow. They seated themselves under one of the trees on chairs. The girl's skirts spread out so widely that her chair was completely obscured, so that she seemed in the dim light to be sitting on air.

"I am very nervous, sire," she said. "What I told you was true. I am not good. Not good enough, certainly, to play on such a fine instrument."

Napoleon's eyes were studying the effect of the moonlight on her hair which was held in place by a narrow band of black velvet. "It seems the good fate of this instrument to rest always in the hands of lovely women," he said. "Now, Betsee, you must not be too modest. Let me hear what you can do."

Betsy allowed her fingers to wander over the strings. After a moment she produced an air with a familiar lilt.

"That is a French song," declared Napoleon.

" 'The Song of Dunois'," said Betsy. "You should know it very well. Didn't your niece, Queen Hortense of Holland, have some part in writing it?"

Napoleon pondered this for a moment and then nodded. "Yes, you're right. The little Hortense did help with the air. She had more music in her than her mother. But the royalists took it as their own, for some reason, so I didn't encourage its use. Still, it's a tuneful bit. Sing it for me."

"I know only the last three lines. I'll have to play it through and sing only when I come to the finish."

Accordingly she played the air with a quite sure touch and at the finish began to sing the words in English.

> *"And grant, immortal queen of Heav'n,*
> *was still the soldier's prayer,*

> *That I may prove the bravest knight*
> *And love the fairest fair:*
> *That I may prove the bravest knight,*
> *And love the fairest fair."*

Napoleon was watching as well as listening, and perhaps his eyes were more attentive than his ears. "Your voice is much improved, *ma petite*," he said, after a moment. "But then you have changed so much that I can hardly believe it has all come about in such a short time. How does it happen that there are English words for this French song?"

"I believe Sir Walter Scott translated it."

"H'mm! That's how you get your songs in that benighted island."

"Please, sire, it's such a lovely evening. Can't you speak more kindly of us?"

There was a pause and then Napoleon sighed. "You must not begrudge me the satisfaction of venting my spleen. What else have I left?"

"Will you listen if I sing an English song? It's new and it's quite lovely, I think."

When he nodded, her fingers began to draw a sad and haunting melody from the strings while she sang:

> *"The harp that once through Tara's halls*
> *The soul of music shed,*
> *Now hangs as mute on Tara's walls*
> *As if that soul were fled.*
>
> *So sleeps the pride of former days,*
> *So glory's thrill is o'er;*
> *And hearts that once beat high for praise*
> *Now feel the pulse no more."*

"I heard Grassini sing that," declared the listener. "With Italian words, of course. It is a pleasant air. And you sang it with nice feeling."

"Grassini? She was one of the Others, I think."

Napoleon nodded. "She proved very bothersome, that one. She wanted me to acknowledge to the whole world that she had become the lodestar of my life. I said No and I cancelled her lease on the Rue de Chantereine."

265

Betsy looked startled. "The Rue de Chantereine! The same house?"

"No. Not the same house. She's in Russia now, I believe. Of course, I made a settlement on her."

He rose to his feet. Taking the guitar, he replaced it in the rosewood box which lay on a table near the door. Returning, he resumed his seat. There was silence for several moments.

"Betsee, I was pleased with the music. But it was to talk that I brought you here. I want to talk seriously, *ma petite*. Most seriously. You have become a beautiful woman. I have known many beautiful women but you"—with one of his infrequent smiles—"you are, I think, the *fairest fair*. Now, being a beauty offers great opportunities but it also creates responsibilities. You have a mind as well and a tongue to express what you think. You can rise to great heights."

"But, sire," said Betsy, "how can a woman rise to great heights in a world you have made a man's world?"

He nodded seriously. "That is true about women in general. Their part in life is to marry, to be good wives, and raise children. But you will become a recognized beauty wherever you go—Paris, Vienna, Rome, London, even New York. I am going to be very much disappointed if you don't achieve the destiny I can see for you.

"It's not hard to tell," he went on, "what will happen on this little island where all the eligible men—if any of them can be called eligible—are officers in an English regiment. You are going to sweep them off their feet; they will stretch out their long legs on your porch and fill your ears with inane talk. But not one of them is good enough to touch the tip of your little finger. I know you must dance a little, and also flirt, but I shall be very angry—no, I shall be enraged, I shall be furious—if you let yourself become entangled! You must never give one of them a serious thought!"

"But, sire," said Betsy, after a long pause. "Suppose I never leave this island? It seems quite possible that my family will always remain here."

"No, no! Put such thoughts out of your head!" he exclaimed. "You must believe in your destiny. If you do, your chance will come. Think of the ladies who have played big parts in this world you say is of my making. That fine Lady Holland in England, the Staël creature, Récamier, Madame Roland, Aurora Königsmark—no, she was a generation earlier but she was a rare beauty. *Ma foi*, I could name scores. But perhaps you should persuade your father to go to New York. There are chances to make great fortunes there."

"New York!" cried Betsy, in a dismayed tone. "So far away from everything that counts!"

"The world is due for another change. I made it a world for soldiers, where a stout heart and a clear head meant more than blue blood. And now America is going to make it a world of industrial giants. Millionaires, they call them. A fascinating world. And such brilliant prospects! If I had known what I do now, when I was a half-starved student in France, I might not have gone into the Army. Instead I might have made my way to New York and started in the business of building fast ships. That," he sighed, "is where I should be now.

"Betsee," he continued, after a moment, "it won't be hard for you to get away from this island. You have read about a certain family who lived in Corsica and whose name was Bonaparte?" He motioned toward the house. "From the tone of their voices in there, they are becoming a little annoyed with each other. That means they are enjoying their whist. Well, let us stay out a little longer. Perhaps it would strengthen your resolution for what lies ahead of you if I told you about this family and how the second son selected his own particular star —and proceeded to follow it."

Betsy leaned forward eagerly. "Yes, please do, sire. I would like to know all about that second son."

Chapter Three

1

In the heart of Ajaccio there was a quiet old quadrangular square. It lay back of the cathedral and the streets which ran into it were narrow and shaded by elms and plane trees. On one of these streets, the Rue St. Charles, there was a stone house which stood four stories high. The walls of this old and rather quaint dwelling had been covered with a yellowish plaster and all the windows, two to each floor, had shutters painted a rather severe gray.

Ajaccio was not a city of great wealth but in the section back of the cathedral the houses had an air of gentility and were occupied by members of the old Corsican families. The home in question belonged to the Bonapartes, who, at this early stage, enjoyed one distinction, that of being unusually numerous. There had been twelve children, but four had died, and so eight of them were left to fill the large and sparsely furnished rooms and the drafty halls with noise and song and dispute, with heads bobbing out from behind the shutters, with daring ascents to the flat roof and with games in the street and the narrow alleyway.

The head of this family, Charles-Marie Bonaparte, generally called Carlo, was a lawyer and both eloquent and fierce in partisanship. He was tall and slender, with a handsome nose and an olive skin and eyes which sparkled and danced and smoldered and never seemed still. The mother, Letizia, had belonged to the noble family of the Ramolinos and so had brought a dowry with her; a small enough one, it was true, seven or eight thousand francs and no more. She had been quite a beauty when she married Carlo at the age of fourteen, with fine dark eyes and an intelligent as well as attractive face.

There was in the house on the Rue St. Charles, a large couch in what was called the *salotto*, high of head and foot.

It is with this comfortable but somewhat dilapidated piece of furniture that the story of the Bonaparte family really begins.

2

Carlo was a strong partisan of Paoli, who led the independence party in Corsica when the overlordship of Genoa was transferred to France. Two daughters had been born by this time and had died very young, Joseph had been brought into the world and was showing every indication of remaining, and it was apparent that another child was on the way. Letizia decided, nevertheless, that wherever her beloved Carlo went she also must go, and so she was with him when he made his way into the mountains to join the clans under Paoli. For several months they lived in caves or slept out in the open, and were harried about through the mountain passes and over swollen rivers. "The new child will be a man and a soldier," declared Carlo, "for surely no military career ever began so early." He was quite right. The new child would be a man and a soldier.

They were still playing hide and seek with the French forces when it became clear to Letizia that her time was near. She broke the news to her husband with a worried frown. "Please, Carlo," she said, "I want our son to be born in our own home and not here under the brushwood. Can we not go home now?"

Carlo had been taking the war making with great seriousness. He had half a dozen pockets on the front of his shirt and there was a pistol in each. He fumbled with one of these as he considered the problem.

"Dear little Letizia," he whispered finally. "I am not taken into the general's confidence but it seems to me that things are not going very well. Actually there is nothing I can do. We shall return as you wish to our own home. Even though the French in Ajaccio may look at us with sour eyes."

The day they reached the city, the expectant mother knew they had not started a moment too soon. "I think," she said to her husband, "I must go at once to Mass." Old Uncle Lucciano and one of the female relatives who lived with the family promptly brought out an ancient cane-backed chair and in this she was carried to the church. The chair was deposited back of the last row of seats, which was fortunate, for, with the first sound of the priest's voice, the labor pains began. Zio Lucciano, who had been archdeacon at the cathedral but was now retired and badly crippled with rheumatism, took one side of the chair while Carlo, a prey to deep anxiety, took the other.

"Not too fast!" protested the old man, holding up his side with difficulty.

"No," agreed the father, "but pray, Zio Lucciano, that we go fast enough."

Their best speed proved barely sufficient. When they reached the house, it was too late to carry the expectant mother to her own bedroom on the floor above. And so the child, who would be a man and a soldier, was born on the couch in the *salotto*.

He was a somewhat puny child with a large round head but even in his first hour of existence his eyes seemed to take in everything about him. It is on record also that the child did not announce his entry into life with the usual plaintive, mewing sound of the newly born but instead with a cry which was strong and even strident. One who heard it declared years after that it was as though he were trying to say, "Well, here I am at last and I wish it understood that everything I shall want in life I intend to take."

He was given the name of Napoleon.

In the meantime the army of Paoli had suffered a serious disaster and the resistance to French occupation practically ceased. Carlo decided he had done all that could be expected of him and made his submission. He made himself so useful, in fact, that he was appointed to the post of assessor to the court of Ajaccio with a salary of sixty pounds a year. This seemed such affluence that he proceeded to build a new dining room on the old stone house and to project out from it a nicely grassed terrace where the family could sit of an evening.

But the yearly salary failed to suffice for the family when the husband and father was full of such extravagant ideas, and so Carlo found it expedient to practice a little law as well. He would walk to his office in a velvet coat with lace at his wrists and wait for clients. Children, alas, continued to arrive with more regularity than clients and so the family continued to experience many ups and downs.

The order of succession in the family was as follows:

Joseph, Napoleon, Lucien, Elisa, Louis, Pauline, Caroline, and Jerome. Without exception they were bright and handsome, some of them (the luckier ones) more indebted to their brave mother, the rest having qualities which stemmed directly from their lighthearted father.

3

Even in the earliest years, while father Carlo was still alive, the family lived on a narrow measure of subsistence. Carlo was brilliant enough and he had a gift for making friends in the highest places, but somehow he could never succeed in keeping a family such as his in food and clothing. The problem, therefore, rested on the shoulders of his wife, the once beautiful Letizia (she retained some of her fine looks to the end of her days), with her deep sense of duty and her great common sense. Somehow she always managed to keep food in the house. Her fingers were never idle. She made all the dresses for the girls and she rotated the suits of the boys with much ingenuity.

Joseph, the oldest of the eight survivors, was destined for the law. Actually he was better suited to banking, having a gift for the acquisition of money, even as a boy, and a sound idea of how to keep it. Many times, when the handsome father had failed to bring any contribution to the flat family purse, Napoleon heard scraps of conversation between his mother and the bland older brother.

"Maman, Maman! How can I do what you want? I am not made of money."

"Now, Josepha, you *always* have money. I know you very well, my good son. I am proud of you, though where a boy like you can get so many coins to fill his pockets is something I do not understand. But, please, just once more."

"It isn't fair, Maman. Why doesn't our father—"

"That will do!" Letizia never permitted any criticism of the magnetic man to whom she had given her love. "These bankers you work for, they will help you out. Do you want your brothers and your lovely sisters to go hungry?"

Joseph always gave in, of course, and so there would be fish, purchased cheaply at the docks, or occasionally a leg of the wonderful Corsican mouflon. After the unreliable Carlo died (of cancer in a French hospital to which he had been sent), the responsibility fell still more heavily on the broad shoulders of Joseph, who had been elected in the meantime as a councilor of the municipality of Ajaccio. This was one of the reasons tor the great liking which Napoleon always felt for his oldest brother, and for the crowns which were placed on his inadequate brow.

There was no need actually for the privations which the gallant Letizia and the large Bonapartist brood suffered. There was Zio Lucciano, who had been archdeacon and a prominent figure in the church. In his old age, he had come to live with them, a stooped figure with the sharp beak of acquisitiveness and joints swollen with rheumatism. He had been given a cool room on the third floor and from this he seldom stirred, becoming in time practically bedridden.

The care of the family finances, including what was left of Letizia's dowry, had been put in his hands. His one idea seemed to be that money was something to be kept, to be put to work at interest, and to grow over the years. Under no circumstances was money to be spent. What if a handful of noisy children required food in the meantime? That seemed of small concern to this old miserly bag-of-bones. Somehow they would be fed. That woman downstairs, whom he admired very much because of her industry and courage and her lack of feminine foolishness, would see to the children. She always managed somehow.

And so, when Letizia would come to him with a shadow of distress in her eyes, to beg for aid in tiding over a crisis, he would shake his head and mutter that he did not think there was a sou available at the moment.

"Surely something can be done!" the mother of the family would cry. "Zio Lucciano, I am desperate. I owe money to the butcher and the baker. They are refusing to sell me anything."

He would look up at her from under his shaggy brows and frown in disapproval. "Young woman, have there been extravagances? It must be so or you would not so often ask me to get blood from stones." He would go on frowning and muttering to himself. "Well," he would say finally, "I will do some figuring. Perhaps it will be possible to save a little for you this time. Come back later."

It was suspected that the grasping old uncle kept the family money in his bedroom but no one had any inkling as to where it was concealed. It remained for little Pauline to uncover the secret.

She was the butterfly of the family, a slender child, with so much beauty of feature and such symmetry of figure that Napoleon always contended she was the most beautiful woman in the world. That, of course, was when she had grown up and spent a large part of her days on a couch (at first on the couch where Napoleon had been born, but later on much more costly ones) where her admirers gathered about her and amused her with their talk. As a young girl she was a pixyish figure and infinitely engaging, who broke all the rules of the household. "Marie-Pauline!" her mother would say in exasperation, "why do I allow you so many liberties? Why do I not punish you for the naughty things you do?" "But, Maman," the child would say, "am I really naughty? I don't mean to be." Of all this charming brood, little Pauline was Napoleon's favorite; and she kept her hold on his affections until the end of his days.

One morning the restless Pauline climbed up to the third floor and looked through the open door of Zio Lucciano's room. He was so sound asleep that a fly sitting on the tip of his nose had not disturbed him.

A short time later there was an uproar in the bedroom with its own high window looking down over the square. Great-uncle Lucciano was screaming with rage. "Woman! Letizia! Come! At once!"

Letizia ran up the narrow stairs as fast as her feet could carry her, to discover that the old man had rolled his bent body over to the edge of the bed. He was shouting imprecations at a completely unconcerned Pauline, sitting on the floor with her skirts gathered up above her small white knees. The girl had found the bag in which the funds were kept. The bag, she explained later, had been hidden under the mattress where it could only be reached from below.

Very pleased with herself, she had untied it and had spilled out the gold and silver coins on the floor. When her mother arrived, she was calmly stacking them up in even piles.

"See, Maman," she said. "Money, oh so much money!"

"This child, she must be punished!" spluttered the archdeacon. "When I saw what she was trying, I told her to leave. She paid no attention to me. She is a very bad child, this one."

"But, Zio Lucciano, where did all this money come from?"

273

The old man had his explanation ready. "It is not ours. It belongs to a man in town who listened to me when I preached at the cathedral and who knew I could be trusted with it. I see to the investing for him. Take it away from this wicked little imp! How could I replace it if a piece of gold were lost?"

Letizia took his word for it, believing him a holy man and above any evasions. After sending Pauline out with a sharp reprimand, she scooped up the money with hands which trembled and poured it back into the bag.

"There, dear uncle," she said, placing the bag in his eagerly clutching fingers. "It is all there. You must not be angry with the child. She is a good little girl and did not know what she was doing."

Uncle Lucciano's rage subsided to some extent. "Well," he muttered, "I don't want her coming back. See that she stays out of my room."

When the old man died a few years later, it was found that it was family money after all, quite a sizable nest egg. Letizia knew the many good uses to which it could be applied. But she put her foot down firmly. This money must be reserved for the education for the boys. There were so many of them still, Napoleon, Lucien, Louis, and a tiny little fellow, the final one to arrive, who had been named Jerome. All of them must go to schools in France. The family could struggle along somehow. She had always managed to keep them fed, and would continue to do so.

4

The Bonaparte children must have seemed a contradictory lot to anyone with opportunities for close observation. They were, in many respects, as different and individual as the members of the most large families. The quiet, businesslike Joseph, the repressed but strangely gifted Napoleon, the glib Lucien, the lovely Pauline, the plump and opinionated Caroline; here, surely, was variety in physique as well as in qualities of mind and temperament.

But in many important respects they were a unit. In a century generally considered brilliant and advanced but which had not learned the advantages of the bathtub and considered the use of perfumes a proper substitute, the Bonaparte children were scrupulously clean. Madame Mère had laid down a dictum, "A bath every day for all of you." She had no difficulty in enforcing it. All of them clamored for their turns in the one cramped and much dented family tub. It became a fetish with them, one moreover that they enjoyed. Probably all of them retained this sense of cleanliness as long as they lived. Certainly Napoleon did. After every crisis in his life, every battle won, every diplomatic struggle ended, after every state function concluded, he sought first of all the solace of steaming hot water.

They seem to have suffered from the same maladies at the same stages. If Joseph had measles at seven, then Napoleon would have it in the same year, with Lucien and the rest trailing along with similar visitations. They laughed at the same jokes, and mourned the same misfortunes. Except, perhaps, Lucien; he was the one loose cog in an otherwise tightly fitted chain.

With their love of hot water and cleanliness, the Bonapartes were pagan in their lack of inhibitions. They would walk to the bath and emerge therefrom without either clothing or towels to save themselves the embarrassment of other eyes upon them. In this connection there is another story to be told about Pauline.

She seems to have been the least inhibited of them all. Thinking nothing of running about the house in the condition generally called *stark naked*, she even invaded the out-of-doors in a similiar state. When Letizia first observed this quaint demonstration, she took Pauline by the ear and led her back into the house.

"But, Maman," protested the girl, "what have I done wrong? I am pretty—I think I am *very* pretty, don't you, Maman?—and so it is a pleasure for people to see me. It's only if you're fat or skinny or have knobby knees that you should keep bundled up in clothes."

"Understand this, Marie-Pauline. There must be no more of this—this indecent parading outside without clothes. Even the commonest woman of the streets wouldn't display herself as you have done."

Pauline giggled. "The commonest woman of the streets would look *terrible* naked. She would know better than to try it. She wouldn't want to lose—"

"Pauline, Pauline! How can you say such dreadful, wicked

275

things! Where have you learned them? I can see that I must take your education in hand myself."

5

A constant factor in the life of the island was the vendetta, and there was a strong appreciation in the Bonaparte clan of its importance. An insult to one of them was a blow to the family pride and must be repaid by concerted action.

Which leads to the story of the Signora Sanluzzi and the pot of household slops.

Napoleon returned from a French military school to find his brother Lucien firmly ensconced in the affections of the senior Bonapartes and the younger brothers and sisters. The thoughtful second son had never felt any great liking for the confident and contentious Lucien and it annoyed him somewhat to find everyone turning to the latter for advice and leadership. An episode occurred very soon thereafter, however, which made it possible for the family to draw a comparison between them.

For reasons of economy the Bonapartes had leased the top floor to a connection by marriage, Signora Sanluzzi. She was a widow and lived alone. She was, moreover, very outspoken and liked her own way, considering herself bound by no social laws. For some time she had chafed at the spectacle of the handsome Carlo strutting about in velvet and laces and tossing money around with a much too lavish hand. Finally she could not stand it any longer and one morning she carried out a pail of slops which she emptied over him as he paused at the front door before setting out for his office.

This was the worst of insults. Napoleon was back in the little shed which had been constructed for him when he was a small boy, and which he still used. Louis carried back a message to him. "Brother, the name of Bonaparte has been besmirched. You are needed at once." He came to the house in a great hurry and found all the children assembled with the exception of Lucien and, of course, Joseph, who was still in France. They were looking very solemn, even the little Caroline and the still smaller Jerome who was not yet four. When the situation was explained, Napoleon's fighting frown took possession of his face. He sat down and began to think.

Lucien entered the room with a satisfied smile.

"It is settled," he announced. "I have persuaded Maman that we must bring a suit at law against her. This will cost her a pretty penny."

Napoleon turned in amazement. "You seem to have forgotten something," he said. "The meaning of the word vendetta."

Lucien was surprised at any member of the family being ready to dispute with him. "Vendetta?" he said, with an easy laugh. "Of course, Nabuleone. But how better can we repay her than by striking at her most vulnerable spot, her purse?"

"Insults are never settled in the courts." Napoleon continued to stare at his brother for several moments and then turned to the circle of faces behind him. "It is our duty to avenge this bitter offence. Being a woman, she can't be called out. Nor can we resort to violence in any form. We must humble her pride. I shall now tell you of the parts each of you must play in the plan I have devised.

"You, Elisa," he went on, "and you, Pauline, and you, little Caroline, will have passive parts but it will be most important for you to carry them out properly. Since her knees gave out, she seldom leaves the house and depends on you to supply her appetite for talk. From this moment on she must exist in a vacuum. No one will speak to her. No one will look her in the face. She must be ignored when she comes downstairs."

"One moment, if you please," said Lucien. "What right have you to take things in hand this way? I have settled on the proper procedure after talking with Maman. We need no advice from you, Master Nabuleone."

Napoleon turned on him sharply. "It seems the reports I've had of you are true, Lucien. There are stripes on the back of our little horse. And, what is more, you possess a knack for getting on the wrong side of everything. We'll hear nothing more from you, if you please."

"And now, Pauline," he went on, turning to the beauty of the family, "what is it you are to do when this woman comes down the stairs and speaks to you?"

"I will say no more than 'Good morning, Zia Caterina' and then turn my back on her."

"No, no! Pauline, you must not say a word. You must keep your eyes lowered and never look at her. It must be as though she does not exist. As though she has turned into a ghost or some kind of disembodied spirit. Do you understand now?"

Pauline was such a gay and happy child that this role did not please her. Nevertheless she said, "Yes, Nabuleone, I understand. I am not to say a word."

"And you, little Caroline?" asked Napoleon.

Caroline was a chubby child with a trim ankle and a nicely rounded little behind. Her complexion was high and so was her temper.

"You say I mustn't speak to her, and so I won't," she declared. "But, please, couldn't I take off a shoe and throw it at her? Or perhaps, if she steps on that loose rug in the hall, might I yank it out from under her?"

"Your wishes do you credit, Caro. But I assure you it will hurt her more to be ignored."

Lucien got to his feet at this point. "I am still a member of the family," he said. "But would anyone, listening to all this, believe it? Try things your way, Nabuleone. We'll see what happens."

He stalked from the room with a red and angry face. No one seemed aware of his departure.

Louis was fairly boiling with desire for a part in the comedy. "What am I to do?" he demanded. "Could I go out at night and sing under her window?"

"I have noticed, Louis," said Napoleon, "that you carry up to her each morning a supply of water from the well. From now on she won't have a drop of water unless she comes downstairs and gets it herself."

"She won't like that!" said Louis, grinning delightedly.

"Everything delivered for her is left downstairs. Her mail, her groceries, her meat. One of you always races up to deliver it. From now on it will accumulate downstairs unless she takes it on herself to hobble down."

"She'll burst her stays over that!" cried Louis.

"That bell in the hall which we ring when visitors come for her, will never be used. We will say to visitors: 'We have no dealings with Signora Sanluzzi. She has ceased to exist as far as we are concerned. What is more, we will regard it as an affront if you go up to see her.' That is the proper procedure in a vendetta. Those who are for the other side are against you. There is no halfway position. And so, I think, she will have no visitors at all."

"Finally," went on Napoleon, "there is another task for you, Louis. If that pipe, which hangs over the back of the roof, were plugged, the rain water would back up and run down the walls in her bedroom and kitchen. The first time she goes out, you must fill the pipe with mud and stones. Then we'll sit back and pray for rain."

"It won't be long," he concluded, "before she comes down and begs our father's forgiveness. *On her knees.*"

Late that afternoon the signora came to the top of the winding stairs. There was no one in sight. Not a sound reached her ears from below. Finally she called out: "Where is everyone? I saw you, Elisa, running into the dining room. At least I think it was you. I can hear Pauline giggling somewhere. Now this has gone far enough. Why hasn't that lazy Louis brought up the water for me? I saw Pozzi Canletto come to the back door with the meat. He must have left my order."

Silence. She called several more times but did not succeed in arousing any response from the family. She walked back into her rooms with a set look on her stern features.

The next morning she was up at an early hour, early enough to hear Carlo come out to the front door and pause at the stand for hats. She hobbled out to the landing.

"Do you know what's going on here?" she called down. "I want you to speak to those little fiends. I haven't had a drop of fresh water since the day before yesterday. No one answers when I call. Now, then, Carlo Bonaparte, I want all this to stop! Do you hear me?"

The head of the household apparently did not hear her. At any rate, he selected a hat, put it on his head and walked out, closing the door with a loud and satisfying sound.

The irate woman then began to call the others. "Letizia! Elisa! Lucien! Louis!" Not a sound rewarded her efforts. No door was opened, no head appeared.

Late in the afternoon the now thoroughly aroused tenant of the top floor took a large pitcher in hand and began the descent of the stairs. She stopped every few steps to rest and listen, hoping for some signs of relenting. She was disappointed in that. As she was returning from the well, bent almost double with the weight of the water, she had the luck to intercept Napoleon on his way to the house from his shed in the backyard.

"You!" she cried, setting down the pitcher and addressing herself to him with a furious glare. "I suspect this is all your doing."

"Your suspicions are well founded," he responded. "Now, don't draw any rash conclusions, Zia Caterina. I am speaking to you only because it is necessary to let you know our purpose. Henceforth no one in the family will address a word to you."

Breathing hard, she asked, "How long will this persecution last?"

"That depends on you. It will last until you have gone to my father and begged his forgiveness. On your knees."

"I have my pride!" cried the signora. "I would not dream of asking pardon of that coxcomb! Do you understand? Never! Never!"

Napoleon gave her a satiric bow. "I leave the matter, then, in your hands."

Suddenly reaching down and raising the pitcher, she threw the contents in his direction. But Napoleon had been anticipating some such action and skipped aside so nimbly that not a drop touched him. He reached the door and closed it behind him.

Two weeks passed while the younger members of the family watched the skies hopefully. Nothing marred the beauty of the weather. The days were clear and fine and the sun poured down a continuous heat on the old stone house. Then a cloud showed in the eastern sky. It may not have been larger than a man's hand in the beginning but very soon thereafter it filled the whole Corsican sky with a black threat. For two days it rained while jubilation filled the lower stories of the house.

The third day fell on a Sunday. All members of the family were ready to start for the cathedral for early Mass, when the upstairs door opened. Signora Sanluzzi emerged with a tragically stony face. She began slowly on the long and painful descent.

"She carries no white flag," whispered Napoleon to his mother. "But, ma certes, she is capitulating."

"Poor Caterina, I am beginning to feel very sorry for her. She has always been so proud!"

The beaten tenant of the top floor took her time in getting to the bottom of the stairs. With a tightly knuckled hand on the newel post (which was, prophetically perhaps, a rather badly carved eagle's head) she stood there and glared about her.

280

"My walls upstairs are dripping from this rain," she said. "Why should the roof suddenly leak in this way? I have my suspicions there is more than the hand of nature in it. Well, I can't hold out any longer. I give in." She turned to the head of the family. "Carlo, I ask you to forgive me. I shouldn't have done it."

Napoleon took it on himself to respond. "There was another clause in the terms, Zia Caterina. The left knee was supposed to touch the floor. But I think my father will agree to suspend it."

Carlo with all his faults was one of the most friendly disposed of men. He smiled and extended his hand. "You have done enough, my dear Caterina."

Letizia was the most anxious of all to establish things again on an amicable basis. "You must come to Mass with us, Caterina," she said. "It will show the neighbors that we are all friends again."

"Louis," said the father, "be sure there is fresh water upstairs for your aunt when we return."

"Caterina, you must have dinner with us," declared Letizia.

Pauline carried the day's mail up to the top floor the next day.

"Child," said the signora, "I am sure all this was Napoleon's doing. When did this change come over him? He used to be such a quiet boy. Now he's completely different."

"Yes, Zia Caterina. I guess he's going to be the most different man that ever was seen."

6

Once Letizia was asked which day she considered the most pleasant in her life and replied without hesitation: "There was a wonderful day, an Easter Sunday, I think. It was just before my dear Carlo died."

"It hadn't any connection, then, with the great events in the family—the victories or the crownings?"

"No. It was—well, a rather quiet occasion."

"What was so unusual about that particular day?"

"It was the only time when all of our family were together for a meal. Even little Jerome. It's true he was so small I had to hold him on my knee but he waved his spoon with such energy! I remember . . ." she paused and allowed her voice to fall ". . . that all the ones we had lost—all of them so young, so very young—were back with us. Particularly my sweet Maria-Anna, whose face kept appearing and smiling at me. I suppose all that part was a dream. Ah, yes, it was a beautiful day."

Which is, perhaps, the best way of introducing a feature of life in the Bonaparte household which is essential to an understanding of the various members; food, meals, table talk.

The meals, it must be conceded, had to be cautiously arranged because they were so carelessly attended. The head of the family, who remained handsome and ostentatious almost to the end, objected to dinner being served before his arrival and yet was seldom on time himself. It became necessary to post little Caroline at a point where she could see her father when he turned into the street on his way home. She would race into the house, crying excitedly: "The papa is coming! I saw him."

Napoleon's presence, when he was home on vacations from his French schools, was never to be counted upon, but this did not pose a problem for his hard-worked mother. When he came in late, he would content himself with anything that was left, eating with a bent back and a preoccupied air. Pauline would sometimes return and sit beside him. Once she asked him what he was eating and he looked at her with a blank air. "I don't know, Pauline. It was on the platter. So I took it." She examined the food with a frown. "I think it must be something that was scraped up for you. Do you like it?" Napoleon studied the dish for a moment. "Now that you mention it, I don't believe I do."

Lucien was a frequent delinquent. "Where is your brother?" Letizia would ask, as she took her place at the end of the table. Someone would answer: "Lucien? He's out with his *awful* friends. He'll be arguing with them and probably won't bother to come home."

Lucien was always arguing; at home, outside with friends, during meals, after meals, on the streets, at the Jacobin Club, wherever he could find a listener. He was convinced that he would become an inspired orator and most of the family agreed with him. But this did not make up entirely for the inconvenience to which they were put.

Pauline was rather troublesome. She was convinced that a

lady should not sit at a table for her meals but should recline on a couch. "That was what they did in the days of the Roman Empire, Maman," she would say. "The men did the same. So it must have been right."

"Do you really prefer to eat sprawled out on that couch?" her mother would ask. "Isn't it very uncomfortable?"

"Oh, no, Maman. I enjoy my food so much more. You ought to try it."

"Who would serve the meals if we all lay around on couches?"

That point did not concern the lackadaisical member of the family. Sometimes she got her way about it because, if Zia Geltruda, a childless aunt, were present, she would steal out to the other room, taking some food with her. When upbraided for this, she would say: "It's such a pleasure to watch her. I've never seen such a *nice* eater. Do you know, she can finish a bowl of soup lying flat on her back and not spill a drop?"

But this is getting slightly afield. The point at issue is food. The Bonapartes, who have always been described as a quarrelsome family, never saw eye to eye, certainly, on the question of what dishes should be served. When asked about the meal she recalled with so much pleasure, Letizia would say with a reminiscent smile, "It was such a quiet meal." Few meals were quiet. When Mammuccia Caterina, the one servant kept by the family, came in with the main dish, there would be an instant clamor of dissent and someone was certain to remark, "It's very clear who's the favorite of this family," meaning the one whose preference was being served on this occasion. Each had a favorite dish and was displeased when anything else was brought in.

Those who had been for any length of time in France had, of course, acquired French tastes. They liked unusual foods now, strange sauces, heavily spiced entremets, and very rich desserts. Even the fine Corsican mouflon was no longer to their taste unless served with side dishes. They now wanted rice, strange vegetables, and tomatoes. The tomato created a sharp conflict between the visiting members of the family and the stay-at-homes. It was still called a love apple in Corsica and it was very expensive. It was believed, moreover, to be an aphrodisiac and no self-respecting matron would have it in the house, which meant it that it was never on the Bonaparte table. The visiting members would, therefore, look at a fine roast of lamb served alone on a platter, and sigh with regret.

It was the same with fish. The island had many fine varieties, including *razza, soglie, murena* and, above all others, the great island trout. This favorite dish was cooked in boiling oil and served with a great deal of pepper. From the very first all members of the clan had preferred it to other dishes.

But now they were less partial. Joseph would take some of it and be so careless that the bones would have to work their way out at the corners of his mouth. "It seems to me," he would complain, "that the trout nowadays has more bones than it used to have."

Even the once popular dessert, the *inoleata*, a cake made with flour, sugar, and white wine, had lost its appeal. Letizia would look with despair at the plate from which no more than a piece or two had been taken. "They seem to think their poor old mother is a very bad cook," she would think.

The divergence of opinion on the subject of food seemed to add an extra edge to the differences which arose in the table conversation. "Perhaps they would behave better if we had more guests," the distracted mother would say to her ailing husband or Mammuccia Caterina.

"They should be more like our little Nabuleone," the servant would say. "He eats everything and never speaks unless he has something worth saying. I mustn't mention names but some of the others—*Hé!* It's a wonder they have any hats left, they talk through them so much!"

One of the chief bones of contention at the table was who should carry Zio Lucciano's tray upstairs to him. On one occasion it was agreed that Pauline's turn had come. She protested with more vigor than was usual with her. "Poor Zio Lucciano has the gout," she said. "It won't do him any good to see me. He's always been so suspicious since I found where he kept the money."

"I think," smiled the very ill Carlo at the head of the table, "Zio Lucciano's gout won't be made any worse by the sight of you, my pet."

But father Carlo's judgment was not sound. Pauline returned in a very few minutes with more than a hint of guilt in her manner.

"Please, Maman," she said. "I didn't mean to do it."

"Do what, Pauline?"

284

"Well, Maman, when I went in, he looked at me and frowned. A very mean frown, Maman. He said, 'Oh, it's you, is it? Don't they think I'm suffering enough as it is?' Maman and Papa Carlo, I think I lost my temper."

"What did you do, child?" asked the mother.

"Well, Maman, for one thing, I wanted to get out as soon as possible. I forgot all about his gout. I slammed down the tray-right on the tip of his big toe!"

7

One day Letizia invited a young stranger to dinner. This was some years after the death of the head of the family. Napoleon was home on furlough from his regiment of La Fère and Joseph was located again in Corsica. The stranger arrived in good time and was introduced to the family, each hearing the name differently—M'sieur Gritt, Greet, Grill, or Grim. He was probably a year or two older than Napoleon and not more than an inch taller.

It was clear that he was in good circumstances. His coat was of black broadcloth and, though the tails were long enough to touch his knees, it was double-breasted and so short in front that his waistcoat, a riot of color, could be seen. His breeches were a handsome shade of plum and of superlative cut. His hat, which the small Caroline had captured and deposited on the end of the memorable couch, was broad of brim and sported a gold buckle on the front of the band.

At first glance Napoleon decided he came from the other side of the English Channel, for there was a John Bull-ish note to his long nose and longer jaw and a glint of the same in his gray eyes.

The visitor sat on Letizia's right and the three oldest brothers faced him across the table. Lucien was more than usually talkative that day and inclining to slash at Joseph, whose cheerful conservatism was a constant source of irritation to the ebullient third son. Did Joseph know, he asked, that a leader to replace the late M. Mirabeau would be found either in the ranks of the Jacobins or the Cordeliers? Had it yet reached his ears that the Austrian queen was planning to flee the country?

Joseph hemmed and hawed, and Napoleon watched with a

285

brooding expression in his eyes. Finally Lucien turned to the latter.

"Do you agree with Joseph?"

"No."

"*Hé!* then you agree with me."

"No."

"But you must agree with one of us."

Napoleon had been watching the Englishman at intervals to see what effect this kind of talk was having on him. It was clear that M'sieur Gritt, Greet, Grill or Grim was listening with interest but at the same time doing full justice to the excellent *langouste* which happened to be the main dish.

"I never agree with you, Lucien. Why? Because you are always talking about things you don't understand."

After dinner the guest approached Napoleon. He desired to talk with him, he said. Napoleon suggested that they go to the terrace at the back of the house. On the way there they came to a halt in front of the mantel in the *salotto* while the young Englishman examined a small metal cannon painted a bright green.

"I was given a cannon when I was six years old," he said. "It was larger than this and I believed it was meant to be used. The first day I stuffed it full of gunpowder and set it off. Every piece of furniture in the room was ruined and every pane of glass broken. My father decided that the ambition I had been entertaining of becoming an artillery officer when I grew up should not be encouraged any further."

"My father saw this one in a shop window one evening on his way home," explained Napoleon. "He decided it was what I needed, so he went in and bought it. He had just enough money in his pockets to pay for it, so he reached home without a sou. The money had been needed for some special purpose but my mother just smiled and nodded her head. I have always treasured it."

When they reached the terrace, Napoleon asked his guest for enlightenment on the score of his name. "Our mother's way of pronouncing names leaves much to the imagination," he said.

"It is Greer. John Knox Greer."

"Then you are Scottish. I am glad to hear it."

The guest smiled. "The Scots and the English are getting pretty well merged, you know."

"No, there is still a very clear division. That is evident at

286

least, to outsiders. Did an ancestor of yours arrive with James in 1603?"

" 'Pon my word, m'sieur, you know something of our history, don't you? Yes, one of the old boys, about six 'greats' back, came down with King Jamie. When the East India Company was formed, my ancestor, who seems to have had a shrewd head on his shoulders, got himself a post at a factory in India. Ever since there have been Greers in the business, each one richer than those who went before. My gov'nr—"

"Governor?"

"The pater. An Englishman. He reaped the benefit of all the efforts and savings of all the earlier Greers. He is fairly rolling in wealth."

"I expect your company is a private one now. Could it be the Bengal and Eastern, by any chance?"

"Yes. The Bengal and Eastern."

Napoleon's eyes were wide with interest now. "*Ma foi*, how very lucky for you! I have studied the history of the East carefully. You stole India from France, you know."

"Who," asked Greer, with a twinkle in his eyes, "did the French steal it from?"

Napoleon gestured. "We'll have to get it back some day, M'sieur Greer. If it hadn't been for your man Clive—"

"The gov'nr says Clive was the greatest Englishman that ever lived."

"Not entirely accurate, m'sieur. The second greatest."

"Ah. What was the first?"

"Oliver Cromwell."

The guest was startled into an exclamation of surprise. In fact, his eyes opened wide and his mouth showed a tendency to follow their example. "Really! Cromwell! Come, you are joking. That murdering destroyer of property and beauty and—everything worth while."

"You haven't been a close student of history, M'sieur Greer. You were fighting a civil war and it had to be ended. The Cavalier lords wouldn't give in, so it was necessary to batter down the walls of their castles. Can you shell walls without breaking a bit of bric-a-brac or damaging a family portrait? Then the Scots and the Irish kept invading England and *that* had to be stopped. Cromwell did it all. Then he found himself with a country to rule and nothing but religious fanatics around him. A fanatic may have uses but certainly his place is never in a governmental post. So again

287

Cromwell had to do it himself and he ruled the country so well it became again a first-class power.

"He made only one mistake, your great Cromwell. At the last moment he let his expiring spirit indulge in silly family pride. He appointed his amiable but stupid son his successor. I don't believe any Frenchman would make such a mistake. I most certainly would not."

Greer had recovered sufficiently to smile at this. "Do you expect some day to face such a decision, M'sieur Nabul-on?"

Napoleon did not go to the labor of answering. Instead he asked a pertinent question.

"What are you doing in Corsica?"

"Frankly, I am wasting my time. You see, the gov'nr has an idea our concern should broaden its scope. As I'm the only son, and he's a sick man, the poor pater, he wants me to look the world over and learn to speak a language or two. He hopes I may become some kind of—well, I expect, a modern Jacques Coeur."

"*Hé!* Then you know something of French history. Jacques Coeur, yes. A great man. One of the greatest Frenchmen. But I still don't understand how you happened to come here."

"Well, he wanted me to go to Canada first."

"Which you also stole from France."

"Not at all. You're entirely wrong there. But it would take too long to go into it and I would have to do a lot of slanging of both our governments. I refused to go to Canada. It's too cold. And those blasted Indians with their tomahawks! Not a pleasing prospect at all, that. I came here, instead, thinking I would have a good chance to rub up my French and get a sort of toe hold on Italian at the same time. You know, I expect, that I've been working in the offices of Grammini and Destinn. They're correspondents of Bengal and Eastern and very nice chaps indeed. But their problems are different from ours in London, you know."

"Where will you go next?"

"Venice. For a few months. Then, Ho for the Far East where French francs and Portuguese moidores can be scooped up and converted into solid English pounds, the basis of all good currency. To say nothing of the stream of eastern gold coins, the rolling ribbin from the caves of Ali Baba which tumble into any convenient pocket, preferably an English one, like orphans in search of a kind home."

"M'sieur is something of a poet."

John Knox Greer leaned back in his chair and looked at his host with a speculative eye. Napoleon, in his opinion, cut a rather meager figure. He was thin, although his legs were shaped well enough. His cheeks were almost cadaverous and his hair lank. His clothes (he was not wearing his red and blue uniform) were of cheap material and had seen too much wear. The sleeves of his coat, in fact, were losing ground in the race with his wrists. But as the man from beyond the Channel studied his companion more closely, he became aware for the first time of the strange power in the young Corsican's eyes. Napoleon seemed to be looking through him rather than at him.

"I am a dull dog," said the Englishman. "Hardly a scrap of poetry in me. But has it never occurred to you that there's an affinity between poetry and trade?"

"No. Poetry is of the spirit."

"And trade isn't? Come, m'sieur! You French like to call us a nation of shopkeepers and you think our empire is a lot of shops at convenient places in the world. Have you forgotten how Clive conquered India with a handful of followers? Have you ever heard of Captain Cook and the way he took over those great island continents in the South Pacific? Consider also how we took possession of the Pillars of Hercules and turned Gibraltar into the most powerful fortress of all time. You see, we're a combination of two races—the Normans who were practical and acquisitive without a trace of sentiment in them, and the Anglo-Saxons who were not practical but were packed with poetic instincts from their bare toes to their sodden eyebrows. M'sieur, there is more poetry in trade than in war and almost as much as in religion."

Mammuccia Caterina brought out a large pottery dish on which reposed a fine ripe melon and placed it on the table between them. Pauline had followed closely on her heels.

"Please, Nabuleone," said the girl, "might I have some of the melon?"

Greer was on his feet immediately and Napoleon took a moment before following suit. "May I serve mam'selle?" asked the guest. On Napoleon's nod, he cut a slice and handed it to Pauline.

"Thank you, m'sieur, for giving me such a large piece. I am *very* fond of melon."

Greer watched the dainty motions of her hand as she cut the fruit into small squares and then conveyed them to her mouth. It became *very* clear that she had a great liking for melon as she left nothing but the bare rind. Then she gave their guest a sudden close scrutiny with her heavily lidded eyes before returning to the house.

"How old is Mam'selle Pauline?"

"Not quite ten years."

The Englishman was astonished. "She is tall for her age. I was sure she was in her teens." Then he allowed his feelings to get the upper hand. "Hell and damnation, what a beauty she is! If she were a few years older, I swear I would be begging the right to ask for her hand."

Napoleon answered in a tone which expressed indifference. "Pauline has had that effect on many. I am sure, M'sieur Greer, that our mother would be gratified to listen to you. But unfortunately I must inform you that I have other plans for her."

"You? But you are not the oldest brother."

"That is true. But in matters of the future, the family consider first what I have to say." There was a brief pause. "Please understand me; I am highly pleased you think so well of her. But there are many things to consider."

Greer glanced back over his shoulder at the weather-beaten stone of the old house. He thought of the shabbiness inside, the pathetic rents in the curtains, the sag in the cane seats of the chairs, the unskilled mending which had been done on all the carpets. Here, most clearly, was a family in financial straits.

"If I should ever come back," he said, "and your plans for the very lovely Pauline have not matured, and if she had on me then even a small part of the effect she has now—well—the matter of settlements is considered of importance, I believe. I am not boastful ordinarily but—well, confound it, I might as well come right out and tell you that some day I shall have enough of the golden ribbin of the East to fill the hull of a merchantman and to pave a square or two in good old London as well."

"There is no denying that we are very poor," said Napoleon, smiling grimly. "It will probably be necessary for us to leave the island and settle somewhere in France. So you see how uncertain things are going to be with us."

There was a moment of silence and then the brooding expression so often observed on the Napoleonic countenance, became most noticeable. "M'sieur Greer," he said, "I have a deep-seated feeling—a premonition, if you like—that all through my life, no matter what I become or where I go, I am fated to have trouble with England and Englishmen!"

Greer's eyes wrinkled up in an amused smile. "Naturally, my dear fellow," he said. "Frenchmen have been having trouble with England and Englishmen for centuries. First, there was that steamy state of things, the Hundred Years' War. Then the little difficulty known as the Wars of the Roses—with the two countries at each other's throats the whole time." He indulged in a chuckle. "There's no reason why it should always be that way, though. The French people are coming around to some of our democractic ideas. At least, I gathered as much from the things your brother was saying, the young, hotheaded one. Give us a chance to—to knock those premonitions out of your head. Come over and stay with me for a while. You could look around London and perhaps get to like us a little better. I'll postpone my visit to Venice so I can take you in hand."

Napoleon shook his head. "My regrets, m'sieur. It is quite impossible. I have a commission in the Army and I must return next week. There is so much I must still learn. All my spare time is devoted to studies."

"You are an officer and you still study? Gad, m'sieur, I wish the officers in our Army felt the same way. But, tell me, what is it you are studying so attentively?"

"War," said Napoleon.

8

His leave of absence came to an end and Napoleon faced with mixed feelings the necessity of returning to his regiment. On one hand he was eager to get back to his work and his studies. On the other, he regretted leaving the pleasant life of his native island with its fine, even warmth and the grandeur of its rugged hills.

John Knox Greer was leaving on the same ship, having decided to return to England before venturing further eastward. They stood together on the wharf and waited for the tender to come in for them. Napoleon was back in the uniform he had not used at home because of the dangers of wear and tear. To the Englishmen he looked older and much more commanding. The extent of his poverty was implied, however, by the single piece of luggage he was carrying, a medium-sized bag which apparently had seen long usage before it came into his possession. Greer carried nothing himself. His man, a stolid type of Englishman, had capacious satchels in each hand and more bags suspended on straps around his shoulders.

"Can you manage it all, Pinser?" asked Greer, with a sudden attack of solicitude.

"Yus, sir. Quite, sir," said the man.

"How long do you think it will take?" asked Greer, studying the lateen sails of the stout three-master in the roadstead.

Napoleon gestured doubtfully. "It has been done in as little as two days. Sometimes it takes two weeks. Depending on the weather."

"Egad!" commented Greer. "I hope we get one of the better kind. I must confess it; I'm a damn bad sailor. I keep finding excuses for not going on this terrible voyage to India."

"I'm sorry to leave home," confessed Napoleon. He was keeping his eyes on the line of high granite hills which formed a majestic background for the pleasant little city of Ajaccio. The summer *raffiche* was blowing down from the heights and across the bay. He drew the enticing odor deeply into his nose with a gusty enjoyment.

"There is no place to compare," he said to his companion. "Why should I allow the call of ambition to drag me away from a place which fills my being with such delight?"

"But you are doing it."

"Yes. But I'm still torn in two ways at once. Perhaps I should turn around before getting into that miserable harbor boat and go back to devote myself to the cause of Corsica's freedom and then to a quiet life writing history."

"A dull life that would be," asserted the departing visitor. "No choice between the two. And damned well you know it."

All members of the Bonaparte family had come down to see Napoleon off and even the tenant of the upper floor, with smiling forgiveness, had arrived in the only sedan chair on the island. She was already regretting that she had hired it, for it was a creaky affair and swayed dangerously between the two inexpert islanders carrying it. Lucien had left the party when they passed a door painted red in one of the ancient buildings at the water level. "I will be back at once," he had said. Joseph had grunted. "That's the Jacobin Club. We won't see Master Lucien again for hours."

They had some time to wait for the arrival of the tender and Napoleon used it to discuss in low tones with his mother the arrangements for moving the family to France if the political unrest on the island made this desirable. Greer took advantage of the chance to talk with Pauline. She was modestly dressed in printed muslin but, when she glanced up at him from under the brim of her college style hat, he realized that she had a warmth in her eyes beyond her years.

"I find it hard to believe, mam'selle, but they tell me you are still too young for travel," he said to her. "When you overcome this disadvantage—which should be much sooner than they think, yes indeed much sooner—you must come over and see England."

"Oh, oh, I would like that, m'sieur," said the girl. "Even though travel frightens me. You see, I am inclined to be indolent."

"Are you? Are you indeed?" Greer leaned down to get a closer view of her dark eyes. "How very right of you! Do you know, I am rather indolent myself. Oh, I don't sleep late in the morning or loaf about when there are things to be done. But I'm not one of your vigorous fellows who are always in the middle of things like steam engines and blowing whistles to make others clack their heels. I am much of the opinion that indolence is a pleasant trait, particularly in young ladies. It's so much better than going in the other direction and becoming a nagging, prying woman. We have too many of *them*."

"Would there be horses and carriages to ride around in and—and exciting places to go?"

"There's a fine little roan who would be perfect for you. As for carriages, there are at least a dozen. All the way from dogcarts to the stanhope kind of thing where you sit away up in the air like a goddess in the clouds. Come to think of it, I wouldn't give you much chance to be indolent."

There was no evidence of indolence, however, in the way Pauline took possession of Napoleon's arm when he had finished his talk with their mother. "I want to ask you some things," she whispered. "Can't we walk up the pier, away from all these people?"

"Of course, my small one. What is it all about?"

"About you," said the girl. "I didn't hear you speak of it but the others tell me you are not well liked among the officers of the regiment. Did you say that to Maman and Joseph?"

"Not exactly. But I did say they don't welcome me into their innermost circles."

"Nabuleone!" she cried. "I can't believe it. You must be a great deal more clever than any of them. They should be proud to have you. Why, this is absurd! I am very angry about it!"

"It's not absurd. It's just what I had every reason to expect. Look at it this way. I am Corsican and they are all French. They consider me an outsider and a stranger to begin with. I don't speak perfect French yet and the difficulty they have in understanding me annoys them. I believe in burrowing into my books in spare hours and they prefer to play cards or other games, to call on young women in town. The disreputable ones, for the most part. They think I'm a morose fellow, and perhaps I am. So, you see, little sister, they have good reasons for not liking me."

"I hate them!" cried Pauline. "They are jealous of you. That's the real reason."

"Perhaps they are. A little. I am making myself a better soldier than any of them can expect to become."

"Don't you resent the way they feel?"

"No," answered Napoleon. "It makes it easier for me to use my time in any way I like. I don't have to find reasons for not wasting it with them. Pauline, it's a helpful thing to feel superior to those about you, and not show it. That's the way it is between these blockheads and me. I'm willing to accept this lack of good will because secretly, inside myself, I think very poorly of them. I have something here," touching a finger to his forehead, "which they lack. It makes me feel superior to all of them. At first I thought I was going to be an author and write great novels. But now I am sure I am going to be a remarkable soldier. I'm so sure of this in my own mind that I can afford to let them treat me as an inferior. Do you understand me?"

"No," answered the girl. "No, I don't understand it at all. I know I'm more beautiful than other girls but I don't want to keep it a secret."

Napoleon smiled down at her troubled face. "I have one great consolation. I know my lucky star is straight above me in the sky. As long as it is there, nothing can stop me. If I ever feel unsure, I look up—and there it is! It is going to lead me to—" He laughed briefly. "You wouldn't believe me if I told you where this star of mine may lead me in time."

"Yes, I would believe it."

"People here in Corsica think no one can climb very high without the influence of a wealthy or powerful family. They don't expect me to accomplish much. They don't know about this star. So, you see, Pauline, you must not worry about me."

Joseph came up behind them and pressed a small purse into Napoleon's hand. "You'll need this, brother," he whispered.

The kindly Joseph did not know how much Napoleon would be in need of it. The latter had been most uncomfortably aware as he dressed to leave that his pockets were almost empty.

When the two travelers had been taken aboard, they remained standing at the rail, waving to those who watched from the shore. The lateen sails of the *tartane* which would carry them to Marseilles, were ruffling in the breeze as though impatient to catch the full force of the winds. Napoleon's attention was only partly given to those he was leaving. He had already noticed that the vessel carried a small battery of guns and he was impatient to inspect them.

Greer said, "I'm coming back to Corsica, you know."

Napoleon turned and looked at him with surprise. "When?" he asked.

"Oh, a matter of a few years. I want to give that little sister of yours a chance to grow up."

"M'sieur Greer, put it out of your head. France and England will be at war in a few years."

Chapter Four

1

Napoleon had taken an hour in telling this story of his youth, with a number of long pauses to consider which parts he could include and which should be suppressed. At the end Betsy asked a question which indicated the interest she had taken in the only part where the shadow of romance had raised its head.

"Did he return to Corsica?"

"I returned once. Ah, you mean Greer. *Ma foi*, did I not tell him there would be war between England and France? It began in three years. In the meantime Greer had married an heiress and taken her out to India. He contracted some disease there and died. A cousin controls the Bengal and Eastern now." He turned then to the more personal aspects of the story. "Have I made clear the handicaps under which I labored? Would you expect the son of an impoverished family in that little island to rise to an imperial throne? In view of my success, do you still see no prospect of escaping yourself from the bonds of middle-class life in the smallest and meanest bit of rock and sand on the face of the globe? Betsee, you have beauty. You have courage. You have clear judgment. What more do you need?"

"So much, sire, that what you are saying frightens me."

"This has to be considered, that it's not enough to have the qualities needed for success. You must be hard, selfish, unfair, unscrupulous."

"But—but, sire, I don't think I'm as bad as that."

"Of course you're not. I didn't mean you should be hard and unscrupulous yourself—but you must be ready to use such traits when the necessity arises. You must let nothing stand in your way. Now I am not the possessor of all these bad qualities, despite what the world says of me. But I have done things which warranted such a belief. Only when no other course was open, you must believe. And I have never lost sleep because of what I've done.

"A woman is never under such a strain," he went on. "But if she wants to become great, she must set herself an objective and never forget it.

"You see, Betsee, getting to the top is hard but staying there is harder. You must fight every inch of the way getting up; and then, to remain on the crest, you must consider everyone an enemy. With no exceptions, mind you. And you must keep an eye on your star in the sky."

"But, sire," said Betsy, "when I look up at the sky at night, I see thousands of stars. Can I claim one as mine?"

"That comes later. It is actually no more than a sense of belief in yourself. When you have that, the stars seem to be watching you, to be talking to you. Now what I'm trying to do is to save you from falling into the mistake that all women seem to make, even those who have some of your qualities. You must not get yourself involved in the inevitable romance and so remain shackled in marriage for the rest of your life."

Betsy had drawn her feet up on her chair to escape the dampness of the grass. She was watching him intently, her hands clamped tightly about her knees. Napoleon was leaning forward to study her expression.

"*Ma petite*, Sir Jason Greer, who is now head of that firm, is not married. He seems a solid enough fellow and with a wife like you he could become the business giant of Great Britain. If you must marry, that is the kind of match you must aim for. There are plenty of young millionaires in America, keen, bright, attractive fellows. I'm not making a wild guess when I say you could have your pick. You could make yourself the social leader of the new world. And, my Betsee, there are other possibilities, greater than any of these. They can't even be hinted at. But it is conceivable that something might come of them.

"It comes down to this. You must not throw your chances away. It may seem to you that a new life is starting for you here. It will be very exciting for a short time. Be calm about it. The little fellow in uniform who catches your eye today will probably be a stupid, domineering, wine-swilling nonentity in a few years. Whoever he is, he is not good enough for you."

There was a long moment of silence. "Well," said Napoleon, finally, "do you agree?"

"Yes, sire, I am sure you are right."

"Will you make me a promise, then? That you will come and talk to me if you find yourself becoming involved? Before it has gone too far?"

"Yes, sire. I promise."

2

Betsy's introduction to the social whirl of St. Helena came about soon after. She knew that a committee meeting had been called at the Briars to make arrangements for the opening assembly of the season. Jane was a member of the committee and had bottles of port handy for the gentlemen and a good supper prepared of poached eggs, chicken slices, and a really remarkable Spanish spice cake, to wind up the evening. To keep out of the way, Betsy decided to pay a call immediately after dinner on the Veiled Lady. She took along a substantial portion of cake and was pleased to find that her friend enjoyed it very much.

When she was leaving to return home, the Veiled Lady gave her some advice.

"Pretend you are taken by surprise when you enter the room," said the mysterious occupant of the house. "Stand in the doorway for a moment and look about you as though to say, 'Now, what is this going on?' Do you think you can contrive to look just a shade bored—but at the same time, mind you, with a starry-eyedness about you? Yes, I am sure you can. Now, unless I am much mistaken, there will be a panic on the part of the gentlemen to get your attention as soon as possible. They will say, 'Rully, Miss Jane, what a pleasant surprise you have planned for us', or something to that effect. Then you must enter the room slowly, and gracefully, without seeming aware of the presence of strange gentlemen until each one is brought forward and introduced. Be a shade distrait in manner, as though you consider the purpose of the meeting rather too trivial to interest you."

Betsy followed these instructions. When she appeared in the door of the drawing room, where the committee had gathered, Jane called to her to come in.

"You know all the girls," said Jane. "But I'm sure you haven't met any of these—these gallant defenders of England, Home and Beauty who are condescending to help us plan a

298

really brilliant evening. Lieutenant Grannison, this is my sister Elizabeth."

The tallest of the male members advanced a few steps and bowed elaborately. So, thought Betsy, this is the great catch who has kept the whole island so excited, the next Earl of Windelcomb, the heir to such a fortune! She looked up and saw that he was rather tall and rather good-looking in an extravagantly mustachy way. Her first reaction was that he was a young man who was sure of everything, particularly himself, and who was very much convinced of what was right and befitting one in his exalted place. He was wearing his dress uniform, with the long tails and scarlet lapels which were white when buttoned back, and a whole cascade of looped lace punctuated with gold stars.

"I know what the emperor would think of him," was her first formulated opinion.

"Rully, Miss Jane," he was saying, "this *is* a surprise."

Others were brought forward and she got only a hurried impression, except for two. One was a tall fellow with something unpleasant in his pale eyes and loosely held lips. His name seemed to be Spatz-Rakeshaw. The other was quite young, of medium height. His name was High and he was called rather generally Johnny High. He seemed very pleasant indeed.

"I am sure no one will object," said the lordly Grannison, "if Miss Elizabeth sits down and listens to the deliberations. That is, if she cares to."

No one expressed any objections and Lieutenant Spatz-Rakeshaw moved over immediately to sit beside her. "I say," he whispered, "we knew our pretty Jane had a younger sister but none of us suspected the truth. The sheer wonderful truth. You will be at the dance, of course."

"Yes, if I'm invited. You see, I've always been thought too young."

"Egad!" ejaculated the officer, in horrified tones. "We must see to *that!* Really, you know, how silly can mothers get with their rules? And matrons of honor and committee members and so forth. But don't worry. The most determined bachelor of us all—myself, egad—will take this matter in hand."

The chairman, standing in the center, raised a hand for silence.

"We come," he announced, "to the question of programs.

A crisis arose in London recently on this point. The ladies there were detected in a practice that the gentlemen had to put a stop to. They were using a system of double cards, if you know what I mean."

"I don't," said someone.

"Well, if I must explain, each lady came to a dance with two cards. One was all marked up with names, faked names you know, as though she had nothing left to offer. If a gentleman presented himself who did not find favor in her eyes—you know that *can* happen at times, what?—she would fork over the filled card. 'Ooh, la, I'm afraid there is nothing left!' But let a partner she favored step up and out comes the real card—with plenty of dances open. Yes, gentlemen, I assure you that I saw this treachery practiced. With my own eyes."

"Was it ever practiced on you?" aske the youthful John High.

The masterful Grannison flushed to the roots of his hair. "Rather not!" he exclaimed. "I would know what to do if it had!"

"What would you have done?"

"By Jove, I would have turned on my heel and left the floor!"

"Oh, no, now. You wouldn't have gone that far, surely."

"In London," declared the much sought after heir to so much that was desirable, with a hostile eye on his questioner, "it was considered double-dealing of the—of the blackest kind. I heard it spoken of as dastardly and—and perfidious. Were they trying to usurp our privileges? Well, it's the duty of this committee to take action. I'm not sure this double-program practice has been used here. But whether it has or not—"

"It has," said one of the girls.

"Ah! Then the matter seems to be settled. We must follow the example of London. In London the practice was put a stop to."

"But how?" asked one of the girls.

"By abolishing the program system."

"No programs?" asked the ladies, almost in chorus.

"No programs."

"But—but if you have no programs, how do you get partners?"

"By the group plan. There are ten couples in each group. At the start all the gentlemen vote for lady A of group one, and the ladies vote for gentleman A. Then Lady A selects another gentleman. Gentleman A selects another lady. Each one brought in selects another until the group is filled. The members of the group will dance together all evening. Changing partners, naturally. Group B is chosen the same way, then group C. Fortunately that's all the acceptances we have. Just enough to fill out the three groups."

"Oh, dear!" said Jane, looking rather sad. "The poor girls who are not drawn until near the end! How unhappy they'll be!"

The chairman answered brusquely, "Don't waste your sympathies. They'll be on the floor, won't they? That's more than they could expect with programs. And, of course, they'll be the homely ones, the poorly dressed, the spinsters, the widows without property, the stupid ones. In fact, the black sheep and the speckled eggs."

"And," suggested Betsy, "younger sisters who have never been to a dance before."

"This girl is pretty," thought Grannison, "but I suspect she's a bit of a saucebox. It might do her good to be left for the last group. Perhaps I should use my influence to make sure that she is." Then he indulged in a mental shake of the head. "But if I did that, by gad, I wouldn't have a chance to dance with her!"

Mrs. Balcombe appeared in the doorway to the dining room. "Has the committee completed its labors?" she asked. "If so, supper is ready."

The officers came to their feet with an enthusiastic clumping of heels. "Ah, supper!" they exclaimed in unison.

3

The days immediately preceding the assembly were anxious ones for the Balcombe sisters.

"Supposing I'm not called until near the end?" Betsy would say. "Or—I might even be left until the very last! How dreadful it will be, sitting there and trying to smile and wishing there was some hole to crawl into!"

"*You* have nothing to worry about," Jane assured her many times. "You'll be called early. But what about me?"

"Why, Jane, you're one of the most popular girls on the island. Why should you worry?"

"I know that most of the men like me. But they all like others just as much. Perhaps it'll be the others they think of and not me. It could happen that way! I think about it all the time. I even dream about it."

There was no cause to worry about their frocks. The dressmaker spent a fortnight on them, with Mrs. Balcombe running in and out at all hours, to advise, to suggest and to frown when some detail seemed not quite right. The final result was, in the opinion of everyone, perfection.

The younger sister was to wear pink, a rather pale pink net over white satin. Waistlines had been going higher all the time with the result that the pelisse fell away immediately below the narrow band serving as a belt and descended in an ever widening V almost to the bottom of the skirt. This was an early appearance in the world of fashion of what was to become the greatest and most dazzling adventure in feminine dress for half a century, the crinoline. On the pelisse were trimmings of rosettes, in the center of each a small artificial rose of a darker pink. The narrowest possible band was wound around her hair. The general effect could hardly have been bettered, for it had a virginal effect and yet suggested the merest hint of sophistication.

Jane's frock was of light gold satin with frills of cream net banded with darker satin at her neck and sleeves. The crinoline effect had not been attempted. In fact, the skirt fell almost straight for more than half the distance and then turned into flounces which undulated and swished most delightfully whenever she moved. Her skirt was perhaps half an inch longer than Betsy's.

William Balcombe looked up with eyes full of pride when they joined him on their way to the front door that evening.

"If I were judge," he said, "I would call you first and second. But which would be which?" He smiled at his wife. "The like of this hasn't been seen since you were that age, my dear."

Chapter Five

1

The natives of St. Helena were quite poor. The population never seemed to increase and nothing happened to introduce any excess prosperity into the even tenor of life on the island. There were just so many acres to be cultivated for the growth of vegetables or to serve as pasture for a few scrawny sheep. There were just so many mouths to fill, and so never any increase in the number of loaves of bread baked each day. There were just so many chins to be shaved each day and so many suits of clothes to be cut out and stitched each year. In fact, there were just enough deaths in an average year to provide a meager subsistence for the village laystall and for the small profit of putting together plain pine coffins.

But the yamstock had one pleasure in which they competed fiercely, a single extravagance to which each of them yielded at least once in a lifetime. Sailors on ships coming back from the East always had goods to sell surreptitiously. Stolen articles perhaps or at least strange things they had picked up in the teeming bazaars of the East; diminutive ivory elephants which a man could attach proudly to a watch chain, huge jewels of more than doubtful value in spurious gold settings to be used as cravat pins, charms of dark and hidden power which the vendors spoke about in solemn whispers. The ladies found more spectacular temptations when they stopped and spoke to sailors who lounged on the street corners of Jamestown; large ostrich plumes, blue, red, yellow, white; lengths of rich silks and satins, embroideries of breath-taking variety; shawls as ornate as Joseph's coat of many colors. No matter how poor, every woman in St. Helena had at some time or other acquired a plume for her hair and the material for a dress which was good enough for a duchess if not actually for a queen.

303

These luxuries had to last them a lifetime and so they were seen in public on very rare occasions indeed. One evening when they all came out was the annual assembly ball.

2

The Rev. Mr. Stodgkin had agreed to act as announcer and he was already in his chair on the platform in the government reception room when the Balcombe family arrived. Mr. and Mrs. Balcombe found inconspicuous places at the back where they had some difficulty in keeping their two daughters in sight because of the bobbing plumes all about them. They watched with a certain amount of nervous intensity because the balloting had already begun. The girls were voting for Gentleman A in class one and the men for Lady A. An usher was collecting the slips of paper for counting on the platform.

The clergyman untangled his long legs and rose to his feet when the two reports were handed to him.

"Ahem, Gentleman A in section one," he called. "The result is probably not in any degree unexpected. Lieutenant Cyril Grannison."

Grannison got up, bowed and went to the chair at the head of the line.

"And now Lady A in section one. The voting shows—" Mr. Stodgkin squinted down at the slip as though he found it hard to read or, perhaps, to believe. "It seems to be—Miss Elizabeth Balcombe."

There was much loud handclapping on the part of the young men but a rather noticeable lack of enthusiasm among the young ladies.

"Jane!" whispered Betsy, in a sudden panic. "I can't believe it!"

"I'm not surprised. Get up, Betsy, and take that chair you've won."

Then a sudden and all-pervading light suddenly filled Betsy's mind. This wonderful honor actually had come to her. It was as though an orchestra had started to play and was filling the crowded room with celestial music. With cheeks slightly flushed, she walked the open space between the two rows of empty chairs to a position opposite the future Earl of Windelcomb. He took a step or two over to meet her, wearing a somewhat restrained smile.

"Well," he said. "A bit of a surprise, what?"

"I'm just as much surprised as you are," said Betsy.

"I confess I didn't expect this. But nevertheless—I may as well confess, young Miss Betsy. I had made up my mind and was on the point of marking my ballot for someone else when you came in. And before I knew it, I had put your name down instead."

"Thanks for this most flattering information."

"Odd how things work out sometimes. Very." An anxious expression settled on the long-nosed, long-chinned countenance of the Great Catch. "We'll be dancing the first one, you know. A minuet. Do you know all the steps?"

"I'm afraid I'll have to watch you closely and follow your lead."

"Then I expect we'll do quite well. What is your favorite dance?"

"Oh, the waltz, of course."

He looked quite impressed at this. "Really! Now that's downright interesting. How did you learn to waltz?"

"At home. Jane and I waltz together a great deal. I've never tried it outside or with another partner."

"Are you good?"

Betsy looked up at him. "Yes, I think so. I love to waltz. It's like being wafted off into fairyland."

"Odd. Dashed odd. That is, for one as young as you. Perhaps you'll be the answer to my problem. You see, I'm going to need a good waltzer for the first dance after supper. No one else knows this but it's going to be a waltz." He looked about him cautiously and lowered his voice. "You see, the committee decided not to have waltzes. It's a German dance and is being taken up madly in Paris. So all the slow-coaches on the committee decided it would be safer not to have one. But I've taken it on myself to arrange with the orchestra for a waltz immediately after supper. Now then, I must have a partner ready to take the floor at once to get things started. If the rest get grumpty about it and don't come out, then it might become an exhibition dance. Do you think you could go out with me and be ready to perform alone?"

Betsy was delighted at the prospect. "Certainly. I would enjoy it."

At this moment Betsy heard Jane's name called and saw

her sister coming out to join them. "Now everything's right," she thought.

Betsy found that her tall companion was letter-perfect in the many phases of the minuet, although prone to frown when she displayed any hesitation. In addition, he seemed to consider himself responsible for everything that was going on.

"Gad!" he whispered furiously to his partner at one stage, "I thought we came out even. Then what's that inconsiderate creature doing there? All by herself. When did she come in?"

"That's Tilly Shade. Her father has a feed shop. She came in just a few minutes ago."

"What impudence, to be late! Now what in thunderation are we going to do about her?"

"We can't let her sit there all evening, can we? And this will make us one man short."

They were separated for a few steps. When they came together again, Betsy smiled up at him to let him know she had the solution. "I'll trade places with her for the next dance. I'll sit that one out."

"But see here, isn't Johnny High your next partner? He's not likely to care much for the substitution."

Betsy sighed. "Yes, it's Johnny. Tilly's a very bad dancer and I hate to do this to him. But he'll understand. I'll speak to him first, of course."

For the rest of the evening the other girls followed Betsy's example. One would sit a dance out and surrender her place to the late arrival.

"You're too dashed goodhearted," said Cyril, in one of the intervals. "Still it's got us over a bad spot, hasn't it. Do you suppose that girl is grateful to you?"

"Not a bit," answered Betsy easily.

"Well, we'll see things through. Steady the Buffs, what?"

While all this was going on, Betsy had been aware that she was being watched from all parts of the room. People smiled at her and nodded. Mr. Stodgkin, who continued to occupy his chair on the platform, never stopped staring at her over the tops of his eyeglasses. She was not aware of his particular absorption in her, however, until Jane called it to her attention.

"Stodgy has you singled out, Bet," the latter whispered to her. "Don't let him get you as his partner for supper."

The signal for supper brought everyone out on the floor. The back benches were soon empty of plumes and beautiful

306

silks maltreated by local dressmakers. Betsy saw Lieutenant Grannison making his way in her direction through the press, with the clergyman not far behind. Before either could reach her, one of the governor's aides came to her side.

"Lady Lowe desires a few words with you, Miss Balcombe," he said, offering his arm. "Permit me to escort you to the consulting room."

Looking back over her shoulder as she walked away, Betsy saw the tall officer and the almost equally tall clergyman standing shoulder to shoulder and looking very much taken aback.

3

The consulting room served many purposes but it was used chiefly by the judges during the spring and fall assizes. There were rows of pegs along one wall on which hung the black and funereal robes of the law and a few wigs, which had been collecting dust for many seasons and could not conceivably be given place again on any reasonably fastidious head. Another wall was covered with bookshelves which had more open space than books. The governor's wife was seated in a high-backed chair.

Betsy entered with some hesitation, having no idea why she had been summoned and having, moreover, some fear of the formidable Lady Lowe. As she came farther into the room, it became apparent that the latter had a pleasant eye and friendly smile.

"Come and sit here beside me," said the mistress of Plantation House. When Betsy obeyed by taking a rather low chair close at hand, the lady studied her closely. "My, you *are* a pretty child. Have you been enjoying the dance?"

"Very much, my lady. This is my first dance."

"You seem to be having quite a triumph. Something to remember as long as you live. I recall my own first dance so well. I was younger even than you and I confess I was frightened. I came through without being a sitter-by but I had many bad moments."

The governor's lady was not considered a handsome woman but there was no denying that she had a good figure. Her neck and shoulders were white and finely modeled. She seemed prone to take advantage of this by a free use of her

307

arms. At this point she leaned over and patted Betsy on the hand.

"There is an explanation I want to make. You and the other members of your family seem to be friendly disposed toward General Bonaparte."

Betsy hesitated before answering. "Yes, my lady. He was a guest with us for some time. For over two months."

"I have been told he was a most pleasant guest."

"Yes, my lady. We all came to like him very much."

"Neither you nor your sister have been invited to Plantation House. You have plenty of sense, I am told, and can put two and two together. We are speaking in confidence, my dear, because I have never heard the governor himself say what I am going to say to you. His Excellency, you see, is in a most difficult position. When General Bonaparte was at Elba, he was not guarded closely enough. He escaped from the island—and fifty thousand men died in battle as a result. The responsibility for seeing that this doesn't happen again rests on my husband's shoulders. He would be blamed if Napoleon escaped a second time.

"Do you mind if I call you Betsy?" she went on. "Well, Betsy, I am the only one who knows how heavily this responsibility weighs on the governor. He finds it hard to sleep. Every night I hear him get up and make his way in the dark—he doesn't want to disturb me by lighting candles—to one of the windows. He stands there and studies the semaphore at Alarm-House. He's always afraid some bad situation has developed during the night. Has Napoleon escaped? He thinks of little else. He gets up in the mornings gray with worry. Is it any wonder that he insists on knowing everything that is said when visitors have talks with the prisoner at Longwood? He believes he may discover some references which will help him to maintain the necessary degree of surveillance. I am certain there are few people on the island who appreciate how difficult his position is."

"My lady, I have heard my father say what you have just said."

Lady Lowe looked at her with wonder and some degree of doubt. "That is—is most interesting. Does your father ever allow such feelings to show in his relations with the governor and his staff?"

"I don't know." Betsy was sorry now that she had allowed

herself to become involved in such a discussion. She paused to consider how far she might go.

"Don't hesitate, child, to tell me anything you have in your mind."

"My lady, my father is a patriotic Englishman, even though he did get to like Napoleon. But I am sure he never has a chance to display his feelings. He is—well, my lady, he is kept in his place. He is treated as a grocer. He is sometimes called that to his face."

"I see. Your father objects to being called a grocer?"

"I have never heard him say so. But, my lady, he was an officer in the Navy and later an official of the East India Company. The company he is with now was formed to handle the importing of food and all other supplies and it was given the purveyorship for the household at Longwood. My father isn't ashamed of this. I've heard him say that the trade of the Empire is largely in the hands of gentlemen. My father, Lady Lowe, is one of the gentlemen."

"I suspected there was some such reason. I have heard a great deal about your father and mother since coming here. All favorable—except in the matter of your relationship with General Bonaparte. Is there anything you want to add?"

"I shouldn't have said anything at all, Lady Lowe. I feel very guilty."

"I asked you a question and you have had the courage to answer me. You mustn't feel guilty. This talk we have had might lead to better understandings. I will try to find a good opening but the source of my information won't be revealed under any circumstances." The governor's lady became aware that the orchestra was resuming in the assembly room. "My dear, I don't want to rob you of a dance. You must run along. My carriage is here and I am leaving in a few minutes."

4

Cyril Grannison was standing outside the door and, quite literally, gnawing his nails with anxiety.

"We must run!" he exclaimed. "There's barely enough time to get there!"

Seizing Betsy by the hand, he began to race in the direction of the assembly hall. "Gad! I was afraid that woman would keep you too long. That would have been a pretty state of things, what?"

"Whom did you take in to supper?" asked Betsy, a little breathless from the speed at which they were traversing the dark and dusty hall.

"A very pretty and very charming woman—your mother."

"Oh!" exclaimed Betsy, delighted. "And what happened to Papa?"

"He took one look at the wine provided for supper and decided to enjoy a walk in the fresh air instead."

As they entered the hall, the orchestra leader was in the act of raising his baton. In a moment, the strains of the most seductive music began to fill the air. Grannison stepped out on the floor and bowed to Betsy.

"May I have the honor, Miss Balcombe?"

Betsy stepped into his arms and they glided out to the center, with all eyes in the room fixed upon them. Although she had declared her willingness to undertake this test, she had been indulging in some anxious afterthoughts. They left her almost immediately.

Under these circumstances, the waltz was like a beautiful dream. The music was strangely enticing, her partner was an adept at the long whirling measure of the step and she herself found it easy to follow his direction. Her long skirts swayed gracefully with each step, her cheeks took on a glow as pink as the delicate hue of her crinoline, her eyes, not quite at the level of her partner's shoulder, became rapt and dreamy.

"How lovely!" she whispered.

"A beautiful dance for a beautiful lady," he responded.

No one else seemed disposed to come out on the floor. They made the full circumference of the hall twice with nothing to divert the close interest of the spectators. Then there was a sound of feet behind them. Johnny High had brought Jane out to the floor.

Almost immediately the space began to fill. "It's getting them interested, what!" exclaimed Grannison.

The music stopped. Grannison drew away from his partner in order to clap his hands and cry: "Encore! Encore!" The baton was raised again.

The dancing space seemed to shrink and draw in around them. So many dancers had come out that it was no longer possible for Betsy and her partner to take the long slow steps which constitute the great pleasure of the waltz. The other

310

guests had come out to try their hands, or rather, their feet in this seemingly intoxicating exercise. Betsy became aware that there were plumes on middle-aged heads nodding about her, and heavy masculine feet stumbling along in efforts to catch the rhythm of the new dance. Twice Grannison gave the "Encore!" signal. When he paused and made no move the next time that the music stopped, there were immediately cries for more and an almost general clapping of hands.

"Gad!" exclaimed Grannison, in a delighted whisper. "It's a success, Miss Betsy Balcombe. Reverberations of this great event will reach every dance floor in the British Empire. We've made a success of the waltz, right here in St. Helena, the last place in the world for it to happen. We've made history! And, Betsy, you deserve most of the credit. Gad, how they watched you! I'm not a bad dancer, egad, but no one was aware that I was on the floor!"

On the drive home Mr. and Mrs. Balcombe were in the front seat and each of the girls had pre-empted a corner of the rear, in which to curl up and rather sleepily review the events of the evening.

William Balcombe was the first to break the silence. "Well, Betsy," he said, "I'm of the opinion that you've made a most unusual debut."

Chapter Six

1

Betsy had become the acknowledged belle of St. Helena overnight. The first to realize this with certainty was, perhaps, her father. He was seated in his office the next morning when it was announced that the Rev. Mr. Stodgkin desired to see him.

Mr. Balcombe frowned and said to himself, "Now what does that pest want?" He called to his secretary, a middle-aged man wearing paper cuffs, "Bring him in, Sluicer."

The reverend gentleman had gone to great pains to make himself look his best. His hair had been cut and was combed back neatly His collar was fresh and his clothes had been brushed with a vigorous hand.

"Good morning," said William Balcombe. "Take a chair."

The curate sat down and folded his fingers together tightly over his chest.

"Mr. Balcombe, I am early. You see, I have something—er, momentous to discuss with you. I have come to say that I desire the hand of your daughter in marriage. I am asking your consent to speak with her."

Balcombe sank back into his chair and stared at his visitor. "Mr. Stodgkin, Jane's mother and I prefer not to think of her yet as—as ready for matrimony."

"But it is not Miss Jane. It is your younger daughter Miss Elizabeth."

"That," declared the father of the two girls, "makes the suggestion still less acceptable. Betsy is a mere child. And too young to consider seriously the prospect of matrimony. I have most decided views on this matter, Mr. Stodgkin."

"Many girls are married and have children at her age."

"True. But," and Mr. Balcombe's tone became more decided, "that is not the kind of start in life that I want for my daughter."

The clergyman cleared his throat and shifted his position uneasily in his chair.

"I appreciate your view, sir. Ordinarily I would be—not happy, no, but willing perhaps to abide by your decision. In other words, to wait for a reasonable time. But there is an important point to be considered. A vacancy has been created by the death of the vicar of Eastblow-in-the-Vale. My own country, Mr. Balcombe. It has been offered to me."

"My congratulations, sir."

"There is a stipulation. They feel the need of a married man. The parish is largely rural and they think I will need a wife in the parochial work. She, your daughter, will like the country. The vicarage is of good size, in fact capable of housing a large family. It is well furnished with a splendid ecclesiastical library, even a few novels. We will be able to afford a maid to do the heavy work. You may rest assured that little Betsy is going to be happy with me."

"Wait, wait!" exclaimed Mr. Balcombe. "You speak as though the matter has been settled."

The clergyman smiled with every evidence of confidence. "And why not? I have much to offer her. I may climb, sir. The soundness of my views has been noticed in elevated circles. With approval." He nodded with an even easier smile. "I was a wrangler, you know. I wrote Greek verse. I still toy with light verse in the vulgar tongue, and am almost persuaded to offer it for publication. I have been careful and have money in the Funds. There's a wealthy aunt who has me in her will for two thousand pounds. What more is there to say?"

"This, sir. If Betsy wanted to marry you, I wouldn't stand in the way. The decision is hers to make. But I think I should tell you that I believe she will say no. If I were in your position, I would go no further with it."

"Sir!" The clergyman sat bolt upright in his chair. The color which flooded his face was the result of surprise, even it seemed of indignation. "Are you in earnest?"

"Quite."

The Rev. Mr. Stodgkin rose to his feet and fumbled with his hat, which had been placed on a corner of the desk.

"Really, sir, I am not convinced you represent your daughter's views. I prefer to speak to her. If you have no objections, sir, if you have no objections.

"None."

There was company at the Briars that afternoon. No fewer than six officers had arrived in time for tea and they were now seated about a table on the front porch, engaged in the pleasant and bantering talk which usually follows.

Jane, whose eyes happened to stray to the stone gates at the entrance, gave an exclamation of dismay.

"Oh, dear, there's not a crumb left. And here's Mr. Stodgkin driving in!"

The vehicle in which the clergyman was wont to make his rounds was one of the curious variety known as single-horse carts. In a matter of a few years it would become quite popular for family use under the name of dogcart. The two wheels were high and suspended between them was a body about four feet square which made it capable of accommodating one adult and three children. He presented a somewhat comic appearance, his chin and knees being practically on the same level.

Betsy's hand went with a feeling of dismay to a pocket in which she had hastily placed a note received from her father earlier.

> Betsy,
> Beware! Creaky-knees is going
> to pop the question.
>   Papa.

The two sisters walked to one side.

"What does he want?" asked Jane.

"Papa sent me a note. He's going to propose. I'm—I'm afraid it's me."

"Betsy, I'm sorry. I hoped I would have the bother of rejecting him. Oh, well, you'll just have to be firm."

The clergyman seemed uncertain as to whether he should alight. Finally he hopped ungracefully from the uncertain footing of the cart and threw the reins around the trunk of a tree. Jane went forward to receive him.

"I'm sorry you're so late, sir," she said. "Our guests have been rather greedy and there isn't a scrap of food left. But if you'll be kind enough to wait, we can get something for you."

"Thank you, no. I came for a purpose. But it can wait un-til—until later. I shall speak to each of the young men and

314

then be on my way." Betsy had now joined her sister, without any show of warmth or eagerness. "Ah, Miss Elizabeth, it is a pleasure to see you looking so well."

"Thank you, sir. Come and join our circle."

"Not today. Tomorrow, I think. If you will be free then."

"There's no telling," said Betsy, quite willing to discourage him. "They just drop in, you know. But come in any case, Mr. Stodgkin."

The clergyman's eyes were fixed on the younger sister. "There is a matter I desire to discuss with you."

"Tomorrow, then."

The next morning Betsy received a note from the clergyman, informing her that he would arrive about four that afternoon. He desired a serious talk with her about a matter of deep mutual interest. Undoubtedly her father had already told her what was in his mind.

"It's to be this afternoon," she told Jane. "I dread it. But I'm going to be brief and firm."

She felt a certain relief, nevertheless, when Lieutenant Grannison put in an appearance at three-thirty, followed very shortly after by two more officers of the regiment. The one-horse cart turned in at the gate almost immediately after and Betsy went over to greet her suitor with a sudden sense of hesitation.

The Rev. Mr. Stodgkin did not leave his seat. He frowned angrily as his eyes took in the familiar bright uniforms on the porch.

"I expected to find you alone, Elizabeth. You had my note?"

"Yes. Oh, yes."

"Was that not sufficient reason for keeping these idle young men away?"

"They came unexpectedly. I couldn't be rude and send them off."

"But you know what I want to discuss with you?"

Betsy nodded, keeping her eyes lowered.

"I should have thought under the circumstances you would be eager to find means to get rid of them." He sat for a moment in a smoldering silence. "I have so much confidence in your good sense, Elizabeth, that I feel convinced of your decision. It irks me to press for confirmation with so many eyes on us but I cannot wait any longer. Is it to be yes?"

Betsy shook her head. "I don't want to be married yet. Not for a long time, Mr. Stodgkin. It is an honor to be asked but—my answer must be no."

"You are a foolish child," said the clergyman, frowning darkly. "I know I can convince you if I have a fair and proper chance to talk with you. There is a week before I sail—well, say five days, allowing for the arrangements at the end. If necessary," raising a clenched hand in the air, his favorite pulpit gesture, "I shall come every day in my determination to clear your mind of doubts. Why it should be necessary is beyond my powers of reasoning; which, I protest, are rather considerable. I have everything to offer you. Must I say that I find it hard to condone your attitude?"

"There are so many things you can't condone, Mr. Stodgkin."

His face assumed an even redder hue. "Am I to understand you are expressing a doubt of the soundness of my views? Really, really, I had not expected this." There was a long moment of silence. It was clear that he was casting up the points on each side, the evidence of her obduracy against the total of her charms. "Nevertheless, and in spite of everything, I am going to persist. You will see me tomorrow and I insist that none of your feather-brained friends are to be here."

Lieutenant Grannison walked across the lawn to meet her as the little vehicle and its thoroughly angry occupant disappeared in a swirl of dust. His face had taken on an entirely new expression. Such doubts as he had been entertaining were gone. Watching her at a distance and observing the graceful sway of her skirt and the glint of the afternoon sun on her golden hair, he had said to himself that anything which concerned her had become a definite responsibility of his.

"Betsy," he said, "I have a suspicion about this genial gentleman. I think he's trying to ballyrag you into marrying him."

"Well," said Betsy, "I really shouldn't discuss it, you know."

"But?"

"But, yes. He is."

"You've turned him down, of course."

"Of course. But he's coming back tomorrow. In fact, he swears he's going to devote all his time to changing my mind for me until his ship sails."

316

"Why doesn't the silly ass pack up his pride and get off the landscape?"

"You don't know how much pride he has. He can't seem able to believe that a girl might not want him."

"Well, my gal, a little rallying around may not be out of order."

What seemed to Betsy an astonishing thing occurred the next morning. Two of her new military friends, Cyril Grannison and an amiable oaflike young man named Burden (whose father had made a fortune in army contracting), came galloping up before ten o'clock. Grannison dismounted and consulted his watch.

"Seven and a half minutes! That's good riding, Toby, what?"

"What are you doing here at this hour?" asked Betsy, in complete perplexity.

"You'll understand in literally no time at all."

The truth of this statement was almost immediately evident. The swaying cart, containing the ubiquitous suitor, appeared around the bend of the road.

"Ha!" cried Grannison, in triumphant tones. "We knew he was coming—and here we are. Do you want to hear how we knew?"

"I am wondering," said Betsy. "Just a few minutes ago I happened by the merest chance to be looking in the direction of Alarm-House and a signal was given which I had never seen before. Two short flashes and one long. Does that have anything to do with it?"

The masterful Grannison roared with delighted laughter. "Has it anything to do with it? What do you say, Toby?"

"I say, what! Does it now, does it? Ha, ha, really!"

"I will explain later," declared Grannison, "in the meantime there is this clerical nuisance to be dealt with."

The clergyman's face was a study in anger and futility when he saw uniforms confronting him in the garden. He reined in his horse and sat in stony silence. Betsy crossed the lawn and held a hand up to him. It was disregarded.

"I told you we must see no more of these stupid young men!" declared Mr. Stodgkin.

"I had no idea they were coming. But, after all, sir, the roads are free."

"I refuse to talk to you unless I have the opportunity to

expound my views properly." After a moment of sullen silence, however, he changed his mind to the extent of drawing a slip of paper from one pocket. "Perhaps *this* will have some weight with you. I told your father we would be able to afford a general maid in the vicarage. I have gone into the matter more fully and am now convinced that we could do better. In addition to the maid, we would have a man— part gardener, part coachman." He was watching her face closely to see how much this was impressing her. Perceiving less effect than he had expected, he added hurriedly: "And a boy in the scullery! Yes, a boy in the scullery! You would, of course, have a riding horse of your own. A carriage—with the Stodgkin crest on the panel!"

"You are most kind. But—"

"There are still four days," asserted the clergyman grimly. "Four days, if necessary, in which to convince you. I am prepared to use every minute of them!"

When the one-horse cart had turned back on the road to Jamestown. Lieutenant Grannison entered on an explanation.

"It's this way, little Miss Elizabeth. We were not engaged at Waterloo, worse luck, but the 53rd has always been a fighting regiment. Perhaps you've heard we are not very happy here. Well, it's true. Isn't it, Toby?"

"Quite. Quite."

"We don't relish being kept here to act as jailers over—well, over a great soldier. We're sick of all this drilling and having to keep a watch over our shoulders on those silly, unnecessary signals all around the island, set up by this stern, unyielding, inflexible Sir Hudson Lowe. If we must have the beastly things glittering in all directions, we can at least make use of them."

Betsy indulged in a laugh which had a slight touch of hysteria. "Do you mean—do you really mean that what I saw was a signal you were sending out? A signal that he was coming here?" When Grannison nodded, with a gleam of pride in his eyes, she clapped her hands. "What a wonderful idea! Who thought of that?"

"Did I think of it, Toby, or did you?"

"Well," said the second officer, "I may have had the first faint glimmer of it, but you took it, by Gad, and wiped its face and put its hair up in curls and sent it out into the world with a spank on its—ahem!"

"That was the way of it!" cried Grannison proudly. "At

first we thought of a white rag as a signal, shaped as much as possible like a clerical collar. But they would have caught on to that in no time. So we arranged the flashes instead, to be sent out as soon as one of our fellows in town spied him setting out in his cart. And now, by Gad, we know we can beat him here from camp. And there you are!"

"Glorious!" commented the second officer.

"But won't it get you into serious trouble?" asked Betsy, beginning to feel decidedly nervous about the plan.

Grannison gestured confidently. "What care I how wrath they be? I'll sell my commission and step out, if this little martinet at Plantation House gets his hackles up."

"But really," protested Betsy, "I can settle things with one more talk."

"And spoil this fine comedy situation we've developed? No, no! What I say is, on with the play! We want to show we're not the vapid fellows everyone seems to think we are."

For two days things went on as before. The signal would flash, an officer or two, or even three, would ride over furiously from camp, and the still determined suitor would arrive too late to unlimber his heaviest argumentative guns.

On each occasion he brought out a pad and read off some new concessions he was prepared to make. They constituted a formidable list, or so he thought.

Five pound a year all for herself but which must cover wardrobe expenditures.

Two dresses a year.

One new hat each year [hastily corrected to two].

A pianoforte (Did she know how much a pianoforte cost?).

A visit once a year to his brother, who was in the wool business at Hull and had a house on the water.

A complete silver tea service (including an Argyle).

None of these glittering inducements had any effect and he would ride away in a mood of constantly deepening exasperation.

On the last day before the ship was to sail, Betsy and Jane sat alone on the porch. It was getting close to four o'clock and Betsy kept an anxious eye over one shoulder on the semaphore at Alarm-House. There had been no sign of the now familiar signal. When she shifted her gaze to the road from Jamestown, there was nothing to disturb her. Not a speck of dust rose in that direct on.

Finally a horseman approached the Briars, having come apparently from Plantation House.

"It's Major Housthorpe," said Jane. "Do you suppose he's coming here?"

It became apparent quickly that he was. Dismounting from his horse and tossing the reins to Mantee Timms, he walked over to join them. The temporary commanding officer of the regiment was verging on fifty; a well-set-up figure with a crinkle of humor lines at the corners of his keen gray eyes. He sat down between them.

"I've been in trouble," he said. "Should keep a closed mouth about it but I can't bottle it all up inside me. These young scatterbrains playing hi-diddle-diddle with the governor's precious semaphores! Whew, is he upset! He walked up and down in a fine fury, his nostrils white and twitching with rage. Had I no idea of discipline? Why did I allow such things to happen? It did no good to say I didn't know anything about it. I should have known! Well, there we are. There's to be no more of it. If anyone interferes with his signal stations, they will be cashiered!"

"I was afraid of this," sighed Betsy. "I begged them to give it up. But they were all enjoying it too much."

"To be honest about the situation," said the major, "what can you expect? They don't enjoy snooping around like jailers, with keys in their belts. I told him that. He made no response but his eyes accused me silently of black treason, fraternization, and a willingness to see King George spilled from his throne.

"But," went on the major, a smile returning to his ruddy cheeks, "there's a piece of good news too. A certain party, who never found any favor in my eyes, has gone aboard his ship. A very disgruntled party, I may say."

"So, Betsy, you may rest easy now," said Jane.

"Don't be too sure of that." The major looked approvingly from one to the other. "I may fall into the habit myself of dropping in here quite often."

Early one afternoon Comte Bertrand turned in at the Briars and was lucky enough to find Betsy in the front gardens.

"It's you I want to see, mam'selle," he said. "The emperor desires to speak with you. Something has happened which disturbs him very much."

"When does he want to see me, m'sieur le comte?"

"I think you had better ride over this afternoon and stop at our house. The emperor said he would be there at four o'clock." The grand marshal then indulged in a smile. "We hear you have had a narrow escape from matrimony."

Betsy smiled back. "My mind was firm from the start. But it was hard to convince the gentleman."

"There was a widow on the ship. On her way home from India. She came ashore and from all reports, she's a determined person. She'll have him by the time they land."

Chapter Seven

1

Napoleon arrived promptly at four. Madame Bertrand disappeared, leaving them in sole possession of the drawing room.

The emperor did not seem in a disturbed mood. He smiled warmly at Betsy.

"*Ma petite*," he said, "it was an amazing trick you played, you and those young officers, on the unyielding clergyman— and the equally obdurate governor."

"But, sire, how did you hear about it?"

"Every scrap of gossip comes to us here sooner or later. *Ma foi,* all Europe will roar with laughter in due course. Ha, what a use you made of that greatest absurdity, that string of signal towers on this tiny little island. It was a resplendent idea of yours."

"But, sire, I didn't think of it. They did, the officers."

"Nonsense, Betsee. Those weak-minded youths couldn't have thought of such a beautiful stratagem."

"But, sire, I assure you—"

"Of course," interrupted the emperor, "it will be wisest to let people think that. It will save you from any hostile action on the part of the great and masterful Sir Lowe." A frown took possession of his face. "He is beginning to strike out in all directions. The first blow came today. The marquis and his son were taken in charge."

"M'sieur Las Cases?" Betsy found this hard to believe. "But, sire, on what grounds?"

"As far as I can tell, there is no case against them. This morning I heard sounds of unusual activity in the wing where they are located. I went to a window and I saw troops engaged in removing all possessions of the marquis and packing them in carts. In the distance I saw Las Cases and the boy being taken down the road to town. It seems," he went on after a pause, "that the good marquis was guilty of an indiscretion. But nothing more."

"What did he do?"

"He entrusted some of his notes to a man named Scott who was returning to England. They had been transferred to lengths of silk in the smallest of script. Now, of course, they will search him for more evidence and they'll keep all his papers for examination."

"But," asked Betsy, in tones of alarm, "will they be held as prisoners?"

"In some form of confinement until all the papers have been examined. Then they will be packed off on the next ship for Europe. I am sure there was nothing in the notes that would involve any of them in any form of spying and so they can't be punished."

"I think it will be a good thing for poor Emmanuel to get home," said Betsy.

"Yes. But he's still somewhat of a—what is that foolish word of yours?—ah, yes, a cod." Napoleon indulged in a speculative frown. "I am laboring under a suspicion that our good friend is not adverse to being sent home. He has been here long enough to serve his purpose. His books are crammed with notes. He has enough material to write a large fat volume of memories now. If they are published at once, he will make a fortune. Sir Lowe has made another serious error. He should have left the marquis to grub along here for a few more years." He was picking up a few Englishisms. "Now the story of Longwood will be spread to the wide world."

Betsy was thinking, "And I labor under a suspicion, dear sire, that this has been planned between you." All she said aloud, however, was another reference to the sad plight of Emmanuel. "I have always felt sorry for him."

"And now a word of warning, my child," said Napoleon, a deep frown showing on his broad white brow. "You must be very careful. This is why I wanted to see you at once. Sir Lowe is striking out like a cobra. He and O'Meara are at daggers drawn. The doctor will be sent back to England very soon. A most unfriendly eye is being fixed on the Balcombe family. Your father is skillful and diplomatic, but one false step—and back to England you would all go. Even a mistake by you, my best little friend. Think, dear Betsee, how sad it would be for me if you were not here!"

"I think, sire," said Betsy, "that we are all conscious of the need to be cautious."

They sat in silence for a few moments, looking into each other's eyes. Then, after the exchange of an understanding smile, Napoleon's frown returned. "You are being seen too much in the company of that very superior person whose name escapes me. I refer to the officer who was born with a look of condescension on his lofty brow."

"I think you mean Lieutenant Grannison."

When Napoleon nodded, Betsy said in a casual tone: "I've been riding with him. Twice."

"I recall telling you that it would be necessary to dance and perhaps flirt a little. But, *ma petite*, don't carry things too far. Not with this fellow. I do not approve of him, and nothing will make me change my mind."

2

The detainment of the Marquis de Las Cases in a small room in Jamestown caused a great sensation. He wrote long letters every day to the governor in his small cramped hand, and Sir Hudson Lowe answered them. From the length of the correspondence, the pair must have spent the bulk of their time with pens in hand. In the meantime the notes entrusted to the man Scott and the great bundle of sheets taken from the rooms of the marquis at Longwood were submitted to the closest scrutiny. Nothing was uncovered which dealt with a possible escape for Napoleon. Las Cases made no effort, however, to get permission for an extension of his stay. He seemed willing to leave and arrangements were made for him to board the first ship which arrived in harbor.

On the final afternoon, when the vessel would sail with the turn of the tide, Mrs. Balcombe and Jane were sitting on the front porch and engaged in conversation about practically nothing at all. The last named, who had kept her eyes fixed on the entrance gate, exclaimed suddenly, "It must be!"

"It must be what?" asked her mother.

"The coat. You know, Mamma, the one that's been hanging in the window of Tringlane's tailoring shop for so long. Ever since Lawyer Finch said it didn't fit and wouldn't pay for it."

"So it is," affirmed Mrs. Balcombe. "There's no mistaking

those awful magenta buttons, is there? Whoever it is wearing it seems to be coming in."

"I think it's Emmanuel Las Cases," said Jane.

In a few moments her opinion was confirmed. It was the son of the marquis and it was in his mind quite clearly to pay them a call. He was wearing the double-breasted coat now familiar to all residents of St. Helena. It was a little large for him; and, for that matter, so was his tall felt hat which came very close indeed to concealing his ears completely from view, and so was the shiny black cravat which spread almost from one shoulder tip to the other.

The rapid gait at which he was approaching them brought his trousers into special notice. They had lost all claim to fit from continuous wear but perhaps the splendor of his shoe-shine made up for that, to some extent at least.

The visitor removed his hat when he reached the steps and bowed to the two occupants.

"Madame and mam'selle, I am your humble servant," he said.

"Good afternoon, M'sieur Emmanuel," said Mrs. Balcombe. "You have come to bid us farewell, I think."

The sober dark countenance of the French youth broke at once into a pleasant smile. Emmanuel had been acquiring a knowledge of the English tongue but his use of it was largely confined to the stilted phrases he had acquired in books.

"Yes, madame, I depart this afternoon with my father. The voice of authority has said we must not wait for a ship sailing directly back to Europe. Instead we go to the Cape of Good Hope and wait there for a vessel going north." He looked about him with a sudden sobering of mood. "I do not perceive Mam'selle Betsy. She is home, I trust?"

Mrs. Balcombe shook her head. "She went riding half an hour ago. I hope she'll be back soon. But you can never tell. Sometimes she rides for hours. Betsy will be very much disappointed if she doesn't see you, Emmanuel."

"And I would be most unhappy not to see her."

Emmanuel reached into a side pocket of his double-breasted coat and brought forth a small article in the form of a cross of the Crusades. This he consulted carefully.

"Time flies most distressingly fast, madame," he said. "This watch of mine is most accurate. I must be at the wharf in thirty-five minutes."

"That is a most interesting watch," said Jane. "I don't believe I've ever seen one just like it."

"It is the only one of its kind ever made, Mam'selle Jane. My grandfather had it designed in this shape because we were a crusading family. This is the first occasion I have had to use it, for my father has been averse to trusting me with it."

"You have good reason to be proud of it, Emmanuel," said Jane.

The youth nodded. "Our family was much in the Hundred Years' War also and later had their part in the wars of the Sun King. But I am not to be a soldier. My father thinks I should devote myself to the management of our estates in Languedoc. I am wearing a new coat which I am afraid he will not approve. Being confined to this one room, he could not get out to select a coat for me. And so I had to do the best I could."

"It is a most unusual coat. Your father no doubt will approve of it."

The youth nodded to Mrs. Balcombe rather eagerly. "I chose it because of the buttons. They are so large and such a very fine color."

"Sit down, M'sieur Emmanuel. You can spare us a few minutes. Are you walking back?"

"Yes, madame. No conveyance was available. In any event I doubt if my father would have felt justified in such an expense for my—my convenience." As he talked he kept his eyes turning in all directions. "It seems unlikely now that Mam'selle Betsy will get home in time for me to see her."

There was a moment of silence. "Some day," went on Emmanuel, "I hope to see you all again. It will be when my father no longer requires my aid in preparing his manuscript. I may return to St. Helena. But certainly I shall go to England. It is necessary for me to study the box."

"The box?" Jane asked the question with a puzzled frown.

"Yes, Mam'selle Jane. You must know what I mean." He indulged in a rotary motion with both hands. "The box. It is an English game."

"Oh," Jane began to laugh. "You mean boxing. But, Emmanuel, why do you want to box?"

The expression on the youth's face changed at once. His eyes burned darkly.

"For revenge," he said. "My father, who is innocent of all

wrong, has been confined in a small room for weeks. It is monstrous that this has been done to my father, the head of one of the oldest and noblest families in Languedoc. Not the land of the modern *oui* but the ancient and honorable land of *oc*. He has been confined like—like a criminal. As this governor is English, I must punish him in an English way. By assaulting him with my fists and giving him in public the much earned black eye!"

His listeners would have found it hard not to laugh if it had not been for his intense earnestness. His mood changed abruptly, however, and he gave another long glance about him. Then, very slowly, he rose to his feet.

"I must go now," he said. "I am very sad not to have seen Mam'selle Betsy. Will you convey my regrets to her? And tell, I beg, that she will be much in my thoughts. I hope to see you all when I go to England to learn the box."

He replaced his jeweled watch in the pocket of his coat, bowed to each of them in turn and then took his leave. "Adieu, madame and mam'selle," he said. "It has been a pleasure to know you. And please convey my message to Mam'selle Betsy."

He walked away briskly and, when he turned on to the Jamestown road, he clapped one hand to his head to keep his hat in place and set off at a run.

"Do you know, Jane," said Mrs. Balcombe, "I suspect he's in love with Betsy."

"Of course he is. I've known for a long time. Whenever he was in the room with us, he would keep his eyes on her face. Betsy is losing a most devoted admirer."

Mrs. Balcombe sighed. "The poor young man," she said. Then she added, "The poor nice young man."

Chapter Eight

Permit No. 41
For Lieut. C. Grannison and companion to visit the estate of Longwood.

Time, 3,15 on this day to 4,15.

No extensions or changes in time.
Holder to be allowed to speak to General Bonaparte if the latter is agreeable.

IT IS UNDERSTOOD THAT NO TALK OF A POLITICAL NATURE WILL BE INDULGED IN AND THAT SAID HOLDER WILL BE PREPARED TO REPEAT TO HIS EXCELLENCY, THE GOVERNOR, EVERYTHING SAID AND DONE.

ANY INFRINGEMENTS OF THESE REGULATIONS WILL LEAVE THE HOLDER SUBJECT TO SEVERE PENALTIES.

Cyril Grannison drew the above ticket from his elaborately striped waistcoat and waved it with languid triumph before Betsy's eyes. She took it from him and read it with an amused smile.

"You *have* influence," she said. "Did he knew who the 'companion' is to be?"

"Not at first. He was on the point of scratching his name on it when he stopped and pointed at the word with his pen. 'This companion,' he said. 'Who is he?'"

Grannison then proceeded to tell the story in full detail. He had informed the governor that the companion would not be a man but a lady. The suspicions of the governor had been aroused at once. "A lady?" he said. "A young one, no doubt. Now why, may I ask, would a young lady want to go *there?*"

"It happens this young lady knows General Bonaparte."

"So! I was afraid of something like that. Who may this young lady be?"

The lieutenant had not enjoyed this interrogation. "I am taking," he had said, "a very good friend of mine. Miss Elizabeth Balcombe."

"'Ha, I thought as much. Are you aware that I have been refusing permits to members of the Balcombe family? Surely some other companion could be found just as agreeable."

Grannison reached for the permit and proceeded to tear it into small pieces.

"Wait, wait!" exclaimed the governor. "Don't be so impulsive. Now it will be necessary to make out another card."

"I accept no dictation in my choice of companions."

"There will be no dictation, lieutenant. You *are* an impatient young man. I wonder if you understand—well, I am sure you will observe all the regulations. I'll have another card made out for you."

"He was most reluctant about the whole thing," reported the lieutenant. "His face was red and he hemmed and hawed as he signed his name across the lines. He made me think of a pig jibbing at a gate. Well here we are. Shall we start?"

The two visitors rode up to the Longwood gates a few minutes ahead of the time set.

"I am under orders, Lieutenant Grannison, sir," said the noncommissioned officer who came out to inspect the card, "to point out that you are ahead of time. Three minutes and ten seconds early."

"Is that sort of thing done with all holders of permits?"

"Indeed, yes, sir. Always, sir."

"Then," said Grannison, "we'll make up for being early in arriving by being late in leaving. And it may be a lot more than three minutes."

The young officer was still grumbling as they walked through the gates. Then he stopped and looked about him. "This is the closest I've ever been to this place," he observed. "Gad, it's small, what? I say, there are over thirty people in the household. Now how can thirty people exist in this run-

329

down domicile for domestic animals? Must be like a pigsty inside."

"It is, rather," said Betsy.

Napoleon received them in the drawing room, looking quite fit as to girth and very tidy as to dress. It had been his custom to pinch Betsy's ear whenever they met and his hand automatically went out. Then he allowed it to fall.

"You are of the regiment, of course," he said, speaking very slowly in French. "It is always a pleasure to talk with soldiers. Civilians I find tiresome and objectionable." Then he turned to Betsy. "Ha, *ma petite*, it is a long time since you have been here. I have felt much neglected."

"It is only because of Lieutenant Grannison's influence that I am here now," said Betsy.

"I have been hearing much of your companion. You, sir, will sit in the House of Lords in course of time. I am sure Sir Lowe was ready to go down on his hands and knees to you, although he doesn't rank emperors very high. Would you care to see over the Louvre of St. Helena? You come at a moment when we are at our fustiest because of the mildew."

Grannison, who was brimming over with curiosity, answered that he would like to see all of Longwood. He would like, also, to speak to some of the household, if this would not be breaking the laws.

"I suspect," said Betsy, "that he is going to write a book. But he'll never get it published because the printer would run out of 'whats' in the first few pages."

Napoleon smiled at her and then said to the officer: "She is of an impudence, this one. But I put up with her because my regular companions run the 'gamut in conversation from dull, duller, to dullest."

The Captive summoned Santini and explained that their guest was to be shown over the house and the grounds and was to meet the Baron Montholon and the baroness and any members of the household he desired. In the meantime Miss Balcombe would remain with him.

"We will talk when you come back," said Napoleon to the lieutenant. "There are many questions I want to ask you."

He then led the way to the library where the billiard table was still kept. As she followed him, Betsy looked about her with a pang in her heart. The interior of the house was being allowed to fall into even greater disrepair. The paper was peeling off the walls and ceilings, the curtains showed rents, the carpets were full of holes. She drew in her breath with distaste, finding the atmosphere heavy with the fustiness of which Napoleon had complained.

The billiard table was piled higher than ever with books and reports and rolled-up maps, so that there was little of the surface showing. As the bottoms of both chairs had been broken through and not repaired, Napoleon placed his hands at the back of Betsy's knees and elevated her to the occupancy of the limited table space. Here she sat and teetered her feet back and forth as they talked.

"That hole in the ceiling hasn't been repaired," she said, looking up. The gap was so large that she could see some of the beams in the steaming hot darkness of the attic. A shudder ran over her as she detected the scratch of rat nails on the wooden surface of the flooring above.

"The hole has been repaired three times. It keeps breaking and I wonder if it is worthwhile having more carpenters. It gets larger every time they touch it."

"Sire," said Betsy, "I go home and weep after I have been here. It is so dreadful! How can you stand it?"

He looked at her with a slow smile which revealed the depth of his affection. "Then you must contrive to come oftener. I forget all the annoyances of my life when you visit me. Every time you come, you seem by some magic to look more and more pleasing to the eye. That little bonnet, how charming it is, *ma petite*. Even though you seem to have reserved it for use when you have this tall gander with you."

It was in every respect a beautiful hat, on the order of the cottage, or "poke" bonnet but raised back so far from her face that the black lace forming its base could be seen. It was of a delicate shade of blue, crisscrossed with narrow bands of golden grosgrain. It framed her face to perfection.

"No!" exclaimed Betsy. "Oh, no, sire. I've had this bonnet for weeks and this is my first wearing of it. I waited until you could see me in it."

"Am I to believe that, when you are devoting all your time to young nobodies in their tawdry uniforms?" An expression compounded of vexation and severity settled over his face. "There are many things I must learn the truth of. You went to a service in the church with the commanding officer of the regiment. He is an old man and, *ma foi*, he is dull."

"He came for tea, and Jane and I accompanied him to the church. He's not dull and he's not much older than you—al-

331

though he looks much older." This had a touch of slyness, for Major Housthorpe was several years younger than Napoleon. The latter accepted her explanation with a confirming nod of his head.

He continued at once with his interrogation. "You went to a dance in the town with that officer whose name—" He raised a hand below the level of his head to aid in the matter of identification.

"High? Oh, Johnny High is a beau of Jane's. She couldn't go to that particular dance, so I took pity on him. He is a great admirer of yours, sire."

"Then there's a most vicious fellow. Something-Rakeshaw, I believe. He has called seven times at your house."

"Sire!" cried Betsy. "How do you find out about such things?"

"Early in my official career I came to realize that a spy system was essential. I have always had a good one."

"I suppose I should feel complimented that you go to such pains to know what I'm doing. It is true, he has called exactly seven times. He came always of his own accord and was rather coolly received."

"Now," said Napoleon, frowning darkly at her, "I come to a more serious matter. Your escort today. You are seen with him everywhere. Seventeen times. Am I correct again?"

"I would have to count back, sire."

"Are you in love with him?"

"N-no."

"Has he proposed marriage?"

Betsy shook her head. "Not yet. But he is going to. The symptoms are unmistakable. Some day soon he will say, 'What, what?' and I will be supposed to blush a little and then say, 'Yes, my good lord and master.' Or something of the kind. Then we will both know it has been settled."

"And are you going to succumb to this highly romantic and most passionate form of courtship?"

Betsy paused for such a long time that the frown on the emperor's face grew even darker. Finally she shook her head. "No, sire," she said.

"Is it so hard to make up your mind?"

"No."

"Can you tell me your reason? I am taking it for granted that you don't love him."

"I have several reasons. One, if I married him that star

you said was directly above me would move to some other part of the sky. It would lose all interest in me."

Napoleon's reception of her reasoning was characteristic. He smiled lightly, then rather broadly. This he followed by throwing back his head and laughing loudly. He reached out and, taking her face in both hands, gave it a shake. This he repeated several times and finally kissed her on the tip of her nose.

"It is so pretty, your nose. I could not resist it, *ma petite.*"

"Lucky nose," commented Betsy. "To be so greatly honored."

There was silence between them for a moment. Betsy thought: "I shouldn't have said that. He may misunderstand me." Apparently Napoleon read into it more than she had intended. Stepping closer to the table and gathering her into his arms, with a whispered, "Betsee! Betsee!" he kissed her many times; not contenting himself with the tip of her nose or brushing her mouth but pre-empting her lips squarely and wandering to her eyes as well.

She fell into a panic and began to struggle. This caused her to lose her balance and she found it necessary to reach with both arms to the rail of the table behind her for support.

"Sire, this is wrong," she said, breathlessly.

Napoleon stepped back at that. After a few moments of reflection, he said, "Yes, *ma petite.* It is wrong. But it's clear that you and I must have a serious talk. Come, we'll go into my study where there are actually chairs in a reasonable state of repair. And it has a fireplace which this abominable room lacks. We'll be more comfortable there."

Betsy had folded her hands together in her soft and slender lap. He took possession of them and helped her down to the floor.

"Are you very much upset?" he asked, smiling at her. "I see that you are, my small one. It is indeed time for that little talk."

Longwood was singularly lacking in halls and, in fact, most of the architectural devices for communication between rooms. One chamber opened off another. When they emerged from the library into the dining room, they encountered Madame de Montholon, who looked at them in a startled manner which changed quickly to suspicion. She was rather elaborately dressed; in something she had donned hastily, no doubt, for the benefit of the young English officer.

"Ah, madame," said Napoleon. "Where is m'sieur le sous-lieutenant?"

"My husband and I had a pleasant talk with him. He is now at the stables, as he is much interested in horses. Archambault is with him."

"Have him brought to the study when his tour is completed, if you please. Mam'selle Betsee and I will be there."

The lady turned with more than a flutter of disapproving skirts and walked to the door which led to the kitchens. "Is it your wish, sire, that the young man be detained in further talk?"

"No," responded Napoleon sharply. "But, observe, if you please, the usual rules. Let me know when he is coming in."

The Captive's personal study was about the size of his bedroom and was in some respects the most dismal apartment in that house of gloom and disorder. The furnishings had been obtained by a search through such storehouses of discards as the island possessed. But it did have two chairs with recent upholstering. Napoleon seated Betsy in one of them and then drew up the other so he could face her.

"Jealousy," he began, "is a sign of weakness. It is mean, sly, and uncouth. And yet, Betsee, I am now compelled to ask your pardon for my display of this objectionable trait."

"Perhaps I thought it a compliment," smiled Betsy.

The Captive proceeded with his own line of thought. "Here am I, a man of fifty years and not in the best of health. Fate has turned against me at the decisive stage of my career and I have been robbed of my power in the world. My possessions have been riven," accenting the word dramatically, "from me. I am confined for life on this horrible volcanic rock. And yet I am still capable of jealousy and the bitterness which goes with it. Because of you, *ma petite*. You were the one who made life tolerable for me when I was put ashore. I have always felt you belonged to me. And now you are devoting all your time to young men who are, I must allow, of the proper age for you. I am not able to accept this change gracefully. I don't believe I had realized how deep my feelings for you had become until I saw you perched out there, smiling at me from that useless billiard table and swinging your feet back and forth like the little girl I remembered so well."

"But, Betsee," he went on, "I must speak frankly. The empress, my second wife, has not written to me since I was sent to Elba. She has placed my son in the care of her imperial parents. A divorce is impossible because of her rank and her religion. But even if something happened to remove the obstacles, I still could do nothing. I must not endanger the position of my little son. That must be my first consideration."

"Naturally, sire," said Betsy.

"We have talked at times about the ladies in my life. I think you call them the—"

"The Others."

"There have been a number of them—"

"Many, sire."

"If complete accuracy is desired, then we must concede there have been many. Some of them have been great ladies, some of—of lower degree. All of them have been beautiful." He paused. He was studying her face, and his eyes had lighted up with the glow which comes often at the glimpse of a work of art. "I think, *ma petite*, that you are more beautiful than any of them."

"You can't mean that, sire."

"But I do mean it. I am in earnest." Napoleon began to cast back in his mind over the years. "My Josephine was not a great beauty. She had daintiness and charm but—her teeth were bad. Marie Louise was young and of a fresh complexion but in time I came to realize that her habit of letting her mouth fall open at moments of surprise or distress made her look stupid. La Bellilote—yes, my little Madame Fourès was very pretty but I am compelled to say she had about her a certain hint of commonness. Mademoiselle George, my laughing, romping comedienne, soon became *gaillarde*—"

"In English," said Betsy, "we are inclined to call it *chunky*."

Napoleon bobbed his head in agreement. "A rather good word for my handsome Mam'selle George. Now Maria Walewska was different from all the others. She was lovely and, *ah*, of so much courage and loyalty. But her beauty was—a little solemn. Her smiles always came slowly. She did not sparkle or—or, shall we say, bubble with gaiety, as others I could mention so often do."

"Now you, *ma petite*," he went on, after a long moment, "brought something new into my life. I remember our walks so well, just the two of us, sometimes hand in hand. I would say things against the English for no other reason than to see

335

your face take fire. You would always say exactly what you thought, yes even to the great Napoleon! *Ma foi,* how outspoken you were! The things you would say to me! You became most lovely when you were angry with me. No one had ever faced me that way before.

"I began to feel then that you belonged to me. As you grew up, I saw less of you but I never considered that I had lost the little girl back at the Briars. And now, Betsee, you are fully grown up and you have become exquisite—and you can't belong to me any more! I cannot marry again. And, *ma petite,* you can never be one of the Others—that shadowy band of almost forgotten charmers, whose existence seems to concern you so much and me so very little. You are too good for that. And my affection for you is too real and deep. Am I making myself clear?"

"Yes, sire. I understand."

There was a long pause. Napoleon kept his eyes lowered but it was possible to see that they had narrowed as he considered the advisability of saying more. Finally he glanced up. "There is always a chance that my position will improve, that I will be freed from this degrading captivity. The people of France may demand my release. The English Government may awaken to the barbarity of their treatment to me. Perhaps my star is still showing up there above me. The chance that I may emerge again is an infinitesimal one, I confess. But if it happened, *Mon Dieu,* it would change everything!

"And so, Betsee, I want to warn you again. Don't throw yourself away. I want you to have the best of everything. Wait at least until you return to England. None of these long-shanked *hommes de néant* will do."

There was a rap on the door. "M'sieur le sous-lieutenant," announced Santini.

"Come in, sir, come in," said Napoleon. "'Have you been impressed with the beauties of this tropical Versailles which your government has provided for me?"

Chapter Nine

Margette had been picking up some random bits of English and Betsy was not surprised when the girl paused after opening the gate for her.

"Mist'us ill," said Margette.

Betsy laid an importunate hand on the girl's arm. "Is Madame very ill?" she asked.

The girl struggled to find the words she needed and ended by drawing a handkerchief from her belt. She coughed and then pressed the square of muslin to her lips. "See!" she said, holding it out as though for inspection.

"You mean she is coughing blood? Margette, this is very serious. Has a doctor been called in?"

The maid repeated the word "doctor" several times before getting any meaning from it. Then she shook her head. "No. No doct'. Mist'us say no use."

When she found herself in her usual seat near the dark inner window, Betsy looked about her with an augmented sense of the dismay it always brought her. "My poor Julia!" she thought. "This is worse than Longwood."

The voice of the Veiled Lady was cheerful enough when she stationed herself on the other side. "Well, my gay young friend," she said, "and what have you been doing? In what mischief have you been playing the leading role? No more signaling over the semaphore, I trust."

"I have had a long talk with the emperor," answered Betsy. "But I don't want to speak of it until I've heard what you have to tell me about yourself. Margette seems very much disturbed."

"It would be foolish of me to say that she isn't right. I think—well, Betsy, there is no cure for what ails me. I received a letter a few days back which helped my spirits a

337

very great deal but is now having the opposite effect. I am feeling an intense regret for what might have been."

"The letter was from England? From your family?"

"From England, yes. But not from my family. I have no close relatives. This—was a proposal of marriage."

Betsy gulped at the unexpectedness of this piece of information. "Why, Julia!" she exclaimed. "Were you—pleased?"

There was a long silence. Then the voice came in more subdued tones from the other side of the opening. "I think I shall have to tell you now the whole story of how I happen to be here. You remember what I said before? How I fell in love with a married man, an associate of my father's? What I held back was that his wife was a woman of an intense pride and a furious temper. When she learned about it, she came to see me—and threw acid in my face."

Betsy had difficulty in restraining an exclamation of horror. She had heard of such things, of course, but found it hard to conceive of her gentle friend being involved in such a tragedy.

"That explains why I live here like this," went on the voice. "Only one side of my face suffered from the acid but it was turned into something—something quite inhuman and beyond description. My doctors urged me to cover the injured side with a mask and take up my way of life again but I could not bear to try. My father had left me with very little; not enough to keep on as an invalid all my life. To save the wife from legal punishment, her wealthy and powerful relatives created a fund to provide me with an income. One stipulation was made. I must leave England and settle somewhere as far away as possible. St. Helena was chosen. And here I have been ever since."

"Won't time cure the scars?"

"No, Betsy. They are too deep. I lost the sight of the one eye, of course. I am so sensitive that I keep that part of my face covered all the time. Even Margette has never had a glimpse of it," she sighed deeply. "Perhaps you will believe me now when I say that the state of my health does not cause me any concern. The—the inevitable climax can't come too soon."

Betsy had indulged in many speculations as to the reason for her friend's rigid refusal to mingle with people but this explanation had never occurred to her. It was hard for her to believe but there was no mistaking the note of tragedy in the low voice.

It was some moments before the story was resumed. "Poor Andrew has had a worse time than I have. His wife died some months ago. He wrote me at once and urged that I return to England and marry him. Can you conceive of anything finer under these terrible circumstances? It was a wonderful letter, without a line or a word to indicate any inner reluctance on his part. He told much of what had been happening. As soon as I left England, his wife's brother called him out. Andrew carried the loaded pistol to his post but refused to raise it on the signal. The brother's bullet came within an inch of his ear. He and his wife continued to live in their home but they spoke very seldom. Fortunately there were no children. What a dismal life! I sometimes think it has been much harder for him. He said in his letter I would be shocked at his appearance, for his hair has turned gray and his face 'resembles a map of Napoleon's campaigns!'

"Of course, I replied at once and said how happy I had been to hear from him. But I said I was sure what he proposed would not be wise."

"But why?" asked Betsy.

"I think," said the inmate of the dark room, "that I am as proud as his wife. In my own way. A single glimpse of my scarred face would bring him a feeling of loathing. *That* I could not bear. In any case, Betsy, I am really very ill. It won't be long now. So—so I decided to continue in this way to the end and not impose on my poor Andrew the responsibility for the little time left me. I wrote him a very long letter to convince him it would be a mistake."

Inevitability is something that the youthful mind does not easily accept. "Are you quite sure the scar is not improving?" asked Betsy.

"Quite, my dear." After a few moments the voice went on. "I can never tell you how much pleasure I have had from your visits. I suppose you have sometimes wondered what I look like?"

"Often. You told me once that you are rather dark and so I carry a mental picture of you with no more than that to go on. I am sure you are lovely."

"Perhaps I should do nothing to disturb this pleasant supposition. But, Betsy, I would like to have you carry more of a picture of me than that. A matter of pride? Yes, I suppose

339

it is. You see, the left side of my face is quite untouched, although this sickness is making it seem thin and drawn."

There was a sound movement on the other side and then the ring of a bell reached the girl's ears from a distance in the house. Almost immediately they heard the solid footsteps of Margette crossing the courtyard from the kitchen. She appeared in the doorway, carrying a platter and two glasses of wine.

"Thank you, Margette, for anticipating my wants," said the Veiled Lady. "I would also like two more candles. The largest you have."

Margette looked surprised as she turned to leave the room. She was back quickly with two quite long yellow candlesticks.

"Give one of them, please, to Miss Balcombe." A thin white arm, bare to the elbow, reached out through the opening and took the other candle. Her friend's hand, Betsy observed, was beautifully formed, the fingers long and tapering.

"Come up a little closer, please."

What followed was almost like the materialization of a spirit in the darkness. Out of the shadow there grew what seemed like a very beautiful life-size cameo, pale, almost white, under a crown of abundant black hair. The single eye in the cameo, which was kept lowered, conveyed an appearance of intelligence and high spirit as well as beauty. In the soft light of the candle, the nose stood out slender and rather long. The only note of tragedy was in the line of the mouth.

"Julia! Julia! How lovely!"

"I am glad you feel that way. There never seems to be any end to vanity. I can still feel it, even I, with my frightening scars. This is how I want him to remember me and I can't risk the possibility of letting him, or anyone, see the dreadfulness of the other side. Not all the time in the world nor the skill of all the surgeons can do anything to remove the scars. I shall continue to the end like the Rose Noble of Thring. Do you know that story, Betsy?"

Betsy did not know it, so she continued. "It's said that a long time ago an English king stumbled over a coin while visiting a battlefield. It was one of the first of the rose nobles minted in the reign of Edward the Fourth. He began to restore it at once with his own hands, having a great interest in old coins, and he succeeded in making the side with the snow rose of the House of York glow like new. Before starting on the other side, which was tarnished and pitted and worn by time, he became aware that the wife of his host was extraordinarily attractive. He gave it to her, seeing that as it stood the coin was an unmistakable token. It was understood between them that she would send it to him whenever her husband was away on a tour of his other estates." A brief ironic laugh interrupted the telling. "It's not a very proper story, is it, Betsy? Because, of course, the husband was away a great deal and the token came just as frequently into the hands of the king."

"But," protested Betsy, "the king could have restored the other side as well."

"No. The side with the rose had rested against a flat stone surface which protected it from much of the ravages of time. The other had worn away almost to nothing, like the side of my face you haven't seen."

The candle was extinguished in the inner room. Betsy blew out the one which had been placed beside her.

"And now," said the voice, "you have something to tell me about this great man who has become such a friend of yours."

Betsy proceeded to tell everything that had happened during her visit to Longwood, and to repeat the conversation as fully as her memory allowed.

"His intentions seem honorable," said the listener at the finish. "Quite remarkably so, in view of his romantic record. But, my dear, I still feel you must act with a great deal of caution. A small incident can sometimes upset the most honest purpose. Such as the rustle of a silk petticoat or an unexpected glimpse of a pretty ankle, even the sparkle of an eye under the scoop of a becoming hat. Try not to be alone with him in his private suite and avoid any such episodes as sitting on a table and needing to be helped down. Napoleon has not changed, you know, even though he's convinced now that you are a new experience in his life.

"But," went on the voice, "there is a matter of still greater moment. You may find it easier to control the conduct of Napoleon than that of your own heart. How, my dear, did you feel when this was happening?"

"What you are asking is, am I in love with him?"

"Yes, that is what I am asking."

"I don't know," answered the girl, promptly. "I'm not at

all sure I know what love is. Certainly I don't feel anything different for my new friends. I enjoy being with them and I find we all have mutual interests."

"That," said the Veiled Lady, "is unusual to begin with. At your age you should be on the point of falling head over heels in love with someone. If it isn't one of these officers, can it be Napoleon? That is the point that disturbs me."

"The emperor fascinates me. I feel that all men are more or less alike—except Napoleon. I watch his eyes and wonder what thoughts are going on behind them. They are different thoughts, I am sure, than those of all other men. He is—he is—oh, how can I say it? It's impossible to describe him with words."

"You are aware, of course, that any relationship would have to be of the—the left hand?"

Betsy nodded her head. "I realize that, of course. Does it matter, where the man is so far above everyone else?"

"In time you would discover that it does. Moreover, do you realize that he is on the verge of old age? When there is such a disparity in years, all the adapting must be done by the woman. All the fitting in, the controlling of likes and dislikes, of moods and beliefs. It is easy to believe that you find him fascinating but Betsy, do you *like* him?"

"I like him very, very much."

"And will you always?"

The girl did not answer at once. She seemed to be weighing the question with great care.

"All I am certain is, that I will never be able to fall in love with any other man as long as I continue to have a share in Napoleon's life. Even though it may be a very small share."

"Or until someone comes along who is quite irresistible, shall we say? A young man who seems different also from all others."

"He would have to be very different from those I've met so far."

"For your sake, Betsy, I hope this young man comes along very soon—and I hope I can see you often in the meantime."

"You can depend on that. We seem to need each other, don't we?"

Chapter Ten

1

From a corner of the Bertrand house Napoleon could stand behind the shutters and see a large part of the Deadwood course where the annual horse races were held. The Bertrands were staying home on the opening day. Spyglass in hand, he retreated into the house with an irritated frown.

"Madame," he said to the countess, "I don't see Betsee."

"Betsy isn't going. She can't ride her pony any longer, you know. She's outgrown it. And all the family horses are in use. So it was decided she would stay at home."

"This, madame, is outrageous!" declared Napoleon. "They know how pleased I always am to see Betsee. Something must be done."

After a moment's thought he summoned Marchand who was waiting outside. "Had m'sieur le docteur left for the day?"

"I think not, Your Majesty."

O'Meara put in an appearance promptly. His relationship with Napoleon had become more cordial during the past year, largely because of the breach which had opened between him and the governor. He grinned broadly when he learned what Napoleon had in mind.

"He won't like it," he said, referring to Sir Hudson Lowe. "It will rouse the bile in him but that's an additional reason for going on with it. I'll speak to Archambault at once. It won't take him long to get Mameluke ready."

"It will have to be done quickly. They seem to be organizing the races now. Remember, the gray is to be well groomed. The saddlecloth of crimson velvet is to be used and the best side saddle. The gold bridle and the gray plumes, of course. Nothing too good for our young friend. I want you to go along with Archambault."

"Glad to go, Your Highness. I like to study the scowl

343

which comes over the fine open countenance of Old Mutter-and-Mumble whenever he sees me."

"The wind seems to be freshening a little."

"It's a little sharp. Nothing to bother an Irishman but I suppose it's enough to send shivers down the thin spines of these islanders."

"Then she must have a warm cloak. Something in keeping with the grandeur of my fine Mameluke. Ah, I have an idea. Omurr," he always had difficulty with the Irishman's name, "why don't we send her the Robe of Marengo, to use if the winds really begin to blow?"

"The Robe of Marengo!" The doctor, clearly, was shaken by surprise. Napoleon took so much pride in this historic article that it was as though he had suggested finding a coronation robe for the occasion.

"Have it folded neatly and placed across the saddle, in case of need. And be quick about everything."

"If necessary, Majesty, I'll apply the toe of my stout Irish shoe to get Archambault started."

The ladies' race had been run when Betsy arrived at Deadwood but this she did not mind. The fact that practically every pair of eyes had opened wide when she appeared was ample compensation. She heard people talking about her on all sides. "She's riding his favorite horse!" "Yes, it's Mameluke, covered with silver and plumes!" "Well, she *is* lovely, isn't she!" and "Pretty brazen, I call it."

Count Montholon whispered to his wife, who wore bright red as usual: "That's the Robe of Marengo folded over in place of saddlebags! This is unbelievable!"

In a matter of seconds the officers of the regiment had gathered in a body about the new arrival. They exclaimed over the magnificent trappings of the big gray.

"It's a dashed shame you're so late getting here," said Grannison. "The ladies' race is just over. You would have won in a walk."

"We've come to an agreement about the next one," said Johnny High. "We're all going in. Some of us are riding plow horses. It's going to be a wild free-for-all. No telling who'll win in such a mishmash as this."

Grannison, who rather fancied himself as a rider, did not agree. "Oh, I expect real class will tell. Though I'd lay a few sovereigns that you'll come in pretty well near the end, Master High."

"Having seen what I've got to ride, I'm not betting on my chances."

"By Gad!" cried Grannison. "I've got an idea. Why shouldn't Betsy come in with us? It's not for the championship of the regiment or anything of the kind. It isn't going to be one of those tough ones with everyone riding at top speed. You might not do badly at all, Betsy."

"You mean," said Betsy, with a hint of meekness, "that I might not come in last?"

Grannison pursed up his lips. "N-no. You might do well enough. A few of them might come trailing in after you, High, for instance. You have a devilish good mount, you know."

"And you don't think I would disgrace myself?"

"I think," said the originator of the scheme, "that you might surprise yourself. I really do."

All the rest joined in. It would be good sportsmanship on her part. There had been no excitement in any of the events and her appearance might stir things up.

"Would your father object?" asked Johnny High.

"He's not here."

"And Lord Hogen Mogen has just left," said Grannison. "Taking all his staff with him. That sort of clears the air, doesn't it? Betsy, we can fix things so you won't be in any danger at all. We'll start you off to one side, so you can keep clear of all the starting and stopping, and the kicking and all the galomphery before the signal's given."

"That's *very* kind of you!"

Betsy's eyes were busily searching for her mother. She finally located her in a cluster of ladies far off at one side. They were deeply engaged in conversation.

"Well," she said, "why not?"

A cry from Napoleon drew Bertrand to the corner where the emperor was standing. A spyglass had been shoved out through a hole in a shutter and he was keeping an eye glued to it.

"This will be worth watching."

"Yes, Your Imperial Highness?"

"Betsee is going to ride against the officers, from the look of things. I wish I had gone down to watch."

"Isn't there time still?"

"No, they're lining up now. *Ma foi*, Bertrand, these young men may be in for an eye opener."

"Betsy rides quite well," conceded the marshal. "But can she be expected to hold her own against army officers?"

There was silence for several moments and then the sound of a pistol shot reached them from the direction of the course.

"They're off!" said Napoleon. Almost immediately he indulged in a dance step. "Mameluke came out like a cannon shot. And you ought to see Betsee! She's riding easily and beautifully. *Mon Dieu!* What a fine hand on the reins!"

Finding that he could see little with the naked eye, Bertrand went back to his work in another room. Madame Bertrand came in, attracted by shouts of the emperor.

"What is it, sir?" she asked.

"If we had another glass, you would be able to watch something worthwhile, dear madame," declared Napoleon. "This is going to be a great race, egad, she's out in front." He began to jump up and down with excitement. "Ride, Betsee, ride! Bear in toward the pole, child, don't stay so far out. Save yourself ground. Ah, just look at her, my little Betsee!"

Only a portion of the course could be seen from the Bertrand house. When the contestants vanished from sight, Napoleon stepped back from the window and folded up the spyglass.

"Has she a chance, sire?" asked Madame Bertrand.

Napoleon seemed to have cooled down a little from his first enthusiasm. At any rate he displayed a note of caution. "She seems to be doing well. Of course, the hardest part of the run is ahead of her. But, *ma certes*, she started well."

He walked into the room to which the marshal had returned. The latter looked up from his papers enquiringly.

Napoleon repeated himself. "She's doing well," he said. "Would you care to lay a bet on the race?"

Bertrand, as Napoleon knew well, had a full share of the gambling instinct. He frowned and gave some thought to the suggestion.

"What do you propose, sire?"

"I am disposed to gamble on Betsee. After all, she is riding my own favorite. Well, marshal, what do you say? *Compte rond?*"

"Compte rond?" Bertrand clearly had not expected to be offered even money. He glanced sharply at the emperor. "That's more than fair. Do you mean it, sire?"

"I must show my faith in Mameluke. And in her."

"Then, I'll take you, sire."

2

At the close of the afternoon Betsy rode Mameluke to the Bertrand gate where Archambault met her. She sprang easily to the ground.

She patted the nose of the big gray. "My sweet fellow!" she said. "How beautiful you are! And how fast!"

Mrs. Balcombe and Jane rode over in the delivery wagon to pick up Betsy and take her home. The Bertrands came out to greet them. The two ladies, who were on a most friendly basis, whispered together while the marshal stalked about with a pleased air.

Napoleon walked the distance between the two houses with his arms linked behind his back. He wore a frown such as no member of the Balcombe family had ever seen on his face. Stopping beside Bertrand, he held out a sovereign. The latter accepted it with a pleased bow.

"Betsee!" exclaimed Napoleon, in a rasping voice. "You lost! How can you explain it?"

Betsy looked surprised and hurt by the sharpness of his tone. "No, sire," she said. "I didn't lose. I didn't finish the race."

"You mean you dropped out?"

"Yes, sire."

"But why?" he demanded to know. "Didn't you think you could win?"

Betsy was watching him with a troubled air. "Yes," she said, in a hesitating tone. "I was sure I could win. I was well ahead. But when we reached the last sign, I took the wrong turn."

Napoleon swung angrily on his heel and began to walk away. "I have never known you to be stupid. How could you miss the turn? Was the sign not clear?"

"I—I missed it on purpose, sire."

The emperor stopped and glared back over his shoulder at her. His expression could be described by one word only, ferocious. There was fire in his eyes and the corners of his mouth had been drawn sharply down.

"*Tonnerre!* You missed on purpose! Betsee, I do not understand. Why did you do this? Didn't you want to win?"

"No, sire. As soon as it became clear that Mameluke was too fast for them, I knew that I shouldn't have entered. It wasn't fair. All the others had such poor mounts. So—when I came to the last turn, I realized what I must do. I went over to the left instead of taking the inner course. And, then, naturally, I couldn't get back."

"How often have I told you," he demanded, "that you must always win? Winning is the most important thing in life! No matter what you are doing, you must strive with every nerve in your body to win. Haven't I spoken of this many times?"

"Yes, sire."

It was clear that he was not only angry but very much puzzled. His forehead had become wrinkled into an expression that showed his complete lack of understanding. "Betsee, what was your reason? Why did you enter the race if you didn't intend to do everything in your power to win?"

"They wouldn't have invited me to enter if they thought I had a chance. They didn't even expect me to make a good race of it. You see, they couldn't afford to be beaten. Everyone would have laughed at them. In the regiment it would be considered a disgrace. To have a girl beat them all! No, sire, it wouldn't have done. The word would get back home in time and the poor 53rd would become a laughingstock."

"Laughingstock? I don't know what that means."

"When I became sure they were not going to catch up, I either had to pull Mameluke in or pretend to be mistaken about the turn."

"This," declared Napoleon, waving his arms in his exasperation, "is one of those absurdities they teach you in England. Fair play—is that what you mean? I am astonished, Betsee, that you could behave in such a childish way. If you are to take advantage of the fine qualities you possess, there must be no more of this. You must win, win, win! It's no concern of yours if the feelings of others are hurt. The spoils in life go to the strong, never to the magnanimous, the kindly, the weak, the stupid." He began to walk back to the Longwood entrance. "I am disappointed in you. I am disturbed and angry."

As Betsy rejoined the others, her thoughts in a turmoil, she heard Madame Bertrand ask her husband, "Gratty, when did you make that wager with him?"

"I think it was after the horses had ridden out of sight."

Betsy hurried on, not wishing to hear anything more.

"Did you know," continued the countess, "that Betsee was well out in front at the time?"

"No. He said she was making a race of it."

"Ah, I thought so." She was silent for a moment. "Was it a sovereign he gave you?"

Bertrand nodded. "Yes, a fine, shiny sovereign."

"We could make such good use of it! Still, Gratty, I think it would be wise to send it back."

The marshal smiled. "I've already done that. As soon as he turned his back, I handed the coin to Marchand and told him to lay it on his desk. Nothing more will be said about it."

"Why was he so indignant with the poor child?"

Bertrand spread out his hands. "He was completely sincere in what he said, you know. This is a matter of principle with him. It's part of his philosophy of life. Always win, no matter what the cost. It's proof of the interest he takes in the girl that he thinks she should be taught to follow his principles. I'm sure he had no conception of what she meant."

3

After lunch the next day, Mrs. Balcombe drew Betsy off to one side. It was clear she was very much disturbed.

"Did you notice how quiet your father was?" she asked.

"He *was* quiet, now that you mention it, Mamma. But Jane and I were doing so much talking that neither of you had a chance to put in a word."

"Betsy!" Mrs. Balcombe shook her head, solemnly. "He had a better reason that that. He was summoned to Plantation House this morning. The governor was in a great temper. Because of what you did yesterday."

"Because I raced against the officers?"

"No. It was chiefly because you went there on Napoleon's favorite mount. He is sure the story will get back to England and be accepted there as proof that sympathy for him is running high on the island."

"It is, of course, Mamma."

"He calls it treason."

"Mamma, I sometimes think that man is mad. Doesn't he realize that Napoleon was our guest and that we all became very friendly? Does he expect us to turn on him now?"

Mrs. Balcombe sighed deeply. "Well, he made it clear to your father that he may decide to send us all back to England. He regards us as—as a hostile influence."

"But, Mamma, that's unfair. Papa was in town when Mameluke was sent over. Did he explain that?"

"I don't think so, child. He didn't want to be blaming you. He didn't make any defense. But he was deeply disturbed when he came back. He didn't want to talk about it. Even to me."

There was a long silence. Finally Betsy said, "Mamma, don't you think it will be a good thing when we leave this island?"

Mrs. Balcombe nodded her head with sudden emphasis. "Yes! I do. Your father is entitled to a much better post. If he would only make use of his influence. But it might be inconvenient to return at this moment. Financially, I mean."

Betsy sat down to think the situation over. She could not see why the happenings of the previous day could be construed as an evidence of wrong feeling on their part. Napoleon's chief reason for not attending public functions was because of the way the islanders swarmed about him to ask questions. If such a thing happened would Sir Hudson Lowe feel he should deport the whole population? "That wretched little man!" thought Betsy. "Daring to talk to my father this way!"

She decided finally that an explanation of the occurrence should be made. She went upstairs and changed to a more suitable dress. Then she selected one of her most becoming hats and returned downstairs. No one was about so she went to the stables and had a horse saddled for her.

When she reached Plantation House, she was surprised to see that the Juggernaut was waiting at the main entrance. This was a name given to the oldest, the creakiest, the least reliable vehicle on the island. Many years before, when it was new and shiny, it had belonged to a high official, a governor, perhaps. When the first owner left St. Helena, he sold it to one of the farmers and it had remained in the possession of the same family for many long years, getting more dilapidated and less safe all the time. What, she asked herself, was this relic of the past doing at Plantation House!

The answer was supplied when the representative of the French Government, the Marquis Claude de Montchenu, came out through the front door. He was looking fully as run-down and timeworn as the carriage. His hat had lost its nap, his clothes were sadly out of shape and his neckcloth suggested a distant laundering. The worthy marquis, always complaining about the meager stipend paid him, had become the most frequent borrower on the island.

"That old toad!" thought Betsy. "He's falling lower all the time. He must have borrowed the Juggernaut."

Montchenu, ready to let bygones be bygones and recognizing her with a rheumy gleam in his eyes, bowed very low.

"Ah, mam'selle!" he said. "You are looking charming. Most beautiful indeed. I must be getting old, for I can't find words to tell you how—how beautiful you are."

Betsy's first impulse was to make no acknowledgment of his presence. Second thoughts, however, dissuaded her from this course. She gave him the benefit of a frigid bow and walked away to the entrance of the administrative wing.

She was admitted after some delay and found Sir Hudson Lowe seated at his desk, with his eyes fixed straight ahead of him. He neither looked up nor spoke when she approached.

After several moments of embarrassing silence, Betsy felt she must state her reasons for coming. "Your Excellency," she said, "I wish to make it clear that my father knew nothing of what occurred at the races yesterday until he returned home for dinner. Mameluke was brought over by Dr. O'Meara early in the afternoon—"

"Ah, O'Meara!" The governor still kept his gaze averted. "Always O'Meara! This confirms me in the decision I have reached."

"But, sir, he was acting on orders."

As this elicited no response, the girl continued with her explanations. For a time Lowe did not move nor make any further remark. Finally, he got to his feet and, leaving her standing beside his desk (she had not been offered a chair), walked across the room to speak with one of his secretaries. There was a whispered conversation and then the governor stalked from the room.

Betsy waited. Surely he was coming back. She had not yet

been allowed to give him a complete explanation. But the minutes passed and there was no further sign of the governor. Finally she could stand it no longer. She crossed the room to the desk of the secretary.

"Can you tell me if His Excellency intends to return?" she asked.

The secretary, a recent addition to the staff apparently, for he was a stranger to her and very young, leaned back in his chair. Then he shook his head.

"He did not inform me of his movements, miss," he said.

Betsy's temper rose at this point. It was bad enough to be treated discourteously by the governor, but there was no excuse for a subordinate officer to show her such lack of consideration. Suddenly she stamped the floor with one foot.

"Stand up!" she exclaimed.

The secretary was so startled that a flush took possession of his pimpled face. After a few moments of hesitation, he got slowly to his feet.

"Now you at least look like an English gentleman," said the girl, storm signals flaring in her eyes. "Haven't you ever been told about standing up to speak with a lady? Or were you acting under orders? Now that you *are* up, I have a request to make. Will you be kind enough to inform His Excellency when he returns—if he returns—that I have left. He apparently did not wish to see me again. Whether or not he had anything further to say, I have no intention of waiting longer here."

"I—I will so inform His Excellency."

"You will also tell His Excellency this. He may not have had anything more to say to me when he left the room with such rudeness. But I had much more to say to him. Things he would not have enjoyed hearing, I am sure."

"I will report what you have said."

"A final word. There must be a book on etiquette in the library here. Study it some time."

Lady Lowe, as it happened, emerged from the drawing room in time to see Betsy on her way to the side entrance. She noticed the rigidity of the girl's figure and concluded that she was leaving in a state of indignation.

"I am afraid," thought the chatelaine of Plantation House, "that I have not been successful in restoring the peace."

352

4

Dr. O'Meara came to the Briars that evening with a long parcel under his arm. He accepted a glass of port and settled down to drink it, resting the parcel across his knees.

"I have good news," he said. "I have been discharged and am leaving for England in a matter of days."

"Do you consider that good news?" asked William Balcombe, with a glance of friendly commiseration.

"The best. As long as I stay here I am cut off from all free communication with the outside world. He, my Lord Butmenobuts," motioning with a thumb in the direction of Plantation House, to indicate that the reference was to Sir Hudson Lowe, "reads every line I put to paper before allowing it to go. He puts my letters under a microscope and gives them acid tests. What chance is there to get the truth circulating about the way he's running things here? But when I get back to dear old Frog-and-Toe"—a slang name for London—"I'll be free to talk."

He stretched out his legs luxuriously and proceeded to enjoy his port. "I believe, William, that you have the best cellar on the island. The stuff *he* serves is poisonously bad. Now this," glancing approvingly at the fine ruby liquid, "this is wine for gentlemen. Have you ever given advice to Butmenobuts about the wine he should serve for his official entertaining?"

"No," drily. "I have found him rather averse to accepting advice on any point. At least, from me."

"Well," said O'Meara, "the newspapers are going to hear plenty of truth from me when I reach England. I'm going to write articles and I even think of publishing a book. Don't you suppose he sees the danger in turning me loose like this? I swear the great blockhead must have a mind like a colander. Full of holes."

Betsy, still in an upset state of mind over the reception she had met at Plantation House, heard something of what was being said. She knew they would miss the breezy Irishman but she was glad that he was returning. "And I hope," she said to herself, "that he does tell the whole truth!"

On his way out, the doctor dropped the parcel in Betsy's lap.

"A gift, I suspect," he said. "So mum's the word. If he

353

hears about it, that fellow will have it taken to pieces to see if it contains any messages from Napoleon."

Betsy took the parcel upstairs to be opened. There was a note attached which she opened first.

> "This," Napoleon had written, "was given me by a member of my family who loves me very much. So it seems fitting that I should give it to one for whom I have a very deep feeling."
>
> N.

"I think he wants me to know he didn't mean the things he said last evening," she said to herself, drawing much consolation from the thought.

Chapter Eleven

1

Napoleon had been one of the last to yield to the popular swing in favor of trousers for men in place of breeches. He considered trousers vulgar and unfit for public wear. "These baggy monstrosities!" he would say. "An Anglo-Saxon notion, fit only for field workers, swine sloppers and—and English shopkeepers!" No one had dared to appear before him in the offensive garment while he was in power.

One day, however, when the sun was high in the St. Helena heavens and the heat about Longwood was almost unbearable, he had noticed that most of his staff were wearing trousers as they went about their duties. He promptly summoned his valet. Marchand responded, attired in breeches which fitted him with a snugness threatening the safety of the seams.

"Marchand," he said, "these abominations they are wearing out there, these English *trousers*, what are they made of?"

"Cotton, I believe, Your Majesty."

"Where do they get them?"

"At a shop in town, Majesty. They are very cheap, as might be expected."

"Are they comfortable?"

"I am told so, Highness."

Napoleon's own clothes literally were sticking to his frame in the inescapable heat. He walked to a window and shuddered when he saw how the so-called English innovations flapped about the shanks of their wearers.

"They are hideous, Marchand. But perhaps they are suited to the climate of this hellish island. Have you felt a desire to wear them?"

The valet hesitated. Then he said, "Yes, Highness, but I have never given in to it."

Napoleon walked back from the window. "Get a pair and try them. Then report to me."

Marchand's report was delivered with a hesitant smile. "Your Imperial Highness, I must be honest," he said. "They are most comfortable. They are actually cool."

The emperor gave in with a reluctant sigh. "Get a pair for me," he instructed. "Those coats they are wearing, are they of cotton also?"

The valet nodded. "Yes, Highness."

"Get one for me. And those wide, floppy hats. Are they actually made of straw?"

"Yes, Your Highness."

"They are incredibly ugly and vulgar. Do they keep out the sun?"

"So I have been informed, Highness."

"I might as well go the whole distance if I am giving in at all. Get me everything—trousers, coat, waistcoat, and one of those absurd hats."

This trivial passage led in a short time to a situation Napoleon would gladly have avoided. He found himself facing one of the most dramatic incidents in the course of his exile while attired in the baggiest of cotton trousers and wearing on his head a very wide straw hat. In Paris he would not have been recognized. In fact, if he had approached the gates of the Louvre in such garments, he undoubtedly would have been chased away by the threat of bare pikes in the hands of sentries.

He was standing near the trave at one end of the stables and was watching the younger Archambault shoe a horse. Glancing over his shoulder, he became aware that Bertrand had emerged from his house, carrying as usual a spyglass for a glance around the horizon. There was something about the behavior of the marshal which caused Napoleon to study him carefully. Why had he swung the glass back over his shoulder so abruptly? And why was he now standing in the heat of the morning sun with nothing on his head?

Napoleon did not pause long to ponder. His reaction to what he observed was rapid and instinctive. But as usual he gave no sign of what was passing through his mind. He did not make the mistake of running for his own spyglass, because he knew this would seem suspicious. Instead he walked with a steady step to the gate between the two properties, waving the sentries back when they converged on him with drawn bayonets.

"M'sieur le maréchal!" he called. "I have a few matters to discuss. There is no great hurry about it but come over in a quarter hour or so. And, *Mon Dieu*, put on a hat. The top of your head is red already and covered with perspiration. Do you want to have a sunstroke?"

When Bertrand arrived at Longwood there were tears in his eyes, and Napoleon's heart jumped, in spite of the outward calm he maintained. He recognized the sign as good.

"It is so, then?"

"Yes, sire."

The marshal choked back his tears but Napoleon was disturbed by the pallor of his cheeks and the way he was rolling his tongue between his lips.

"We must appear casual, Bertrand. In the name of heaven, act as though we are discussing a bill for a saddle of mutton. There are spies in our own household, you know, and the guards at Alarm-House get you under their glasses the instant you come over." Napoleon went to the extent even of slipping both hands into the pockets of his trousers, as a proof of his own calm. "Our ship is in?"

"Yes, sire. It is out in the roadstead. It has an enormous superstructure but the main mast is trailing over the side. Much of the rigging still attaches to it."

"Can you make out the name?"

"No, sire. The ship keeps turning in the wind."

"You—you are quite sure, Bertrand?"

"Completely, sire." The marshal paused and seemed to stagger a little. "Can we take a seat? I feel, sire, on the point of collapse."

"I would order wine for you but I fear it would arouse too much curiosity."

They seated themselves in the shade of one of the garden trees. Bertrand drew out a handsome silk handkerchief and dried his forehead. He was breathing rapidly.

"Lean back and take your time, Marshal. We have waited two years for this so we can afford to let a few minutes pass us by."

Napoleon's composure under the circumstances seemed remarkable but, if anyone had been close enough to study his face closely, it would have been apparent that the pupils of his eyes had grown large. When he spoke again, however, he gestured with a steady hand.

"Everything is ready," he said, in a low tone. "I have gone

357

over the details a score of times. All possible contingencies have been provided for. Never on the eve of a battle was I able to feel as much confidence as I do now."

Bertrand was slowly recovering his wits. He sat up in his chair.

"Yes, sire. Each day I give some time to thinking over the details. I find no flaws or omissions."

"There is only one danger I can foresee. The man Roberaud knows my habits and characteristics well enough to deceive the most suspicious eye. But he knows nothing of the people here. It will devolve on you, Bertrand, to coach him; for I, God willing, will be on my way to Rio. No one must be allowed to see him for many days. It can be given out that the fall into the ravine has left him in a weakened condition. The new doctor won't suspect anything, so you can afford to let him pay some visits. You must be on hand when anyone else is allowed in. Even the Montholons. Even Madame Bertrand. In the meantime you must keep drilling him in what he must know. The people I like. Those I dislike. What is to be said to this one and what to that. His real identity must be kept a secret for as long as possible; for, certainly, a month. By that time I will be far out of the range of the British Navy, and it won't matter if they discover there is a cuckoo in the nest."

Napoleon's calm seemed to be betraying at last a tendency to desert him. A faint spot of color showed near his cheek bones. There was a glitter in his eyes which Bertrand had often observed on the beginning of an important battle. The knuckles of his hand which gripped the arm of his chair were white with pressure.

"The Balcombe family must be kept in the dark. Even Betsy. She has sharp eyes and would detect the imposture quickly. I will leave a letter for her, to be delivered at your discretion. Within a few days, I think."

A moment of tense silence ensued. Bertrand's cheeks had recovered some of their natural color, although trying thoughts were running through his mind: "My God, will I be able to play my part well? So much is going to depend on me!"

Napoleon got slowly to his feet. "Better return now, Marshal. According to plan the men from the ship will arrive at that shop—"

"Spotts and Clinch, the ship chandlers."

"Yes. They are to be there at two-thirty. Is Madame Bertrand letter-perfect in what she must do?"

"Yes, sire. She can be depended on."

2

The shop of Spotts and Clinch was on the main street and quite close to the junction with the promenade. It was so close, in fact, that from the window a view could be obtained of the far reaches of the roadstead; provided one could get near enough to the window through the conglomeration of articles packed into it (which was well nigh an impossibility), and then succeed in peering through the long unwashed glass, a feat to defy the vision of a catamount. The shop was deserted when Madame Bertrand entered, save for a dingy little man perched on a high stool in the rear. He came forward, picking his way in the darkness created by lengths of rope and sail hanging from the ceiling.

"M'sieur Spotts?" she asked.

The dingy little man squinted at her through a profusion of whiskers and eyebrows. "No, Clinch. Good thing for you, ma'am. Spotts was always Against."

"I—I don't believe I understand." Madame Bertrand, because of her Irish descent, had started with a small command of English and had been augmenting it slowly but surely.

"You're Ma'am Bertrand, ain't ye? Well, you must know the people of this island is split up. Some for Boney and some against. Spotts, he was Against. If there was something ye wanted to buy and Spotts waited on ye, he would hop up the price like sixty."

"And you, M'sieur Cleench? Are you For or Against?"

"Well, ma'am, I'm not exactly For. I'm just sort of For. And I'm allus disposed to offer our French cust'mers a fair price."

"This makes me curious, M'sieur Cleench. Does not your partner know that having us here, and the regiments and the ships, brings a great deal of trade to your shop?"

The second partner nodded his head. "A great man for figgers, Spotts. Worked out profits to the last dec'mal, and they was one hundred and eighty-six point eighty-seven over the old one. If the ships and troops had been withdrew, he would have taken the longest rope in stock and hunged hisself. Well, ma'am, Spotts is dead and buried. Dead two weeks and gone. Now, what was it you wanted?"

She explained that the Count de Bertrand thought of doing some fishing, purely for pleasure, and he needed a proper pair of sea boots. "Was not this the shop where one might find sea boots?"

"Yes, ma'am!" Clinch rummaged in the utter confusion of the window stock and produced a pair of hip-length boots which undoubtedly could be described as proper. "There y'are, ma'am. Best to be had on the island. So much the best that we've had it in stock, Spotts and Clinch, for five years."

The customer said she was not quite familiar with what was needed in sea boots and that she would not have come in herself, except that she wanted them as a surprise. It seemed to her, she continued, that the price he was asking was very high. Was he adding on interest for each of the five years?

"Guess you should've had Spotts waiting on you after all. You'd've been a pair."

At this moment the jangling of a bell warned of more customers. Madame Bertrand could not see who had come in because a great assortment of goods was suspended on a gimbal across her line of vision, such as signal lanterns, bells, brass lamps, and tall candles. She glanced back over her shoulder at a ship's clock on the wall. The hands pointed to two-thirty.

One of the newcomers was speaking in a loud and confident voice. "This is the shop. Un-mis-tak-ably."

The use of the word "unmistakably" was the signal Madame Bertrand had been told to expect. She parted the goods hanging on the gimbal and saw that two men were standing just inside the door. The speaker had the ruddiness of cheek which bespoke a seafaring life and a jauntiness of manner which indicated to her that he came from across the Atlantic. He caught sight of her at the same time and he stopped speaking. Taking advantage of the fact that Mr. Clinch had turned his back to her, she held up the boots and pressed a letter into the toe of the right foot.

"I think, m'sieur, I shall take the boots," she said. "But I have other errands to do and will call back for them a little later."

The new arrivals stepped aside to let her pass without as much as the quiver of an eyelash to indicate an interest in her. An hour later she returned and the boots lay where she had deposited them, on a chest near the entrance. She paid for them, took them up and walked out to the street where the Bertrand carriage, a rickety affair of long lineage and broken springs, awaited her.

It had been a trial for her to shop in the town, even in fact to put in an appearance there. Because her husband was acting as mouthpiece for Napoleon in his never ending disputes with Plantation House, an instruction had been passed out that the Bertrands were not to be received socially nor allowed credit in any of the shops. She was thinking of this as the carriage followed the tortuous course of the Longwood Road and wondering if the notes exchanged by way of the sea boots could conceivably point to a time when they would all return to France. A passionate desire for the gracious old life welled up inside her, particularly when the carriage stopped in front of their house. She sighed deeply as her eyes took in the meager and commonplace lines of the dwelling.

Her husband came to the gate to greet her. He did not say a word but his eyes propounded the question which clearly filled his mind.

"I think," she said, in a low tone, "that all went well. The boots are in the carriage."

"We must not seem too interested," said the count. "I'll get them after a few minutes. In the meantime come in and tell us about it. He is here."

3

Napoleon was sitting in complete silence in the diminutive drawing room. He looked up as they entered and Madame Bertrand felt an intensity in the glitter of his dark eyes such as she had never observed there before. Having discarded his loose and comfortable trousers, he was in uniform again, with sky-blue breeches and a coat of the darkest brown.

"Madame has brought them, sire," said Bertrand.

"Ah!"

"It seemed advisable, sire, not to give any hint of haste or urgency. I left everything in the carriage. I'll send a servant out now to bring the parcels in."

"Stand in the door and watch," advised the emperor. "Take the boots away from him before he has a chance to examine them."

In a few moments the sea boots had been deposited on the table.

"I left the note in the toe of the right shoe," explained Madame Bertrand.

The count felt down in the boot and said with a satisfied smile: "They took it. At any rate there's nothing there now."

Napoleon frowned darkly. "No note in reply?"

"Nothing, sire."

"I'm sure I put the note in the right shoe," declared Madame Bertrand.

Napoleon spoke in an impatient tone. "Try the left shoe."

Bertrand followed the suggestion and his face lighted up. "It's here! It's here! What a relief, sire."

He drew out a note and handed it to the emperor, who promptly sat down at the table where he spread out the sheets. They were covered with writing in a small and familiar hand.

"The good abbé!" said Napoleon. "I urged him to come, although he's always been a victim of seasickness. He has had a bad time, as can be told from the handwriting."

He lowered his head and started to read. Before turning the first page, he came to a stop. Feeling tension in the air, Bertrand glanced anxiously at his wife. The sheet of paper dropped from Napoleon's hand.

A long silence fell on the room. The Bertrands did not dare ask a question. Napoleon sat as motionless as a wax figure.

"Bertrand!" he whispered, finally.

"Yes, sire."

"We are lost! Our plan, our splendidly detailed plan, cannot be carried through." There was another pause, more painful than the first. "Everything was working perfectly. Except for one thing. Roberaud was killed. Two men were carried overboard when the mainmast broke. Roberaud and one of the sailors. Neither body was recovered."

He got to his feet and stumbled blindly to the door. "I'll read the rest later. I must have some time alone. *Mon Dieu*, Bertrand, to have this happen!"

There was a couch in the hall and they heard him throw himself on it. The Bertrands looked at one another like prisoners who had been informed that a reprieve was denied them. The hopes which Madame Bertrand had allowed herself to consider as she drove from town had faded away.

It was some time before Napoleon returned. He did not

speak but proceeded to read the letter through carefully. Then he handed the sheets to his marshal.

It took Bertrand some time to decipher the hastily scribbled lines, pondering and frowning over them. Napoleon sat beside him in a state of complete despair.

"Was it a trick of fate?" asked the emperor, when Bertrand completed his reading. "Or was it, perhaps, the Hand of God?—I thought every contingency had been provided for. I foresaw this possibility but there was no certain way of protecting ourselves. Of the four doubles I used in Paris, two had died and no trace could be found of one other. We had to pin our hopes on Roberaud who was the best of the lot and the most loyal. I warned the abbé to treat the man like a precious piece of Dresden china. Have you any idea how a ship careens when there is trouble aloft? He should have been taken below until it was all over." He rose slowly to his feet. "Perhaps there is some other way. We have the fastest ship in the world at our command. Surely, surely, my inventiveness will not desert me when my need is so great!" He added after a moment: "I need time to consider the situation. Come over in an hour and discuss it with me."

4

Napoleon's face was white when he received Bertrand in his small study. He had removed his coat and loosened the cravat at his neck. There was a physical limpness about him which suggested he had lost his strength and purpose.

"You have given some thought to the abbé's suggestions?" he asked.

"Yes, sire. I must say I feel that my confidence has been restored."

"Ah, because he has brought some of the old guard with him?"

"Yes, sire. Fifteen of them. The best soldiers in the world. It was a splendid idea to have them disguised as artisans for employment in the East."

"Yes, it was a good idea. If we had succeeded, they would have been most useful as a guard against assassination wherever we went. But only fifteen! He seems to think they give me a sufficient force to use in slashing my way to freedom. The abbé has a shrewd mind for diplomacy but he has no conception of fighting and no knowledge of the conditions here. Even a hundred of my stoutest fellows would have no chance. They might cut a way through the English companies around Jamestown and enable me to reach the water. But there are gun emplacements along the rocky walls above the roadstead. They have been trained on our ship ever since it came in. A few rounds of shot would send the clipper to the bottom."

"No," he went on, "the original plan was the only one that held any chance of success. It had to be so timed that we would go on board while the island still seethed with excitement over the recovery of my wounded body in the ravine. And for that we needed Roberaud. The abbé's idea would call for a hundred miracles. What chance would that give us? A very small fraction of one per cent, perhaps. We would all be killed. At one time, Bertrand, I would have been ready to risk the loss of lives, including my own. But I seem to have changed. Why send all my fine old veterans to certain death in a lost cause? Why sacrifice the ship with all on board? As far as my own life is concerned, it would be a relief to end it in this way."

"But, sire," protested Bertrand, "as you have said, we have the fastest ship afloat at our doorstep. The men the abbé has brought with him are the best soldiers in the world. Surely, surely, there is still a way!"

"I see no way now," declared the emperor. "Have you anything to propose?"

Bertrand answered with a show of eagerness. "Let us forget Jamestown. There is a path down the face of the cliff which takes you to a narrow beach opposite the roadstead. The guards could be landed at night to attack the guns and put them out of action. In the meantime you take the path down the cliff to a boat waiting for you on the beach."

"I have often studied that path," said Napoleon. "Only expert mountain climbers or wild goats could use it. Heights make me dizzy and I would lose my balance with the first few steps. It would not serve our purpose for me to commit suicide in that way."

"You could be lowered by ropes, sire."

"Where could we get enough rope for the purpose? Many hundred yards of it would be needed."

"The captain could buy more than he needs to make his repairs."

"Everything he gets will be scrutinized closely. Suppose they allow him to overestimate to that extent, how would he get the rope to us? Are you aware that there is a squad on guard at the head of that path day and night?—Don't you know that the platform on the face of the cliff swarms with gunners and that the rocks around them make a natural epaulement?"

The emperor got stiffly to his feet and began to pace about very slowly. Finally he collapsed on the couch and let his head fall back against the wall.

"Bertrand, Bertrand, this is the end. They will keep me here until I die."

"You spoke of miracles, sire. Perhaps there will be a miracle."

"An earthquake to bury these English regiments and open a path down throught the rock? A great storm to scatter the fleet but leave our clipper ship safely at anchor? No, Bertrand, the only miracle we may still hope for is a change of heart in the English Government. It seemed possible for a time but now I have no hopes in that quarter. No, I am here for the rest of my days. The spar which carried Roberaud into the sea settled my fate."

Chapter Twelve

1

The news spread across the island that Napoleon was seriously ill. He had taken to his bed, so the story ran, and had remained in the dark for four days, seeing no one but his valet, and eating nothing.

Sir Hudson Lowe's face wore a frown when he heard this. "He has some deep purpose," was his expressed opinion. "He is in as good health as when I arrived."

But the governor was entirely wrong. The story was true. It was not until the morning of the fifth day that Napoleon rang for his valet.

"How is the weather, Marchand?"

"Your Imperial Highness, it is much like a midsummer day in desert country. It will be very hot when the sun gets up."

Napoleon sighed and with some difficulty attained a sitting position. "I must rouse myself. Open the shutters, Marchand. This morning I shall try some breakfast. It must be very light. A roll, a cup of chocolate. No more."

"Your Imperial Highness is feeling better, then."

"A little, Marchand. But I am in constant pain. Across here," passing a hand over the region of his stomach. "Sometimes it is more severe than at others. But it's always there."

After nibbling at the roll and drinking some of the chocolate, the Captive threw back the covers.

"I am a truly frightening object. *Ma foi*, I need a shave as badly as a gorilla. When you are through with me, see to it that a message is sent to M'sieur the marshal. I must talk with him."

Bertrand came over with great eagerness on receiving this message. He found Napoleon wrapped up in a cotton dressing gown, in spite of the heat, and with a red handkerchief bound over his head. The first glimpse was in the nature of a shock, for the Captive had lost a great deal of weight. His cheeks seemed to have fallen in during the brief period of his seclusion.

"Sire! I have been over a score of times in the hope of seeing you. You indeed look ill."

"I am not well, Marshal. You must not tell anyone yet but for several months I have been feeling pains as my father did in the first stages of his trouble. It may be that the shock we have suffered has accelerated the advance of the disease. Certainly, I have been very ill." Bertrand was showing such deep concern that the emperor added: "I won't die this week or the next. There will be a slow decline, during which I shall suffer more than any of my soldiers who died in battle."

"The man, Professor Antommarchi, who has been appointed to take O'Meara's place, will be here very soon."

"That's true, Bertrand. But remember, he was selected by my uncle, Cardinal Flesch. That doesn't arouse in me any favorable expectations. The cardinal is not of a discerning judgment. From the little we have heard, I feel a particle of resentment toward the man already."

"Then, sire, we must demand the services of a competent physician at once."

Napoleon shook his head. "It would do no good. The doctors, who know so much about some diseases, seem to have no understanding at all of this. They could do nothing for my father and they will do nothing for me. I am reconciled to that. It will be easier to face it alone instead of jangling continuously with the kind turnkey at Plantation House." He gestured in dismissal of the topic. "What have you heard about the ship?"

"They are not ready to sail yet. The mast has been set up and reinforced with steel struts but there's still much work to be done in replacing the damaged rigging. It will be another week before they sail."

"Taking with them my heart—and my last hope! Have you received any further word from the abbé?"

"A single note. It was smuggled through the handyman at the chandler's shop. He tried to get a permit to land but was flatly refused. He still believes you could escape with the aid of the guards."

Napoleon snorted. "Observe! I am as weak as a newborn kitten." He returned to the question of his health. "What I need is a doctor for the spirit, not for the body. I am weary

367

of all my people here. Bring Madame Bertrand for dinner tonight. And ask the Balcombes to come also."

"Sire, we have no visitors. The island people are under orders to stay away."

"Then it must be Betsy alone. *She* won't hesitate to disregard the turnkey's orders. Get her as far as Hutt's Gate and I'll find a way to smuggle her through the sentry lines."

The sentry lines were drawn tightly around Longwood as soon as dusk fell but in the hours of daylight there was nothing more than a thin patrol maintained about the property. When Napoleon ventured out for a walk, the sentries had a tendency to follow his course so that he could always be kept in eyesight.

Soon after his breakfast one day, the emperor aroused himself to undertake a walk in his free area. He went very slowly and found it necessary to use a cane. As he took an easterly direction, the two sentries began to follow after him, leaving a wide space empty behind them. Casting occasional glimpses back over his shoulder, he was rewarded finally by the sight of a red hat which bobbed into view at intervals. The wearer of the hat finally disappeared from sight in the Longwood gardens.

He was pleased at the success of the maneuver but could not refrain from venting his disgust at such stupidity. "Heads of mutton!" he muttered, referring to the regimental officers responsible for the control of the lines. "A military band, blazing away on their brasses and with rolling drums, could march through undetected!"

Betsy was standing in an arbor which screened her from view when he reached the gardens. She took a few steps toward him and then stopped.

"Sire, how thin you are!" she exclaimed, studying his face with anxious eyes.

He regarded her pensively, thinking how young she was and how beautiful. Then he looked up at the towering wall of rock which closed off all view of the sea, and above which a rack of clouds warned of rain. If the rain came, it would be no more than a warm drizzle, with no relief in it.

"Betsee, my star has fallen from the sky," he said, in a hollow voice.

This startled her so much that she gasped. Seldom at a loss for words, she found herself now quite speechless.

Napoleon seated himself and motioned to her to do the same. *"Ma petite,* I had decided not to tell you. But why should there be secrecy between us? Can it matter now? I found a way of escape from this dreadful rock. I was sure it would succeed. But the one man I needed most was killed; and the scheme blew up like smoke from a cannon when it has been fired. It offered me the only chance; and now that one chance is gone. I must stay here until I die." He added, with a deep sigh: "And I am ill. Very ill."

Bertrand had said to her when she stopped at Hutt's Gate: "His life may depend on a change of mood, an escape from this feeling of despair. Try to make him feel better. Make him smile. Make him laugh, if you can." Accordingly she had come prepared to be cheerful, considering it fortunate that she had chosen her brightest and most frivolous dress, one of light red with the matching hat he had spied as she slipped through the sentry lines. But now she realized that the task was not going to be easy.

They sat and looked at each other gravely across the table he used for dictation in the mornings.

"Betsee," he said, after a few moments, "I am an old man. And you—*certes,* you are still so very young. I ought to say to you, Go and live a normal and happy life. Forget all about this sick and defeated man they are keeping here like a common thief."

"Sire, please believe that my greatest happiness is in seeing you." She was silent for a moment. "I was told I must try to get you into a cheerful frame of mind. But I find I'm not feeling very cheerful or frivolous myself." After applying a handkerchief to her eyes, she added, "I thought of a few things to say but now I realize they are much too trivial."

"Suppose you tell me what they are."

She knew that Napoleon had a weakness for gossip concerning people about him and so she began with several anecdotes of the kind. He listened, and occasionally there would be a slight flicker of amusement in his eyes. Once he emitted a sound which might have been described as the distant cousin of a laugh. But he had no comments to make.

"I have failed," she said finally. "You are not in a mood for these silly things I am telling you."

"The fault is mine," touching a forefinger to his brow. "I have not yet recovered from the effects of these misfortunes. You will accomplish your purpose best, I think, by just sitting where I can see you. It seems to me you are looking especially well, *ma petite*. Is it because of the new dress?"

"It is nice, isn't it? The skirt is something *very* new. The pleats will never come out." A few years later this kind of skirt, having achieved wide popularity, would be called accordion-pleated. "The material was sent out and Mamma made it herself."

"Madame Balcombe has a skilled hand quite clearly. But how did you manage to get the material through from Paris?"

"It didn't come from Paris, sire. It was made in England."

"Absurd! The English are not capable of planning anything as novel as this. I know a great deal about dress and style. Did you know I designed the official costume for ladies at my court?"

"No, sire, I didn't know that. But then I have only the slightest conception of how versatile you are." She hesitated. "But, sire, the material did come from England. You see they have been wearing kilts in Scotland which fold over in a much wider style. The idea grew out of that."

"Since you are convinced you know more about such matters than I do, I shall content myself with saying that if it had come from Paris the style would have been better. The skirt would have been longer. As it is, I have seen the tip of a shoe several times since you sat down. That shouldn't be."

Betsy appeared very much distressed. "One's feet should never show. I must have been careless."

"It's an attractive shoe, to judge by the mere glimpse I have had."

Betsy leaned over and used both hands to wrap her skirts tightly about her ankles. Then she raised her feet high enough from the ground for him to study the design of the shoe. He frowned approvingly and even touched a finger to the embroideries of silk thread.

"Ah, ah! It is as pretty as those foolish comfit boxes ladies carry about with them. The shoes, at least, came from Paris."

"No, sire," corrected Betsy. "They came from London. Oddly enough the English make fine shoes. Much better than the French."

"Nonsense!" said Napoleon, sharply. "You must cure yourself of this bad habit of making rash statements without any knowledge of the subject. Paris leads the world in all matters of style—in the designing and making of dresses, hats, cloaks, gloves, shoes. England is so far behind in everything as to seem absolutely benighted."

"But, sire, these *were* made in London. Mamma always went to a funny little man named Mr. Quint, who has a tiny shop on Tweedly Place, just off Berkeley Square. He made beautiful shoes for her. He's very old now but he still sends them to her. So she asked him to make some for Jane and me."

"And how could this M'sieur Quint, from his shop in the place with that silly and typically English name, achieve such a perfect fit without seeing you?"

"Oh, we had to send all the information he needed. Jane made a drawing of my foot and I made one of hers. We sent all the measurements he said were necessary. Pages of them, figured to the smallest fraction of an inch. He is a very great artist in his way, that old Mr. Quint."

"And you are a very great exaggerator, Betsee. But what interested me actually was not the style of the shoe but the size. I swear I didn't believe it possible for anyone to wear as small a shoe as this."

"Sire! You are flattering me."

He began then to indulge in one of his favorite pastimes, that of drawing comparisons which were generally ill-natured in tone. "I mean it. My sister Pauline has a beautiful foot but I'm sure she couldn't wear a shoe like this. I have observed that beautiful women almost always have feet that incline to be plump. Even my two wives. I swear that some of these beauties have feet as broad as a peasant woman's. Consider Mam'selle George. *Sacredieu!* She did some dancing on the stage and it ruined her feet."

"Perhaps, sire, they should all have gone to old Mr. Quint at Tweedly Place to get their shoes."

Napoleon scowled darkly at her. "Are you aware how fantastic that would be? A Frenchwoman of refinement and taste depending on a shoemaker in London? *Ma foi*, would you have them send for their hats to those islands in the South Seas? Betsee," his voice rising to an angry pitch, "how absurd you are!"

"But from what you tell me, the poor ladies were quite badly in need of a decent shoemaker."

It could not be said that his face flushed. It was too pale and drawn for that. But it was clear that he was deeply annoyed.

"There is no sense to this argument. Why, why, do I condescend to discuss such matters with you? Always you speak of how things are done in England, which to me is of no consequence whatever. Are you trying to make me angry?"

Betsy turned her head so he could not read her expression. "Yes, sire. I am trying to make you angry."

"Then you have succeeded. But why do you act this way when you find me ill and cast down with my misfortunes?"

"If you can't be made to laugh, sire, then the next best thing is to make you scowl. Anything to arouse you from this apathy."

At this moment a most unexpected change came over him. He had allowed himself to subside at an easier angle in his chair. Much of the strain lifted from his face.

"Betsee!" he whispered, as though afraid that the powers determined to undo him might hear. "For the last few moments I have felt no pain!"

She leaned forward eagerly, the much discussed shoes completely hidden under the pleated folds of her skirt. "Oh, sire, how wonderful! Perhaps all this talk about foolish things has done you good after all."

"Can it be that I was too pessimistic? That Bertrand was right in saying that the pain I felt here," touching the seat of the trouble with one hand, "is the result of shock?"

"Oh, sire, God grant it is no more than that!"

"I have always had an inclination to melancholia. I mustn't give in to it any longer. My plans have failed but I must not abandon all hope. The spirit of France may be aroused to demand my liberty. The conscience of England may awaken. There may be great years ahead for me after all.

"What a relief!" he went on. "Not to feel that nagging, incessant pain. But I must not allow myself to be carried away by these hopes. You have helped me to forget my troubles but they will come crowding back. I can't say yet, *tout va bien!* I told Bertrand, who wanted to have doctors sent for at once, that the only one I wanted was Doctoresse Betsee, who might be able to make me forget. And you've done it. By making me angry."

"Perhaps I should think of more absurd things to say."

"It's clear you must come to see me as regularly as a good physician does. There must be no excuses for not coming. No staying away because of other engagements."

372

"Other engagements will never stand in the way, sire."

"You must not allow these stupid officers to take up your time. Particularly the one I am most jealous of at the moment."

"Which one is that?"

"That doddering old simpleton who's in command of the regiment. I forget his tongue-twister of a name. You will find, Betsee, that when a man of his senile years falls in love with a young girl he will be more persistent than any of the callow youngsters." He concluded in stern tones, "You must remember always that you have a very sick patient."

"Sire, you will always be my only consideration."

"I suspect that there should be no more talk now. I am tired. I'll just sit here for a time and revel in this freedom from pain. And watch my little visitor and physician, which will be the greatest pleasure for me. I must gather up enough strength to go for another walk. I must lead the sentinels far enough away for you to leave as successfully as you came."

Chapter Thirteen

1

The ire of His Excellency the governor had been aroused to such a degree that getting to Longwood without a permit was a most difficult feat. Betsy had to fall back on transit in the delivery wagon for her second visit. On coming within sight of the rambling building, she crept under an empty potato sack on the floor and, as a result, had a streak of dust across her face when she greeted Napoleon.

For the first time she was seeing him in cotton clothing and was shocked to observe how thin he had become. His eyes seemed lost and sad. Nevertheless he proceeded to do something quite unprecedented. Getting rather painfully to his feet, he went back to his bathroom and returned with a damp towel. This he used to wipe the smudges from her forehead and cheeks.

"There, my brave Betsee!" he said. "Risking the anger of that bad man!"

"There was a moment when I didn't feel brave at all. The sentinel came over to look into the wagon and I was afraid he was going to whisk off the sacking to see what was under it. They say"—with a brief tendency to giggle—"that he's going to have all potatoes and turnips and cabbage cut open from now on. He suspects you are having letters smuggled to you in the vegetables."

"He is capable of any folly." Napoleon turned and walked to a window where he could see the towering black rocks of the Barn. He stood there in silence for several moments.

"Here is the evidence. Beyond that cliff the sea rolls for thousands of miles, dotted as far as the eye can see with the sails of the British Navy. And here am I, a sick man. So ill, in fact, that it is supreme folly to think I could create confusion in the world if I should contrive to escape. The will to set nations at war has gone. But still he sits up there in his handsome house and bites his nails over what I am doing, even what I am thinking. Even more to be deplored, he wonders what other people are doing and thinking. You and your family in particular, my only real friends. And he makes it necessary for you, my Betsee, to hide under potato sacking in order to pay me a visit."

He continued to stare out the window, his head sunk forward, his fingers tightly laced behind his back.

Betsy had been appalled on entering the house to find how much it had been allowed to deteriorate. There was a suggestion of neglect everywhere. The curtains sagged and showed many rips and stains. The rugs had been trampled on by too many muddy feet. The clock on the mantel had stopped and it was evident from the amount of dust with which it was encrusted that it had not been wound for a long time. Catching a brief glimpse of his bedroom, she was distressed to see that the bed had not been made.

Finding her nose unpleasantly assailed by the sourly familiar odor of mildew, she summoned up her courage to protest.

"Sire, don't you realize that the staff here are neglecting their duties?"

He nodded his head moodily. "Yes, it has been apparent for some time but—it is of such small consequence now."

Mrs. Balcombe was a thorough housekeeper of the old school and she had instilled much of her own spirit into her two daughters. Betsy felt her sense of protest rising.

"Sire, something should be done about it. It's had to escape the mildew in the damp season but they don't seem to be making any effort. I would enjoy making them step lively."

He smiled at her affectionately. "I am sure you will make a fine housekeeper, or wife, for—for someone. But you can't take a hand in things here. They are jealous enough of you as it is. *Mon Dieu*, there are nothing but black looks about the place for at least a day after you've been here."

He had returned to the narrow couch in his study on which he had been lying when she arrived. It was so old and out of repair that it seemed likely to give way under him.

"When a man has been immersed in certain duties all his life, he sometimes reaches a stage where he can't continue. My success was due in part to following up personally the orders I issued. I never considered a thing settled when I had given an order. I made certain it had been obeyed. This was not only my rule on the campaigns but in the administrative offices in Paris as well. Looking back, I believe I issued scores of orders every day. And I saw to it that every one was carried out to the letter.

"Betsee," he went on, after a pause, "I became so weary of it that now I am giving no orders at all."

"But," she protested, "there's your comfort to be considered."

"Marchand is a splendid valet. He looks after my personal needs without being told. He does everything silently. The chef is an artist. Although we always have trouble—to which Bertrand attends—about getting fresh butter and flour and the best quality of beef, the good Lepage serves wonderful meals. So, *ma petite*, I live in comfort.

"As for the rest," he continued, "if they want to allow this slipshod kind of housekeeping, they suffer from it more than I do."

Betsy studied his face more closely and was able to understand why he was willing to let the establishment take care of itself and to enjoy freedom at last from the burden of constant supervision.

"My poor Nabuleone!" she exclaimed.

Napoleon's attention quickened at once. "What did you call me?"

"Sire, forgive me! I didn't intend to take such a liberty. It slipped out by accident."

"A pleasant accident, Betsee! It made me very happy to hear it on your lips. It took me back to those early days." Then he returned to the point they had been discussing. "You are right, of course, about the carelessness here. Something must be done about the mildew. I shall speak sharply to Perron and I may even have a few words on the subject with Madame Montholon."

"And the rats! They seem to be increasing all the time."

He smiled at this. "No, Betsee," he whispered. "The rats may prove of great help to me. The facts about them have been sent to England. They are in the hands of members of Parliament who will see to it that the whole nation is informed. Nothing will serve as well to arouse the sentiment in my favor. So the rats must be allowed to increase and multiply.

"You've heard," he went on, "about prisoners who are visited in their cells by rats or mice and who make pets of them? I can understand it. In the dining room there is a hole in the baseboard, a large one. There is a huge fellow who puts in an appearance at every meal. He's such an enormous specimen that I'm sure he must be the emperor of the rats of Longwood. I've become accustomed to him and I call him Caligula, because of all emperors Caligula was the one who most resembled a rat. He stares at me as though he senses that I have been an emperor also in my time. Can you believe that if anything happened to this bold fellow I would feel badly?"

2

The talk between them subsided. Napoleon obviously had outdone his strength. He sank back on the couch and closed his eyes. It was some time before he opened them again.

"Everything that happens to me now is painful," he said. "I came here, Betsee, without illusions. I knew things would be hard. To maintain a proper standard of living I would need to be severe about etiquette and household rules. I told my people before they elected to accompany me that we would follow court procedure as closely as possible. They all saw the necessity for it and agreed. Have you observed that Marshal Bertrand never comes into my presence except in uniform? That he never addresses me first but waits for me to speak? He has been most punctilious, my thoughtful Bertrand. But now that I am a sick man the rules are beginning to break down. A few days ago I sent word to the marshal that I required his presence at once. He appeared quickly, wearing the tunic of his uniform *over a pair of civilian trousers!*"

Betsy could not repress a smile.

"I realized, of course, that the mistake was due to absent-mindedness and that he lacks an aide to call such mistakes to his attention. But it would not have occurred before. Now that they serve an invalid, they are no longer alert."

Betsy's curiosity had been aroused and she asked, "Sire, did you call the mistake to Count Bertrand's attention?"

Napoleon shook his head. "No. I left it for him to discover himself. The shock would be greater that way. As for the servants, they don't dare relax in my presence. But behind the scenes—ah, that is a different matter! This morning I decided

377

to pay a visit to the stables to see our fine old friend Mameluke. I knew he hadn't been getting enough exercise and I suspected he would be carrying too much fat on his splendid frame. Before I went in I heard a conversation being carried on inside. Archambault—the elder, if you please—was giving Mameluke a grooming and talking to someone at the same time. I heard him say: 'Old Mammy is in bad condition. He pants and he wheezes like an old hack on the street cleaning. But it doesn't matter. *He* will never ride again.' "

"Sire, what a cruel thing to say!"

There was more of sorrow than anger in the Napoleonic face as he continued. "No, it was casually said. I did not mind his comment on my health, for they all know how ill I am. It was the way he said it. The proper way would have been, 'His Majesty is not in good health' or 'His Imperial Highness will never ride again.' But he said '*He*.' Betsee, I ceased to be *He* when the golden circlet touched my brow at my coronation."

"The man was just careless, sire."

It was evident from the tensity of his expression that Napoleon found no satisfaction in her comment. "They are forgetting that this dismal place is still part of an imperial establishment. And I am too ill to make them realize it."

He straightened up at this point. "The pain was bad this morning but it seems to have eased some. Is it because you have come to see me? I think that is the reason, *ma petite*. You must stay for luncheon and I will send for the grand marshal and Madame Bertrand to join us." He indulged in a rather bleak smile. "I will suggest that he wear a *complete* uniform this time.

"First," he continued, "I must send instructions to Lepage at once so he can prepare some of the things you like. You may not know it but you are a favorite of his. I have observed how his eyes light up whenever he sees you. *Eh bien*, like master, like cook! He will be happy to prepare some special dishes for you."

3

When they approached the dining salon they found the Bertrands and the Montholons waiting outside the door. There was warmth in the greeting Betsy received from the grand marshal and his wife but the Montholons were not friendly in any degree. Napoleon was aware of this lack of cordiality and took an obvious pleasure in seating Betsy on his left hand. As the chair on his right was the prerogative of the marshal's wife, Madame Montholon had to be content with a seat on the other side of her husband. She compressed her lips and frowned in a way which manifested her dissatisfaction with this arrangement.

Betsy had once spoken glowingly of Lepage's way with lamb chops and so she was not surprised when a platter filled with them was carried in and placed in the center of the table. They had been sautéed to a fine brownness and were surrounded by stalks of asparagus, an almost unattainable luxury.

Napoleon leaned forward to inspect the asparagus. "This, without a doubt, was intended for dinner. But that scoundrel out in the kitchen has sent them in now because you are here, Betsee. This is favoritism carried to an extreme."

Madame Montholon, bending over her plate with a set expression, shared this opinion. But she kept it to herself.

The emperor had no appetite. He refused dish after dish. "I had breakfast this morning," he explained. "You can't expect me to have any desire for another meal so soon."

Betsy, however, was hungry. Without any apology she had two of the chops and even allowed herself to be helped to some of the fillets of fowl *à la béchamel* which followed. She was still interested in food when the entremets began to arrive. She recognized orange *gelée* with pleasure, was equally pleased with the Bavarian cheese and was quite delighted with the final dish, a *gâteau praliné* served on a pedestal cake plate. The *gâteau*, she could see, was stuffed generously with almonds and garnished with whipped cream.

Napoleon cut a slice of the cheese but it was not for his own use.

"Perron," he said, motioning to the slice, "this, of course, is for our four-footed guest. *Ma foi*, he is a gourmet, that one. He wants only the best cheese to be had." He turned to his left. "Have you also noticed that, Madame Montholon?"

The lady shuddered. "No, sire. They make my blood run cold. I never enter a room any more without looking around first to see if any of them are there."

"And you, Betsee?"

Betsy felt a shrinking of the flesh. She was so conscious of the unpleasant scratching of rodent feet on the floor that she wanted to draw her own feet up and tuck them under her on the chair.

"Is he—in his usual place, sire?" she asked.

"He is right behind you. Turn and have a look at him."

"No thank you, sire. I am so afraid of them that I am almost—but not quite—losing my appetite for this wonderful *gâteau.*"

The mention of the cake took Napoleon's eyes back to the table. Betsy saw them suddenly open wide in surprise and then harden in a way she had never observed before. His knuckles rapped sharply on the table.

"Perron!"

"Yes, Your Imperial Highness?"

The emperor motioned to the cake plate. "It is not the rule that both plates must be placed on the board? Even if one of them is empty?"

The face of the butler went white and he gulped uneasily.

"Your Imperial Highness, there is a reason. The other one has been broken."

Napoleon shoved back his chair from the table. He stared about him with no trace left of the geniality he had displayed in the matter of feeding the rat. A blazing fire seemed to have been lighted behind his eyes.

"Broken! When? Why was I not told?"

"If you please, Your Highness, I did not hear of it until I came in to inspect the table. The pieces were found, swept into a corner of the kitchen. Everyone denied any knowledge of the mishap. I—I intended to inform Your Majesty but found no opportunity."

There was a long silence. Napoleon's gaze was fixed straight ahead of him and he seemed to be striving to find a course of action suited to his mood.

"Perron, I have a cane with a hooked handle. Ask Marchand for it and then bring it to me."

"That poor Perron!" thought Betsy, with sudden alarm. "Is he to be chastised publicly?"

Napoleon turned to her so sharply that she dropped her spoon on the plate in front of her.

"Betsee, have you noticed this pair of pedestal plates on my table?"

380

"Yes, sire, many times."

"I will tell you about them while Perron is out. They are not antique. I don't suppose they could be considered valuable. But they had a great value in my eyes. They belonged to Madame Mère. Perhaps they were brought to Corsica when her family moved there from Italy, although I am inclined to think they were made in Corsica. They were among the things my mother took with her when she married my father. They were always on the table in our old house under the cathedral. They were associated in my mind with good things to eat.

"When Madame Mère," he went on, "set up her establishment in Rome, she took the plates with her. There had been so much damage done with so many children in the house and they were all that was left of her *dot*. You can imagine how much she loved them. But when she heard I was being sent into exile a second time, she sent them to me at once, thinking they would be a reminder of better days. I was happy to have them."

The frown he had worn on hearing of the accident returned to his face.

"And now one of them is broken! By some heavy-handed simpleton of a footman or a lazy *saligaude* in the kitchen! And I—I was not told!

"Betsee," he went on, "you can see, can you not, how unhappy my thoughts will be if I see again the one that is left?"

Perron returned with the cane and handed it to his master with a suggestion of apprehension in his manner.

"I am not blaming you for the breakage but I am angry beyond words that you did not find some way of informing me at once. Do you think I am too ill to care or to do anything about such things? I am noticing this tendency in everything that goes on here."

Then he stretched out the cane and hooked the end around the pedestal of the plate. With a quick movement of his wrist, he jerked it off the table. It took a course between the Montholons and crashed on the floor, breaking into many pieces. The *gâteau praliné* was spilled over the carpet.

He handed the cane back to the butler and rose to his feet.

"Come! The pain is back. It is worse, I think, than I have

ever had it. I will not be fit for human company for the rest of the day. Betsee, will you be kind enough to return now with M'sieur the marshal? He will get you home by the little strategem we discussed earlier."

Chapter Fourteen

1

Betsy watched Marchand carry the Sanctorious from its place in the bathroom. Feeling a personal responsibility, she asked, "Where is it being taken?"

"It will be stored in one of the attics," answered the valet. "You see, mam'selle, it is no longer needed. The weight, it does not go up. On the contrary, the weight keeps going down. So it is best not to have this machine to remind us."

A thought flashed through the girl's mind and she was still turning it over when Napoleon came in to greet her. He had been shaved closely and was wearing proper breeches again and the white silk stockings which went with them. In spite of the pallor of his cheeks, he looked more like himself. There was again, in fact, the almost overpowering air of distinction about him which he had lost in his baggy cotton clothing.

"Sire," she said, "I have been putting two and two together. And I know how you intended to make you escape."

"So!" He sat down facing her and broke into an amused laugh. "You have put two and two together. What answer did you arrive at? Six, eight, ten, hein?"

"No, sire. Four. Right on the snook, as we benighted English sometimes say."

"And what then was the plan?"

Betsy's face lighted up. "Even though something happened to spoil matters, it was a wonderful plan. I discovered about it when I saw the Sanctorious being removed just now. I remembered that when we found it for you, it was needed at once. You had to lose a certain amount of weight within a definite time. That gave me the clue. There was to be a substitution and you had to weigh exactly the same as the man who was coming to take your place."

Napoleon's smile turned to a look of concentration which

he turned on her. *"Ma foi!* Right or wrong, Betsee, you have an idea. But tell me, my wise one, how I was to get away from the island after the substitution had been made?"

It was now the girl's turn to smile. "All the time that disabled ship was lying there in James Roads, I kept thinking, if only it had been a French ship and not American! And now I am thinking, What reason have we for being sure it was American? It was manned by Yankee sailors but the ownership could be French. Sire, I think the man who was to take your place arrived on that ship. And I am sure you planned to get away on it."

The emperor sat very still for several moments while he studied her face. *"Eh bien!"* he said, finally. "Some day I will feel free to tell you if you are right or wrong." He sank against the back of the chair and sighed with the relief that the more relaxed position brought him. "You haven't been here for five days, *ma petite*, and I have missed the moments of release from pain that you generally bring me."

"I think I am being watched," she said, with sudden gravity. "They always seem to be on the *qui vive*. I wonder if they are taking advantage of that trick we taught them and are sending out signals when I leave the house? Two days ago I was stopped. I had ridden behind a party of visitors who wanted a glimpse of Longwood. I intended to leave Monty at Hutt's Gate and then watch for a chance to cross the line. A sentry held me up when I tried it and asked me a long list of questions. He read them off from a paper."

A silence of some moments fell between them. "All the ladies in my life—we've discussed them often, haven't we, *ma petite!*—were beautiful. Some more so than others. But only two of them have had anything much here," touching his forehead, "Some even seemed *sans cervelle* at times. They were afraid of me, I suspect. Certainly they accepted whatever I said or did as beyond dispute. Of the two exceptions, the first was responsible for bringing me into the world. Madame Mère. She was never afraid to speak out when she thought I was wrong. And sometimes, alas, I *was* wrong. The second is you, Betsee."

"Sire! I—I can't believe you mean it."

"The first and the last. The oldest and the youngest. And of those in between I asked for nothing more than what they had to offer—charm, liveliness, a bright eye, a trimness. I can't

384

recall now that any of them influenced my decisions in any way."

At this point Betsy observed over her shoulder the approach of the grand marshal accompanied by the newly arrived admiral of the fleet, Sir Pulteney Malcolm. "Sire," she said, hurriedly, "perhaps you will allow me to ask you some questions later. But I see that the admiral is on his way here with the grand marshal."

Napoleon sat up at once in his chair. He had seen Admiral Malcolm several times and they got along very well together, the head of the fleet being urbane and pleasant.

"I must see him, Betsee. And it won't do for him to find you here. He is fair-minded and would think little of it. But he might let a hint of it drop outside and that bloodhound at Plantation House would pick it up and start to bay. We'll have to find a hiding place for you."

"I noticed," said Betsy, "that the hole in the library ceiling hasn't been repaired. Suppose I climb up there?"

"Do you realize that it will be very hot?"

"I think I can stand it."

2

When the commander of the fleet left, the emperor sent Marchand in search of his first visitor. The valet returned with a most sober face.

"Please, Your Imperial Highness, she's not there," he reported. "I climbed up myself. The attic was empty."

"Start a search for her at once. Perhaps she went out into the gardens."

Betsy was soon found but it was necessary to carry her into the studio in an unconscious condition. The valet deposited her limp figure on the couch.

"Your Imperial Highness, she had draped a curtain over the billiard table and had crept under it. She must have been overcome by the heat."

Napoleon gestured excitedly. "Don't stand there and talk, Marchand! Hurry! Find restoratives. There must be no delay."

A bottle of hartshorn was quickly produced and waved under her nose. When Betsy opened her eyes she was astonished to find Napoleon hovering over her with an air of alarm and

385

deep solicitude. He had taken possession of her hands and was chafing them feverishly while he murmured, "*Ma petite! ma petite!*"

"I am so sorry!" she managed to say. "What have I done? I must have fainted."

"Yes, Betsee. Ah, how white you are!"

"I was going to climb into the attic," she said, after a pause. "But I heard scratching on the ceiling and I knew there must be rats. I could not go up but I had to hide quickly, so I found a robe and draped it over the billiard table. I crawled in under it."

Napoleon turned to the valet and held up his first two fingers. "That much of brandy, Marchand. It will do her the most good."

The brandy proved effective and in the course of a few minutes the color had returned to the girl's cheeks. She sat up on the couch.

"Will you forgive me for causing so much trouble?"

"Betsee, you were trying so hard to spare me embarrassment. Are you feeling recovered?"

She was watching him with grave intentness. "I have often thought this and now I know it is true. You have the sweetest smile in the world."

"I reserve it for you. For all others, the scowl, the frown, the critical air. Yes, only for you, this special smile. Does it betray how deep my feeling is for you? Ah, Betsee, if you had been born forty years ago! What might have been, what might have been!"

The recuperative powers of youth, reinforced by the brandy, had clearly dispelled the effects of the stifling hour she had spent under the table.

"Forty years ago! But, sire, I would have married and I might be a grandmother now. Because I wasn't born earlier, I was able to come here with my family. I can't think of any other circumstance which would have allowed me the chance to—to catch a glimpse of you."

Napoleon seated himself on the foot of the couch. "Naturally it would have depended on a complete reversal of the plans which are made for all our lives. In the first place, your mother would have needed the common sense to be a Frenchwoman or an Italian, or better still a Corsican. Under no circumstances an Englishwoman."

"That would have been a very considerable change in plans, wouldn't it?"

"It would have been necessary also for you to be just as you are now. Ah, *ma petite*, if you had been in Corsica and just a few years younger than I! If I had seen your lovely hair glowing in the ardent Corsican sun!"

Betsy was listening eagerly, her eyes responding with warmth.

"If I had seen your eyes as I see them now! So lovely, so full of life! If I had heard you some morning whistling in those narrow old streets around the cathedral! I would, of course, have fallen instantly in love with you, and we would have been married. Even if you had been as reluctant as Josephine was in the beginning."

Betsy shook her head. "No, no, sire. I don't think I would have been reluctant at all."

"Think back to what I told you about my boyhood. There was no hint of what I was to become in that thin, gloomy, silent youth who was called Nabuleone. The beautiful butterfly might at first have scorned the drab moth. Still, let us assume that by a happy accident of birth I met and married you. It might have made a difference in my whole life."

"Perhaps, sire, you would have followed your first thought and became an author instead of a soldier."

He shook his head positively. "The instinct for soldiering was too strong. But the whole course of things might have been changed. I wonder if there would have been a 'whiff of grape' to bring me so quickly to the top? I am sure I wouldn't have attracted the notice of Barras and his like soon enough to get the Italian command.

"You see, Betsee," he went on, "there is always a point, generally when a man is young, when a momentous decision must be made. Two paths open before him. One entails a great gamble. If I had been married to you, happily of course and with a young family, I might have been less disposed to take the gamble when I stood at the inevitable crossroads.

"And, if you hold back once, the chance is never likely to offer itself again," he added. "The course of history might have been changed. I might have been content, shall we say, to remain First Consul or even to be commander of the armies of a republican France. In that event my battles would have been fought in the Low Countries and along the Rhine and the Alps. There would not have been the Egyptian mistake nor the tragedies of Spain and Russia."

"But wouldn't there have been times," she asked, "when you would regret the chance to climb higher? To wear a crown?"

Napoleon paused thoughtfully. "Almost certainly," he said, finally. "Always I have had the urge to climb. Higher and higher. I might inevitably have reached the stage where I would no longer listen to my two sage advisers. But I think there would have been enough scope without taking the highest step. There would have been continuous fighting, because the monarchial powers of Europe would have invented pretexts to crush a republic. I would have won all the battles easily, of course."

"You would have been the Cincinnatus of France, sire."

Napoleon shook his head with a suggestion almost of violence. "Do you think I would have been content to return to the plow after each battle? He was a stupid peasant, that Roman general. Could a man capable of winning real wars have been content to follow a team of oxen? No, no, my victories would have been much too great for that. And I would have been more demanding in the matter of rewards. I wouldn't have taken orders from the venal politicians who swarmed in the Forum. The orders would have been issued by me. But I think it possible I would have been content to remain the undeclared ruler, the Cromwell who refused the semblance of a crown, the director of the victorious armies of democracy. Perhaps my place in history would have been surer that way. Perhaps even higher."

He was so pleased with his consideration of this different approach to greatness that he got to his feet and stalked, somewhat unsteadily, up and down the room. His mind was filled with the magnificence of the battles he might have won and the acclaim with which time would have resounded to his stern republican rectitude. Certainly it would not have ended this way: with the sullen roaring of the sea constantly in his ears and the sweep of the trade winds over the rocky declivities of St. Helena.

Finally he stopped beside the couch and leaned over to study its occupant. Betsy's cheeks were recovering their usual color but she seemed content for the time being to lie curled up in the comfort, if it could be called that, of the sagging and shabby ottoman. "This," he thought, "has been different.

It has been idyllic and so fitting in my—my last love." He was content to do no more than pinch her ear.

"Ah, Betsee, if *that* had been the way my life was lived, the outcome would have been different in one respect, at least. All the beautiful ladies, these Others as you insist on calling them with a hint of scorn, who now will become familiar and glamorous figures in history, would never have been heard of at all."

Chapter Fifteen

1

Betsy had realized early that he benefited most from her visits if she had something to read to him and she made a point of taking a newspaper, a review, or even a book with her. He would snatch it from under her arm and thumb it over hastily. "Ha!" he would exclaim. "It is English! Always something from England! It will be antagonistic and unfair to me. And stupid, of course. All English writing is stupid."

"Then," she would say, "you would rather I didn't read to you today."

"I did not mean that. It is interesting to discover how wrong these countrymen of yours can be."

He had a favorite armchair in his bedroom, one of the few fine pieces in the house, a capacious enough chair with the straight and simple lines of the Directory period, covered in golden yellow silk. This he would have carried into the library and would take possession of it there, crossing one leg over the other. Betsy would find a stool and seat herself in front of him. She would read slowly, in a serious effort to achieve a fully understandable translation. Sooner or later he would discover some statement with which he was in furious disagreement and then he would lash out in criticism. Betsy, believing that a soft answer was needed to turn away his wrath, would have little to say about his first attacks. Inevitably, however, he would go too far. Her eyes then would catch fire like the point of the new flame lighters called tinder matches, and she would plunge into the point at issue. They would be at it hammer and tongs. It was chiefly about politics and international affairs that they disputed: what the Irish meddler (Castlereagh) was doing in England or what the satanic Austrian (Metternich) had up his sleeve. Betsy was well enough read in such matters to talk him into the round occasionally.

390

"Enough!" he would say then. "I cannot bear any more of this. What little health I have left will be destroyed."

"On the contrary, sire. An argument does you good."

Once she got up to detach a small mirror from a wall. "Observe," she said, holding it in front of him. "When I came in you were tired and very, very gloomy. The corners of your mouth sagged. Your color was *terrible*. And now what do you see? Your eyes are alive, you have color in your cheeks. You may be angry but it does you good."

Napoleon raised his hands in surrender. "As usual, Betsee, you are right. I don't know what I would do without you."

Once she was reading to him from a London newspaper which had arrived after being shipped to Cape Town and was therefore unusually old. All the news it contained was familiar and the commentary was of small interest. She was hunting desperately for something to read when her eye lighted on a very short news item datelined Paris.

"This has a familiar ring to it," she began. Then she stopped abruptly, realizing it was something he should be spared. She turned the page quickly.

Napoleon reached out and chained her wrist. "This news with a familiar ring to it," he said. "Why are you passing over it? Do you think it should be kept from me?"

She hesitated. Then she said, "Yes, sire."

"Someone is dead?"

She nodded..

"Then read it. *Ma foi*, am I a child that I must be spared from knowing things?"

"It is dated December of last year, so it has been a long time in reaching us. It records the death of Countess d'Ornano. No details are given."

Napoleon remained in deep and somber thought for some time. "You recognized, I judge, the name," he said finally.

"Yes, sire. You told me once that Marie Walewska had married a Count d'Ornano. I—I felt sure it must be the same."

There was a long silence. Napoleon had slumped deep into his chair and, judging from the brooding look in his eyes, he had fallen into an introspective and saddened mood.

It was in late summer of 1814 and Napoleon was at Elba, where he had been sent by the allied powers after his first abdication. It was vastly different, as he would learn to his sorrow later, from St. Helena. It was a little island of low hills off the Italian coast. It enjoyed clear skies, and, although cloyingly hot at times, it was as gentle as its people, and as subdued. The members of the Old Guard, who had been allowed to accompany him, some seven hundred or more, found it a lazy and relaxing place. It had the same effect on his beautiful sister Pauline who had arrived on a corvette called, of all names, the *Inconstant*. Madame Mère had come over from Rome and had established a Spartan ménage, because she feared that her son would need all the substantial support she could provide.

Even in this captivity of velvet bonds, and despite his intention of not staying there long, Napoleon had kept himself busy, revising the laws, improving the courts, and studying the social conditions. He had imported mulberry trees and he had built roads. He had remodeled his residence in the capital, Portoferraio. He had erected for himself a country residence of white stone up in the chestnut groves of San Martino, and had taken over a curious little wooden house of four meager rooms on the highest point of the island, almost under the spreading granite wings of the rock called the Eagle of Marciano. To this little hideaway he had given the name of the Hermitage.

His chief concern of the moment was an overwhelming wish to bring his wife and their little son, the King of Rome, to the island, a desire in which the quiet Elbanese shared. There had been rumors that Marie Louise was to pay him a visit; and so, when a vessel from Naples put in at the port and a half dozen people came ashore in the shades of early evening, it was easy for the watchers to accept the identity of a blond young woman and a boy of three who were of the party.

A carriage and several saddle horses were on hand for the accommodation of the new arrivals. They did not stop at Napoleon's curious house in the port but turned up the winding road which led to the interior of the island. From a post on the highlands at Pomonte Napoleon had watched them disembark and he met them before they had progressed far. The carriage came to a halt at a point in the relatively cool highlands where two large tents had been raised. The beautiful young lady with fair hair and almost startlingly blue eyes was to occupy one of them. The boy was to share the other with the attendants.

Despite the lateness of the hour, Napoleon and his charming visitor seated themselves in camp chairs in front of her pavilion and talked together for several hours in low and earnest tones. The inhabitants of the island were never to learn that the mysterious beauty was not the empress but his Polish paramour, Marie Walewska, and that the boy was their three-year-old son, Alexandre. She had come to assure Napoleon of her undying devotion and of her desire to share his exile.

It was of this they talked as they sat side by side through the early hours of the night and on the following morning when the discussion was renewed. He was gratified by her continued love for him but he was at the same time apprehensive. The hope was still in his mind that Marie Louise would finally decide to cast her lot with him by coming to Elba. Above everything, he did not want to take any step which might give his Austrian wife any excuse to keep the King of Rome from him.

It was decided between them that she would give up the idea of coming to Elba, and the next day the party took to horse and carriage to rejoin their ship which was still docked at Portoferraio. The trip was made in the middle of the day and the inhabitants swarmed eagerly along the route to see the unnamed visitor. They undoubtedly gained the impression that she was more beautiful than the reports they had received of Napoleon's wife, and certainly that she had much more of dignity and character than they had supposed.

Napoleon watched them depart from a post in the hills. He returned to the Hermitage in a mood of silent constraint.

Marie Walewska gave him another proof of her constancy as soon as he had escaped from Elba and had made his triumphant return to Paris. She hurried there and took possession of the house he had given her some years before. She visited his offices unsummoned and was unfortunate enough to find him immersed in the mad excitements of the early stages of the Hundred Days. He was sitting at a desk, white and tense, letters piled about him, the floor strewn with campaign maps. Davout, the most capable of his marshals, had joined him at once and was acting as Minister of War but the emperor believed in superintending everything himself.

A lady to see him? Send her away.

But, he was informed, this was a rather particular lady, the Countess Walewska. This compelled him to give the matter some thought. Inform her, was his final decision, that he was happy she had come but that at the moment he was too busy to see anyone.

She returned a second time and again found him with his office filled with staff officers and the floor still covered with maps.

Not today, she was told. He would inform her when he would be free.

But he was never free and he sent her no message. When, deeply apologetic, he wrote her a letter much later, he received no reply. She had left Paris. He never saw her again.

All this ran through his mind while Betsy sat in silence and waited.

"My poor Maria!" he thought. "She alone was willing to share the troubled days with me."

But that, he realized almost at once, was neither true nor fair. Madame Mère had always been fiercely loyal and ready to place her last sou at his disposal, and also his beautiful sister Pauline, in her indolent and somewhat detached way. And Josephine.

In the height of the exciting days of preparation for the heavy fighting ahead, he suddenly decided he must go to Malmaison. This was the home he had shared with Josephine for so many years and where she had died after the divorce. Ah, that gentle, vivacious, thoughtless, undependable, unfaithful Josephine! Her death had been a shock in spite of everything and he now felt compelled to visit the home she had animated with her charm.

At his first glimpse, he felt a sinking of the spirit. There was an air of disuse about the place. The gardens were unkempt, the grass was rank and uncut, the flower beds wild; and there was an accusing look in the eyes of the sole gardener which seemed to say, "And all this is your fault." But inside he encountered at once the proofs that the once gay spirit of Josephine seemed to pervade the place still.

Nothing had been changed. There was nothing new to

catch his eye, no new paintings on the walls, no startling statuary, no piles of new books (which would never have been read), no new furnishings or costly hangings. When he visited his own bedroom, he was astonished to find that everything was just as he had left it when he made his final departure. His old and rather shabby dressing gown of purple and white was lying across the foot of the bed, his slippers were at the side.

"Josephine, Josephine!" he murmured. "Did you really care this much!"

She had not changed in one respect. Her apartments were filled with the articles of clothing she continued to collect almost until the end. A new housekeeper, who seemed overwhelmed at the need to address him, gave a detailed accounting. There were nearly six hundred pairs of white silk stockings (never used more than once), by actual count 252 pairs of shoes (some of which had been worn twice, none more), two hundred white muslin dresses, five hundred lace-trimmed chemises, over two hundred hats. He frowned sharply when the housekeeper stammered her surprise that they had been able to find only two flannel petticoats and one pair of cotton drawers. "These couldn't have belonged to her!" he asserted, indignantly. "She never wore such things!"

The visit resulted in a startling discovery. In a small room on the ground floor which had served them jointly as a household office, his eye lighted on a carefully disguised wall cabinet under one of the windows. "Ha!" he thought, "the receptacle of our secrets."

His first glimpse at the contents made him smile for it proved how incorrigibly careless the chatelaine of the house had been. There was a belt with a broken gold buckle, too expensive to be thrown out, a torn envelope from which the letter had been extracted, a few valuable buttons, a sketch of Josephine (a very bad one, the work no doubt of some friend), a sheet of music containing variations on the one air she had ever attempted on her harp, a comfit box with a broken lid. There was a faint reminder of her favorite perfume about the contents and this he traced to a package in one corner, wrapped in black velvet.

It was a jewel box of large size. When he opened it, he went suddenly silent. It contained nearly twenty pieces of exquisitely designed and extravagantly expensive jewelry. He recognized them all.

These were the consolatory gifts he had presented to her at the termination of each amatory adventure. He had gone to great lengths to find the most perfect jewelry in all the markets of Europe. There were necklaces, bracelets, brooches, rings, chains, all set with large and perfect diamonds, radiant rubies, somber sapphires, engaging emeralds, and pearls. Each of them might have served as a king's ransom; which was what they were, having been intended to purchase an emperor's release from a sense of wrong.

Napoleon's memory was retentive in all such matters. He recalled each piece and what he had paid for it. He thought, "These, Josephine, I must always keep, to remind me of you."

He returned in late afternoon to Paris, with the case under his arm, to find Davout waiting for him. The Duke of Auerstadt (Davout owed this proud title to his personal victory in the wars with Prussia) was in a disturbed state of mind. A flush which covered his usually pale cheeks had spread well up over the bald arch of his head, and his thin fringe of side-whiskers seemed in a state of agitation.

"Sire," he said, "I am most disturbed over the artillery contracts."

Nothing could have won Napoleon's attention more surely. He had always depended first on his artillery. A study of his victories showed that they had been won by the masterly concentration of the guns at the right spot and, of equal importance, at the right moment. If he were to break up the combination of the English and Prussian armies before the Austrians and Russians arrived, he was going to need guns, guns, guns!

"Well?" he demanded, seating himself at his desk.

"As we expected," said Davout, "the supplies voted by the lower house are insufficient."

"Disregard the house! Spend whatever is necessary."

"But the funds are not available. The manufacturers say the costs have risen and they cannot turn us out so many cannon at such short notice without large advance payments. Can we go to the bankers and wring the money out of them like water from a wet sail? I have talked to them and their attitude is damnably firm."

"Then," said Napoleon, "we must go to the lower chamber and demand additional appropriations. The necessary pressure can be applied."

"But, sire, you know the temper and the ways of these blundering politicians. They will waste weeks in debating it. Each one must get up and have his say at great length. They are idiots with a sense of self importance. And at this stage we can't afford any delay. The guns must be cast at once."

Napoleon indulged in some deep thought, his head bent forward over his chest.

"I will see what I can do," he said, finally. "Come back—in the morning. Early."

Most of the purchases which made up Josephine's secret store had been bought through one house in Paris, a family concern of long standing. The message that Napoleon dispatched to summon the oldest brother passed the Minister of War in the courtyard.

M. Paul, the senior partner, came in response, and his elaborately curled mustaches twitched with excitement when the black velvet cloth was spread on the desk, causing the jewels to sparkle with a brilliance beyond that of a bank of ballroom chandeliers.

"M'sieur, you remember them?"

"Yes, Your Imperial Highness. All of them. Even the few which we did not have the privilege of obtaining for you."

"I have been computing the amount paid for the lot. The total is—rather staggering. But also satisfying. Because we face, as you must realize, a summer of hostilities. I am raising every franc I can get my hands on."

There were a few moments of silence while the jeweler cast up the total in his mind. Then he mentioned a figure, Napoleon gave his head a savage and negative shake.

"Low! Quite low." He himself named a figure. "That, m'sieur, is what they cost me."

"But Your Majesty is reckoning the prices he paid for the jewels. Which is much in excess of what could be obtained for them today."

"Are you telling me I cannot realize the full value of these wonderful pieces of jewelry if I try to sell them now?"

"That is the realistic way to consider the situation, Your Highness. Particularly if you desire to obtain the money at once."

"Why is this?"

M. Paul's face had gone pale and his eyes glittered with apprehension under the heavy black thatch of his eyebrows.

397

"Money, Your Majesty, is tight. With the air full of war rumors, it is running to cover. It is almost impossible to get loans from the banks—even with security as gilt-edged as these."

"Then you do not wish to purchase the jewelry back from me?"

"I did not say that, Your Majesty. I am endeavoring to make it clear that even a house as well established as ours lacks the means to purchase such a princely, nay such a fabulous, collection at the prices you paid over a period of years. If we go to the bank we will meet with point-blank refusals."

Napoleon leaned back in his chair with his arms folded over his chest. M. Paul hesitated to break the silence which ensued. Finally, however, he said: "It would be necessary to form a syndicate, Your Majesty. And that takes time."

This elicited nothing further from the emperor. M. Paul's nose, which was long and pointed, twitched nervously. A clock on the wall above Napoleon ticked away three minutes while the silence held. Then the head of the state straightened up in his chair.

"It is far from my intention to accept a heavy loss in parting with these priceless jewels. I prefer to deal with your house. But, if necessary, I shall seek the opinions of others. Do you desire to consult your brothers?"

"Yes, Your Majesty. By the greatest of good fortune, they are all in town. I may be able to find them at their homes at the dinner hour."

"Then you will let me know this evening what you propose to do?"

M. Paul looked startled, even frightened, at this suggestion. "Your Majesty!" he stammered. "It will be utterly impossible to arrive at a conclusion in such a short time."

"My needs are such that there can be no delay. Make the rounds of your brothers, M. Paul, while they dawdle over their dinners. They are rather numerous, I believe."

"There are seven of us, Your Majesty."

"That makes it impossible for you to visit each of them. Send word around that they must forego their dinners and join you at once. You will have a busy evening, M. Paul."

Davout was shown into the emperor's presence at seven o'clock the next morning.

"M. Paul and his six brothers," said Napoleon, "shared

a most unsatisfactory meal last evening, consisting of that abominable form of food invented by the English, the cold sandwich. They grumbled a great deal but not entirely because of that."

He placed a check in his minister's hand. Davout gazed at it and gasped.

"For the guns," declared the emperor briskly. "Set the wheels turning, my brave comrade. Keep prices down and insist on early delivery. We are going to be hard-pressed up there in the country south of Brussels. We must smash the English and the Prussians before the armies from farther east can join them."

3

Napoleon roused himself from these memories with a realization that was perhaps new to him. He had thought himself in love many times but had it ever been quite as great and real as he had imagined? Certainly there had been in his life a controlling passion far greater than any which could be traced to a beautiful face. What he had been most concerned in having all his years (even going back to the little green cannon his father had given him) was an ever abundant supply of artillery. He hurried away from romance when the need arouse to fight, willing to forget the reproachful faces of his charming ladies until the masterly handling of his guns had blown the enemy into defeat and destruction.

"And that has been the truth," he said to himself. "My chief interest in life has always been for guns!"

Then he became aware that he had an audience of one to be considered.

"I am sorry, Betsee, if I have seemed rude. I have indulged in a few minutes of thought about the past."

"Half an hour, sire," corrected Betsy.

"Nonsense. A few minutes only." Then he paused. "Do you recall the talks we have had about what might have been if you were born years ago?"

"Very well indeed, sire. I think I could repeat what you said on the subject word for word."

"There was one possibility I overlooked and which honesty compells me to mention now. I never allowed anything to stand in the way of my duty, my career, or whatever you want to call it. Would this compelling force have influenced me as much in the event which—which we discussed? Betsee, I must be candid and say that it would.

"There has always been one siren in my life," he went on. "One to whom I have responded blindly. She is not beautiful like the others. Her nose is a snout and she is as dark as iron. Her breath is the breath of death."

"I think, sire, you are describing a cannon and not a lady."

"Yes, dear Betsee. I am."

Chapter Sixteen

1

It fell out that most of Betsy's visits to the Captive at Longwood had to be paid in the mornings. It was during the early hours that deliveries were made and that artisans shambled up the road from town to attend (in their easygoing way) to any repairs which were needed; thus creating a steady activity about the place. Moreover, the light of the sun, reflecting on the spyglass in the hands of Sir Hudson Lowe, never came skipping and flitting in and around the gardens and the house until the afternoons. So, all in all, the little stratagems which had to be devised to get her across the line were more easily carried out in the first half of the day.

On one occasion she arrived before the great man was ready for company. She was informed that he was in the hands of his valet and that she had better find something to read in the meantime. The library could be reached only through the dining room and, when she stepped into that most dismal of chambers, she was astonished to find the iron field cot, in which Napoleon insisted on sleeping, stretched out in front of the fireplace. She turned to Perron who had delivered the message and was now preparing to disappear into the succession of pantries and kitchens which resounded with the stoking of stoves and the rattle of crockery; in great contrast to the lowing of the cattle which had once occupied the same space.

"What is the emperor's bed doing in here?" she asked.

"Well, mam'selle, I guess the dining room was bound to get its turn."

"I don't understand. Does the emperor have his bed moved about?"

Perron nodded. "Drafts, mam'selle," he said. "They're bad things, drafts. And this place has more of them than all the palaces and mansions and chateaux in Europe combined."

"Is the bed going to be left here?"

The butler, who was so fat and short that he looked very much like a large tennis ball in his white cotton clothes, shook his head.

"He didn't like it here. So tonight it will be set up somewhere else."

When Napoleon put in an appearance, looking as though he had found his night's sleep far from refreshing, she brought up the subject at once. He shook his head gloomily.

"The wind whistles in through the chinks in that chamber of horrors they call a bedroom. I tried the bed in every location but no place was safe from it. I am very susceptible to colds and I wakened each morning with my head as heavy as a cannon ball. I had Marchand drape blankets around the bed and then I nearly suffocated from the heat. We've tried the drawing room, the library, the study. The winds get in and hunt for me in all the corners. Last night I had it moved to the dining room and there at last I was free. But there was something worse: the odor of mutton, of fried food, the sourness of wine in the air. I hardly slept at all.

"It will be necessary," he went on, "to move back to the bedroom after all. Perhaps with heavy curtains draped over both windows, I won't suffer from drafts. I will have a lesser evil to endure, of course, the lack of fresh air."

Later he came back to the subject. "Have you noticed anything strange about the winds we get here, Betsee? They don't come up swiftly and then go racing beyond. They seem to come to a pause and then they slink about the house, trying to get in at the windows or under the doors. As I lie in bed and listen, it seems they are muttering out there." He moved his head with sudden vehemence. "Betsee, since this illness fastened on me, I am subject to strange fancies. At night I find my mind filled with fantastic ideas. I should be able to shake them off even in my dreams, knowing them to be absurd. But I can't escape them as easily as that. They even linger on for a time after I waken. Do you suppose my mind is weakening as well as my body?"

"No, no, sire!"

He paid no attention to her vigorous negative. *"Mon Dieu,* sometimes I am certain it isn't the winds I hear but the voices of those who plotted my downfall. Talleyrand, Fouché, Marmont; whispering, scheming, conspiring. I always knew they were false but I did nothing about it. They were useful in their way and I was sure I could keep them at heel. But now they seem to be combining to hold me here, to poison the minds of the French people who have never lost faith in me.

"But," he continued in a tone which suggested a shuddering disinclination to add anything, "that is the least of my fancies. I sometimes think what I hear are the voices which reached me in the nights after a battle. When the surgeons were at work but could reach a few only of the wounded and the dying." He paused. "Can it be that in my final hours of defeat I am to be forced to endure these reminders of the price of victory?"

2

One morning Betsy did not put in an appearance, and, to make matters worse, a rainstorm of unusual violence came up most unexpectedly. There was a furious wind back of it which contorted the clouds into fantastic shapes and drove them in a frantic scurry across the sky. There was about it the kind of terror which sometimes causes imaginative children to fear the Day of Judgment has come at last and to stare up with frightened eyes into the blackness, expecting to discern the stern face of Jehovah behind it.

The house became so dark that the servants were busy lighting candles in all the rooms, and shivering as they did so.

Napoleon stood at a window in a typical mood of impatience. He had something of the greatest importance to discuss with Bertrand and did not want to wait for the storm to finish its seemingly spiteful visit and continue out over the turbulent ocean.

"Marchand!" he called.

The valet, as always, was waiting outside the door. He came in with the suddenness of a jack-in-the-box.

"Yes, Your Majesty."

"I am going to see the grand marshal. Find me a large cloak."

"Your Majesty! In this rain? It's certain to be over in a few minutes."

"Now! Do you hear? Now!"

So Marchand wrapped him up to the eyes in a voluminous cloak and in this he went out with insistent steps into the storm. Bertrand, observing his approach, came to meet him half way. Not having paused to find himself any kind of protection, the marshal was soaked to the skin by the time they gained the protection of Hutt's Gate.

"Change! Be quick about it, Bertrand. I have something to tell you."

What he had to say was this: "My mind is weakening. Come, I want no protestations. Who is in a better position to know? I tell you, Marshal, I have nothing to cope with here. I sit around and read. I quarrel with a stupid Englishman. Always before I had problems to face, decisions to make, losses to retrieve, successes to fashion. All this kept my mind fresh and sharp. No problem was too hard for me to solve. *Mon Dieu*, what a difference now!

"That, Bertrand, is the tragedy I face. Can you conceive how maddening it is? Always my mind has been like a fire burning in my head. Sometimes it seemed banked but always it was capable of exploding into flame in a moment, until it would be crackling and roaring and sending up ideas in all directions like sparks. All my life I have had a great mind to call upon. And now it lies dormant.

"There is one consolation. At night it has a tendency to revive. While I lie in bed, I become aware that my mind is escaping from its state of waking coma. This is even more true when I am asleep for I sometimes have wonderful dreams. Brilliant plans occur to me. They get twisted and awry, of course. In dreams an idea turns fanciful and extravagant, and you need the corrective instinct of a sound waking mind to detect the flaws and correct them.

"This brings me to my reason for coming," he went on, after a moment. "Last night my mind took hold, in a dream, of the problem of getting away from here for a few years of decent peace and comfort. I went over all the conditions and came in like a ship to the right mooring." He paused. "Tell me, Bertrand, who is the dominant figure in Europe today?"

The marshal hesitated. "Metternich?" he ventured.

"No, Bertrand, no! Not Metternich. *Ma foi*, he's a skilled puppetmaster, no more. If it came to the point of a major decision among the monarchs in Europe, the voice of Alexander of Russia would be the dominant one."

Bertrand assented eagerly. "Of course, sire. Why did I make such a mistake? They are all a little afraid of the tsar. His strength is so—so incalculable."

"Alexander," declared the emperor, "has the seeds of greatness in him. He wants to do the best thing for his people, for the little people of the whole world, in fact, but he lacks stability and can't follow a straight line in his thinking. He will never accomplish anything. But if he could be persuaded to speak out about what is happening here, the other monarchs would come to heel and listen to him. I'm certain they would give in."

"We know, sire, that all information about the situation here is being kept from him. It is filtered through the officers of his chancellery. He believes you are living comfortably in a large country house set in a fine wooded park. He has been convinced your health is good."

"Exactly, Bertrand, exactly. And so we must find a way of getting to him. We must send people to him who can convince him of the truth."

"But—but—"

"I appreciate the difficulties. It can be done in one way only. Through the good offices of the pope. Alexander's allegiance is to the Russian church but I know he has always felt a great respect for the man in the Vatican. More respect than I had. I realize now how badly I treated that fine old man." He sat for a few moments in a scowling appraisal of his mistake. "But he's attached to Madame Mère and has done innumerable kind things for our family. I am certain he could make the arrangements for the people I would like to send to Alexander. He, the tsar, has some shreds of liking left for me, in spite of the capture of Moscow and the hatred he conceived for me at that time."

Bertrand had stripped off his outer clothing and was wrapped in an ancient dressing gown. There were ripped seams at the shoulders and a wine stain on one lapel. They made an odd combination to be discussing plans of world-wide consequence. Madame Bertand glanced in and made a face when she saw how her husband was attired. He waved her away.

"How old is the Signora?" asked Napoleon abruptly.

"Do you refer, sire, to Violetta Gravina?"

"Who else? Her voice always thrilled me. Is she still active?"

"Yes. She sings in the best houses in Italy and occasionally visits London and Vienna. Her voice has developed flaws. She can't reach the high notes any longer but in the lower registers she is still magnificent."

405

"Good. And her husband, Jacopo." He smiled briefly. "It was his name which set my mind to working in the right direction. One of the servants here is called Jacopo. Last evening I heard someone calling him in a shrill voice, 'Jacopo! Jacopo!' It came back in a dream in the night and I realized it was the key to unlock this prison house."

Bertrand quite clearly was puzzled but he commented: "An odd little fellow, that husband of the Signora's. He barely comes to the shoulder of his magnificent spouse. But he's a genius in his own way. What magnificent sketches he makes! There is no artist anywhere to compare with him."

Napoleon's face lighted up with satisfaction. "You see, then, what came into my mind. I want to hear the Signora sing again. Would she accept an invitation to come here, think you?"

"She would be highly honored and delighted, I am sure. But could it be arranged? Would the English Government agree?"

"I think the pope could arrange it. Send the invitation at once, Bertrand. Jacopo must come, of course."

"He goes wherever she does."

"And he must bring his charcoal pencils with him."

A light began to dawn in Bertrand's eyes. "Sire!" he cried, excitedly. "You would have him make sketches of you while the signora sings."

"Yes, Bertrand. I would insist on being depicted realistically, knowing how much I have fallen off the last few months. Can you think of a better way to convince Alexander of the truth? In addition, I would have Jacopo make sketches of this place, inside and out. Even going to the extent of showing the hole in the library ceiling, the ugliness of the bedroom, the vulgarity of the bathroom. What a dismal picture he could make of that common dining salon!"

"These sketches," he went on, "could be smuggled out with them. If necessary the Signora could pin them to her petticoats. Even Sir Lowe would not risk having the *grande dame* of music searched."

"That brings me to the rest of my plan. He would assemble a party to travel secretly to Russia when the pope had secured Alexander's consent. The Signora, Jacopo and his sheath of sketches, Dr. O'Meara to discuss the medical side of things, Las Cases and—Betsee."

Bertrand looked startled. "Betsy? Sire, would that be wise?"

The gloom which seldom left Napoleon's face in these last days, lifted briefly in a smile.

"Betsee, of course. Alexander is susceptible and he would be easily won over to her. Can't you picture the scene? This great Greek god of an Alexander and all the rest in the deputation saying, 'Yes, Your Majesty,' 'Of course, Your Imperial Highness,' and 'Live forever, O Alexander'—and then Betsee standing up to him and even correcting him when he made a misstatement! Besides, Bertrand, she would be the ideal witness, telling him of the happiness I enjoyed in that little wooden shell of a pavilion, of my reluctance to leave, of my feelings about this shambles where I have lived for years in sheer degradation. An English girl telling this, with golden hair and a sparkling blue eye and enough feminine guile to show the tip of a neat foot beneath her skirt. Ah, yes, Betsee would be the star witness. Betsee and the Jacopo sketches."

"But," said Bertrand, "wouldn't it be considered unpatriotic of her, being English?"

"There are thousands of English people who say openly that I should be released. Besides she would be playing a part in an event of world importance. What better chance would she ever have to get herself on the pages of history?

"Bertrand, I am sure Alexander would be won over. And if he came out and said to the others, 'This is a mistake, this man Napoleon is no longer to be feared, this petty persecution of him must stop' the rest of them would fall into line."

By talking of this plan which had suggested itself while he tossed and turned in his narrow iron cot, Napoleon's manner had changed. He seemed like himself again and he spoke with the incisive quality he had displayed when the threads of world control were in his hands.

"How long would it take to do all this, Bertrand?" he asked.

The marshal began to make calculations of time and space. "Three months to get the invitation to the Signora and Jacopo. Three months for them to arrive by ship from London. A month here, perhaps. Three months to return. Two months perhaps in negotiations between the Vatican and the tsar. Then a month in Russia, and longer to conduct the correspondence between the capitals. Finally, three months to send a warship here for you. All in all, sire, I think it would be a matter of nearly two years."

Napoleon nodded in a suddenly sobered mood. "A long time, Bertrand. Would I live to see the end of it?"

"Of course, sire. I am aware that you put no reliance in this new man, Dr. Antommarchi but his reports are not unfavorable. It is worth trying. Yes, yes, sire, the effort should be made."

3

The following morning Napoleon emerged from the hands of his valet at an unusually early hour. He walked into the garden and looked up into the sky which was almost cloudless.

"Why am I concerned about the weather?" he asked himself. "For me it is always bad. And now—I must expect to suffer from it for all the time that is left."

Detecting a tremor in his legs, he called to Marchand to bring him a cane. With this in hand, he began to walk haltingly in the direction of Hutt's Gate. When a sentry came charging over and stationed himself a few paces in the rear, the emperor waved the cane at him in a sudden rage.

"Back!" he cried. "Stand back where you belong, you dolt!"

The sentinel remained stationary for a few seconds and then proceeded to follow at a more discreet distance.

Napoleon sank into a chair on the Bertrand porch. The marshal, hurrying out to join him, said to himself that he had never seen his master look worse. Napoleon's skin had a waxy look to it. His eyes had no hint of the usual fire, the vibrancy. He seemed to be breathing with difficulty.

"You concluded it might take two years to see the tsar and open his eyes to the truth," he said, after a long pause. "I have come to tell you—that there is no use trying."

An expression of deep disappointment took possession of Bertrand's face. He stood in front of the sick man and studied him intently.

"But, sire," he protested, "why have you changed your mind?"

Napoleon shifted his position in the chair, seeming to find the effort a tax on his strength. "You may laugh at me, Bertrand. But I must tell you of a dream I had last night."

One hand still rested on the head of the cane. With the other he pointed impatiently in the direction of the road which led past the house toward the town.

"I am getting forgetful. Just down there a short distance, what is it called?"

"Do you mean the Devil's Punch Bowl?"

"No, no. A little beyond that."

"I think then you must mean Geranium Vale."

"That is it. Geranium Vale. Why Geranium? I've never seen geraniums there. Still it's green and sometimes cool. The willow trees give a splendid shade. I went there last night in my dream."

Bertrand waited, making no comment. Napoleon proceeded in a low tone. "It was clear enough when I started. I was all alone and I felt rather well. The pains had left me and I don't believe they came back for some time. At least I didn't need a cane."

"When I reached this vale I stopped. The moon had come out suddenly and I felt that everything had taken on a glow. There was a softness to the moonlight and I fancied there was a trace of green about it. It was—perhaps a little uncanny. Certainly it was different than I had ever seen before."

"I stood at the edge of the road," he went on, "and I said to myself that at least there was something different about the vale. I thought, 'What have they done?' I decided to climb the short distance down from the road to see. But I took no more than one step. Something seemed to be holding me back. I felt that an intangible but demanding hand gripped me by the shoulder."

"So I remained where I was by the side of the road and looked about me. I noticed first that some of the iron railing they put up around that new house had been moved down into the vale to form an enclosure. Inside the enclosure there seemed to be a grave. There was something odd about it, because the gravestone was lying flat on the ground. In old and ill-kept burial grounds the stones will often be found flat on the ground. But this was a new grave. It had not been there when I visited the vale a few weeks before. I tried to recall if there had been a funeral and I decided that nothing of the kind had taken place. And why would they use Geranium Vale? The spring there gives us such fine, cold water and people seem to find it a pleasant place to rest. Young people make it a meeting place. I've seen them sitting there and holding hands. Why turn one of the few pleasant spots on the island into a burying ground?

"I was turning this over in my mind when the moon freed itself of all the clouds. All about me it was as light as day. I saw that beyond any shadow of doubt there was a grave inside the enclosure. The restraining force on my shoulder was no longer there, so I left the road and walked down toward the enclosure. I came to the iron railing and leaned on it while I studied the gravestone. Bertrand, it was blank!"

"No name on it at all?"

"None. 'This is strange,' I thought. 'This is very strange. It's plain enough that someone is buried here but who can it be?' Then I looked closer and I saw that there was something on the stone after all. At the bottom there was a date, chiseled in small figures."

He hesitated before continuing with the story. "Bertrand, I knew then that I had been given a glimpse of the future. I turned and ran from the place in a state of fear, even of panic." He seemed to be struggling to find words. "*I knew I had been standing beside my own grave.*"

Bertrand tried to find words to reassure him, He pointed out that such dreams were common enough. They meant nothing. Napoleon paid no attention to what he was saying.

After a few moments the emperor continued in a low voice. "Bertrand, I am sure there will be no time to win the support of the tsar. You said it would take two years. Now listen to this. The date on the foot of the stone, which I saw with my own eyes, was—May 5, 1821."

Chapter Seventeen

1

Sir Hudson Lowe scowled at a slip of paper which one of his aides had laid on his desk.

"What's the meaning of this?" he demanded.

"It's the talk of the island, Your Excellency, that General Bonaparte is in much worse condition than we've believed."

"There's no basis for such talk! And in any event why does it concern them?" He motioned with an impatient hand at the paper. "Six of them! And they want to call on him in a body!"

"Well, it's being said, sir, that he eats little food. The only thing that seems to stay down is dry champagne. This little group of officers want to take him a case of the best."

"But—but—" The governor hesitated while an indignant flush spread across his face. "What concern is it of theirs?"

"They think—"

"They think! Why should they think? Their duty is plain. They are here to guard against any escape. And I have made it very clear that any expressions of sympathy are entirely improper and—and out of order."

"Then, sir, you wish me to advise them that you refuse permission?"

The governor sat in bitter silence for several moments. Then he gave another glance at the list, his eye lingering over the name of Lieutenant Grannison.

"I thought better of them. Still, I don't want to make an issue of it. Tell them to make their call and—and take their wine. But under strict conditions. An hour only. Not one instant longer. And they must report here to me after leaving him. I must be told every word that was spoken during the call and I must know everything that was done. Make that clear to them."

411

It was agreed later by all who had taken part in the visit that it was the most exhilarating thing that had happened since the arrival of the one time emperor of France. Napoleon had gone to great lengths to make himself agreeable. He had answered all their questions. He had laughed and joked with them and he had stated his opinions freely on all points of military interest.

He was standing in front of the fireplace in the drawing room when they were shown in. That one of his neatly shod feet was placed on a dark stain in the carpet and that behind him the yellow paper was hanging loosely from the wall went unnoticed. The six young officers had no eyes for anything but the compelling figure of the great soldier. Napoleon was wearing a state uniform and his breast blazed with orders and decorations. They could not help noticing, however, that he was surprisingly thin.

"Gentlemen," he said, in halting English, "this is—this is an exclusion. Soldiers only. No civilians. No ladies. No officials. This makes it very pleasant, does it not?"

His guests laughed. "Yes, general," said one of them.

"We—we, us, seven, will talk shop, *eh bien?*"

Six pairs of eyes sparkled with increased animation. He was treating them as equals, dashed if he wasn't! They exchanged gratified side glances.

Napoleon turned to the senior officer. "I would like to continue this discussion in your language. But, alas, I have gone as far with it as I can. I am informed you speak French, so I shall depend on you to act as interpreter. If you will be so kind. My suggestion is that they ask me questions. I will do my best to answer all of them."

So, for more than half an hour, the visitors plied him with questions. Napoleon had been compelled to seat himself after the introduction of his guests but the six officers disregarded the suggestion that they sit down also (there were only four chairs in the room and the seats of two of these were broken through) and stood about him in a highly excited circle. Most of their questions were about explicit battles. How had he made his troop dispositions at this one? Why at that one did he hold his cavalry back until such a late point? Which was his greatest? Who were his best marshals? What was the secret of Murat's great success as a leader of cavalry? Finally one of them summoned up enough courage

412

to ask the question which interested them most. What was his opinion of the Duke of Wellington as a general?

"Villainton," answered Napoleon slowly, "was well served at—at that battle. I was badly served. I regret we did not meet under more even conditions."

"You mean—the weather? The heavy rains in the morning?"

"That, yes. But there was much else. The memory of that day—I do not care to dwell on it."

He proceeded after a moment, however, to amplify his feeling about his opponent at Waterloo. "His campaigns in Spain were good. He defeated some of my best marshals. Of which you are all aware."

Then the ex-emperor burst into a laugh and thumped the back of the one nearest him, who happened to be Cyril Grannison. "Come, we have discussed your good duke long enough. After all, he was—"

"The hardest opponent you faced?" demanded an eager voice.

Driven back to his defense lines, Napoleon frowned. Finally he nodded his head. "Yes. I think I must say yes."

His youthful audience would have continued to bombard him with questions for the balance of the afternoon if Perron had not appeared in the doorway.

"Your Imperial Highness, the collation is served."

In response to a motion by Napoleon, the six guests followed Perron into the dining room. There a remarkably fine tea had been spread out on the mean and meager table. It was an English tea, prepared with a Gallic interpretation of what that meant. There was a dish of Westphalian ham *à l'essence*, an abundance of cold *dindon* (a voice, "I say, that's turkey!"), hot rolls and a wide range of sweet entremets. One of the latter found quick favor with everyone, a huge platter of miniature tarts called *darioles*, in which a rich and delicious mixture of cream was contained in the flakiest of pastry walls. After his teeth had crunched through two of these, Cyril Grannison whispered to his nearest neighbor: "I say, this is truly capital! How does it compare with those soggy treacle tarts we have shoved at us whenever we go to Plantation House?"

"Treacle seems to be a favorite dish with the governor," was the low answer. "But isn't it 'strordinary to find such bully food served on such cheap dishes? Look at the knives and forks. Wooden handles actually!"

"Haven't you heard he had to melt down his silver service and buy cheap crockery on the island?"

The other man's eyes showed surprise. "No, 'pon my word, I hadn't. This is a state of things, isn't it?"

Napoleon excused himself from joining his guests at the meal but he had a glass of the wine they had brought for him. He disliked champagne but he did not allow it to show. He sipped appreciatively and nodded to each in turn over the rim of his glass.

Back at Plantation House, the governor went over the events of the afternoon in full detail, repeating his questions time and again, and checking one man's version against those of others. "Now how did he phrase his answer?" was his most frequent demand. "I want his exact words. Nothing left out and no ands or buts, if you please." When they came to the question about the Duke of Wellington he straightened up expectantly in his chair.

"Ah! And what was his answer to *that?*"

Cyril Grannison took it on himself to answer. "He said, sir, that the duke was the hardest opponent he had faced."

This was in the nature of a disappointment for Sir Hudson Lowe. He had hoped, quite obviously, for a derogatory remark which could be sent back to England where it would reach the ears of the Iron Duke himself.

"So! He said that, did he. Are you sure you are repeating him correctly?"

"Quite, sir."

"Hm! Well, we'll come back to that later. What I am most concerned about is whether any word was dropped about the possibility of escaping from the island."

After a long and grueling session, they were allowed to leave. As he turned with his comrades, Grannison's elbow brushed against the pocket in the side of his tunic. The pocket contained something, something which rustled.

Having believed it empty, he felt inside and brought out a sheet of paper. It contained a few handwritten sentences in French. This convinced him that someone at Longwood had taken advantage of a chance to deposit the paper where he had found it. As his knowledge of French was practically nonexistent, he placed the sheet on the desk of a secretary on his way out.

414

"I don't know what this is. Someone must have slipped it into my pocket."

The secretary smoothed it out and proceeded to read what it had to say.

"Well, this *is* interesting. When did you find it?"

"Just now."

"It says we must examine a consignment of wine that's coming through. And if there's a drop of wax on the label of one of the bottles, we must look at the cork—well, well, this is *most important*. Thank you, Lieutenant Grannison. I'll give this to the governor."

2

Betsy had not seen her friend Julia for several weeks. A barrier had been raised at the Square House, as it was often called by the people of the island. Whenever Betsy rang the bell at the gate, Margette would hurry across the cobbled courtyard and would shake her head dolefully. All efforts to teach the girl a few rudiments of English tongue had been in vain.

"Seeck," she would say. "Ah, very seeck. No one—see."

"Not even me?" Betsy would ask, tapping her breast.

"No one see."

Late one afternoon Betsy rode over to make a more determined effort, feeling that her friend must be in need of assistance. Henry Trottle's horse was tethered at the gate, recognizable by the leather bag attached to the saddle in which the amiable old doctor carried his supplies. On this occasion Margette pointed to the house and then to the horse which was striving to crop the few blades of grasses which grew forlornly along the base of the house.

"Your mistress is very sick today?"

The girl, whose eyes were red, shook her head emphatically. Clearly a point of crisis had been reached. Betsy spoke in a lowered tone. "I'll stay here and speak to the doctor. I *must* know how my poor Julia is."

Margette seemed to sense her purpose. At any rate she smiled wanly and returned to her duties on the other side of the court. It was about ten minutes later that the medical man came slowly into the courtyard and out through the gate.

"Dr. Henry, how is she? I haven't been able to see her for such a long time."

The doctor gave his head a slow shake. "I brought old Henrietta Watts with me. She will stay until—it's over. I don't believe, Betsy, that the poor lady will last through the night. You know that the trouble is with her lungs?"

"Yes, Dr. Henry. The last time I spoke to her she—she explained. She said her strength was going fast. She couldn't speak above a whisper."

He untied the rope and was on the point of climbing into the saddle when he decided apparently to ask her some questions.

"Have you ever seen her?"

"Once. It was her wish. But she showed me only one side of her face. What a beauty she must have been! Of course, we had many long talks."

"She told you her story then?"

"Yes, Dr. Henry."

"That's more than she's done for me. I've asked her outright several times how she came by such injuries but she always refused to tell. She must have been the victim of some terrible accident. Have you repeated the story?"

"No. Not to anyone. Not even to my parents. I gave my promise."

The little doctor was familiarly known as Hatless Harry, being the only man on the island to go without a head covering. As a result perhaps of the exposure, his round pate was covered with curly spirals of hair which sprouted up in all directions, with a rather comic effect.

He seemed to find it hard to believe that she had remained so loyal to her promise. At any rate, he rubbed his knuckles over his head and frowned.

"My wife should have been a man," he said. "Gad's word, what a lawyer she would have made! Let her cross-question the Sphinx and she would get his life story out of him. Can you conceive of the pressure I've been under to find out about this unfortunate lady?" He shook his head rather grimly. "I dread having to tell her that the poor lady is taking her secret into the grave with her!"

It was not hard for Betsy to appreciate his position. His wife was notoriously the worst gossip on the island. Half of the people called her Curious Carrie and the rest preferred to speak of her as Tattle Trottle.

416

"When your poor friend is gone," asked the doctor, "will you feel free to tell what you know?"

"No, Dr. Henry. You see, there are people at home in England who must be considered."

"What a pity! I was hoping you could help me out. Now I *will* catch it!" He paused for a moment. "I must say, young lady, that I admire you for keeping your promise this way. Most of the people on this island would burn up if they had to button a secret like this inside themselves. There'd be smoke coming out of their ears."

He did something to the bridle and seemed on the point of mounting. Then he stopped and stared at her across the saddle. This was quite a feat for him, being a very short man.

"Everybody will be at you about it. Do you think you can hold 'em off?"

"Of course."

"Wouldn't be surprised if Mr. Plantation House himself took a hand. He may scent a Napoleonic plot in it. Think you can resist official questioning?"

"I think I can."

The doctor clapped his hands together. "That's the way! Steady, the Buffs! Stand by your guns, my dear; even if the face of authority gets black with indignation."

He swung himself up into the saddle. Betsy's mood had taken a sharp turn. She was on the point of weeping as she walked over closer to the window behind which the sick woman lay. For a moment she stood still and listened. No sound reached her ears.

"Julia!"

When there was no response, she spoke again. "Julia! Julia, my dear, dear friend! I know you told me it was better this way. But it's hard, it's very hard."

No sound broke the silence from inside the room. Betsy could no longer restrain her tears.

"Good-by, dear Julia! Good-by, good-by!"

Betsy found it difficult to climb into her saddle for by this time her eyes were blinded with the tears.

"You had better ride along with me, my child," said the little doctor.

Chapter Eighteen

1

Betsy arrived late for dinner. The food was on the table and Sarah Timms was hovering about with a worried look on her broad face. The boys had cleared up their plates and disappeared. Betsy seated herself beside her father and then, noticing the main dish on the table, said, "Oh!"

"I know you don't like stewed veal," said her mother. "But it seemed impossible to get anything else."

"It's not that I dislike it so much. I do dislike it, of course. It's—well, do you remember that we had it the night when Napoleon came ashore? And now we have it when"—she turned and studied her father's face intently—"when I think Papa has something serious to say to us."

"What, child?" William Balcombe clearly was taken by surprise. Then he looked at the others and nodded his head. "I don't see how you could have guessed it. But—yes, I have something to say. We are under orders to leave the island and return to England."

"I was certain that was it," commented Betsy, with an expression seldom detected on her face; a hint of fear.

Mrs. Balcombe and Jane were, quite apparently, taken completely by surprise. "Oh, William!" said his wife. "How dreadful for you." Jane did not seem as much disturbed. Perhaps she had been entertaining an unexpressed wish to get back to the pleasant life they could find for themselves in England.

"Stewed veal, the beginning and the end of the most important event in our lives," said Betsy.

"The governor sent for me this afternoon," explained the head of the family. "I was with him for over an hour and at times we had it hot and heavy. No explanation I could make would satisfy him. He was determined to see the last of us."

418

He looked soberly at his wife. "It will be given out, my dear, that your health makes it advisable for us to return."

Mrs Balcombe spoke up gallantly. "And that is quite true. This climate isn't good for me. I'm sure I'll suffer from hepatitis as long as I stay. But you must all realize that I will go as unwillingly as any of you."

"When must we leave, Papa?" asked Jane.

"On the first ship. Lowe can't bear for us to remain an hour longer than is necessary. One is due in from Cape Town next week. We will sail on that."

"Is it a small ship?" asked his wife.

"I'm afraid so, my dear. If the weather turns bad, it will pitch and toss. But we may be lucky enough to have good sailing."

Silence fell on the group. They all kept their eyes on their plates, preferring not to reveal the depth of their feelings.

"You are sure, William, that we won't find ourselves in a financial crisis?"

"I can provide for my family under any circumstances. You must not worry, my dear."

"Perhaps," hinted his wife, "you will now feel disposed to take advantage of your influences at home."

The suggestion aroused Betsy from the mood of shock and anger into which she had been plunged by her father's words. She was sure what his answer would be to her mother's question, remembering what had happened when she accompanied him on his visit to that odd but kindly old man at Windsor Castle.

William Balcombe remained silent for several moments, a hint of stubbornness taking possession of his usually amiable face. His answer, when it came, could not have been less brief or more decided.

"No!"

"But—but, William, you may need influence to secure another governmental post."

"I don't feel that another governmental post is essential to our well-being. Please, don't think I am neglecting our best interests. But I have been standing on my own feet so far. I prefer to go on that way."

Betsy said to herself, "Good for Papa! He isn't going to let them turn him into a toady!" She felt as he did, that it would be better for them to live their lives in their own way without any begging, based on that secret (which was not, she considered, so very much of a secret now) in her father's life. It was doubtful if they would come to him; but, certainly, he must not approach them with his hat in his hand.

"We won't try to take much furniture back with us," declared William Balcombe, intending perhaps to change the subject. "We know from experience what a battering it would be subjected to. We'll take a few personal things and I'll sell the rest to the company for the use of the new occupants here."

"Yes," agreed Mrs. Balcombe, in a dispirited tone. She was finding it hard to repress her tears. "So much to be done in such a short time! How will we ever get through?"

"Sarah Timms will look after the packing. And it's my notion that we ought to take her with us."

His wife's spirits revived slightly at this suggestion. She brushed her eyes with a handkerchief. "It will be a comfort to have her. But *must* we take Mantee as well?"

"Certainly not. Sarah has too much common sense to object if we leave him behind. She knows he would be a complete nuisance at every step of the way. Of course, we could always arrange for her to return if she wanted it that way."

"Will we be allowed to visit Longwood before we leave?" asked Jane.

This question had been uppermost in Betsy's mind. She wanted to be the one to inform Napoleon and had been wondering, in what amounted almost to panic, if she would be allowed to see him.

The tones of the head of the family sharpened as he answered. "After spending an hour in the company of the amiable man at Plantation House, I am sure he will do everything he can to prevent us from seeing Napoleon. Once they got the letter out of the cork—!"

"You didn't tell us about that, William."

"Didn't I? Well, a number of cases of special Spanish wine have come through in the last two years or more. They were always put on at Cadiz and delivered to us. I sent them on at once to the customs for examination and did not give them another thought. It seems now that notes have been concealed each time in the cork of one of the bottles. They come from a special agent that Napoleon used in Paris, a churchman, the Abbé Force."

"He's not putting the blame on you, surely," said Mrs. Balcombe.

420

"He's ready to believe anything. Anxious to, in fact. I assure you, my dear, that I knew nothing about what was going on. But I was mentioned in the note they got their hands on yesterday. It was no more than a reference to the good feeling we have always entertained for Napoleon since we had him as a guest. Lowe, of course, pounced on this as confirmation of his suspicions. He has always been searching for something to justify him in proceeding against me; and now he declares he has it." He paused and then turned to answer Jane's question. "My dear, he will refuse any requests for passes on the ground that we might be given messages to be delivered when we arrive in England."

Betsy's heart sank at this confirmation of her fears. Must she leave without seeing the emperor, without a chance to let him know how deeply she felt?

"I hear," her father was explaining, "that the number of sentries around Longwood is to be doubled. The brave little governor isn't going to take any chances." He sighed wearily and reached for the bottle of port. "I have no appetite, so I think I'll content myself with a glass or two of wine."

As he raised his glass he glanced uneasily at Betsy who was now turned in her chair and gazing steadily through one of the windows which gave an abbreviated view of the pavilion.

"Betsy?"

She did not seem to hear him. At least, she made no answer. William Balcombe glanced anxiously at his wife as though expecting her to rouse the girl from the spell of depression into which she had fallen. But Mrs. Balcombe had risen from her chair and was motioning to Sarah Timms to remove the untouched food and clear the table.

Betsy spent the next hour in a lonely tour of the grounds. Jane called to her once but received no response. Then the younger sister disappeared and was not seen by anyone until some time later when she emerged from the grounds about the pavilion. She was carrying a small china cup in one hand. This she held out for Jane's inspection.

"The handle's broken off," commented the practical Jane.

"Does that matter? Jane, I found it in a closet up there and I recognized it at once. *He* used to drink from it. I saw him with it many times. Don't you remember how pleasantly he would smile at us over the rim when he was having his chocolate in the mornings?"

"I never saw him in the mornings. The gate was barred to me."

"How thoughtless people can be! I suppose it was tossed into the cupboard after it was broken."

"His people were always slovenly. But, Betsy, for goodness sakes, there is nothing in this to—to *moon* over."

"Stewed veal and a broken teacup!" commented Betsy bitterly. "They will always be among the things I remember. Of course, I have the beautiful banjo his sister sent him. And the piece of plate ..." She stopped abruptly. That was a secret she must keep from everyone, at least, until they were safely back in England. But Jane was too concerned with her own thoughts to notice what had been said.

Another half hour's silent communion with herself brought Betsy to a less passive acceptance of her father's announcement. She left her chair on the porch and walked back to the dining room. Here she found her father with a partially empty bottle of port in front of him.

"Papa!"

"Yes, Betsy." William Balcombe pushed his glass away from him and turned to study his daughter's face. "My dear child, you are taking this too seriously. I'm very much disturbed about you."

"Do you think I'm to blame?" she asked.

He shook his head. "Certainly not. The governor, that gentle and fair man, was very much annoyed because he knew you were visiting Napoleon secretly. But he couldn't use that as a reason for sending us back. He needed some bit of evidence he could twist to convict me of using my business relations with Boney to get messages to Europe for him. He has no shadow of a case, of course, but his sponsors in the government will be ready to accept his word. No, no, child, you mustn't blame yourself."

There was a spell of silence between them. "Papa," she said finally, "I intend to come back."

"You mean, to return here?"

"Yes, Papa. Napoleon will miss me very much. More than you, or anyone, will know. I must make every effort to find the means of getting back."

Her father indulged in a wry smile. "And what form would these efforts take?"

"I've never forgotten how kind that old man was when you took me to see him. He wanted so much to help you. I know

422

he has lost his mind but surely there must be others who *know*. Papa, I intend to go to them! I am going to demand—yes, demand!—that they arrange for me to come back."

Balcombe leaned over to pat her hand which she had placed on the table, with her fingers gripping a handkerchief with something almost of passion. "In the first place, Betsy, I wouldn't allow you to do anything of the kind. In the second place, it would do no good. This is a political matter, you see. You could expect nothing from these others, even if they condescended to see you, except cold stares." The habitual kindliness of his expression was lost in a serious frown. "Do you realize, what this infatuation of yours for the emperor—I can't think of any other word—may do to you—to your future? There has been a great deal of talk again, you know. I've said nothing about it because I understand you. But I've been very angry. You are still young, dear child, and the talk will soon subside. But if you returned to the island!—It would become an open and never to be forgotten scandal."

Betsy thought to herself, "Perhaps a scandal would help." She nodded with a suggestion of indifference. "I'm prepared to face it. Papa, I don't care. Let the tongues wag. I've done nothing wrong. Few people realize how ill Napoleon has become. I'm happy in the belief that in a sense I've been necessary to him. He's always been upset on the days when I haven't been to see him." After a moment she added in an almost belligerent tone, "I'm prepared to have my reputation blackened for life if I can help to bring him some ease of mind in his last days!"

"Come, come, Betsy, don't you see you will be throwing away any chance for a normal life of your own? Don't you want romance and—and a happy marriage with children?"

"And live in a vicarage or a deanery or a little house in some dreary suburb? With a husband who might be kind but at the same time as tepid as a cup of weak tea? Do you think afternoon calls on neighbors and the excitement of an occasional evening of whist will make a *full* life for *me?* No, no, no, Papa! I can forego all such prospects without a single pang."

"You may think so now, child. But what about the long slow years when you are older and have lost all pleasant contacts? What will life have to offer then?"

Betsy answered quietly. "Memories. Memories, Papa." She remained silent for a moment while she took his hand and squeezed it affectionately. "You are so kind that I don't want to cause you any moments of uneasiness. But, Papa, a vivid recollection of a great moment in history in which you have played some part can be much more worthwhile than the dreary realities of a humdrum existence."

William Balcombe spent a few moments removing the cork of another bottle of port. He poured himself a glass but failed to find pleasure or compensation in it. "This is all beside the point," he remarked. "Don't you realize you can't either stay here or come back later? I assure you it will be impossible."

"One thing I've learned in my long talks with Napoleon. You must never base all your plans and ideas on one possibility. You must consider everything and have alternative lines of action. Perhaps I've acquired a very small share of his inventiveness from listening to him. I may not be able to return to St. Helena later but there are other ways in which I can be of help to him."

"What ways do you have in mind?"

She responded by asking a question. "When will there be another election in England?"

"I expect they'll go back to the country very soon."

"When they do, Papa, I could offer my services to the opposition. I could make speeches and let people know how badly Napoleon is being treated. The opposition would give me the chance, I'm sure."

Her father indulged in a smile. "I suppose they would be glad enough of something novel such as a pretty girl getting up and slam-whopping the government. But why are you so sure you could stand in front of a noisy crowd and make a speech?"

Betsy answered with an air of confidence. "I haven't any real talents. But somehow I feel certain I could make speeches."

"Have you ever heard of heckling? Every speaker faces the certainty of having Johnnie Raws in the audience who throw insults at them. It's very disconcerting."

"I believe I could hand back as good as they gave."

"Well, then, consider what the government supporters would do. They would dig up those silly old rumors and invent enough to go with them to create a real scandal. And, of course, you would be charged with lack of patriotism. That is always the cardinal sin, you know."

424

"It's an evidence of real patriotism to point out mistakes your country is making."

"To be practical this kind of a campaign would take a pile of money. Politicians are great promisers but in the end they leave you with nothing for your pains. You would have to pay your own expenses. You wouldn't dare accept a sou from the Bonaparte family."

"I've thought of that too. I would go to Lady Holland who is a great admirer of Napoleon's. I think she might help me to get some demonstrations under way. It would help if people were stirred up to march on London in large groups, carrying signs with slogans. *Why Torture a Dying Man?* and things like that."

"I see you've been giving some real thought to it."

"If none of this does any good, I have another plan. This is very secret, Papa. Napoleon told me in the closest confidence something about his finances."

"Be careful, Betsy. Should you tell me?"

"Yes, Papa. I know you will bury it away in the very last cell under that spot where your hair is getting a little thin. He's a large owner in a shipping line. An American company. Supposing the president went on one of their ships which was to call at St. Helena and took his wife along with him. Supposing I went as her companion. I would always wear a hat pulled down over my hair and the darkest green spectacles and I would wear the duddiest clothes. The three of us would be allowed to call on him."

"It's very ingenious, Betsy. But what good would it do?"

"It would show him what risks I was willing to take to see him again. A small matter, yes. But when he was very ill, it might raise his spirits. If it made him feel easier in his mind for an hour, it would be worth the effort."

"For all this," declared her father, "you would need a hide like a crocodile. And endless determination."

Betsy smiled for the first time. "Papa, I don't believe you have any conception of the amount of determination I have."

William Balcombe smiled. Then, almost immediately, the expression on his face changed. An anxious frown gathered about his eyes.

"Betsy," he said, "that's all very well. You have enough determination to do for a whole family. I'm sure they are things you could accomplish out of all these plans. Particularly the electioneering. But child, you're forgetting something. For the time being—for quite a time, in fact—our part must be one of silence. We mustn't get into the newspapers. The government must not be provided with any excuse for coming down hard on us. After a time, a long time, it might do. But not yet. No, no, my dear, no playing a lioness. The mouse must be more in your line."

"Couldn't I be a lionlike mouse?"

He patted her on the head. "Wait. Let's see how things go."

2

Cyril Grannison came to pay a call the next afternoon. He was in low spirits and had little to say. Finally, Mrs. Balcombe got up from the tea table.

"I've *so* much to do," she said. "Will you forgive me if I take Jane and go back to the thousand and one tasks we have ahead of us? Betsy will pour you another cup of tea."

This was what he had wanted but, when alone with Betsy, he seemed at a loss for words.

"I've a confession to make," he blurted out, finally. "It's because of something I did that you are going home. Did you know that?"

Betsy, who was also showing signs of a depressed mood, looked at him closely. "I didn't know. What did you do?"

"I suppose I'm not a brainy fellow at all, what? I know I'm not quick at getting into meanings and that sort of thing. Well, after visiting Boney the other day, we had to report to the governor. It was like being in the bottom class at a second-rate school. He insisted we tell him everything. I think if we'd volunteered to tell him how many crumbs we spilled on the carpet of that abominable dining room, he would have perked up his ears. When we were leaving, I found there was a paper in the pocket of my tunic. Odd thing, what? I hadn't put it here. I jumped to the conclusion that someone at Longwood had slipped it into the pocket. Oh, I realize I acted without thinking. I should have waited until I got away before letting anyone know. Then I could have let the eagle eye examine it to see what the whole thing was about. Instead I said to myself, 'It's your duty to turn this in', and I
426

walked over to the secretary and handed the miserable note to him."

"And what you gave him was a hint about the bottle of wine?" said Betsy, in a tense voice.

"Yes, Betsy, it was about that beastly bottle of wine. You've guessed it. I turned it in like a good little man. Of course, I'd have done it sooner or later. Duty to king and country, you know. But why did I have to be in such a dashed hurry about it?"

"Why indeed? Still, Cyril, you mustn't blame yourself. I think at least one man in twenty would have done as you did. There are so many kinds of duties, aren't there?"

He looked at her with a puzzled frown. "Do you know what I'm thinking of doing? Selling my commission. Seriously, mind you, I may get out of the Army. There are no wars ahead of us, since Boney's out of the running, and dashed if I want to devote more of my life to police duty on this miserable island. And of course, if I returned home, I would be able to see something of you, what, what?"

"I am grateful that you would like to see me again. But, Cyril I don't think you should do anything so reckless. There *is* your duty and—and I have no idea where we will go finally. The company may place Papa in India. Or he may be stationed in Cape Town. Or even Australia. You can never tell."

"But—but—it's this way. If I stay here, I'm sure I'll never see you again. If you catch my drift, that would be a pretty hollow state of things, what? But if I go back to England, Home, and Beauty, I could—well, let's put it this way—"

Betsy gave her head a shake. "Dear Cyril," she said. "I think we had better leave things as they are."

A look of consternation took possession of him. "You mean—that you don't—"

"Yes, Cyril, I'm afraid that's what I do mean."

Chapter Nineteen

1

On the morning of the day they were to sail for home under the cloud of the governor's high displeasure, Betsy and her father took a stroll in the gardens. At first they had nothing to say, for the strain was beginning to tell on them. Even the two boys, who at first had been exuberantly in favor of returning to England, had shown regret in the last twenty-four hours. They had departed for the wharves to superintend the loading of their special belongings, with hands sunk deep in pockets in a way which hinted at despondency.

William Balcombe inspected the fast-growing pines and the already ponderous oaks they had planted to offset the grim unfamiliarity of the banyans, and then said: "Sorry to leave them, Betsy. Do you remember how much we disliked those," pointing to the banyans, "when we first arrived?"

"Rather. Do you remember how I called for help when I first went in under them? The branches looked like the crooked fingers of witches stretching out to prevent me from leaving. I never thought I was a coward like most other girls. But I guess I was."

"We've really accomplished a kind of minor miracle here."

Betsy agreed with a decided shake of the head. "The rest of the island is bare and ugly. But here it's like England, isn't it?"

"At any rate we toned down the tropical effect. I wonder how long this will last? The new people may not take any interest. In that case, nature would take hold immediately."

"I hope that won't happen to the sod," commented Betsy. "It's so gray and dismal everywhere except in this corner of ours. Look, Papa, how the gorse is weaving patterns of gold through it."

"Gad, you're getting poetical. Have you been reading the stuff of that little fellow back in England?"

428

"John Keats? Oh, a little. But I haven't much poetry in me, I'm afraid. Still, Papa, you must realize that I'm no longer a young girl. I was bound to outgrow the tomboy stage sooner or later." She sighed deeply. "These last days have had their effect on all of us. Even on me."

He turned to face her more directly and studied her intently for several moments. It was clear she had been under a strain. Perhaps she had not been sleeping well, for there were shadows under her eyes.

"You mustn't take things so seriously," he warned. "I'm becoming convinced that the future holds out bright prospects for all of us. I've been growing tired of standing between two such antagonistic forces. What I'm hoping for is to get out of the commercial side of things and into—well, the administrative. As for you, Betsy, you had little to look forward to if we remained here permanently. Except marriage."

"Which is not the only answer to a maiden's prayer. At least, not the kind of prayers I say."

She turned suddenly and looked with surprise toward the house. Mantee Timms had brought the delivery wagon up to the front porch and was standing there with the lines twisted through his hands. "We're not due to start for at least four hours. Was Tee instructed to come around this early?"

"Yes, I gave the order. You see, we are going to pay a farewell call at Longwood."

"Has the governor changed his mind about giving us a pass?"

William Balcombe gave his head a shake. "I haven't asked him again. But an hour ago I sent word to the Great Panjandrum that we were going to see Napoleon. Just that."

"Papa!" cried Betsy ecstatically. "How wonderful! I was sure you would stand up to him."

"This may get us into trouble. But," taking out his watch, "he'll have to move fast if he has any intention of preventing us from making our call."

"Let's get started right away," said Betsy eagerly.

"Yes. I sent word to Bertrand at the same time. He'll make the arrangements at that end."

She turned and ran toward the house with an eagerness which showed that bitter experiences had not completely effaced the tomboy in her. "Hurry!" she cried to Mrs. Balcombe and Jane. "We're going to Longwood and there isn't a second to spare!"

When her father arrived at a more sedate pace, she was already ensconced on the front seat, and her dog Snooky (who was going back to England too) had curled up at her feet with his wet nose pressed against the immaculate white of her shoe "I want to drive, Papa," she declared. "I don't trust any of you to go fast enough!"

William Balcombe put a foot on the metal step but paused to look around before getting into the wagon. "For us this is the last scene," he said, "in the combination of tragedy and comedy which is being played on this island."

Betsy drove with relentless speed up the winding road to Longwood. None of the fears assailed her which she had felt when Napoleon would take her out with him in the early days and would order his coachman to fly around the hairpin turns and above the yawning depths. Over her shoulder she caught a glimpse of Jane sitting on the back seat with closed eyes and blanched cheeks. Poor Jane was as frightened as she herself had been on those occasions; and so she lessened the speed as they swooped down through Geranium Valley and up to the awesome heights above the Devil's Punchbowl.

The tall semaphore at Alarm-House rose up above them on the right and she heard her father say, "Well there's been one sensational possibility we haven't lived here long enough to see—the blue banner fluttering out from up there."

Betsy, having been told the story of the planned escape, smiled to herself. "You have no idea, Papa," she thought, "how close we really came to seeing the blue flag flying from every semaphore on the island."

For the balance of the drive her mind was devoted to what might have followed if the plan had been carried out. Where would Napoleon be now? Perhaps he would be occupying a large office in a shipping concern in New York and devoting all his energy and his great gifts to making himself the richest man in the world. More likely, however, he would still be hidden in the secret apartments under the broad mansion his brother Joseph had built on the Delaware River, while international agents sought to solve the mystery of his whereabouts. Would her part in the story have ended when the Yankee Clipper hoisted her new sails and majestically departed from the roadstead at Jamestown? Or would Napoleon have sent for her, after achieving some manner of security, that she might share his new life in some small way? He had hinted at the possibility but there had never been anything to give her reason to expect such an intention on his part.

She realized, suddenly and completely, that there was no part she could have played in the balance of his life.

2

There was no cloud of dust on the road behind them to indicate the approach of messengers so Betsy was content to drive at an easier pace after turning at Hutt's Gate, where two small Bertrands waved at them from behind a picket fence. The Valley of the Nymph, which stretched immediately ahead of them, seemed unusually quiet although they could see the sunlight glistening on the bayonets of sentries.

"They won't let us through!" thought Betsy, her hands tightening their grip on the reins. Would she dare set the horses to a gallop and force their way into the Longwood gardens? The sentries would not have their bayonets set and ready unless they anticipated some such action.

Usually during the hours of daylight there would be one sentinel only on the line between Longwood and the road leading from Hutt's Gate. Now there were three and an officer as well. He was walking over hastily to intercept them.

"That's Johnny High," said Jane, sitting up and displaying her first spark of interest.

Betsy had been too much concerned over the problem of what she should do to look closely at the officer. Now she turned in his direction and saw that Jane was right. She reined in as they reached the Longwood entrance.

It was clear that their good friend Lieutenant High, was quite disturbed. He was wearing a solemn expression and seemed at a loss for words.

"Sir," he said, addressing Mr. Balcombe, "I have received orders from the governor."

They waited for him to continue. "You are to be allowed to pass, sir. But there are conditions. First, the visit must be a short one. Thirty minutes."

"That seems unusually brief, Lieutenant."

Johnny High swallowed hard before continuing. "It seems so to me. But the order from Plantation House is most explicit, sir. To make sure you leave on time, I am instructed to sound a whistle two minutes before."

Balcombe frowned. "Does that mean that when we hear the whistle we must drop everything?"

"I am afraid, sir, that is pretty much the meaning."

"Well, Lieutenant, we won't blame you. I suspect you are finding this task somewhat distasteful. We'll strive to make things as easy for you as possible. When we hear the whistle, we'll leave at once."

"Captain Nicholls is to be in the room during the visit and he must be close enough to hear everything. Immediately on your departure, he and I are to ride to Plantation House and report to the governor. He will expect to be told every word, said."

"I understand that has been the usual procedure," said Balcombe. "Even the allied representatives are expected to repeat to His Excellency all their conversations at Longwood." He indulged in a brief smile. "It annoys them very much. I don't believe they've been as co-operative in this matter as our worthy governor thinks they should be." He drew out his watch. "The time granted us will be up at exactly—fourteen minutes to three. We will be punctual."

"Thank you, sir." The young officer glanced now at Mrs. Balcombe and the daughters of the family. "You are quite right, sir: I find this most distasteful. I—I feel very sad that you are leaving the island. It's going to be a dull place without you."

"We are going to miss you very much, Johnny," said Jane, quietly.

"Yes, Johnny," affirmed Betsy. "You have been one of our very best friends."

"One of our fellows is talking of selling his commission and going home. I—I would like to do the same. But it may not be possible. Family reasons, you know." He stepped closer to them and said in a whisper, "Everyone on the island is saying this is—is a beastly shame."

The grand marshal appeared in the entrance and bowed to them. "His Imperial Highness," he announced, "is ready to receive you."

An orderly put in an appearance and took charge of the wagon and horses. He was an old acquaintance of Betsy's and was looking very unhappy.

"We'll miss you, mam'selle," he said.

There were many others who would miss them also. Heads were appearing in all windows of the service wing with expressions of regret. Marchand, with a uniform draped over one arm, called a greeting to them through the bedroom window. Two gardeners dropped their tools and came forward to voice their respects.

Betsy looked around before entering the house. She caught John High's eye and then ran back for a whispered word with him. "Johnny," she said, "I don't want to get you in any trouble. But, please, our time is so very short that I don't think you should begin to count until we are shown in."

The young officer nodded. "That's what I intended to do. And, Betsy, I've taken the risk of setting my watch back a bit."

As Bertrand stepped toward the door of the drawing room, Betsy looked curiously at a group which had gathered along the walls. They were all familiar, and all friends: the butler Perron, frowning unhappily; Marchand, still holding the uniform and brush; Lepage wearing a troubled smile for her benefit; the brothers Archambault in riding boots; a full score of others. It was quite apparent that the imperial household had a high esteem for the members of the Balcombe family.

The room, as a result, was crowded, and Betsy realized how easy it would have been for someone to slip the note into Cyril Grannison's pocket without being detected. She decided it must have happened when the group of officers were making their departure. "That great zany of a Cyril," she said to herself, "would be so puffed up by the lively conversation with Napoleon and so filled with rich food that he wouldn't notice when she brushed by him." It may be adduced from this that Betsy had no doubts as to whose hand had passed the note. She decided it was a good thing that the lady in question was not in evidence. It would not have been possible to be civil to her.

A footman threw open the doors leading into the drawing room.

3

Napoleon rose from the chair in which he had been sitting. He bowed to the visitors and smiled with the great warmth he scrupulously reserved for those who enjoyed his unqualified liking. His dark blue coat had been ironed to a high perfection and the cut of his white satin breeches verged on the miraculous. The breast of his coat glittered with decorations.

Betsy followed her parents into the room with diffident steps, feeling more awe than she had ever experienced before. This was the Napoleon she had never seen, the emperor who had been a great stickler for form, the conqueror who had frightened into submission the crowned heads of Europe.

He began to speak in English, pausing over each word. "I am filled with regrets that you are leaving. Ah, how I shall miss you—you who threw open your doors to the unhappy exile, the prisoner in a strange land!"

Having gone this far in an alien tongue, he nodded to Betsy to take up her role of interpreter and then reverted to French. He proceeded to speak at some length of the pleasant times they had shared together, recalling the things which remained greenest in his memory; the games of blindman's bluff, the practical joke which failed (because Sam Creepy had to be returned to his owner), the highly diverting use which had been made of the island system of semaphores. All this consumed many minutes. When Bertrand moved in the direction of the door into the dining salon as a sign that there was just time enough left for the collation which Lepage had prepared, the emperor said in conclusion: "I hope it will be understood that the kindnesses lavished on me by M'sieur Balcombe and his charming family have all been dictated by personal good will. Never has anything been said or done which could be held against them by those who control this island. I shall never see any of you again and so I am grateful for these last few moments allowed us."

Captain Nicholls had been hovering about at the rear of the room. The departure of the three older members of the family posed a problem for him, because Betsy remained where she was. He hesitated and then compromised by stationing himself between the folding doors and allowing them to close until only his uniformed sleeve was visible. In this position it was practically impossible for him to see or hear anything.

"You are not hungry, *ma petite?*"

"No, sire. It is many days since I've been hungry."

The emperor smiled for the first time; a brief and not too successful effort.

"Even though the good Lepage had prepared so many

things for you? But he will not be too disappointed. I have ordered baskets packed and put in your carriage. There will be enough to save you for a while from the horrors of the food served on English merchant ships." The last trace of his smile disappeared. He looked at her sadly. "Betsee, this is the last time I shall see you."

"No, sire!" she exclaimed. "No, no! I intend to come back. Very soon, I hope. My mind is made up. I have plans. Several plans, and all of them good, I think."

"You have plans?" He glanced at the door to convince himself that the regimental listener was not able to hear what they were saying. "This is interesting. You must tell me about these plans."

He listened while she repeated the ideas she had discussed with her father. At the finish he shook his head.

"The plans are good. And you have learned from me that there must always be more than one. You have been an apt pupil. But listen to me, child. Your father will be against any suggestion of approaching those who have influence. In this he must be the judge."

"He has already said no."

"I was sure of it. It happens also that my financial interest in the shipping company has been sold. To an American syndicate. They will have no reason for putting in here. So that leaves the one plan which you could follow, to make speeches against the government. Even though it is too late to hope for any relenting on the part of the English hypocrites, I would be very proud to know you had the courage to stand up in public and speak for their sick prisoner." He paused before adding: "But again, Betsee, it would be of no avail. I do not want you to come back."

Betsy's eyes revealed the surprise and dismay she felt. "But—but, sire, I thought you found my visits agreeable. You have told me so."

He nodded his head. "And I meant it. You have been the only tonic to rouse me from my depression. It has been so from the first. From the day when I rode to your father's place and saw you standing there with your sister. Such a pretty little girl! And I could tell at a glance you had a mind of your own."

"It was then you whispered to Count Bertrand and called me *La Petite*."

"You heard?"

"Yes, sire. I think you were sure no one could speak your language and you could say what you liked."

"And you have remembered! Betsee, that was years ago."

"I am not a scholar and not very clever, I'm afraid. But I *have* a good memory. I think, sire, I could repeat all the things you've said to me since. All the things that *count*." She hesitated before going on. "That is why I can't believe when you say you don't want to see me again."

"Ah, Betsee, this trouble which has fastened itself on me! It is of a slow nature and I can see before me a period of long and painful decline. I would rather have my friends remember me as I was in the past or, at the worst, as I am now. And of my friends, you in particular—you, *ma petite*, above them all. For you to be close at hand during what will follow can only serve to fill your mind with unpleasant memories. No, Betsee, it is better that you go now."

It is hard for youth to foresee the irrevocabilities that the future holds. Betsy, her eyes brimming with tears, tried to convince him that a reprieve was possible. "Sire," she declared, passionately, "you have so much physical strength to call upon! You have told me of the many sicknesses you have survived. And of the misfortunes which would have broken the hearts of other men. Surely, surely, it can happen again."

He shook his head solemnly. "Over all these years I have fought so many battles. We made a list of them when Las Cases was here. Sixty major battles. And I won them all. No," after a pause, "all but one. There were difficulties in most of them. I overcame them. But, Betsee, this one, the last battle of all—this is the only one where I have no chance to win."

As they talked Betsy had been thinking that Johnny High was going to dangerous extremes in setting back his watch. At this moment, however, the whistle sounded from the patrol path. She thought desperately, "This, then, is the end. What will be left in life for me? What kind of existence will I have?" Since that first day when she had heard the emperor call her *ma petite*, she had felt little concern about anything else.

Napoleon rose to his feet. "The signal. A shrill tin whistle! Have they never heard of bugles?" And then suddenly his whole attitude changed. He drew himself up stiffly. Color flooded into his cheeks. His eyes blazed. "Betsee, perhaps you are right. I still have my will. Misfortune will never break it. I can throw off this disease, if I will myself to do it. I can do now what I should have done at once: throw my fate into the hands of the one great friend I had, Alexander of Russia. I can convince him that I should no longer be left here to die of the heat and disease. Ha, my iron-hearted jailers, beware the day when my voice is heard again in France! When, who knows? there will be a rumble of cannon and the sound of my cavalry carrying the eagles on the road through Flanders!"

Betsy was watching him closely but could see out of the corner of an eye that her family had emerged from the dining room on their way out. She heard her mother say in a low admonitory tone, "Come, Betsy!" But she saw something else, that Napoleon had lost his balance and was feeling blindly for means of support. She took both of his hands in hers and helped him back to his chair. The momentary animation had deserted him. He subsided at once and his eyes closed as his head found rest against the tapestry back.

The two minutes were up. They would be waiting for her at the sentry line.

"Betsee," whispered Napoleon, "I am old—and sick. They are sending you away and I can do nothing about it!"

Betsy gave no heed to the members of the staff who had come into the room. She put her arms around his neck and rested her damp cheek for a moment on his shoulder.

"Ah, sire," she said, in such a low tone that never after could she be certain that he had heard her, "what might have been, what might have been."

Postscript

I desire to make it clear that this story of Napoleon at St. Helena and the English girl who figured in his last span of years, is neither a biography nor a piece of fictionalized history. It is a novel, although based largely on established facts.

Permit me first to point out that there was no scrap of historical truth for that most spectacular of historical novels *The Man in the Iron Mask*. Dumas had departed much farther from the truth than, perhaps, any novelist had ever dared before or since. This has not been held against him nor has the book suffered in popularity, although the full extent of his improvisation has always been recognized. I hasten to say that such additions as I have made to the story of Napoleon and Betsy seem very slight in comparison, being concerned chiefly with detail. I do not believe I have been guilty of exaggeration in presenting this high-spirited English girl as the last love of the unhappy Captive.

During the months that Napoleon lived as a guest of the Balcombe family on his first arrival, he became very fond of the pretty tomboy daughter. Later, as the girl grew up and the lot of the one time master of Europe in his crowded quarters at Longwood became more and more distasteful to him, his affection for Betsy kept pace with the development of what her daughter in later years called her "truly exquisite beauty." He was intensely jealous of the English regimental officers who took her to dances, he found ways to have her visit him without the seldom granted permits, he gave her presents of the kind usually reserved for those in deepest affection, he loaned his great charger to her to ride in the Deadwood races. All these things are told, sometimes briefly, in the reminiscences left by Las Cases, Gourgaud, Montholon, and Bertrand; although there is much divergence in the versions they present. There are guarded references in Betsy's own short reminiscences, written years later, which show the effect of the stilted atmosphere of early Victorian England. I have taken the liberty of using some anecdotes in different guise from the forms in which they have been presented.

In order to build a story out of what is conceded to be fact, it has been necessary to take some liberties with the sequence of events, to change a few names and to introduce a number of purely fictitious characters.

What followed the departure of the Balcombe family from St. Helena may be told briefly. William Balcombe was appointed treasurer of the great island continent of Australia and took ship with all his family save Betsy, who had been married in the meantime. Jane died on the arduous sea voyage and William Balcombe did not survive long in his new and important post. Descendants of the two sons remain in Australia today. One of them, Dame Mabel Brookes, wife of the great tennis star, Sir Norman Brookes, has written and published recently a most excellent and intensely interesting book with the title *St. Helena Story*. In this she raises the curtain on certain points (sometimes with no more than a hint) and seems to make it clear that there is more which could be told. It was Dame Brookes who purchased the Briars (the pavilion still stands in a somewhat dilapidated condition) and made a gift of the property to the French Government; a friendly gesture which, as she phrases it, placed her hand for a brief moment in that of Betsy's.

Betsy's marriage was a short one, and she was left in rather straitened circumstances. Many visits were paid her by Joseph Bonaparte after he sold his American holdings and was residing in England. Their talk was all of Napoleon and of his life in the island prison. Later the ex-emperor's nephew, Prince Louis Napoleon, visited her constantly during his years of exile in England. Again the talk of Napoleon and of the sad years at St. Helena. Both visitors found Betsy charming and still a pleasure to the eye. When Louis Napoleon made himself emperor by the *coup d'état* of 1851, he gave her an extensive grant of land in Algeria.

Delving into the past is a difficult task, and, with the best of intentions, a writer must always feel a certain presumption in his purpose. I became so fond of Betsy during the task of preparing this long version of her relationship with Napoleon that I hope my efforts to envision the story will be read with lenient eyes.

440